A FLASH OF LIGHT

Ali Ings

Ali Ings

Cover design by: W. V. Rainy

CONTENTS

CHAPTER I

"Marla, come on. The books are here."

The broom clattered to the ground. Marla spun, ignoring it. "Coming."

She darted up the stairs, the cellar door slamming behind her. Marla tore through the kitchen, dashing out the back door. Her boots thudded against the packed dirt path around the house. The noise from the crowd reached her. She sprinted down the road.

Three wagons waited on the main road, parked in the middle of the street. The massive and sturdy cart horses dozed, heads lowered as they napped, ignoring the crowds. Men wearing cream-coloured robes opened the wagon shutters and doors, exposing racks and racks of books.

"Everyone form lines. There's plenty for everyone," a man called as he walked along the wagons.

Marla stopped near the closest wagon and bent over, her hands on her knees. She sucked in a breath. Which line should she join? She glanced between the back two wagons. That one. The last and largest wagon. Marla darted over, still taking ragged breaths.

"Here you go." The blacksmith pulled her into line ahead of him, his powerful hands on her shoulders. He smiled. There was no trace of the usual ash or soot on him. Even his clothes were clean and fresh.

She wrapped her arms around the thick man in a quick hug. "Thanks." This was it, her chance to get a new book for the month. What fantastic places would she get to read about?

He rested a hand on her shoulder, his touch delicate, like when he worked on fine tools. "Any time. I know the young have less patience when they're excited."

Marla shuffled closer to the wagon with the line as people selected books and left. She browsed the racks. Books on every science topic filled the racks or were stacked in piles below in drawers. She ran her finger over the spines as she read titles, finding books on medicine and health, or agricultural sciences, and biology and chemistry, among other topics.

"So many new books," she muttered. "Oh, did you see this one?" Marla pointed at a book.

The blacksmith peered over her shoulder. He pulled the book out. "Advanced metallurgy for specialty tools? Thanks. Have fun choosing." He tucked the book under his arm and left.

She eased around the crowded wagon, investigating every book she could find. Which one, though? So many people still waited their turn. Marla lingered in front of the geology section. She grabbed From Mountains to Valleys and held the thick book to her chest. Mountains. There weren't any nearby. What would they look like up close?

Marla scrambled from the wagon and stepped back, making room for others. She strolled down the street, her new book under her arm. The lines were smaller now, from the books for children in the front wagon and adult storybooks in the middle wagon, to the longest line for the science books in back.

The shiny cover was smooth under her fingers. The picture on the front was of a valley between two mountains, with a lake at one end. Her town had many gorges, and the land rose and fell, but the grandeur of all that rock in one place, she just couldn't imagine it. Would she ever get to see it?

Something moved in the corner of her vision. Marla turned and stared across the street. Was that the edge of a cloak disappearing around the herbalist's house? Ava? gripping her new book under her arm, Marla crossed the street.

She peered through the trees and into the forest beyond the herb garden. Nothing moved. The garden was also quiet, with no sign of anyone. She glanced at the flowers and herbs bursting from packed beds and pots as she walked towards the back gate. Something pulled at her, like an itch she needed to scratch. She passed through the back gate, into the trees beyond.

The moss-covered ground was soft under her boots as she started jogging. Something pulled her deeper into the trees, a feeling tugging on her heart. Marla caught sight of the person, the brown cloak blending into the shadows ahead. They stopped and lowered their hood as they kneeled. A pale hand stretched out, reaching for the soil. Was the hand—glowing?

It wasn't just her hand. A yellow glow spread around the woman. She rose, her hand still stretched down, open palm towards the ground. Marla approached slowly, her attention on the soil below the woman. Little specks of green poked through the soil, unfurling and growing into delicate young ferns.

The older woman wandered through the forest; her grey hair rustled in the breeze. Plants burst from the ground behind her in a trail of shimmering yellow lights, tiny shoots pressing up with unfolding leaves. Each step seemed deliberate as she walked on bare feet through the moss and thin undergrowth.

Marla crept along behind her, staying silent as she watched with wide eyes. The forest nearly glowed wherever the woman walked. A fox slunk from the bushes and followed, close enough to touch their nose to her heels. Rabbits and mice darted out and walked along the same path, the fox ignoring them completely. They all watched the woman instead.

She reached a wrinkled hand over her head and touched a branch as she passed under. Flowers burst into bloom, clusters of pale violet blossoms

3

stretching along the branch. A deer stepped from the bushes and followed, joining the growing trail of animals following her. Was she still glowing? Marla rubbed her eyes with one hand. It had to be a trick of the light.

Marla glanced over her shoulder. The village was far behind them now. She was deeper into the trees than most people dared go. A quick glance around proved they were alone, though, aside from the animals. She watched birds flit about over her, joining the growing procession behind the woman.

Bushes parted for the woman, the branches leaning away to create a pathway. She stepped through and kept going, the trail of animals still behind her. Birds darted over, flying ahead to land on branches nearby.

Marla dashed to the bushes as the deer stepped through, their long legs easily clearing the mass of low branches and barely exposed roots. The bushes shifted part way back, leaving a gap just big enough for her to squeeze through. Marla wriggled between the branches and tumbled through the gap, rolling onto the soft grass in a small clearing, her book tucked firmly in her arms.

The woman bent down beside a pond. The water rippled around her finger, spreading over the surface of the water. A frog chirped at her. She smiled and stood, moving back from the water. The woman kept going, passing through the clearing and into the trees again.

Marla held her book to her chest as she followed. The woman never looked back. They passed the pond and stopped at a massive stump; the edges charred and splintered. Lightning? Marla stopped behind a bush and peered around. Where was the rest of the tree?

"Come out, child." The old woman turned and stared at the bush she hid behind. "It's time."

She peeked out as she eased around the bush. "Time? Time for what?"

"Your awakening." The woman held her wrinkled hands out to Marla, palms up.

Marla walked over, the soft moss springing back once she passed. She ducked under the low branches and stopped beside Ava. The old woman's hand was warm as she rested her hand on it.

"What awakening?" Her voice shook. Nobody ever mentioned anything about an awakening before.

"You felt the pull, right?" The delicate grey eyebrow arched as Ava squinted up at her. She held Marla's hand between hers.

Marla nodded. "I think so. I don't know. That tugging inside?"

"Yes. It brought you out here. You are a Wood Walker. I knew it the moment you were born. This is a dangerous time for you, but also wondrous." Ava beamed up at her. Sunlight streamed down through the leaves, surrounding the woman.

Marla squinted in the light. "Dangerous?" Her fingers tightened on her book.

"You are not the only one awakening right now. Don't tell anyone else what's happening. I need time to teach you." Ava patted Marla's hand.

"I don't understand," Marla whispered.

"No, but you will. I promise. But promise me you won't mention this to anyone until I tell you it's safe, alright? Not anyone. We are called to walk a different path in life. Yours will not be easy, but it will be worth it. I assure you." Ava gripped Marla's hand tighter, clutching it between hers.

"I promise." Something rippled from her. The surrounding leaves rustled in a breeze she wasn't certain she felt. It felt almost like magic, but that couldn't be. She didn't have any magic, as Rogar was so keen to remind her growing up.

Ava grinned. "You are strong already. Study hard and be careful. Don't mention this to anyone."

Marla glanced around at the still and quiet forest. The animals all watched her now. "I don't understand."

Ava crouched and pressed her hand to the soil. Her hand glowed that golden colour. She lifted her hand and a tiny green shoot rose from the soil. Two little leaves spread, angling to catch the sun.

"Now you try. Place your hand on the ground. Call to the life already there. Forests are full of life. It'll respond to you."

Marla lowered to her knees. She touched the damp soil with her palm. Call to it? How? She closed her eyes and took a slow breath. Something touched her somehow, like vibrations through the soil. It wasn't a ground shake, though. It was too gentle.

"Wait, is that a heartbeat?" Marla opened her eyes and looked up at Ava.

The old woman nodded, a smile spreading across her face. "The planet is full of life. The forests are all interconnected. We are a part of that, a complex web that includes every living thing, no matter how big or small. Most people can't feel it. Can you sense that connection?" Ava rested a hand on Marla's shoulder. "Listen for it. Feel it. You're part of it."

Marla closed her eyes again. She took another slow breath. There it was, a steady beating, so low she felt it more than heard it. "I feel it," she whispered. What was it? Whatever it was, she was a part of it. She belonged to it, and it warmed her through.

"That is the pulse of life, of creation, and of every living being. Not everyone can feel it. Most people don't. People that do feel it are called to nurture it."

"How?" Marla's own heart slowed with the pulse, beating in time, though twice as fast as the long and steady beats she sensed in her bones.

"We tend to things that grow. You'll learn more about the land and what it needs to be healthy. Most importantly, we help you develop your skills and teach you how to help life thrive." Ava rested a hand on Marla's back.

"Skills?"

"Creation is quiet. It happens in the dark, under the soil or in the womb. The pulse of life nourishes it. We live quiet lives, too. The Light Chargers, they have flashy magic. They're visible to everyone. They forgot how to give, though. We counter that with our powers. We keep them from destroying everything."

Marla shivered. "What do I need to do?"

"For now, find time to sit outside every day. You can come to my garden where it's quiet. Sit and breathe and feel for that pulse. Let it fill you. Practice that all this week. We must strengthen your connection. Don't tell anyone what you're doing." Ava took her hand and guided Marla up.

She walked back towards town with Ava, their hands still linked. "What were you doing to make the plants grow like that?" Marla walked beside the trail of newly sprouted plants.

"As we walk, we can call to life inside seeds. We can give them a boost in growth and get them through the most fragile stage of life." Ava tilted her head up and smiled at the birds circling over them.

"Is this why you visit the farmers' fields after they've been planted?"

The old woman nodded. "It is. They don't know what I do, they just know fields I walk grow stronger and have fewer problems. One day you will do this, too."

Marla walked silently beside Ava now. The deep sense of life was still there, but more like an echo now, not the strong, all-encompassing thing it was earlier. She looked up through the leaves, seeking glimpses of the clouds floating past overhead.

She shifted her book under her arm. "Did you get your book?"

Ava grinned. "There's no need. Come with me."

She led Marla to a worn trail and followed it back to the herb garden. Marla passed through it with her, going into the house through the kitchen door. Ava headed straight for the cellar stairs and walked down them. The cellar? Marla raised an eyebrow.

The sturdy door at the bottom creaked as Ava pushed it open. The old woman snapped her fingers and a tiny flame flickered in the lantern. She wiggled her fingers, and the flame grew. Ava took the lantern from the hook just inside the door. The flame illuminated shelves of preserved foods lining the room. Did Ava just light it with magic?

"Wait, are those doors glowing?" Marla pointed. Faint purple outlines of two doors filled the narrow spaces between some shelves.

"You can see them. Good." Ava walked over to the nearest door.

Ava raised her hand to the middle of a door. Marla watched closely. With her eyes, she saw a dirt wall. Inside her mind, she saw a wooden door with a thin layer of purple mist in front of it. Marla gripped the nearest shelves. A few slow breaths later, the dizziness passed. Her brain protested this new awareness. She was hot and cold at the same time.

"What am I seeing?" Marla reached out and touched the wall, her hand beside Ava's. The wood under her fingers was smooth and old.

"You're seeing through the protective enchantments. The door recognizes you already." Ava pressed on the door. It swung open.

Marla gasped. The room was packed with bookshelves. Every bit of wall space held books or scrolls. Marla darted inside and turned. Even the space over the door had shelves there. There was a small space large enough to fit her hand on beside the door, but that was all.

Ava walked in and set the lantern on the table in the middle of the room. She walked back and touched the empty space with her flat hand. Vines of light glowed, spreading from the space, along the doorframe, and up over the ceiling. The glow illuminated the room, as if the sun was bottled and held inside those vines.

Marla strolled along the shelves, reading titles as she went. "Healing?" She moved along. "Plant care and development. That's a lot of books." Marla kept walking. "History?" She paused and looked over at Ava.

"These are all our history. Not the official history you read in the books they give freely, but the history of our people. The Wood Walkers."

Marla stopped at the next section. She touched the spine of a thick book. Setting her own book on the table, she pulled the thick one from the shelves. Each page was full of pictures and information about places in her country, glossy photo after glossy photo of places she'd never been to. Marla recognized some locations from other books, but some of these had never been photographed, as far as she knew. She shrugged. Obviously. she was wrong.

Ava pulled a book out for her and set it on the table. "Come look at this one." She opened the book with care, turning the brittle pages with both hands.

Marla looked over her shoulder. "It's a list of names, places and dates? What is this?"

Ava turned to the last page and touched a name near the top. Marla's name. "This is a record of all the Wood Walkers. It records where they're from, when they were born, and what happened to them. This is the one for our village."

She leaned closer. Her birthdate was there, but the rest of the information was empty. Marla looked at a few entries above hers. "Some have a death date and the word drained beside it. What does that mean?"

Ava shook her head. "That is why you must be careful. We work in the shadows, in the old and wild places. Places mentioned in that book." She tapped a glossy page in the open book in front of Marla. "We have a power as old as the land itself. Light Chargers don't work as we do. You must avoid them. They can take your powers for their own and use them until there's nothing left of you."

9

Her thoughts spun. Others were awakening, Ava said earlier. "Teanor? He's one of them? He's awakening?" Rogar, too, she realized. The boy who tormented her growing up, until the Light Chargers came for him. But if Light Chargers awakened, how could she also be awakening?

Ava nodded. "He's no danger to you unless he hears you have powers. They'll be coming for him soon, though, and they are a threat to you. Some of them can sense you, like you will learn to sense them. We can't let them find you." Her fingers brushed over another name, the word drained and a date beside it.

The old woman closed the book and straightened. She gestured at the room. "This is forbidden knowledge. Much of it is far older than the information in the books you get from the Light Chargers. Most of it is unknown to them. You can learn more about how our powers work and how to connect with nature fully. You'll learn to heal and why you can. Even how to choose the right seeds for any location, and why they might fail to grow in some areas. Don't tell anyone else about this room. They won't be able to find it, anyway."

Marla nodded. She smiled as she looked around again. "So many books. It's hard to believe it's real." How long would it take her to read them all? She couldn't wait to find out.

Ava chuckled. "I'll leave some on the table for you. When you are done with them, leave them face down, so I know. Come each evening and read, after you're done with your daily chores. I'll talk to your mother, so she'll know."

The old woman bustled about, stopping to select books, before moving to the next shelf. Soon there was a small pile of books on the table, waiting for Marla.

"These are a good start. Come tomorrow. That will give me more time to arrange everything and talk to your mother. After I talk to her, you will be my apprentice."

Marla grinned. "Really? I—thanks."

"Now go. Tomorrow evening, remember. I know you have the botany book, so brush up on those herbs in the meantime. We'll start with the plants in my garden."

"I will. I just—thanks." Marla threw her arms around Ava and hugged tightly.

"Easy, girl. Don't break my old bones."

Marla relaxed her hug. "Sorry," she whispered.

Ava laughed. "Go put that strength to good use. They'll be missing you soon. Shoo." She waved Marla away.

CHAPTER 2

Marla hustled from the room and dashed up the stairs, her new book under her arm. The wood thudded with each step as she climbed. She crossed the kitchen and passed into the herb garden. The sun shone down on her, warming her.

The front gate squeaked as she passed through. Marla glanced up as she latched the gate again. Something moved behind the house and was gone already. She leaned over the gate and strained to glimpse whatever it was. Was it her imagination?

Marla turned and strolled down the street, her mind on the library hidden below Ava's house. It's been there, hidden all this time, and she never knew. Not only that, but she got to use it. She pressed a hand over her heart. With a last glance at Ava's house, Marla turned down her street.

Had she really seen someone in a cloak going around the back? Everyone here used the main door on the street, not the kitchen door. It hadn't been Ava; they were too tall, and she was still downstairs. Marla shook her head. It could have been someone from outside the town, coming for healing, who missed the sign out front.

Shaking her head, she focused on her path. She stopped by her house long enough to drop off her book before heading back into the street. People in the community garden waved at her, stopping their weeding long enough to smile and greet her as she joined them.

"Hey, Marla. The second batch of spring onions is ready for harvesting. Or you can help plant the fourth batch. It's up to you." Narria waved at her over the wall, pruners clutched in her hand.

"Sure." Marla slipped through the gate.

She passed down the paths laid in stone, between the tender shoots emerging from the soil. The earliest plants grew in the sunniest patches, in the back against the warm stone wall. Marla took a basket from the stack as she passed.

The stone path was warm as she knelt on it. The soil beside it benefitted from that heat, that and the stone wall nearby. Her fingers wrapped around the little onions, damp soil still clinging to them, and she pulled.

The onions slipped free easily, and the dirt came loose with a shake. Marla set them in the basket and reached for another bunch. Soft humming came from nearby. Marla hummed the harmony, keeping time with her movements.

A smooth baritone voice sang the words from somewhere across the garden. More people joined in. The garden was alive with song. Ava taught her this one when she was a little girl. She sang now, adding the high harmonies to the melody and deep notes others sang.

Her fingers warmed as they brushed over the soil, gripping more onions. Energy flowed through her. It faltered as she let the song fade from her tongue, stopping completely when she held the onions up. What?

Marla tossed the onions in the basket and picked up the harmony again, her voice blending in with the others. The power was back, flowing through her as she pulled the onions and set them in the basket. They sang a few verses as they worked, of growth and health and abundant harvests.

The song stopped. Someone picked up a new tune, and Marla looked at the empty soil plot before her. Her basket was full to bursting with spring onions. She smoothed the plot with her hands. The next plot over would be ready in a week, the tall green stalks bright and healthy.

Voices joined in the new song as she retrieved a packet of seeds. Marla kneeled, adding her voice to the song. She gently pressed the tiny seeds into the soil, focusing on the words she sang, letting the energy build in her and flow back out into the soil. Were the seeds glowing slightly? No, she must be imagining it.

With the seeds in place, Marla stood and brushed the soil from her leggings. She picked up the heavy basket and hauled it down the paths, back to the main garden entrance. Marla wrestled the basket up onto the low wagon, beside other baskets of fruits and vegetables. A new song began. She joined others weeding among the later vegetables, those just beginning to emerge from their seeds.

When the song faded, Larinar began telling a story. Marla moved closer. This was one of her favourites. She mouthed the words along as his voice rose and fell, sharing how the daring adventurers crossed the rugged wilds. She journeyed with them in her imagination as they reached the promised land of safety and good harvests. The sun crossed the sky as they worked, stopping for water breaks and lunch. By midafternoon, the garden was tended.

"Great work, everyone. Don't forget to grab your basket when you go." Narria stood on the wagon. She pointed at the baskets at her feet, each with a selection of the fresh produce and herbs inside.

Marla washed at the water pump with the others, drying her hands on a spare cloth draped over a drying rack. She inhaled deeply as she picked up her basket. It smelled of fresh herbs and soil. She wasn't much of a cook, but her mother could turn those into mouth-watering delights. With a quick wave back, Marla left the garden.

***

Her knuckles rapped against the wooden door. She waited. No one came. Ava could be with a patient. She opened the kitchen door and slipped inside. If she was with someone, Marla wouldn't disturb her. Her footsteps were silent as she crossed the kitchen and headed down the stairs.

Light glowed from the cellar. The stairs creaked with each step as she descended.

"Marla?" Ava called from the far room.

"Yes, it's just me."

"Alright. Get reading."

She brushed her fingers over the stone wall as she walked down into the golden light. Marla paused at the bottom. Both doorways glowed, but the second room was open. A woman sat in a chair, with Ava standing in front of her. They held hands. Both women glowed faintly.

Ava looked up and met her gaze. "Reading?" She stared at Marla. "Close the door behind you."

"Sorry." Marla hustled over to the library.

The door opened with a light touch of her hand. She closed it behind her again. The lanterns and strange lights already glowed for her. A plate of cookies and a mug of steaming hot chocolate waited on the table.

Marla settled in the chair and pulled the stack of books closer. She scanned the titles, stopping at Magic for Planting and Harvesting. Her hand trembled as she paused. The next book caught her eye, the shimmering blue ink sparkling in the light. Lines of Power: Planetary Circulations. Marla stared between the two books, before choosing the book on planting. Maybe it would explain what happened in the garden when she was singing earlier.

She opened the book as she picked up the mug. The chocolate was still hot, but just cool enough to sip. She smiled at the sweet cream mixed in as she took a long sip. Marla skimmed through the introduction. So, she really could use song to help a garden grow. It wasn't a dream, and she didn't imagine it.

Her magic will grow stronger if she grounds herself. Great. What does that even mean? Marla flipped to the table of contents. Nothing there mentioned grounding. She checked the index. Was it known by another name? Maybe Ava would explain it?

Who was the woman? Why were they down here instead of up in the treatment rooms? She wasn't from the town or immediate area, not even the closest villages. Marla shook her head and focused on the page again.

She nibbled on a cookie as she read. She was two cookies in when her focus wandered. Her mug was empty. Now she understood more about what happened today, and the songs, though she still had so many questions.

Taking a pencil and pad from the table, Marla jotted notes down. She added questions below that. Pages later, her brain was tired, and she couldn't focus on the words anymore. Marla folded the pages and tucked them in her pocket.

Marla gathered her dishes and left. The other room was empty and dark. The lantern still glowed at the bottom of the stairs. She left it burning as she climbed up to the kitchen. Where was Ava? She set her dishes in the sink.

She peered out the window, face close to the glass. It was dark outside, and the window bounced the lantern light back at her. The street was quiet, small patches of light from the lanterns outside showing empty streets. Marla headed out the kitchen door and into the night.

An owl hooted as she passed through the garden. Marla stepped into the street and latched the gate behind her. The huge night patrolman wandered down the street towards her, his sword at his belt and the metal noisemaker over his shoulder. She smiled and nodded as she passed him. He nodded back. His fingers tightened on the long metal cylinder as he peered into the shadows beyond the lanterns.

She turned down her street. Only the sound of her own footsteps kept her company. She climbed the steps and entered her house, the door still unlocked for her. Marla waved at her parents in the kitchen as she passed, heading for her bedroom.

After a quick washup, she changed, tossing her dirty clothing into the basket in the corner. The knob on the lantern turned smoothly as she extinguished the flame. How had Ava done it? Could she light lanterns like that, too? Shaking her head, Marla settled in her bed. Where would she even begin? She pulled the thick covers over her and snuggled into her blankets.

The moon rose outside her window, shining in on her. Did today really happen? Her skin tingled where the moonlight landed on her. She stuck her hands out into the light and closed her eyes. A soothing warmth moved through her. That warmth again?

Marla opened her eyes. The warmth faded, but didn't stop completely. She closed her eyes again and took a slow and deep breath. The warmth moved down, stronger this time, all the way to her toes. It's like being wrapped in the softest blanket and hugged. What was it, though?

She rolled onto her side, curled up in the blankets. The moon caressed her face. She smiled slightly as she tucked her hands back under the blankets.

***

Marla tilted her face up to the sun, her eyes closed. After letting the heat soak into her skin for a moment, she turned back to the shelf. Holding the wire tool between her fingers, Marla pulled it through the block of clay. Taking the new piece off, she wrapped the large block and set it back on the shelf over her worktable.

She took the large bucket and filled it halfway with water. The garden pump moved smoothly as the water flowed. She set the bucket beside her wheel, out in the biggest patch of sunlight in the corner. Marla retrieved her clay and sat on the short stool by her wheel.

With the sun at her back, Marla lifted the clay. She smacked it down on the wheel. A flick of her hand got the wheel started. Her feet worked the double treadle, spinning the clay. She closed her eyes and felt the clay, drawing it up.

The breeze kept her cool enough, even with the sun beaming down on her back. The clay almost hummed under her fingers, harmonious as she shaped it into a bowl. Dipping her fingers into the water as needed, she let the clay help guide the shape. Had clay ever moved so easily for her? She pressed the treadles in time with the slow and steady beat she felt in her bones.

Marla opened her eyes. A beautiful bowl waited for her on the wheel, symmetrical and almost perfect. She took the wire and freed the bowl from the wheel. Cradling it in her hands, she lifted the bowl. Did she really make this?

A bird perched on her drying rack. Marla approached slowly. It flapped its little wings and flew to a nearby tree, chirping at her. She set her bowl on the rack. Marla lowered the thin and gauzy fabric around her rack, tying it into place. It would help the clay dry evenly, protecting it from the breeze.

The bird cheeped at her again.

"I'm coming. Hang on." Marla wiped her hands on a cloth.

She walked to the bird feeder she had made last year. The bird peeped and bounced around as she poured seed into the shallow dish. The small rim kept the seed from spilling out. Marla tucked the bag of seed away and stepped back. The little brown bird hopped down and pecked at the seed.

So close to her? Marla raised an eyebrow. She shrugged and went back to her wheel. The rest of the flock landed, sending seed everywhere, as she washed her hands in the bucket. She dipped the rag into the water and began cleaning up.

"Look at all of them."

The birds flew off, shrieking.

Marla looked up at the back gate. "Jolnir, do you need something?" Why did he need to stop by now?

He leaned against the back gate. The gate shifted under his weight. "Just thought I'd say good morning." His thin beard was still streaked with soil, though to be fair, it was little more than the peach fuzz of youth. He must have been in the fields, but why was he back already? Shouldn't he be helping plant crops?

She turned her back to him as she sat on her low stool. "Good morning. Now, I have a lot of things to do, so—"

"Need any help?"

Marla shook her head. "I'm fine. Why aren't you in the fields?"

"I'm just on my break, so I went for a walk. See you later, I guess." The hinges squeaked and his footsteps faded.

Finally. She sat motionless for a few breaths. Maybe she should build a higher wall, or move her wheel closer to the house? Nonsense. The sun was best here, and she needed the warmth on these early spring mornings. Setting her rag aside, she went and gathered more supplies.

With a clean wheel and fresh water, Marla got another chunk of clay. The bowl was fun, but she had projects to do for other people now. Settling back at her wheel, Marla set to work. Her mind was on the tasks, the projects people needed, but her body still remembered the feel of making the bowl.

The hours marched on as she added pieces to the drying rack. She looked at the assortment of pitchers, mugs, all manner of containers, and some plates. Marla smiled to herself. Her teacher still handled the complicated projects but sent more and more of the everyday needs to Marla to finish.

"Lunch is ready," her mother called, leaning out through the open back door.

"Be right there. I'm cleaning up." Marla waved a clay-covered hand.

She washed her tools and gathered any remaining clay in a covered bucket. With practiced hands, Marla cleaned her wheel. Washing her hands and the bucket, Marla poured the water in the gravel pit in the corner.

Pausing for a moment, she stared at the skin on her right forearm. The scars were fading, but would they ever go away? Her memories were patchy, but she still recalled the lurching feeling and the pain when she landed. Ava made her special home baked treats while her arm healed, and the blacksmith gave her little metal toys she could play with while she was stuck in bed. Pulling herself from her thoughts, she set the bucket beside her wheel to dry in the sun.

With everything sorted, Marla went inside. The kitchen was warm even with the windows wide open, the oven still radiating heat from the baking. A steaming bowl of food waited for her at the table. Her mother ladled the rest of the stew into one of her glazed clay containers. It had two handles, as well as a sturdy wooden carry handle, so she could take it to the fields with ease.

"I'll take this to the Sowers. When you're done, Ava asked for you. She could use help in her garden. Just think, you'll be her successor." Her mother beamed at her.

Marla nodded. "She's starting to teach me things." Her thoughts turned back to the hidden library.

"Study hard. Just don't forget that platter you promised me." Her mother grinned. "Bright colours, remember." She set the lid on the container. "I'll clean up when I get back. Don't keep her waiting."

Marla dipped her spoon in her stew. The vegetables were chopped fine and mixed in with grains. Little pieces of spice mixed in, bringing specks of bright green to the pot. She added a spoon of the nut sauce from the bowl on the table and stirred it in. A dab of Kiri Root paste for flavour, and Marla stirred it one last time.

"Mm." Marla took another spoonful, and another.

She poured some water in her empty bowl and left it in the sink. If helping Ava meant she'd get out of doing dishes, Marla would spend all day in the garden.

CHAPTER 3

People nodded to her as she passed them in the streets. Some had soil on their knees and were coming from the fields, others carried food containers out to the workers, the contents still steaming through the little vents in the lids. Marla walked past the house and wandered right back to the herb garden.

Ava kneeled in a corner beside some pots, a growing pile of little green weeds on the path beside her. "There you are. Did you get a good big lunch?" She looked over her shoulder at Marla.

"I did. What can I help with?" She walked over and kneeled beside the old woman.

"Today we go deep into the structure of the plant, and how it tells you about a plant's needs." Ava gestured at the pots. "If you're going to help things grow, the first step is knowing what conditions you have. Here, I got you your own notebook. You'll learn better if you take notes." She pulled a notebook and stylus from her pocket and held them out.

Marla took the crisp new notebook and opened it to the first page. The paper was thick and white. She ran her fingers over the sleek pages. She took the stylus and wrote her name on the frontmost page, the ink soaking in immediately. The stylus moved so smoothly over the paper. Where did Ava get it? The standard ones given out freely weren't this easy to write with.

Ava reached for a bucket and upturned it beside her. "Sit. Step one is to always protect your body from the strains of work, especially your knees. You'll spend a lot of time down here, so we'll get you a small stool like mine. You don't have to kneel just because your knees still work."

Marla shifted up onto the bucket and straightened her legs a bit.

"What does this tell you about the plant, and where it's adapted to grow?" Ava cradled a leaf in her hand.

Marla tapped the stylus against her chin. "Leaf shape affects how quickly a plant loses moisture to the air around it." She shared what she could remember, how slender leaves lose less moisture to the surrounding air than wider leaves. "But why aren't both plants suffering here?" Marla pointed at two nearby pots. "It should be too dry for that one, but also too wet for that one."

Ava chuckled. "You're right about both plants. I can always water this one to make up for the lack of rain. It takes special skill to help this one grow, though. Today we're going to study water and how the plants use it. Also, we'll look at how you can interact with water to help. First, though, you need to learn to feel the water around you."

She poured some water into a large flat dish. Marla smiled. She made that dish for Ava a year ago. Ava held her hand over the dish and closed her eyes. After a few long moments, she opened her eyes and smiled at Marla.

"You've made many pots for me. I always requested a specific size or shape, and a certain number of drainage holes in the bottom. It's partly how I control how much water stays in the soil. Now, feel for the water. It can't run away, so you have as much time as you need." Ava nodded at the dish.

Marla held her hand over the dish. She closed her eyes. "What am I feeling for? How?"

"Breathe slow and deep. Water is our life. Listen with all your senses. It should call to you, like the flow of life." Ava's voice was barely a whisper. "Just open yourself and let it call to you. That's enough."

She pulled a deep breath in and let it ease out again. The deep pulsing filled her. Now water? What does it feel like? Marla thought of the feel of rain on her skin, or the damp air that followed.

"Good. Let go and let it come to you. You cannot bully water into doing what you want. In time, you can learn to guide it, ease it, and work with it. For now, simply be open to it."

She let her thoughts go as she took another breath. A few drops of water sprinkled over her hand. She smiled as they rolled down over her skin before falling back into the dish. Wait, was that it? Her wet hands on the clay felt like this. A tiny spark, barely a tingle, more like the warmth of the sun.

"Water is life. It can dissolve many useful things, like nutrients and fertilizers, even medicines. It holds heat well or can cool us and other things. There's an ever-changing aspect of water, but it's also unique. Find that uniqueness, and you'll know water."

Marla relaxed and opened herself to the flickers of energy. They were tiny, a little flash of recognition, but nothing solid she could hold on to. It skittered away just as she felt she had it.

Her stomach rumbled, yanking her from the moment.

Ava laughed. "Don't worry. I didn't learn right away, either. It took me a few days of deliberate practice, and I was an amazing student." She winked at Marla. "It comes to everyone in their own time. Now, we've been at it for hours. It's time for some tea."

"Hours?" Marla looked up at the sky.

The sun hovered over the fields, beginning the steady drop to the horizon. Shadows stretched longer over the ground. Her legs ached in protest of sitting so still for so long. How did she not notice?

Ava rested a hand on her shoulder. "When in communion with nature, we can easily lose track of time. Always practice somewhere safe and private, at least until you learn to sense other people. You're vulnerable when you're in the link."

The old woman stood, easing her body up. Marla closed her book, already with pages of notes on leaves and water, complete with her own little drawn illustrations. She followed Ava into the house. Marla would need to make herself a shoulder bag for her notebook.

"Now, I want tea for my joints, and I'll make you some for energy. Help yourself to those." Ava waved at the warming plate on the stove. "Greens and cheese. Your favourite."

Marla headed straight for the stove. She selected a large pastry from the plate, still pleasantly warm to hold in her hands. Each bite had that gooey-ness of cheese blended with some fresh greens from the gardens, including bits of spring onions. Little herb pieces gave a touch of sweetness to offset the greens. She devoured it in seconds.

"Start your reading. I'll bring your tea and more pastries down for you." Ava set a pastry on a small plate and handed it to Marla. She draped a cloth over the girl's arm. "Don't get the pages greasy."

Marla grinned. "I won't." Defile a book that way? Never. Nothing beat crisp pages as she made her way through a book.

She headed down the stairs, one hand holding her plate and the other on the railing. She touched the lantern at the bottom and the light flickered to life. The glowing door waited for her, shining in her senses, but not casting any light in the room. Marla walked over and touched it, pushing lightly. The door swung open.

The stack of books waited on the table for her. Marla set her plate down and settled into the chair. One book was right in front of her, waiting. She wiped her fingers before opening the cover. Points and lines of power? Had she ever heard of such things before? Marla couldn't remember. It wasn't in any science books she had. Still, she almost chose this book last time. Her fingers itched to wander through the pages.

25

She began reading. Nature was full of energy. Right, she felt that for herself already. Ava even explained a little more for her. The energy was everywhere, but it also concentrated in some places. Those were points of power.

The smell of fresh berry tea pulled her from the book. Marla looked up. Ava came in with a small metal tray in her hands. She set a teacup in front of Marla, along with another plate stacked with pastries. Marla finished her pastry and stacked the fresh plate on the empty one.

"Drink up." Ava lifted her own teacup to Marla. She shuffled over to her chair in the corner. The chair squeaked as she settled onto the thick cushion.

Marla wiped her fingers on the cloth. She picked up her teacup and took a sip. Ava must have cooled it already. It was pleasantly warm on her tongue. The honey gave it an extra burst of sweetness. She drank half before turning back to her books.

Strands or lines of power connected points of power. The energy over-flowed the pathways and spilled into the nearby areas. Interesting. Magic would be strongest at a point, and still stronger than normal along any line of power. Would she be able to feel where they were? One day, maybe?

Her teacup clinked against the saucer as she picked it up. Two more big swallows and her cup was empty. She finished her pastries as she thought about the lines of power. Had she felt one and not known? The book had some maps, and her town was right above one. They ran everywhere. Why? What use would the planet or nature have for such things? How did it affect places far from a line of power? Was it why the farms nearby still had good crops, despite the lessening rain?

"Alright, that's enough." Ava closed her book. "Go enjoy the sun before supper. Your evening is your own, since you read now. Bring the dishes."

"Sure." Marla set her book aside and gathered her plate and cup. She retrieved Ava's cup and added it to her little stack on the tray. "The map had different colours. What were the green dots? There's one not too far from here."

Ava glanced over her shoulder as she started up the stairs. "Those spots are special. They are where our magic is strongest. You can read about it tomorrow. Soon we'll go there, and you can feel it for yourself."

Marla set the dishes by the sink. "Thanks for the tea and the baking."

Ava smiled, showing her white teeth. "You need to eat well while you're learning. The tea will give both strength and protection. Rest now. To-morrow is another day for learning."

She waved at the old woman as she headed out the garden door. Marla strolled along the paths to the gate, admiring the plants around her. Would she keep a garden like this one day? Her thoughts turned back to the book. People can measure points of power using a spell. She didn't understand the magic yet. Would Ava teach her?

Could she find that point on her own? The map wasn't that detailed, since it was of the entire country. Still, she knew the direction. She could already sense some of the world around her. Not today, though. Marla looked up at the sun, low over the trees. Maybe tomorrow.

She crossed the street, passing people on their way home after a day in the fields. Soon the crops would be strong and could look after themselves better. For now, there was a lot of weeding and tending to do.

At least she could relax with her new geology book this evening. Marla smiled as she skipped down the road.

***

"Good. You're up. Once you eat, Ava would like you to go over. She could use your help." Marla's mother set a stack of pancakes on a plate and placed them on the table. "Eat up."

Marla smoothed her hair with her fingers as she sat in the chair. One lock of hair refused to stay tucked in her hair tie. Marla gave up and picked up her fork. "Alright."

Bowls of fresh berries and cream waited for her. Marla piled both on her pancakes and poured some syrup over it all. The fruit was sweet and plump, bursting with juice as she bit into her breakfast. She poured herself a glass of juice from the pitcher, ignoring the bitter dark tea in the nearby pot. A cup with traces of tea gathered in the bottom sat nearby. Her father must already be in the fields.

"Her apprentice. Can you believe it? I'm so proud." Her mother poured some tea and sat across from her.

Marla looked up and smiled back at her, her mouth full of pancakes.

"Make us proud. The nearby towns and villages also depend on her, and one day it'll be you." Her mother ran her finger along the rim of her teacup. She frowned.

Marla gulped down her pancake. "Is something wrong?"

Her mother shook her head. "No. I just worry that one day you might be—never mind. We're so far from the capital, you'll be fine."

Fine? The city? What does it have to do with anything? Marla shrugged and shovelled the last of her pancakes into her mouth. She scraped up her last berries and ate them.

Her mother stared at the table as she sipped her tea. "Have any of the young men caught your attention?"

Marla's fork clattered to her plate. "Excuse me?"

"Well, you spend so much time making things for people and helping in the garden, but I don't see you socializing with any of the young men. Do you need more trips to neighbouring markets? Maybe there's a nice young man nearby that suits you?"

Marla shook her head. "I'm not talking about this." She took her dishes to the sink and ran the water.

"You can't wait forever. What's wrong with the boys here?" Her mother peered over the edge of her cup at Marla.

She stared at her plate as she scrubbed it. "Nothing." Well, nothing she could figure out. When she saw them in a group, her heart raced, and her palms sweat. She wanted to run. How could she explain that, though? Even she didn't know why.

With breakfast done and her dishes cleaned, Marla grabbed her cloak from its hook. She wrapped herself in the warmth and stepped outside. The thick wooden door banged behind her. The bright sun streamed down, warming her through. Marla set off down the steps and turned down the street.

"It's a wonder the crops are doing as well as they are, with the rain being what it is." Farmer Cortir leaned against the fence. He wiped a cloth over his forehead. "At least the gardens are thriving."

Malia looked up at him, her head tipped back so her floppy sunhat wasn't in the way. She pulled a thistle from the soil and tossed it aside, her thick glove protecting her. She glanced at Ava's house. "How are the outer fields?"

Marla slowed her step as she passed.

"The closer to the town the field is, the better the crop. It's like that everywhere I've talked to people. Weirdest thing we've ever seen." He took his hat off and spun it on his finger before setting it back on his head. "I wonder why the capitol isn't doing anything, or if the towns and villages are okay because of them? Maybe they're fixing it with magic and don't need to come out here? Why wouldn't they tell us, though?"

Malia spat in the dirt. "They can't do anything like that, can they? They don't work with nature. They only use it and take from it. Besides, if they could actually help, they'd be shouting it to everyone."

29

Cortir shrugged. "They're the reason we have these tools and advanced metallurgy, and the science books. If it weren't for them, we'd still be using horses and oxen to plow and plant, doing things the hard way." He glanced up at the windmill at the edge of town.

Marla looked over. The massive blades spun slowly. The sun reflected off the bright paint. She shook her head and sped up again, abandoning the conversation. Was there anything the capitol could do? Could anyone bring the rain back, or were they at the mercy of the weather?

The old woman was sitting on the porch, a book in her hand. She looked over as Marla came through the gate.

"Morning, Ava." Marla bounded up the steps.

"Good morning. How are you feeling today?"

"I'm good, I think."

The old woman smiled. She pulled a small, wrapped package from her pocket. "Take this to Fillanna in Toramine. Keep it tucked away. Show it only to her. Are you up for a trip like this?"

Marla took the small package and tucked it in her pocket. "I'll be fine. I've made the trip many times. It's not far." She smiled at the old woman.

Ava took her hand. "I know. You didn't draw attention before, though. Be careful. Be safe. Cut through the woods. Don't use the road. The woods are safer."

"Okay, I'll be fine. Am I bringing anything back with me, like trading?" Marla tilted her head and waited.

"Most likely. If she has something for me, I'd appreciate you bringing it back." Ava squeezed her hand. "Go."

With the package safely tucked in her pocket, Marla headed from the garden. The breeze brushed over her face. It was going to be a beautiful day; she could feel it. Marla left the garden and joined the road. The packed dirt was smooth and easy to walk on. Marla left town, a spring in her step. Once she was through the gates and around the bend, Marla slipped from the road and into the trees.

The soft ground cushioned her steps, making them silent. Birds flew overhead, little brown balls of feathers flitting from tree to tree, calling to each other. The occasional small animal ran past. Marla smiled. It was just her and her woods now. Why take the roads when the forest was so peaceful?

She closed her eyes and knelt. Marla rested a palm flat against the ground. Her skin tingled. Tiny green shoots pushed up around her hand, the little leaves unfolding as they stretched up. Little specks of energy moved around her, some in the trees and others among the bushes and groundcover.

She took another slow breath, and the energy took shape. Mice, squirrels, and birds took shape in her mind. Within seconds, they were gone, and the forest was back to normal. Only the tiny new plants proved she wasn't imagining it.

Marla opened her eyes. She no longer saw their presence. They hid in the plants, but she still felt them like an echo. The sensations slowly faded as she stood and walked. Soon it was just her and the forest, as she always knew it before. It was stronger that time, though. One day, would she feel it all the time?

The town wasn't far. She could be there and back well before dark. She touched a tree as she passed. A surge of life burst through her.

Wood Walkers? She'd heard rumours, things the adults said when they didn't think she could hear them. People spoke of them with reverence. They had powers, though nobody mentioned what those powers were. Marla could confirm that. She smiled to herself again. Nobody ever mentioned what the powers were, though. What else could she do?

Ava caused life to spring out around her. Animals followed her without fear, even next to their predators. She even knew Marla was there the whole time. She let Marla watch. And now Marla was one of them? She shook her head. What did that even mean? It meant Rogar was wrong, and she was special. What would he know? He was just a boy when he boasted about how important he was.

She skipped across the stream and up the bank. Foxes jogged into the bushes ahead of her. Normally skittish, they didn't even glance her way. Even the birds weren't flying off like normal. They didn't stop their song once, no matter how close she passed.

Marla turned her head and listened, her hand cupped around her ear. Was that the blacksmith? As she got closer, she could make out the murmur of the crowd and the sound of saws cutting wood. The blacksmith's hammer rang out steadily. She quickened her step. It was close now. She slipped among the trees to the edge of the woods.

The town lay before her, just a few dozen feet away. People gathered in the town square. Marla weaved through the buildings and peeked around the edge of one. Horses in fancy tack danced around the stableboys, fidgeting and stamping their hooves.

What were they doing here? Marla pressed herself closer to the rough wooden wall. She saw a flash of white and looked over at the inn. Men in robes walked up the steps. A woman in a plain cream-coloured shift dress followed them, her shoulders slumped and her gaze down. Two men in simple work clothes, also in that cream colour, walked behind her. They went inside, ignoring the stableboys taking the horses around the building.

Marla couldn't get the woman from her thoughts. Her face was lined and tanned, as if she spent time in the sun. Her eyes were half closed, and she didn't once look up. She didn't have the arrogant stance of the men with her. She had a dark band around her neck, fitted closely. Nobody else had one. What did it mean?

Worse, what were the Light Chargers doing here? Fear surged through her. A flash of a memory barely more than a glimpse ran through her mind. Someone in white chased her. She panted as she ran. What? When did that happen?

She shrugged it off. Marla crept to the road through the narrow paths between workshops. She skirted the edge of town. Fillanna's house was close to the edge, near the main road, just up ahead. She vaulted the low stone wall, dashed across the yard, and rushed to the side door.

Marla crept up the steps and slipped through the door. She closed the door behind her and took a deep breath. Who was that woman with the Light Chargers? How did she end up like that?

"Come in, child."

Marla spun. "Sorry, I meant to knock, but—" Her words failed her, and she shrugged. How could she explain when she didn't understand it herself?

CHAPTER 4

Fillanna leaned against the counter, a mug of tea in her hand. "I know. They are here. Come. Sit. Have some tea."

The older woman got a teacup and set it on the counter. She filled a little mesh ball with tea leaves and set it inside. Steam still rose from the kettle as she poured hot water into the cup. The smell of fruit and flowers filled the kitchen. Setting the cup at the table, Fillanna gestured at the chair before it.

Marla pulled the package from her pocket and held it out. "Ava sent this." She handed the package to Fillanna and sat.

Fillanna nodded at the basket of fresh buns on the table. "Help yourself. The tea will be ready in a couple of minutes." She unfolded the brown paper from around whatever was inside.

Marla nibbled on a bun as Fillanna read a note inside the package. That wasn't writing as she knew, but little symbols. Some kind of code? She dipped the edge of her bun in the tea and ate it. The older woman tucked the note in her pocket. She held a small stone in her hand, the size of a large pebble, and almost translucent. Little flecks of white were scattered through the pale pink gemstone.

"Interesting. Yes, this will take a few moments, but I have everything I need." Fillanna went to a cupboard and took a wooden box from inside.

The box was large, easily as big as her biggest books. The wood was stained red, with gold trim, and a black tree etched on the lid. She took the lid off, revealing wire and small tools. A magnifying glass in a frame sat in one corner.

"Pink with an eagle? That's rare, indeed," Fillanna muttered to herself.

Marla took another bun as she watched. Fillanna set the gemstone on the upturned lid, the inside covered in felt. Taking pieces of wire and tools from inside, Fillanna wrapped an intricate pattern, bending smaller wires around thicker ones. Finally, she slipped a thin wire through the gemstone and added it in where the eagle's eye would be. Marla sipped her tea as the pendant took shape. Wait, the gemstone didn't have a hole in it before. How did she do that?

"There." Fillanna fastened a chain to the top with a loop of wire. "Ava will want this. Put it around your neck, so you don't lose it on the way back. Keep it under your shirt. Don't let people see it." She passed the little wire eagle pendant to Marla.

Marla eased the chain over her head. The metal was warm and delicate. The gemstone caught the light and almost seemed to glow. She tucked it under her shirt, resting her hand over the shape just below her collarbones.

"Is there anything else for me to take back?" Marla glanced at the basket of buns.

Fillanna laughed. She handed the girl two more buns. "No, that's what she's expecting. You should go now, while they're hopefully still eating. Sneak out, and don't be seen."

Sneak? She could do that easily, but why? Why did their presence make her body tremble? Mind you, her mother never let her get too close to them before, either. Did her mother know something she didn't? "Alright. Thanks for the tea and buns."

Fillanna rested a hand on Marla's shoulder. "You are most welcome. And, girl, don't use those abilities until you're home and safe. Especially not while you're still close to them."

Marla nodded. She still wasn't even sure what her abilities were, though. "Thanks. Be safe."

She slipped from the house. Marla vaulted the back fence and ran for the trees. Once safely inside, she skirted the edge, heading back for her path. Hoofbeats? She threw herself into the nearest bushes and huddled down. Marla peeked through the leaves.

From up here, she could see much of the square. The stableboys were bringing the horses back around the inn, fully tacked up in their fancy leather. The men in robes came from the inn and walked to the horses, the woman and other men behind them. The men in white mounted the horses. Slits in their robes down the front and back let them ride, covering their white leggings even while mounted. One man had gold trim on his robes.

One man turned on his horse and stared towards her bush. She ducked down close to the soil and held her breath. She lifted her head just enough to see them. He raised a hand over his eyes and leaned forward, searching. For her? Her stomach rolled and cramped. Marla wrapped her arms around her belly.

After a long moment, he turned his horse and led the group from the town. They headed down the road away from her. The others walked behind, far enough back to avoid the dust. There was something familiar about him. No, she must be mistaken. She didn't know any Light Chargers. Her stomach dropped. Yes, she did. Rogar.

Marla snuck deeper into the trees. Once the town was out of sight, she jogged. Keeping careful watch, she stayed far from the roads. Nobody was following her. Maybe they didn't know she was there? Maybe something else got his attention, and not her?

She took the most direct route back she could, keeping to the thicker trees. The sun rose above her, ready to start dropping again. Who were the people in plain clothing with them? Who was that woman? How did she end up with them?

Jogging where she could, walking when she needed a break, Marla made it back in half the time. Her town came into sight. She ran to Ava's house and went right in, not stopping to knock. Ava sat at the table with a pot of tea, waiting for her with a fresh plate of biscuits.

"Sit, child. How did it go?" Ava waved at the empty chair.

Marla slid into the sturdy chair and took the offered biscuit. "I got there fine and gave her the package. She sent this back." Marla pulled the pendant from under her shirt.

"Keep it. That's for you." Ava poured tea into Marla's cup.

"What? Really? It's beautiful. Why, though?" She ran her fingers over the wire, feeling the little eagle with its gemstone eye.

"You're awakening. That will offer some protection while you learn and grow. Some, mind. It won't hide you completely." Ava reached under her shirt and pulled a similar chain up.

Marla leaned closer and looked at Ava's pendant. A bear with an emerald eye hung on the chain. "That's amazing. Does everyone have one?"

"All Wood Walkers do. We get them when we're awakening. It helps us remain undetected as our abilities charge and settle again. The gemstone is unique to each of us and is chosen by our mentor or discoverer."

"What abilities? Fillanna mentioned not to use them on my way home. Is it the seed thing?" Marla leaned her chin on her hand, her elbow on the table.

Ava raised her eyebrow. "Don't experiment on your own. Yes, our ability to make things grow and nurture new life is one of them. This power, this magic, it keeps us close to nature. We are part of it."

"Undetected by who, though? The Light Chargers?" Marla took another biscuit from the wicker basket. Her stomach still clenched, but the biscuits helped the nausea.

"Yes. They use magic differently. They can drain us and take our power for their own if we're not wary. We work with the land. They take from the land, and from us." Ava tapped her fingers on the smooth tabletop. She wouldn't look up at Marla.

Marla's eyes widened. "The woman—" she mumbled.

"Excuse me?" Ava leaned closer.

"When I was there, there were two Light Chargers. They had three people with them. One was a woman. She looked tired and empty, like the life had been sucked out of her. She didn't even look that old, though she also did. I don't know how to describe it." Marla traced the rim of her cup with her finger.

"Tell me more." Ava held her gaze, her shoulders tense.

Marla told her everything she could remember, answering each question in as much detail as she could.

"Yes, she would have been awakening when they took her. If they get you before your defences are in place, they can steal every bit of magic you have. We make magic our whole lives, though the stolen ones make less each passing year. I'll alert the others. We might be able to rescue her."

Marla's hand shook. Her cup rattled as she set it down.

"Yes, child. You must be more careful. If you see a Light Wielder, you must run and avoid them, even if it means not completing an errand or doing something you promised you would. You can always try again later, but not if they take you." Ava drained her cup.

"I don't understand," Marla whispered. Another flash of memory raced through her thoughts. She tumbled and rolled, scrambling to her feet. Someone in white still chased her. When did this happen? Was it real?

"I know. You will. Know that you are special, and I will train you to do great things for the land. Be patient. Your powers need time to grow, just like plants need time as they emerge from the soil. Now go, get some rest. Tomorrow we'll spend more time in the garden, and I'll teach you more." Ava smiled at her.

"Can I—" Marla held her lower lip between her teeth.

Ava picked up the basket and held it out to her.

Marla grinned as she took another biscuit. "Thanks."

She waved as she walked to the door. The little eagle rested against her skin. She barely felt it, though she did sense something. It's a protective charm? Had she seen anyone else with a little chain around their neck? No, not that she could recall. Ava always wore those light scarves, hiding hers. Should she do the same?

Marla set off across the garden, heading for the gate. All Wood Walkers had one. Did Light Chargers have something like that, something that identified them? Well, the white robes were a big sign. She wandered down the street, lost in her own thoughts.

Did her parents know what she was? Did they know what she's going through? She promised Ava she wouldn't mention it to anyone. That promise echoed in her mind. Marla shook her thoughts free and went inside. How did she get back so quick?

Her mother looked up from her knitting, settled into her favourite worn chair by the unlit fireplace. "Hey, Sweetie. There's some supper on the stove for you. Your new book is here, on your bed."

Marla grinned. "Thanks."

"Eat first." Her mom called as Marla dashed past. "Clean up, then you can read."

"Yes, momma." She headed for the archway instead of the hall.

A thick clay plate held her meal, sitting on the massive metal stove that still radiated heat. She took the thick protective gloves and carried her plate to the table. Marla grabbed a cup and poured some juice before settling at the table.

She scooped up some millet and veggies. Her eyes widened. Citrus in the sauce? She smiled. Little pieces of chopped dates gave bursts of sweetness, too. Did Ava teach her the recipes, or did she learn them from one of her cookbooks?

Her fingers itched to hold her new book and dive into it. Once a month the book wagons came and everyone got to take a book for free, funded by the Academy. The Light Chargers ran the Academy. Her own bookshelf was bursting with all the books she collected over the years. She could return any books she was done with, but Marla couldn't part with them.

This book was unique, though. Ava sent for this one. Travelling merchants and traders would carry books from independent stores and makers if they were paid for their time. Ava mentioned this one came from a different city. Marla tried to recall the city's name, but maybe Ava never mentioned it?

She ate the last of her meal. Her plate was still hot, but she could pick it up in her bare hands now. She rinsed it and left it in the rack to cool. She'd clean it fully later, when it was cooler, and she didn't risk cracking it in cold water.

Marla dashed down the hall to her room. The book waited on the bed, still wrapped in paper, a note fastened on with string. Marla untied the string and pulled the note off.

Marla,

Here's the book I promised. Keep it tucked away when you're not reading it. It holds information older than our society, and some people would rather it be forgotten.

Ava

Marla tore the paper wrapping from the book. She flipped the book over and opened the plain cover. The first page was full of illustrations of plants, fine green line drawings of common weeds found in her yard. No, not weeds, useful plants, she reminded herself.

The writing almost shone. The black ink nearly sparkled. Herbs and Medicinal Plants for the Village Healer, by Jilla Morena Faria. Copied for Marla, the Newly Awakened.

Copied? Just for her? She brushed her fingers over the page, feeling the smooth paper. She flipped the pages through the table of contents until she reached the first plant entry. A finely drawn plant with small white flowers filled the top half of the first page. There was an in-depth description, including how to tell it from similar plants right beneath. The rest of the entry was on its medicinal uses, including how to prepare it.

It can stop bleeding and reduce inflammation? Marla read the recipe for a simple salve. Everything she needed was in here, including how to harvest and dry the plant. An index of recipes completed the entry. Not only was this plant in her front garden, Ava grew a large patch of it in her herb garden.

She flipped the page. The next plant also grew all over town. She even made tea with it before. It's good for upset stomachs, among other things. Marla read that entry as well. The next few plants also looked familiar. Marla skimmed through the rest of the section, recognizing more than half the plants.

Marla stopped at a set of images, lines drawn over maps and diagrams of a human and some animals. She looked up at the title. Energy Pathways. She traced the lines drawn over the person, all the way from their head to the feet. She recognized the map, though. That image was in Ava's book. The lines of power perfectly reproduced on this page for her, only over the human body instead of on a map.

The light dimmed as the sun dropped. Marla moved closer to the window, using every last bit of sunlight she had. Her parents and brother went to their own rooms at some point. Had she read straight through the evening?

When she could no longer read by natural light, Marla wandered into the kitchen. Her mother left a snack plate out for her. She ate, her mind still on the new book and those fabulous drawings inside. She cleaned up and washed herself before returning to her room. Marla tucked her book in her dresser, under her socks. She collapsed on the bed and curled up, sleep taking her swiftly.

***

Marla fastened her cloak as she left the house, shoving the door open with her hip. The sound of many voices all talking at once reached her. She looked down the road. Most of the town gathered in the square, peering out along the road.

"That's great news." The carpenter slapped farmer Senninger on the shoulder, his loud voice booming over the crowd noise.

"I know. My boy. Mine. He's the first in our family in a century." Farmer Senninger held a scroll up. "And he was strong enough they felt him at the capitol."

The young man beside him winced as the farmer thumped him on the shoulder. He wore a white robe with grey trim and sleeves. The young man couldn't stop smiling, even as he rubbed his shoulder.

Ava gripped Marla's sleeve and pulled her down the street, away from the crowd. "Come. We have to go now."

"They're coming," someone called from near the town arch.

Ava tugged her towards her house. Marla stood frozen. Those robes. She knew those robes. Ava narrowed her eyes. The girl bowed her head and followed. Light Chargers didn't come often, they seldom came with the book wagons, and she wanted to see the horses. They wore such fancy saddles, trimmed with precious metals and gemstones. Not the Light Chargers, though. She could do without them.

Ava shooed her up the front steps to her house. Had Marla ever gone in the front before? She glanced down the road, but houses blocked her view.

"This way." Ava dragged her through the hall, to the kitchen, and down the stairs. "You need stronger wards right now."

"Wards?" Marla stumbled along behind her over the packed dirt floor. She lost her footing, and the flash of memory with her stumbling rushed back.

Ava dragged Marla to her feet and to the second door this time. "He might detect you. Not all Light Chargers can, but enough. You need to be careful. I'm not losing you today."

"Detect me? They really can sense us?" Marla shivered. That man in Fillanna's town. He must have felt her.

"Hush and get inside. Yes, some can feel us, though not all can sense us from a distance. I'll set the wards. Don't come out until I come and get you." Ava shoved her through the door and slammed it behind her.

The latch caught. The door shone with a soft golden green glow. Marla stepped back, stumbling as she tripped on her own bootlace. She plunged to the floor and landed on her backside. Her stomach lurched at the brief falling sensation.

The light got her attention. What were those patterns? Lines spread over the door to the frame, where they kept going onto the walls, just like in the library. They circled the entire room, including the ceiling, leaving only the floor untouched. They looked like vines made of moonlight.

Marla eased to her feet and walked over to the door. She touched one of the glowing lines. It hummed faintly, the same pulsing she knew so well now. Something else filled the lines, but she couldn't place it. The lines faded until she could barely see them.

She paced the edge of the room slowly, following the walls as best she could around the furniture. This was definitely a treatment room, just like the one upstairs, with a chair, a bed, and shelves full of remedies. What was it doing down here?

When she returned to the door, Marla stopped. She took a slow breath and closed her eyes. The energy in the lines beside her tingled. What made them glow? She crouched and touched the packed dirt floor, her palm flat.

Energy flowed up into her palm, up her arm, and down through her feet. This wasn't like helping plants grow, so what was happening? The lines on the walls brightened as she took another breath. Even with her eyes closed, she could detect the glow. With each inhale, the lines glowed with more energy.

She opened her eyes. Her breath rushed from her lungs. Little globes of light floated around her, just like they did around Ava that day in the forest. The energy lines were so bright she could see the room like it was daylight.

What does this mean? Is this what it is to be awakened?

Boots clomped across the floor over her head. Marla ran to the far corner and curled up, her arms around her legs. The room went nearly dark, just a hint of the glow in the lines now. She held her breath. The boots circled above her.

CHAPTER 5

W as it a Light Charger? No, why would they be at Ava's house? Why would Ava hide her if there wasn't any danger, though? Everyone else got to wait and watch them come. She closed her eyes and dropped her forehead on her arms.

Memories flowed through her mind, clear as if they were happening now.

She stood at her front fence, her fingers clinging to the top as she balanced on her toes. Marla glanced back at her mom. The woman's eyebrows furrowed. She tightened her grip on Marla's shoulder.

A group of town boys around ten years old or so ran alongside the road, following the men on their grand horses. Their hooves were polished, and their coats gleamed in the sun. The man on the front horse sat so tall as he looked out at the townsfolk. What was he looking for?

The blacksmith frowned and walked back into his forge, his scowl hidden from them as he faced away. Navorra burst into tears and rushed into her house. The children gathered around as the men stopped in the town square. They pointed at the fancy bridles and saddles.

"It is time." The man from the first horse swung from his saddle and stepped down. He looked around at the children. "But not for most of you. You are too young yet." He took a small bag from his belt and opened it.

The children cheered as he passed little brightly coloured items around. Every child got a little sweet before he straightened up again.

"Time to go." Her mother pulled her from the fence.

"But momma, I wanna see." She spun in her mother's arms, one last attempt at watching the fancy horses. Her little hands reached towards the fence as her mother carried her to the house.

What an odd memory. Marla shook her thoughts free. Why had they been upset when everyone else was so excited? Nearly everyone else was there, smiling and bowing their heads respectfully. Why was she so excited in that memory, when in later ones she's running from someone in white? Nobody else wore white, so who else could it be? What happened in that fragmented memory to change things? She ran her finger over the scar near her wrist.

The latch turned, and the door opened a crack. The lines went dark. Ava slipped inside and shut the door. With a wave of her hand, the lines flared to life, the brightest they'd been yet. She held her hand out and a ball of light glowed, hovering over her palm.

"That was close. You were supposed to be hiding, not using your powers." Ava stared down at her.

Marla shrank back. "I didn't mean to. I don't even know what happened."

Ava stepped closer and wrapped her arm around Marla. "It's not your fault. You're so newly awakened, your powers might react without you. He might have sensed your power, despite my wards. He tried to call to it. The ward hid you, but he might know you're here in the town. Only time will tell now."

Marla took Ava's hand. Warmth flowed through her. "I didn't mean to," she whispered.

Ava let the light ball go out as she pulled Marla closer into a tight hug. "I know. What's done is done. Maybe nothing will come of it. Come. Have some tea." Ava led her from the room and back up to the kitchen. "Tea can also be your friend."

"My friend?" Marla sat in the chair, the bright cushion giving her some comfort. "Sure, tea can keep me healthy, but how can it be my friend?"

"This is a special blend." Ava filled the kettle. "It can hide you. I'll send some home with you. Tell your mother it's for a sore ear. She won't question that."

***

The slender weed popped from the soil with little effort. Marla tossed it in the pile nearby. These roots can be boiled. They aid digestion. They'll also choke out the other plants if allowed to grow unchecked. No wonder they were in pots in Ava's garden. Here in her own garden, Marla would gather them and take them to Ava later. At least her own small garden was still thriving.

Teanor left with the Light Chargers yesterday, whisked away for training in the city. He would become one of them. At Ava's insistence, Marla wore her eagle pendant all night. She had half a pot of the special tea before bed, too. It was hard to sleep when she kept imagining someone bursting into her room to kidnap her at any moment. No, the night was calm and peaceful. Why wasn't she?

The memory played in her head again. Why such an old memory? She had a few memories of them coming over the years.

Marla glanced up as a wagon rumbled past. A heavy tool of some kind was in the back, newly made by the blacksmith for tending crops with. Navorra passed on the other side of the street. Marla took a moment to watch her. She'd nod to anyone who greeted her, but Navorra was silent as she headed back to her house.

Navorra and the blacksmith, both were upset in that memory. What happened? Was it the same thing for both, or did they have separate reasons for being upset? Marla shook her head and focused on the weeds again. She didn't know the blacksmith well enough to ask such a personal question, but she had an idea.

She brushed the moist soil from her hands and stood. Marla went inside and gathered a packet of calming tea Ava gave everyone. She tucked it in her pocket. After a moment to wash her hands, Marla left the house. She turned down the street and headed to Navorra's house.

Marla hesitated at the front gate. With shaking fingers, she unfastened the latch and entered the front garden. She walked up the path and knocked on the door. Marla shifted from foot to foot. Should she just go?

The door opened. Navorra stood there, cloak unfastened, and inside shoes still untied. "Yes?"

Marla pulled the little packet from her pocket. "I brought some tea. I thought you might like a cup?"

The woman smiled, her lined face relaxing. "That was thoughtful. Come in."

She followed Navorra through the small sitting room and into the kitchen. Marla walked to the stove and got the kettle. She filled it and set it on the heat. The little mesh tea ball was on the shelf right nearby, so she filled it and set it in the pot.

"What brings you here, child?" Navorra sat. The chair creaked as she leaned down to tie her shoes.

"I—I had a memory. I'm not even sure if it's real or not. You were in it. You and others. I was so little, and it's just a few moments, but still—" Her fingers tightened around the teapot handle.

Navorra shrugged her cloak off and left it over the back of her chair. "Memories can be tricky things."

Marla nodded. "I know. Most of my earliest memories are just snippets of things. Our town hasn't changed much, though." She filled the pot with steaming water and brought it over. It didn't need to boil, not fully.

The old woman laughed. "No, it really hasn't. Nothing much does outside the city. We may get better ways to do things, new technology to make our lives easier, but we're still the same people inside."

She set the teapot on the table and went back for a couple of teacups. Marla settled into the chair. The old woman's hands were shaking as she rubbed them together. "Are you alright?"

Navorra nodded. She stared down at the table in front of her. "Sorry, child. I'm just not feeling my best right now."

"Allow me." Marla picked up the pot and poured the tea. Weak tea was better than waiting. Their next cups would be stronger. She set a cup in front of Navorra. "I was hoping I could ask you something. It can wait, if you don't feel well."

She tucked her grey hair back behind her ear. Navorra pulled her shawl tighter around herself. "You may as well ask."

"I'm sorry if this is awkward, and I understand if you don't want to answer. Why did you get upset when the Light Chargers came?" Marla blew on her tea. The water rippled around the cup before going still again. Doing something, anything, was better than just sitting there.

"Oh, child," Navorra whispered. "I hope you never find out for yourself."

Marla sat in silence. What did that mean? That wasn't an answer. She brushed her finger over the delicate cup handle. The porcelain was smooth and warm. "Why?" She couldn't help whispering.

"My daughter was like you." Navorra rested her trembling hand over Marla's. "She was awakening, too."

49

"Wait, daughter? You have a daughter?" Marla searched her memories. Was there ever a young woman living here? She didn't remember any mourning rites. How long ago was this?

Navorra brushed tears from her cheeks. "I do. She'll be thirty-five summers old now. They discovered her when she was about your age. You were barely a toddler at the time. I'm not surprised you don't remember."

Marla stared at the pale tea in her cup. She pressed her hands to her thighs and took a slow breath. Taken. Drained. How many names had those two words beside them in the book Ava kept? Was her daughter one of them?

The old woman stood. She walked to a shelf and picked up a framed picture. Her fingers brushed over the glass. She turned and showed the drawing to Marla. "Her powers surged when they were here. One of them noticed. They took her right then and there. Just like that, my baby was gone."

"Was that her?" Marla eased from her seat and walked over. She wrapped her arm around Navorra and hugged as she looked at the picture. Whoever drew it had talent.

Navorra nodded. "Mia. The carpenter's son was sweet to her. They might even have made a family one day. He drew this for me right after."

"What happens when they take someone like that? Is she still—alive?"

Her hand shook so hard the picture slipped. Marla caught the picture and set it on the shelf again.

Navorra stood with her hand over her mouth, tears streaming down her cheeks. "I need to lie down. I'm sorry, child."

Marla walked her back to her chair. The wood creaked again as she sat.

"Would you like me to get Ava?" Marla kneeled in front of her and took her hands.

Navorra shook her head. "There's nothing she can do. She's tried. I'll be fine after some more tea and rest."

"If you're sure. I'm happy to help if I can." Marla stood. She glanced at her teacup, still waiting on the table. Ignoring it, Marla left the house as silently as she could.

Ava approached up the front walk, a basket in her hands. "Oh, Marla. Once I drop these off, we should go for a walk. Wait out here for me?"

"Okay." Marla shrugged. She looked back over her shoulder at the door. "She's not feeling well."

"I'll check on her." Ava walked past and into the house without knocking.

Marla wandered down into the front garden. She kneeled and touched the tiny blossoms, the soft petals almost weightless in her hand. Marla looked around, listing in her head every plant she could remember at least three uses for. More than half. She grinned.

She stood and looked down the road out of town. What would it be like to leave with no warning? Sure, Marla wanted to see the world one day, but everyone was counting on her. In such a small town, everyone had a role to play. How could she just leave knowing that? What if she was taken, though? No, she needed to stay close to her family, now more than ever.

The door opened and closed again. Marla turned. Ava came down the front steps.

"Come, child. I feel like a walk."

Marla fell into step beside her. Ava moved like a woman not yet forty summers old, despite her advanced years. They turned behind the house and headed for the back garden gate. Through the gate, down a path, and they were into the trees.

"Navorra is my sister."

Marla glanced over at her. "Really?"

Ava nodded. "Mia was my niece. I wasn't here the day they took her. When you described her the other day, after your trip, I knew it was her. We're planning a rescue. I haven't told her. Navorra, I mean. Rescues are hard, and we don't always succeed on the first try."

Marla touched a leaf as she passed under the branch. "Is Navorra a Wood Walker, too?"

"No. It's in our bloodline, but it doesn't pass to everyone. She's sensitive to energy, but she can't manipulate it like we can." Ava stopped and bent down. She scooped something from under a leaf. "Hello, little friend. You need some help."

Opening her hand, Ava revealed a little mouse. She held it up to her heart and closed her eyes. They both glowed with a warm green light. When the light faded, the mouse stood and shook itself.

"There you go. Be more careful next time." She bent down and set her hand on the ground.

The mouse dashed off, scurrying for the nearest bush.

"How did you do that? Did you just heal her?" Marla smiled as the mouse disappeared. Did it work on people, too?

"I did. You'll learn how, too." Ava set off again, at the same steady pace as earlier. "To heal, you need to focus on health in your mind. Take what is and turn it into what it should be. Believe it can be that way again."

"That's amazing." Marla wrapped her arms around herself. "The Light Chargers. They don't come through here often. It should be easy enough to hide, right?" She worried her lower lip between her teeth.

"You know you're not the only one awakening, right?"

Marla nodded. "He left, though."

Ava nodded. She rested a palm on a tree trunk as they passed, stopping for a long moment. "Yes, but they'll be coming back to check the town once more now that he's gone, just in case they missed someone else." She cupped Marla's chin in her hand. "Which is why you must be careful. Don't let anyone see you using your powers."

"Okay," Marla whispered. They were coming back? "Is that how Mia was taken?"

The old woman slumped, her hand falling away. "Yes. A young man awakened at the same time as her. We warned her to be careful. We told her what he was. She got so scared of him, she'd run each time he came near. He mentioned this to the Light Chargers, and they came back for her. Had we not told her, she might not have—" Her voice shook, trailing off to nothing. "Just be careful."

"I will." Marla squeezed Ava's shoulder.

The faint rhythmic beating of the blacksmith's hammer faltered. It grew silent. Someone shouted.

"What's going on?" Marla gripped Ava's sleeve.

Ava frowned. "They're back, I bet. It's early. Stay out of sight. If it's really them, we need to get you into hiding. You're awakening faster than normal."

"Am I safer out here? I can go deeper into the woods."

The old woman shook her head. "You don't know how to hide yet, or where. It might not be them."

Ava led her back to the town, skirting the edges in the thicker trees. They circled around towards Ava's house, away from the main road. They snuck into the town close enough to see the square.

Everyone gathered in the town square. Some people pointed down the road. The thudding of hooves on dirt reached her. It was them. It had to be. The crowd parted. Marla leaned just a little farther around the building to see.

Three men rode into the middle of the crowd. They weren't wearing white robes. Merchants? No, the cloth was too fine for a travelling merchant, and not colourful enough. They felt like Light Chargers, though, with that same weird buzzing the others had. Wait, she could feel them? Could they feel her?

Ava hauled her back behind the building. Marla squeaked and Ava pressed a hand to her mouth. She stood over Marla with a finger to her lips. Marla nodded, and Ava let her hand fall away.

"This way." Ava gestured back to her house. "Stay low and don't let them see you."

They dashed to the next building, staying in the shadows. The garden gate was just beyond the next road. Marla glanced around the corner. Two men moved about the crowd as the third watched the rest of the town. If they timed it right, maybe they'd make it?

He turned his back and looked out towards the fields.

"Go," Ava whispered.

Marla dashed across the street, racing for the cover of the fence.

"There," a man called from the square.

Hoofbeats pounded on the dirt. Marla sprinted into the trees. Her lungs ached. She hurled towards the thicker bushes, running on instinct. Ava ran beside her. The horses would need to weave between the buildings, or head to the road and come back. How much time did they have?

Ava grabbed her and hauled her into some bushes. Marla fell as Ava disappeared beside her. She landed on the soft soil among the bushes. The hand pulled at her from down a hole. Marla scrambled down after her, ignoring the soil clinging to her.

The short tunnel curved down and sideways. She tumbled out into a small chamber, the ceiling supported by old planks. It was high enough to stand in, and only a few paces across each way. Sunlight barely reached down the tunnel, the only light she had.

CHAPTER 6

Ava took Marla's hand. Energy flowed through her and the ache in her lungs eased. Ava pressed her finger to her lips. Marla nodded. She sat and curled up, huddled beside the old woman in the near dark. Ava dragged her into the far back corner.

The ground rumbled. Hooves thundered past above them. Dirt shook free and floated down on her. The ground went still. Marla took a shallow breath through the dust. They waited in the silence. Neither woman moved. A bird chirped. Another trilled. Soon birdsong filled the air. Ava smiled and stood, brushing herself off.

"Who were they?" Marla pressed her hand to her heart. Her arm almost ached, more like a memory of the pain than anything.

"Light Chargers. That was an elite team. I don't know why they're not wearing the usual white." Ava gazed at the hole, their only way back up. "I hoped they didn't feel you that day. I guess they did. I never expected your powers to leak through the wards."

"How do they feel me? Were you hiding me with magic?"

"I was trying. Usually, we succeed. Few awakeners are powerful enough to leak through the wards." Ava wiped a tear from her cheek. "My niece was the last one we didn't save, and I promised myself that wouldn't happen to you." Ava wrapped her arm around Marla and hugged her to her side.

"You can stay and hope I can hide you, or you can leave and find the Wood Walkers' city."

Marla leaned her head on Ava's shoulder. She looked at the little shaft of light beaming down on the tunnel. Her stomach twisted at the thought of leaving. Wasn't she safe at home? "I don't know what to do. Will they ever stop chasing me?"

Ava shook her head. "No, child. They felt you. They will hunt you until they get you, or we hide you behind special wards. The nearest are around our city."

"How far is the city?" Marla's voice shook.

"It's a few days' run." Ava rested a hand on Marla's head. "You will be running. I can tell you how to get there, and where to find help along the way."

"Will I ever see you again?" she whispered.

"One day." Ava touched the dirt wall beside her. Tree roots glowed a faint green. "Listen closely. This in incredibly important. They cannot detect minor magic like communication and concealment spells. You can hide among small stands of trees or underground like this, as long as you're not using your powers at all. You'll blend into the natural power in the land. Nature is our ally, not theirs."

Marla listened closely as Ava explained how to get to the city. She practiced and repeated them back multiple times until she got it perfectly.

"Take these. You'll want them if you're going to make it." Ava got up and went to the other corner, where a tarp covered something. She pulled a backpack out and handed it to Marla. "It has a canteen, a tarp, a knife, rope, and other portable tools. Also, a basic medical kit, and some dried foods. There are more stores like this around the land. Take what you need and leave what you can, when you can. Our people can guide you to them."

Marla took the backpack and slid her arms through the straps. It was light and comfortable against her back. She snugged the straps and buckled the hip belt. "Thanks. Thanks for everything. I'm sorry." Could she do this? Was she really going to leave, just like that?

Ava pulled her into a tight hug. "Oh, child. You have nothing to be sorry for. I'm just sorry I can't take you there myself." She looked up at the dirt ceiling. "Now go. They're gone. Follow those directions."

The older woman shooed her up the tunnel and back into the forest. With a last glance back at her, Marla turned and headed through the trees. She fought the urge to look back. Her book was still in her bedroom. Would she ever get to retrieve it? Could Ava send it if she got a message to her?

With a heavy heart, she walked away from the only home she ever knew. At least she knew these forests. She was heading for a town she didn't visit often, but she knew the way. Being alone in the forest was safe.

A shiver of fear rushed through her. Why, though? The forest was empty again, and the animals were moving around. Stay close, her mother used to say. Stay close and you'll be safe. One day you'll walk freely again. Freely? Free from what?

For the first few hours, every little noise had her spinning and twitching. No, the birds are singing. They stop when someone is around. Someone other than me, that is. Me or another Wood Walker. I'm fine. Though she still kept watch, Marla calmed herself.

Step one is to find the stream and follow it. It'll lead to a waterfall. Head up the hill there and to the town. A simple task. She'd usually followed the road to the town, but she knew the stream. Marla stopped and listened. No stream yet.

The bushes rustled. Marla leapt sideways, tripping and landing in a heap under a bush. She pushed herself up enough to look around, her heart hammering in her chest. A fox darted out from under the bush and ran off. She smiled to herself as she stood and brushed herself off.

The sun dropped, and the shadows lengthened. Marla kept walking. The birds kept her company. A bird cried with a shrill peep and the flock took off. Marla froze and listened. Hoofbeats? Where? She ducked among the thickest bushes she could see. With her knees on the dirt, she curled up tight and focused on breathing slow and steady.

The sound was distant and muffled. Where were they? She couldn't tell yet. She pressed a hand to the soft moss under her. The sound faded. Marla stayed still. After a few long breaths, the birds started singing again.

Moving slowly, Marla stood. She peered through the trees, but all she saw was forest in all directions. She crept from her hiding place. Keep the sun to my back. I got this. Marla started walking again.

After a short while, she perked up. The stream? Yes, that was definitely running water. She jogged towards the noise, stopping to listen regularly. The water ran fast and clear over a pebbled streambed. Marla dropped to her knees and pulled her canteen out. She nearly drained it, taking massive gulps, before filling it once more.

She sat back on her heels. Her skin prickled. Was she being watched? Marla looked around. Where had the birds gone? She closed her eyes and listened. Foolish. She can't let that happen again.

Marla capped the canteen and tucked it away. Pulling her pack on, Marla slunk into the thicker bushes. She listened. The breeze rustled leaves slightly. That feeling got stronger, like an itch she couldn't scratch. Was it just a large predator? They could be incredibly silent.

A steady, soft thudding approached. Hoofbeats? Marla stayed low, tucked in among the bushes. Don't move. Breathe, soft and steady. Her heart betrayed her by pounding in her chest. She trembled, hugging herself tighter.

"Where is she?" a man muttered. "I swore I saw her."

The horse stomped a hoof, though the moss softened the sound.

A silent image yanked her into her thoughts. She lay sprawled on the ground beneath a tree, her broken arm held to her chest and oozing blood. Someone in white stood over her. It was gone in a flash. She cradled her arm against her chest, her hand over the scar.

Marla pressed her hand to her mouth. He was so close now, just a few bushes over. There had to be a better place to hide. She pressed her palm to the moss. No, she didn't dare. No magic, Ava warned. She closed her hand into a fist and held it to her chest.

The hoofbeats moved on. Marla lay still. Her legs cramped. Her lungs ached as she finally took a deeper breath. The hoofbeats were gone. How long should she wait? How long had it been?

A bird landed in the bush beside her and chirped. The flock followed, singing and flitting about. Easing to her feet, Marla crept from the bushes. She scanned the surrounding forest. Nothing. Just trees and birds. Faint hoofprints headed past her, going up the hill. The same hill she wanted. Her heart sunk.

Getting away and staying safe was the most important thing, but Ava said safety was up that hill. Now what was she supposed to do? Home was safe once. Should she go back? Maybe she should still go on, but not on this exact path? Marla walked until she was just out of sight of the stream, but could still hear it.

There, that should be far enough. She turned and followed the stream by sound, heading up the rise. The sun was nearly down now. How many hours of light did she have left? Would she make it or have to camp out here?

The birds flew off, scattering in all directions. Marla dashed for a cluster of trees. A horse snorted. Another whinnied from her other side. How many were out here? She tucked and rolled in among the bushes between the trees. They'd see her for sure. She curled up and pressed herself low to the soil.

Her foot dropped. She twisted and looked. Her foot hung over an opening. The shadows hid a hole; the branches hanging over it. How deep was it? She pulled herself in, wriggling down. The hoofbeats were getting closer. If they saw her boots, she'd be done for. Please, let this be deep enough.

Marla crawled and shifted. The tunnel opened up, and she slid down into a chamber. She curled and tucked her arms around her head as she rolled on the floor. Her breath rushed from her lungs. Marla sprawled at the bottom, a tool digging into her back.

She looked up. The lower half of the tunnel was darker, though sunlight flowed down into the upper part. The soil was slightly damp, but warm, not cool, like she expected. This had to be one of the places Ava mentioned.

It was just light enough to see once her eyes adjusted. There were supplies in the corner. She sat at the bottom of the tunnel and listened. It was so quiet up there. In the dark, she couldn't see the scar. How could she get it from running from a Light Charger? Wouldn't they have taken her back then? None of this made sense.

Marla peered up the tunnel. It was silent out there and the ground no longer shook. Were they gone? She pressed trembling hands to the soil and waited. How long should she wait?

A bird flew to the entrance and hopped down towards her. She chirped at Marla. Her little wings flapped. Marla smiled. She crawled back up the tunnel to the entrance. Listening closely, Marla poked her head up enough to see. She was alone, just her and the birds.

"Thank you. I appreciate it," she whispered. "Do you know the way?"

The bird peeped again. The bushes rustled. A small rabbit hopped out and sat before her. His nose wiggled as he waved a paw.

"You know the way?"

He hopped a few feet up the hill before stopping and looking back.

61

"Okay, thank you."

Marla followed the rabbit. Her boots sank into the soft soil before springing back with each step she took. The bird flew ahead before landing on a branch and waiting. It peeped. She and the rabbit approached, and it flew ahead again. The rabbit hopped beside her as they followed the bird. They crested the rise, and the ground levelled off.

The bird took off, flapping furiously and screaming a warning peep. Was that the metal of a horse's bit, or hoofbeats? She ducked and rolled into some bushes, following the rabbit. Marla stayed low as she peered through the leaves. She pressed a hand to her chest, over her racing heart.

A wagon rolled by, just within her sight, but too far to see well. Something massive pulled it. A horse or an ox? It passed by and kept going, not slowing at all. She must be near the road.

A horse snorted behind her somewhere. It was hard to hear over the pounding of her heart and the blood rushing through her ears. Those hoofbeats were getting closer. There had to be a better place to hide.

There, a few long paces away, a tree had fallen recently. The leaves were still green. The boulder behind would give her more cover. Marla dashed across and rolled under the tree. She wriggled up among the branches, close to the trunk.

"You, there," a harsh male voice called.

"Yes?" a woman replied.

"Where did the girl go?"

"What girl?"

"She didn't come this way?"

"I didn't see her." The woman sounded so confident.

A tree branch snapped.

"Over here," another man called.

Hooves pounded the soil, sending little vibrations through the ground. Marla curled up as tight as she could and closed her eyes. Slow and deep breaths, she reminded herself. Let them get farther away.

Soft footsteps approached her. She felt them instead of hearing them. How?

"Hey, are you okay?" The woman kneeled beside the tree.

"Yeah," Marla whispered, hating how shaky her voice sounded.

"Stay still a little longer. We're sending them away."

We? Who? Marla hugged her curled legs tighter. She couldn't stop trembling. The horsemen crashed through the bushes, heading away, getting farther with each moment.

"Alright, will you come out for me? We won't harm you." A hand extended under the leaves towards her.

Women were safe, right? She'd never seen one in a white robe. Marla wriggled out, crawling on her belly. Dirt clung to her clothing. She rolled out and sat, her back to the tree trunk. Marla pressed her shaking hands to her thighs. Her ankle ached. When did that happen?

"Deep breath, now." The woman took her hands and held them.

The trembling passed. She took a deep breath with ease. Her ankle stopped hurting, too. How? Her eyes widened. A Wood Walker?

"Thank you. Who are you, though?" Marla met her gaze. She noticed the chain tucked under the woman's clothing, just barely peeking out near her collarbone. She had a pendant, too.

The woman smiled, the fine lines around her eyes crinkling. "I'm Issa. What's an awakening Wood Walker doing out here in the forest, instead of hiding?"

63

Tears leaked from her eyes and rolled down her cheeks. "I messed up. They came for him, but I messed up."

Issa sat beside her and wrapped her arms around the girl. "It happens. Take another deep breath. We'll go when you're ready. We shouldn't linger here, though."

Marla wiped her cheeks with dirty fingers. She straightened up and braced on the tree as she stood. Marla clung to Issa's arm for a moment as she steadied herself.

"Thanks again. What are you doing out here?" Marla looked around. The town wasn't close that she could see or hear yet.

"We're travelling. Come with me. I know someone you need to meet." Issa slung her arm around Marla's ribs and guided her through the trees.

They passed through the bushes until Marla saw the road. She turned at a distant yell, slowing her step. Her gut urged her to run, but her legs felt like uncooked bread dough.

"They won't come back. Still, we need to move." Issa nodded to the wagon ahead. "Here."

The wagon was parked, the oxen standing quietly with their heads low. The closer ox looked at her and blinked slowly. Boxes and crates filled the back of the wagon.

Issa led her to the back, where she lifted the tarp. She pulled a crate out, revealing a small space inside. "Get in."

Marla scrambled up and wiggled into the spot. A couple blankets padded the hard wood.

"Pull that blanket over you as much as you can. It'll help hide you." Issa pointed at a dark grey blanket. "Be quiet. We'll let you know when it's safe." She slid the crate back into place and fastened the tarp down again.

Marla unfolded the thick blanket and curled up, spreading it over herself. Was she supposed to cover her head, too? She tucked deeper under it but kept it off her nose and mouth.

Footsteps approached the wagon. "Did you get her?" Another woman? She had a light voice, soft and almost hard to hear from her hiding place.

"Yes, we're ready." Issa walked to the front by the oxen.

"Come on." The light voice spoke with authority, and an ox snorted.

The wagon shifted. It vibrated lightly as it rolled down the packed dirt road. Marla examined the blanket as she lay there in silence, just the sound of hooves to occupy her. The threads were finely spun, and the fibres were soft. There was something about it she couldn't quite figure out, but the blanket felt like more than a blanket somehow. She itched to examine it with her powers, but didn't dare.

She closed her eyes and took a deep breath. The deep pulse of life wasn't there. Instead, the blankets wrapped around her warmed just a touch. Interesting. How did they do that? Was it blocking her senses? Was it hiding her from them?

Was this the help Ava promised? Maybe she had a chance now. With help, she could get to this city and be safe, if anywhere was safe. What if they wouldn't help, though, or took her the wrong way? Follow the river. What was next? Marla rubbed her temples.

New voices approached, barely audible over the hoof sounds and light rattling from the wagon. Wait, a man? Was she in trouble, after all? Were they really helping the Light Chargers?

No, Issa helped her hide. They must be her friends. She said others were drawing the Light Chargers away. Until she knew otherwise, she had to believe she was safe.

The wagon continued at a slow plod. Marla closed her eyes and settled. This wasn't the main road. Where was she? Recalling maps in her mind,

Marla tried to place where she might be. It helped pass the time, as she couldn't quite make out the voices.

The wagon turned, and the road smoothed out. Did they just join the main road? There were a few towns out this way, according to the maps, but only one was close enough to where she should be. Now she had some idea how far she had come.

Noises filtered through to her. The wagon jolted, and Marla bumped her head on a crate. She rubbed the spot, easing the ache.

"We're here." Issa was beside the wagon, walking to the back.

The tarp lifted, letting the light in. The crate shifted, scraping against the wooden deck as someone pulled it away. Issa held a finger to her lips as she extended a hand to Marla. Marla took her hand and eased to the edge. She dropped to the ground beside the woman.

They were parked in front of a vast building. A couple of people unhitched the oxen. Men opened a set of double doors in the building. It was half full of crates. A storehouse? Issa pulled her away, around the side of the wagon, and towards a stone wall.

"They're here. Stay quiet and follow me," Issa whispered.

"Where are we?" Marla asked, as quietly as she could.

"Somewhere safe. A supply depot. Come."

CHAPTER 7

They walked along the wall, staying low. Issa led her through a gate and turned among the trees. The sound of voices pulled her attention to some buildings among the trees. Issa kept to the thickest bushes as she weaved her way closer.

Marla glanced over and saw the road. It was wide, clear, and smooth where it cut through the trees. She followed Issa, staying low. They reached the back of a building. Issa held her finger to her lips and pointed to the corner of the building. Marla crept over and peeked out.

Two men slid from their horses; their white robes were unmistakable. Two more men in cream-coloured robes stood nearby, a woman between them. Her back was to Marla, but she had the same hunched posture and lowered gaze.

What were Light Chargers doing here? That didn't look like the group who were chasing her, but how could she be sure? Marla tucked back beside Issa, her back pressed to the wall. Maybe she wasn't as safe as she hoped yet.

Issa rested a hand on Marla's shoulder. She took the girl's hand and led her between some buildings, away from the men. "Come. This inn is safe." She stopped at a tiny building made of stone.

"This is an inn?" Marla stared at the small hut.

The door faced the forest, not the town. It wasn't on a main road or anything. Was Issa crazy, or leading her into a trap?

"It is. Watch." Issa opened the thick wooden door.

The inside was a single room with a couple of tables and a counter. Two tall men could stretch their arms out and touch the side walls.

A small woman sat behind the counter. She smiled at Issa. "The usual five?" She raised her eyebrow at Marla.

Issa smiled back and shook her head. "Six."

The woman nodded, her black hair bobbing with each movement. "You know the way." She stood and moved her stool.

Issa wrapped her arm around Marla and pulled her behind the counter. She kneeled and pulled the rug back, exposing a wooden trapdoor. It swung silently back with a light pull. Sturdy stairs led down to a packed dirt floor. Lanterns hung on the walls, giving the space a soft golden glow.

"Go on." Issa nodded at the stairs. "The others will be here soon."

Marla walked down the stairs, holding the railing. They didn't creak, groan, or shift at all. She touched the dirt wall beside her as she walked down. The soil was warm. Each lantern she passed warmed her face, like a tiny piece of the sun had been bottled.

She stopped at the bottom and waited for Issa. Three tunnels branched off, all lighted and welcoming. Wooden supports were evenly spaced, holding beams above her. A safe place underground? They really must be Wood Walkers.

"This way." Issa led her to the right.

She followed Issa down the hall. Wooden doors were spaced along both sides, each with a small rug at the entrance. Two lanterns hung on either side of each door. Woven patterned wall hangings hung in the blank spaces between, bringing colour to the hideout.

Issa stopped at a door close to the end. She opened it and stepped aside. "This is it. Make yourself comfortable."

Marla walked into the room. She smiled as she looked around. Thick wooden timbers supported the walls and ceiling, the wood stained a light golden colour. More lanterns gave off a soft light and gentle heat. Two beds took up most of the room, though there was a small table with a couple of chairs in one corner. A few rugs brightened the place up.

"All this down here? It's impressive," she whispered, as she walked to the nearest lantern. Marla held her hand close to the glass, and the heat warmed her through.

"We have safe houses like this spread throughout the country. Hideouts, rest stops, and storehouses. You know about hiding underground?"

"Ava explained a bit." Marla lowered her hand away from the lantern. "We were kind of in a rush."

Issa raised her eyebrow. "You know Ava?"

"She's my neighbour. Was my neighbour, I guess."

"If you need a snack, check the box." Issa nodded at the table. "I'll make sure the other rooms are ready and I'll be right back."

Marla wandered to the table, crossing a rug. The thick fibres softened her steps, reminding her of moss. She opened the small box on the table, setting the light wooden lid aside. Waxed paper packets were stacked inside. She opened one. They were full of crackers, each one still crispy. Bits of dried fruit and nuts were baked in each one.

Issa closed the door as she slipped away silently. Marla meandered around the room and nibbled her crackers, looking closer at everything. She stopped at a wall hanging, some yarn art of a countryside scene with a sunrise. All this was here, underground? Did all towns have something like this?

She returned to the table and pulled a chair out. The cushion was soft under her. Marla stretched her legs out. It's been a while since she's run like that. She'd never spent so long curled up in a wagon, either. She set her remaining crackers on the table and rubbed her legs.

The door swung open, and Issa stepped into the room. "The others will be here any moment. Come with me."

Marla eased to her feet and walked over. She waited in the hall as Issa closed the door again. There was a little sign beside the door with the number three on it painted a bright orange. The yellow light from the lantern above it softened the colour.

They followed the hall to the end. Issa marched right into the room. It was larger than the bedroom. A large table had eight chairs around it. One corner had some padded chairs and a reading table between them. A bookshelf sat against the wall nearby. Cupboards lined the end wall near the table. The last corner near the chairs had a small mattress or large pad of some kind leaning up against the wall.

Marla settled into a padded chair in the corner. She looked up at Issa, who paced the room near the door. The woman glanced down the hall regularly.

"Are all the Light Chargers men?"

Issa stopped pacing and stared at her for a long moment. "Oh, uh, no. Most are, but not all." She spun and smiled, staring down the hall.

A couple of people walked into the room. They each carried a bowl or platter of food.

"Issa?" A slender woman tilted her head at Marla. She led the others to the table, where everyone set their food down.

"Newly awakening." Issa walked to the table with them and waved Marla over.

Marla eased to her feet and walked over. She sat in the chair Issa pulled out for her. Issa was on her one side, and someone in a loose tunic with short, cropped hair sat on her other side. A man or a woman? No way of knowing. Marla shrugged to herself. It didn't matter. The slender woman sat across from Issa.

"I arranged for some proper stew." The slender woman folded her hands on the table.

"And I have it." A man walked in carrying a massive pot. He set it on the table, right in the middle.

Wait, she knew that voice. He was the one with the wagon with Issa. Marla let out a breath. He wasn't a Light Wielder. They really were just protecting her. She was safe with them. Probably.

An older woman followed him in, closing the door behind her. She set a basket of fresh pastries beside the stew before settling into a chair as well. Issa stood and filled the bowls, passing them out to everyone. The others took more food from the bowls and platters of vegetables and grains. Marla set a little of everything on the small plate someone handed her.

"So, child, how did you end up in the forest, running from the Light Chargers?" The slender woman watched her with pale eyes, almost the colour of sand.

Marla shared how Ava tried to hide her, and how her power leaked out. She explained how Ava hid her again and told her to leave after giving her supplies. She didn't share the directions to the city or too many details, just in case.

"Were you the people who drew the Light Chargers away from me?"

The older woman grinned. "We sure did. We'll need to teach you how to defend yourself and hide yourself better. Or at all. Now, eat up, dear. You need food after all that running."

Marla dug into the stew. She tore a pastry apart and dipped it in the thick broth. Marla tried to sneak a better look at each person around the table as she ate with her head down.

Issa smiled. She split a pastry and buttered the inside. "Marla, this is Kria. She's the leader of our small group."

The slender woman nodded to Marla. She tucked her light brown hair behind her ear as she picked up a mug. "As much as we have leaders, yes."

"That's Tialla." Issa nodded at the older woman.

"I knew Ava when we were girls." Tialla dabbed at her chin with a cloth. "We used to gather herbs together, and work in the vegetable garden."

"You lived in my town?" Marla perked up.

"Oh, forests, no. Ava and I met each other during training. She returned home after that, and I went my way." She winked at Marla.

"Dornir, at your service." The man bowed his head to her. He flashed a quick smile and raised his mug.

Marla smiled back.

"I'm Adris." They bowed their head to Marla, their short black hair swinging down around their face. They looked up and smiled again.

"H—hi, everyone. Where are we, though? What is this place?" Marla gestured around the room.

"This town is a supply depot for us. The shops and makers here all trade with us and help us. They're friendly with our people. Your people. We have a few towns and villages around the country, but until you know which ones, act like every village is a danger." Issa rested a hand on Marla's shoulder.

The juice in her mug sloshed as her hand shook. Marla set the mug on the table. "Okay, but what's actually going on? I was living an ordinary life, maybe even a boring one. The next thing I know, I'm being chased by men on horses. I didn't ask for this. I don't even know what 'this' is."

Adris placed their hand over hers. "It's not something you ask for. It's a gift you are given. The early days are confusing, but if you listen and keep learning, you'll discover how amazing this is."

"How is being chased amazing?" Marla wiped a tear from her eye. That echo of pain ran through her arm.

Adris wrapped an arm around her and pulled her close for a hug. "It isn't. The early days are hard. The thing is, you have no idea what all you can do yet. Once you learn to use all your gifts, you'll never be afraid in a forest again."

Marla peered up at them. "Never?"

Tialla raised a mug. "Never. We pass through the forests like shadows. In the wild places, where our powers are strongest, even the most powerful Light Wielder can't harm us."

"Not unless we get careless and forget who we are," Dornir added. "Awareness is how you stay safe. You need time to learn."

Issa raised her mug. "And we'll teach you."

"Just like that?" Marla looked around at the group.

Kria nodded. "Just like that."

Tialla set a hand over Kria's. "It's time."

Marla set her spoon down in her nearly empty bowl. Time for what? She took another pastry from the plate.

"We have someone else to save here. It's important that you remain here or in your room. If everything goes well, we'll be back in minutes. If not, we don't need you in danger when you can't defend yourself yet. Understand?" Tialla held her gaze.

"Okay?" Marla shrugged.

Kria stood. "Does everyone know their tasks?"

The others stood and nodded.

"Is everyone ready?" Kria looked around the small group, waiting until they all nodded. "Dornir, Adris, go. We're following."

Issa rested a hand on Marla's shoulder. "You can return to our room or wait here. Don't wander the hallways. You can read if you like. It doesn't matter what happens out there, stay here. We won't be long."

The group left, closing the door behind them. Marla stayed in her chair, finishing her meal. Was that all the instructions they were getting? What were they going to do?

Once her bowl was empty and her last pastry finished, Marla wandered over to the bookshelf. There were books on a variety of topics, though the health section was the largest. She browsed the titles, stopping at a book called The Awakening. She grabbed it.

Marla settled into the chair and opened the book. She nodded as she read about the earliest stages of awakening, the awareness and feelings that sometimes happened. Her eyes widened as she read about the next stage. Surges of power will shoot through her. What will that feel like? Wait, hadn't she already had one? That's how this whole mess started, wasn't it?

The door swung open. Adris stumbled in, their arm around a woman, keeping her upright. Issa rushed through and helped support the woman on her other side. They guided her to the corner, taking tiny, shuffling steps with her. Tialla set the cushion down. They lowered her to the pad and stretched her out.

The woman gasped for breath. She wore the same cream dress or long tunic as the other woman had. There was a faint line around her neck where the black band might have been. Kria draped a blanket over her, hiding the rough skin around her ankles.

Tialla kneeled beside her head. "Breathe. You'll feel better soon." She rested her hand on the woman's forehead. Her finger traced the line around the woman's neck, her touch soft and light.

The woman panted, her hands waving in the air. Adris took her hands and let her cling to them. Kria set a hand over the woman's heart. A green glow covered them both from head to toe. The woman went still, her breathing settled, and her eyes closed.

"That's it, love. You'll be fine. Feel your power filling back up." Tialla rubbed the woman's shoulders.

Issa got a bowl and filled it with water. She took a cloth and brought them both to Adris. Issa joined Marla in the corner, settling into the other reading chair. "That went well." She kept her voice low. "They weren't expecting us, because they were focused on finding you."

"Where's Dornir?" Marla whispered. She gripped the armrest.

"He's in his room. He'll give us privacy as we tend to her." Issa nodded to the corner, where the others had removed the woman's clothing and draped the blanket back over her.

"Oh."

"I'm going to help them. Stay quiet. We'll teach you how to help soon." Issa stood.

Marla curled up in the chair. This woman didn't look so worn out as the other woman did, but she still had hollowed cheeks and was thin. She didn't move much, either, laying still as Adris bathed her with the cloth. Tialla stayed at her head, murmuring to her as she stroked her hair.

Wait, this all seemed familiar somehow. Marla closed her eyes and let her mind relax. Yes, she once lay on a table, the green glow around her. It smelled of baking and herbs. Ava's house? The green made the pain fade. What injury would be bad enough Ava would have used magic on her? Right. She opened her eyes and touched her arm. Why couldn't she remember, though?

Issa went to the cupboard and got a couple of bottles and another cloth. She handed one to Kria before kneeling beside the woman's shoulders. Pouring some medicine on the cloth, Issa tended to her chafed neck skin.

Kria opened the other bottle and filled the dropper. With Tialla's help, she got the medicine in the woman's cheek. Tialla lifted the woman's head and shoulders slightly so she could swallow easier.

"There. All clean." Adris pulled the blanket fully back over her again. They stood and carried the bowl of dirty water to the sink.

Issa tended to the woman's wrists and ankles with ointment. How did she get those? Marla wrapped her arms around her legs and hugged herself tightly.

"Let us know when you're ready to sit." Kria cradled the woman's cheek in her hand.

She nodded. Her movements were still weak. When she tried to press herself up, her arm gave out.

"Easy, now. Let us help." Issa slid a hand under her back and helped the woman sit. "There. Slow and easy."

"Marla, would you open that cupboard and get a robe for her? Middle-most shelf, centre pile." Kria nodded at a nearby cupboard.

"Sure." She eased from the chair.

The cupboard was full of linens and blankets on the bottom shelves, and robes and clothing filled the rest. Marla took a robe from the pile, pale green and made from fine wool, and shut the cupboard again. She took it over, kneeling beside Adris.

Wait, that face was vaguely familiar. No, she had to be imagining it. Still, now that she was clean, and some colour was back in her cheeks, something about this woman pulled at Marla. Who was she?

"Here you go. Stretch your arms out. You'll be warm and comfortable in this." Adris smiled at the woman as they unfolded the robe.

Issa helped steady the woman's arms as she stretched towards the clothing. They dressed her, easing the robe over her. Marla pressed her hand over her mouth. Why were her ribs so visible?

Issa met her gaze. "Marla, how about getting her some juice? It's in the cold box. She can use a glass."

Marla shook her thoughts loose and stood. "Yeah. Anything."

She took a glass from the cupboard with a shaky hand. Marla stopped and took a deep breath. This could have been her? Still could, if she doesn't make it to the city? She took the pitcher and filled the glass. Holding the glass with both hands, she carried it over to the woman.

"Thanks." Issa took the glass from her and smiled at Marla. "You're doing great." She brought the glass up to the woman's lips. "Take it slow."

Marla jumped at the knock on the door, quiet though it was. The door opened a crack.

CHAPTER 8

"I've arranged for a group to take her back home." Dornir's voice was slightly muffled by the door.

"Thanks." Kria walked to the door. "She'll be ready in a few days."

"I'll let them know." He closed the door.

"What's your name, child?" Tialla held the woman's shoulders. Her hands glowed.

"Mia." Her voice was shaky and barely more than a whisper. Had she spoken much lately?

Marla gasped and pressed her hands to her cheeks. No, Mia might be a common name. It can't be her.

"Are you okay" Kria rested a hand on Marla's shoulder.

Marla shook her head. "No. I think she's from my town. I think she's Ava's niece."

Kria kneeled beside Mia. "Do you know Ava?"

Mia nodded. Tears filled her eyes and rolled down her cheeks.

"Rest, child. We'll let them know you're safe now. You can't go see her just yet, but we have somewhere safe. You can recover there. When you feel better, write her a letter and we'll get it to her." Tialla held Mia's hand.

Child? This woman was maybe twice as old as Marla. Then again, how old was Tialla? Her grey hair put her past middle age, though she had the energy of a younger woman.

"I'll stay with her overnight," Adris offered. "I'll prepare the recovery room."

Kria nodded. "I bet Dornir already started."

Adris grinned. They bounded up and over to the door.

"We should get some rest, too." Issa wrapped her arm around Marla. "We have a big day ahead of us tomorrow. You'll want to be rested."

"Go. We can see to her." Tialla lay her hand on Mia's shoulder.

Issa steered Marla through the door and down the hall. They returned to the bedroom.

"Choose whichever bed you like. They're the same." Issa turned on an extra lamp.

Marla shuffled to the closest bed and collapsed on it. She kicked her boots off, leaving them beside her bed. She sat, her elbows on her knees.

"Are you okay?" Issa pulled the blankets back on the second bed.

She nodded. "I guess. One minute, I'm just a regular person. I'm no different from anyone else in town. It's daily work and sharing tea with friends. The next thing I know, I'm running through a forest, being chased by the people who run things. I don't know what's going on or why. It's all so confusing." Marla dropped her head in her hands.

The mattress shifted as Issa sat beside her. "How much did Ava teach you?"

Marla shook her head. "Not much. We didn't have time. Just that I could make things grow. Oh, and not to be found by them. She mentioned hiding places and help. I don't even know why I'm running, just that I can't go home."

79

Issa rubbed her back, slow and gentle circles that softened her muscles. "It must be confusing. You leave, simply because someone tells you, and you don't know who to trust. You might not even know where you're going, or who you'll meet when you arrive. It's incredibly brave to go, though."

"I don't feel brave." Marla's hands shook. She straightened up and pressed her hands to her legs. "I feel so scared. What if something happens to me? What if I become like them?"

"We'll do everything we can to make sure you don't. Did you know we have people scattered all over the country? They look for people like you. We find you and bring you somewhere safe. You'll have a chance to learn and grow. We're the ones Ava sent you to find, me and Kria and the others."

Marla held Issa's gaze. Her eyes were an interesting mix of dark brown with streaks of almost a golden honey radiating from the middle. "You are?"

"Most likely. If not us, this area has more groups just like ours than any other in the country, except for the farming belt. If we hadn't found you, our friends would have. You still would have come here, to this Safehouse. We probably would have met, anyway. Maybe it's fate?" Issa smiled. "You look exhausted. Get some rest."

Issa stood and pulled Marla up with her. She pulled the blankets back. Marla dropped onto the mattress and curled up. She closed her eyes as the woman tucked the blankets back around her. Her legs ached from all the running. The warmth and weight of the blanket wrapped around her like a hug, soothing her.

"Wake me if you need anything at all. There's a washroom just down the hall beside the meeting room. If you're not absolutely certain where, wake me. Don't wander, okay?"

"Okay," Marla mumbled.

Issa chuckled. "Sleep well."

The room went dark, except for the faintest trace of light on her eyelids. Issa's bed creaked. A book opened and pages turned. Marla slipped into a deep sleep.

***

"Time to get up. Breakfast." A hand shook her shoulder.

Marla batted at the hand.

"Up. We leave in an hour, whether or not you're ready. You don't want to walk without eating first."

The blankets ripped back. Marla shivered and curled into a tight ball.

"The washroom is free, if you want to clean up first. You have a few minutes, so make the most of them."

Marla rolled towards Issa's voice and opened her eyes.

"Seriously, get in there before Adris does. They take all the hot water, otherwise." Issa tilted her head towards the door.

She pushed herself up and eased to her feet. "The beds are comfortable. I could have stayed all day."

Issa grinned. "Today, we'll teach you how to draw on the magic of nature. You won't be so tired after that."

Marla nodded. She stuffed her feet in her boots. Her legs didn't want to lift fully as she walked, and she shuffled across the room. Marla fumbled at the doorknob.

Issa lay her hand over Marla's on the doorknob. "It's this way." She guided the girl down the hall, stopping at the last door before the meeting room. "We'll be in here when you're done."

Marla stepped into the small room. She filled the sink from the pipes, blending the water so it was warm. Soft cloths sat in a pile on a small table nearby. Marla took one and washed herself. A spare hairbrush waited on the table as well. At least there was a mirror over the table. She fixed her hair. After a chance to relieve herself and wash her hands once more, Marla left the warm little room.

Everyone sat around the table already when she arrived. Kria, Issa, and Tialla sat and talked. Dornir rubbed his eyes. Adris was propped up over a bowl of food, their chin in their hand, their elbow braced on the table.

Tialla waved her over. "Good morning. Come and eat. Big day ahead of you. Have as much as you want." She bustled over and wrapped an arm around Marla's shoulders.

The old woman marched her over to a chair and settled her between Issa and Kria. Tialla filled a bowl full of cooked oats, berries, fruit, and cream, and plunked it down in front of Marla.

"Did you sleep well?" Kria looked her over.

Marla nodded. "I'm not used to waking up without the sun."

Issa rested a hand on Marla's shoulder. "We all wake better with the sun. Some of us can manage better without it, though." She smiled as Dornir caught Adris, their elbow slipping as they plunged towards their breakfast.

"Sit up, love. You eat it. You don't wear it." He sat them back in their chair.

Adris blinked a few times, staring ahead at nothing.

Marla nodded her thanks as Tialla set a steaming mug of tea in front of her. Cinnamon wafted up to her, chasing the sleepiness away.

Tialla touched the edge of the mug. "There. Cooled it for you. You can have some any time now."

"What? Really?" Marla wrapped her hands around the warm mug and raised it to her lips. She took a small and tentative sip. "How?"

"I took some of the energy from it. Shame I couldn't transfer that energy to them." Tialla smiled at Adris, who fumbled with their spoon.

Marla hid her smile behind the mug. "Will I be able to do that one day?"

"That and more. You said Ava's already shown you how to call to life in a seed?" Issa raised her eyebrow.

She nodded. "I've sprouted seeds and started feeling for water. I've also felt that steady rhythm, the slow beat. There wasn't time for much before I had to leave." Marla scooped up some breakfast and set it on her tongue. She closed her eyes as the cream blended with the sweet fruit. "Mm."

"Good, isn't it?" Tialla beamed at her. "Old family recipe. It's the touch of honey that makes all the difference."

"Today, we need to teach her to absorb energy. Waking her was a real chore. Not as bad as that," Issa nodded at Adris, "but it'll help her."

Kria nodded. "There will be plenty of opportunity. We'll leave once everyone is washed."

The rest of breakfast was quiet, other than Dornir encouraging Adris to eat. Marla had a second mug of tea before she was done. The spices woke her fully. Something was blended in with the cinnamon, and it had a light kick.

"Alright, we're travelling light. No wagon. Keep that in mind as you choose supplies. Issa?" Kria held her gaze.

"I'll teach and help her. You can focus on our mission and seeing to Mia." Issa lay her hand on Marla's shoulder. "When you're ready, I'll show you how to prepare for a day trip."

Marla set her spoon down and glanced at Adris. "I'm ready."

"We have a storeroom for this. Everything we need is in there. Come with me." Issa rose from her chair.

"What about our dishes?" Marla gestured at the table.

"I got this, dear. It's your first day, so relax and learn." Tialla waved her off.

Marla followed Issa from the room. They stopped by their bedroom, where Issa retrieved her bag from under the bed. The woman led her back to near the washroom and opened another door. A lantern flicked on as they stepped inside, the flame steadying within moments.

"Everything we need for any trip is in here, no matter how far we are going. Every major rest stop has a fully supplied storeroom, so you can always resupply along the way. That's what we were doing when we found you, actually. Bringing more supplies to restock. The oxen let us move the biggest shipments at once."

Marla stepped closer to some shelves. Open boxes held all manner of goods inside. There were shelves of food like cheeses and crackers, or other dried foods bundled and ready to go. Other shelves held clothing for any season. There were pouches with travel tools folded inside. Coils of rope sat in a corner. The entire room was full of things, including bed rolls and tarps and other forms of shelter.

"How do you know what to take?" Marla turned slowly, looking at every-thing.

"Experience. That, and there are more supplies stashed around, so if we guess wrong, we're still alright." Issa walked to a shelf and picked up a backpack. "Day supplies are here. You'll mostly want food and safety tools."

Marla walked over and looked over her shoulder. "Safety tools?"

Issa unrolled a leather kit. Little metal tools sat in their own straps or pouches. "Scissors, a small saw, tongs for removing splinters, wire cutters, and so on. We'll make sure you know how to use everything." She re-rolled the kit and tucked it in the backpack.

"How long is the food good for?" Marla picked up a package of crackers.

Issa took a packet of crackers and tucked them in an inner pocket. "Crackers, cheeses, and the dried fruits are good for months, even years, if stored properly. That's with no magic to help preserve it. With care and magic, you can store some food for many years." She tucked more food into the pouches. "Here. Turn around."

Marla turned her back to Issa. The woman slipped the backpack on her, easing the straps over her shoulders.

"It's so light. Even with the food." Marla tightened the straps.

"The heaviest thing in there is the cheese. We only need to carry a couple days' worth. Always take an extra day, just in case, though we'll teach you how to forage in the forests. In the warmer months, the forest can provide everything we need. Now, let's go join the others."

Issa led her from the room and down the hall, past their bedroom. Adris slipped from their room and followed behind. Dornir waited at the bottom of the stairs. They all turned at the bottom of the stairs and headed down another hall. Marla glanced up at the stairs.

"There are other ways out," Adris explained. "Ways that don't potentially have a Light Charger at the top."

Issa led them through a thick wooden door. The hall kept going, though there were significantly fewer doors along it. The lanterns were closer together, their light shining around each bend in the tunnel. They turned many times as they walked. North pulled at Marla, so she knew they were heading mostly south. Something in front of her called to her as well. What?

Tialla sat in a chair at the bottom of a ladder, her knitting in her lap. "All ready?" She looked Marla up and down, with that motherly smile on her face.

The group nodded, almost as one. Marla glanced up at Issa, who lay a hand on her shoulder. She looked at the wall hanging, a painting on a scrap of wooden board. The waves almost looked like they were moving. How did the artist do that? Was that what the ocean looked like?

The small group parted as Kria joined them, heading for the base of the ladder. She tightened the straps on her bag. "Everyone ready?"

"We're ready," Issa assured her.

Kria nodded to Dornir. He scampered up the ladder and stopped on a wooden landing. It was dark where he was, but Marla could see him place his hands on the hatch above him. He looked down at Tialla, who stood and tucked her knitting in her embroidered bag.

"It's safe." The old woman nodded. "They left already. Probably to get help, so stay alert, everyone."

Dornir pushed up on the hatch. He slipped from the tunnel and disappeared in the sunlight. Tialla followed, climbing with ease. Issa nudged Marla and nodded at the ladder. The rungs were smooth and thick under her hands. Marla climbed until she could see out, her head above the grass.

The trees were thick. There was no sign of the settlement, no noise except the birds and the breeze rustling the new leaves. Marla took Dornir's offered hand, and he helped pull her up and away from the tunnel.

The others emerged one at a time after her, Kria coming last. Dornir slid the hatch closed. The top was covered in dirt and grass and blended almost seamlessly into the land around it.

She raised a hand over her eyes. The morning sun beamed down on her at a low angle. After the soft light of the lantern, the bright sun made her eyes ache. She blinked and turned her head away.

"Are you okay?" Issa rubbed her shoulder.

Marla nodded. "I wasn't expecting how bright it is."

"You get used to it after a while." Dornir grinned. He glanced at Adris. "Well, those who do a lot of morning travel do, anyway. Eventually."

"This way. We'll be in town by midafternoon if nothing unexpected happens." Kria set off through the trees.

Marla followed, with Issa and Tialla beside her. They headed down a gentle slope.

"This would be easier if we were standing still, but it'll still work walking." Issa shifted her pack and snugged up a strap. "The first step is being aware of the energy around you. You've done that, right?"

Marla nodded. "We were trying to connect with water before I left."

Issa raised an eyebrow. "So soon? Interesting. Alright, once you've felt the energy, invite it in. Let it flow around you and fill you. Don't hold it, let it flow out again. Like this."

She took Marla's hand. Their joined hands glowed green. Energy moved through her, tingling lightly as it passed up from her feet and back down again. Some flowed into Issa through their hands.

"There. Now you try. Don't worry if it's not that strong. See if you can get any energy to move at all."

Marla nodded and took a calming breath. Should she close her eyes? Marla looked down at the tree roots and small shrubs. No, she'll trip and hurt herself. Nothing for it. She took another slow breath. Her mind settled.

The energy hummed around her, faint, but there. The pulsing that usually filled her was distant, but she still sensed it in her bones. She slowed her steps, and the sensations got louder. Drawing up with her mind, Marla invited the energy in. How did Issa get it to move?

"Don't force it. Make space for it. Let it flow. It's like a river, and your body is a channel it can flow down. Guide it and let go."

Softness. Okay, she could do that. Marla let go of her power and lightly imagined it moving up through her. The energy flowed up all the way to her head, where it pressed against her skull. Something nudged it and the energy turned, flowing down again.

"That's the rough idea, but don't forget to send it around you. Your head should be like a river bend, where the water curves back on itself. It's not like a lake where water lingers. Try again." Issa squeezed her hand.

Marla pulled and let go, inviting the energy up into her. It was easier this time, and she let go sooner. One little tug got the energy going. It slid up her, gently this time, instead of the rush of power. As it reached her head, Marla guided it around and down. Little bits of the flow swirled and broke from the main flow, but most of the energy dropped through her in a current.

"That's much better." Issa squeezed her hand again. Some energy moved between them.

The little pools of swirling energy smoothed out and flowed into the main current of power. Issa sent the remaining power down and out, leaving Marla charged and refreshed.

"You just need practice. Rest for a while before we try again." Issa smiled at her.

"I feel a lot better after that." Marla glanced back at the others following behind. The entire group slowed their step for her.

CHAPTER 9

"When you use more power, this is how you keep from burning out. Just remember, you borrow the energy, you don't own it." Issa let go of her hand.

"Is there a limit to how much you can use and keep going?"

"There sure is. Don't overdo it at first." Dornir glanced back over his shoulder at her. "The more practice you get, the longer you can work. It's a gift that nature gives us, but we must use it wisely. Do nature's work and by the time you're Tialla's age, you can go as long as you want."

Tialla smacked his shoulder. "What do you mean by Tialla's age?"

Dornir hustled ahead, lengthening his step. "You are our most skilled and venerable worker. That comes with age." He smiled as he dodged another swipe at him. "My Lady." Dornir smiled and bowed his head. He ducked the stick aimed at his head.

"That was a warning shot," Issa whispered. "If she used a rock, he wouldn't have ducked it. She's amazing with a sling."

Marla grinned. What was she expecting? She wasn't sure, but it wasn't this. It wasn't people who joked and laughed and walked without fear. Maybe it wouldn't all be running and hiding and living in fear. Maybe there was a shred of normal out here, too.

They walked through the morning. The forest was peaceful. Occasionally, Tialla changed their path a bit, but they always headed vaguely southeast. Marla kept practicing for short bursts under Issa's guidance, when Tialla announced it was safe. Each time, it got easier. Safe from what, though? Marla wished she knew more about magic and how to sense things.

"Here. We follow the road. Local offerings are always best." Kria stopped at the edge of a wide road, the dirt well-packed and smooth. "Dornir, Adris, keep her safe. As the youngest, she should choose the offering."

"But—" Issa wrapped an arm around Marla's shoulders.

"She'll be safe with them. I need you two to help gather the rest."

After a long moment, Issa let her arm fall away. She turned on Dornir and Adris. "Don't you dare let anything happen to her."

Tialla took Marla's hands. She whispered, so softly Marla couldn't make out words. A breeze circled her and coated her, lightly rustling her hair and clothing.

"There. A spell of protection, to shield and keep you from their sight. Go in peace."

"Thank you." Marla looked down at her hands. An incredibly thin layer of translucent light coated her. "Won't they see this?"

Tialla's jaw dropped. Adris stared at her with wide eyes.

"You can see that?" Kria held her gaze.

Marla nodded. "Shouldn't I be able to?"

Tialla squeezed Marla's hands. "Most people can't with so little training. A few can. You don't need to worry about it. The magic will protect you. Go, before it gets too late. Oh, and if you see a Light Charger, don't make eye contact. Don't meet their gaze. That's the only way they can see through that shield, unless they are exceptionally powerful and know to look."

"The road is just over there. We'll be there and back in no time." Adris pointed through the trees.

Marla glanced back as she followed Adris and Dornir through the trees. The others split and disappeared into the forest.

"Where are we going?" She hustled to Adris' side.

"We're going to the town market. We want some of the first fruits of the season as an offering." Dornir walked on Marla's other side, matching her pace. "We'll be charging and restoring a point of power. Do you know what those are?"

"I started reading about them, but only had time for the first chapter." Marla shrugged. "They sound interesting."

Adris chuckled. "Yeah, they are. This first one is a minor point of power, so it'll be good for your first one. Minor doesn't mean less important, though. At every point, we place an offering. The youngest chooses the fruit, which was me, but now it's your turn."

"I'm sorry. I didn't mean—" Marla stumbled.

Dornir caught her arm and steadied her.

Adris turned and held Marla's shoulders. "It's fine. There is no shame in growing older. Only honour."

Dornir released Marla's arm and strode into the forest ahead. Marla raised an eyebrow.

"Scouting," Adris whispered.

"For what?"

They grinned. "A good place and time to join the road."

He stopped at some bushes, just in view ahead of them. Dornir slipped among the bushes, reappearing moments later. He waved. Adris hurried

91

over, dragging Marla with them. She jogged to keep up. Dornir stepped through the bushes. Adris pushed Marla after him, following close behind her.

Marla glanced down the road both ways. The road curved around some ancient trees, massive trunks with widespread branches, and she couldn't see far in either direction. It was also empty. She walked with them over the smooth paving stones, tightly fitted together and gently sloping to the edges.

The road made for easy travel, but something seemed off about it. Marla looked down at her feet as she walked. The road tingled slightly with power, but something seemed empty about it, like something was missing. What, though?

Adris took her hand and squeezed it gently. "We won't feel nature's power easily when we're on the roads. They're enchanted to keep them clear and level."

"Right. I read about that briefly in a book, but only in a paragraph or two. I didn't know I'd miss the soft ground so much. It feels much better on the feet."

Adris slung their arm around her shoulders and pulled her closer. "You're a natural. The good news is you're more sensitive to nature's energy than most of us are. The bad news is the same. You'll miss it more when you're away from it."

Marla smiled. "Figures. Wait, more sensitive?"

They walked around the curve and the trees thinned. The town was visible now, right beside the wide road. The clear blue sky called to her, even as the wide-open fields around the town made her heart race.

"Yes, we all have different strengths and sensitivities. The stronger you are, the more you love the deep forest." Adris pulled their arm away. "You'll be fine. It's not far, and this town is usually quiet."

Dornir took the lead as they left the treeline. Marla walked a half-step closer to Adris. Was she sensing danger, or scared because it was new? What if she guessed wrong? Adris smiled at her and took a deep breath. Marla copied them, filling her lungs with fresh air, and let it out slowly.

They passed a massive wagon pulled by a pair of enormous horses leaving the town. The back was empty now, just folded sacks and empty produce crates stacked as high as the side walls. Other wagons were coming towards the town from the other direction, all heading for the open town gates like Marla was.

"The oxen teams leave earlier, since they're slower," Dornir explained, as they passed a small cart pulled by a sleek horse. "They can carry more, but it takes longer to get places."

Hoofbeats pounded the road behind them. Adris pulled her to the side of the road, right near the border stones. Marla pulled her cloak tighter around herself. Her hood hid her face, and she didn't dare look back. The tingling told her who it was. Why them? Why now? Could they feel her, too?

The horses passed at a steady trot. Marla risked a glance at the horses as they passed and turned in through the town gates. The first horse was a typical Light Charger's mount, large and sturdy, wearing the fancy tack. The second horse was almost a pony. A woman rode it. She wore a simple tunic and some trousers, and her hair was braided. The metal band around her neck shone in the sunlight.

"That's unusual," Adris muttered. They moved back to the middle of the road.

"What?" Marla followed them.

"He must be in a hurry if she's riding. She's also in better shape than most. She must be powerful. That, or she's his first capture."

Marla rubbed her cheeks. She barely noticed him, as she was too curious about her. They were already through the gates and out of sight.

Dornir shook his head. "I'll let Kria know. She might be important. If he's younger, a rescue might be easier, too."

"Is it still safe to go shopping? They're in town now." Marla shifted her backpack, adjusting the straps.

Adris smiled. "We'll be fine. Just don't stop and talk to him. He probably won't notice you exist. Tialla's magic is incredibly powerful for shielding the newly awakened." They linked arms with Marla.

"You're sure?" She couldn't help the tremor in her voice.

"He's got her to worry about, and he's travelling alone. If he tries to take you, he leaves her vulnerable, and he knows it. You'll be fine. Focus on your task, and we'll be out of there in minutes."

Marla listened to the market noises as they approached the gates. "Okay, why are we buying fruit when we have plenty?"

Dornir stopped at the gates. "We give back as well as ask. It's most powerful if the fruit is from the area. Look for the freshest fruit you can find. The kind doesn't matter. This early it'll probably be spring apples, or some berries. Choose something ripe and juicy. Size doesn't matter as much as freshness."

She took the offered coins he pulled from his belt pouch. Marla tucked the coins in her pocket. They passed the guardhouse and walked down the street. The market was ahead on the left, tables and carts filling a square, all loaded full of goods.

What was that noise? Wait, looms? A weaving town? Her town had some smaller looms, but these sounded huge. Would she get to see them? The steady clacking thuds came from the far end of town, away from the market. Warehouses blocked her view.

Marla gaped at the dizzying patterns and bright colours of the canopies over the booths and tables. Many stalls had fine cloths with delicate patterns, much fancier than any clothing she wore. Other booths and carts had more workmanlike cloth, and some places had already made clothing for sale.

She stared at the people moving about in shimmering clothing, similar to the Light Chargers', but in hues of blue and red and other bright colours. Even many merchants at the market dressed in such finery. "Does everyone here dress like that?"

Adris smiled and shook their head. "Not at all. You'll find those still working at trades, like farmers and blacksmiths and such, they still wear the thick work clothing. Once they're done, though, they probably change into this." They reached out and touched a bolt of cloth on a nearby table. "This region is known for many types of silk."

"We've got the finest silk around. Take some home to your family?" The merchant held up a box of silk handkerchiefs.

Adris pulled a coin from their pocket and traded it for a forest green handkerchief. They handed the little silk square to Marla. "Here. A memento of your first trip with us."

She took the handkerchief and held it against her cheek. "It's so—I don't even have words for it." Marla grinned. "Thanks. I've read about it, but never seen silk before."

"That's the silk warehouse." Dornir pointed at a massive building right near the marketplace. "See the extra guards?"

Marla nodded. The building didn't have any low windows. All were small and high up, and all the doors had a pair of guards standing at them.

Adris spun Marla around. "The farmers are all in that corner." They pointed to the back of the market, where empty wagons stood along a road just across the wall. "Choose some fruit. Three different kinds are best. I'll get the bread from the bakery right over there. Dornir will visit the apothecary. When you're done, wait there, and I'll come get you. Don't wander. He's probably at the inn."

She nodded. It seemed simple enough. Marla joined the crowd and headed for the back corner, listening to people barter. Local rates seemed a little higher than what her neighbours charged, and she didn't want to be taken advantage of. The crowd wasn't heavy, and she passed into the farmer's area with ease.

Three stalls in the corner were loaded with different varieties of fruit. She selected a couple of spring plums and some berries. Marla handed the coins over and got a small cloth bag with her new produce. One more—she continued to the next stall.

Apples. Perfect. Marla hung her little bag from her belt, freeing her hands. She picked up a shiny ripe apple, small and well-formed. Three apples tumbled from the table. Marla caught two, but the third rolled past her.

"Here you go." Someone with a light male voice held the apple out to her.

"Thanks." Marla took the apple. Her cloak hood partly blocked her view, so she turned. Her heart skipped a beat as she saw his boots. Only one group wore those white boots.

He waited; his hand outstretched with the apple. "Are you alright?"

"I, yes—I—" Marla nodded and took the apple with a shaking hand.

His larger hand wrapped around her wrist. "Do you need a healer?"

Flashes of emotion rolled through her, fear, joy and confusion mixed up inside. The world spun around her and her knees shook. He gripped her elbows and held her up. The sensations passed as quick as they came.

"I'm alright. Just tired from travel, I think." She pulled herself upright, keeping her head down. Marla rubbed her eyes with her sleeve. Something in that flash of emotion still pulled at her. No, don't look at him. He might use magic to trick me. He might see through the shield.

"If you're certain." He relaxed his grip on her arms.

Marla pulled away and turned back to the farmer. She bought all four apples and added them to her bag. Keeping her head down, she sidestepped the Light Charger. "Excuse me."

"Miss?" His hand touched her shoulder and gripped slightly. Something electric shot through her.

Marla froze. "Yes?" Her palms sweat. She gripped her bag tighter.

"Would you care to join me for tea?"

She stared down at his boots, the fine leather shining in the sunlight. "I must go. Thank you for the offer, though."

Marla spun and pulled away, heading for the town gates. He didn't hold tight or try to stop her. Her skin prickled at the feel of being watched. Her arms still tingled where he touched her. Tingled? Wait, did he leave magic on her?

Soft footsteps behind her made her heart race. Marla tensed. Should she run?

"Take it easy. It's me." Adris quickened their step and moved up beside Marla. "Are you alright? Did you look into his eyes?" They draped their arm over Marla's shoulders.

She shook her head. "I'm okay, I think. I didn't look at him. I don't know—"

Adris pulled her around the guardhouse and outside the walls, away from the road a bit. "Take a moment and slow down. What happened?"

Marla leaned against the wall. She pulled the bag of fruit from her belt and held it. With her feet in the grass and the fruit in her hands, the slow pulse of the surrounding land moved through her, calming her. "I dropped an apple. He gave it back to me." She took a slow breath. "I felt something when he touched me. I don't know what it was."

Adris cradled Marla's cheeks in their hands. "Describe it for me."

"I don't know. I got dizzy. Emotions rushed through me, but I don't know where they came from." Marla touched her arm where the tingling still lingered faintly. "How can I tell if he used magic on me?"

"They don't have magic to control the mind, so don't worry about the emotion thing, though I'll mention it to the others. He was a powerful elemental, though. I felt him from across the marketplace. He might have felt you. Maybe even through her shields." Adris shook their head.

Dornir appeared around the guardhouse. "There you are. Are you alright?"

Marla held the bag of fruit out to Adris. She nodded.

"He's heading for the inn now. We should go while we can." Dornir nodded to Adris.

They took the fruit and tucked it in Marla's backpack. "You handled yourself great. I was ready to help, but you got out just fine."

"Let's get back. We have time to do this today if they found their parts of the offering." Dornir smiled at Marla. He slung an arm around her and eased her from the wall.

Her legs still shook as she walked with him. They followed the open road, walking along the edge.

Adris stayed behind her. "There. We're just a group of friends walking home. Keep your hood up and we'll be among the trees in no time."

Marla clung to Dornir's arm as she walked. Don't look back. The trees were so close. Her fingers tightened on his sleeve. She strained to hear hoofbeats, but all she heard was carts clattering as they rolled along.

"He isn't coming this way," Dornir soothed.

She sighed as they entered the forest again. Once they left the road, the energy from the ground flowed up into her, displacing the tingling fully.

How could something so quiet and soft make her feel so safe? Nature's energy felt like a warm bath, where he was like a static shock.

"Now, are you alright?" Dornir brushed her hood back and turned to face her. "You're awful quiet. I mean, more than usual."

Marla nodded. "Just thinking. Everything is so new. I've walked through forests before, but now they feel alive or something. The town felt kind of empty somehow? I don't know. Even familiar things feel so different now."

Adris hugged her. "You're awakening. You're noticing the world around you now, in a way most people never see."

Issa rushed through the bushes towards them. "You're alright?"

CHAPTER 10

S he clung to Adris and nodded.

"There was a Light Charger, but the shield worked." Dornir rubbed Marla's shoulder. "He's not following."

Tialla pushed through the group and stood right in front of Marla. She peered into Marla's eyes. "No trace or markers. You didn't look him in the eye?"

"No. I saw his boots and his hand but wouldn't look up at him."

"He knows she's here. Whether he knows she's a Wood Walker or not, we need to be careful. We'll charge the site and find a sanctuary for the night." Kria walked over and held her hand out.

"Fruit." Adris nudged Marla gently in the shoulder.

Marla stood still as Adris retrieved the bag from her backpack.

Kria opened the bag and inspected the fruit. "Excellent. You did incredibly well. We also got everything we needed. This should go smoothly."

She walked with them deep into the trees, away from the road. Issa stayed beside her. The bushes thickened, and the trees grew closer together. She stepped carefully across the hill as the slope increased. The farther she walked, the larger and more frequent the boulders got.

They rounded some bushes and stopped at a massive cluster of rocks. Kria squeezed between the rocks in a narrow gap. Marla and the others followed her through, where the rocks opened up again. Flat stepping stones led away through a stone arch. Thick bushes grew beyond the arch, in the narrow gully and up the sides.

Kria stopped and faced Marla. "You're coming with us, but remain quiet and watch. Questions can wait until we're done."

Marla nodded. She looked at the stone arch. What kept it balanced there?

The others took their cloaks off. They turned them inside out, so the soft green lining was visible. Adris smiled as they unbuckled Marla's cloak and turned it, flipping it around with ease. Marla smiled back at them as she refastened the cloak pin.

It was so quiet down in the gully. Even the birdsong didn't reach her. Kria walked through the stone arch, her steps confident and head held high. Tialla followed. Issa nodded to her, and Marla walked after them. She heard footsteps behind her, barely detectable on the stone path.

The gully curved around to her right; the path leading the way. She couldn't see around the bushes. The overhanging tree branches hid the sky above. Marla kept close enough to Tialla she could reach out and touch her cloak. A surge of panic rushed through her. A fragment of a memory filled her, with her laying at the bottom of a gully like this. She fell. Her arm broke because she fell. How does the person in white fit into this?

She pressed her hand to her mouth and gazed up at the cave entrance. Runes were carved into the rock, and each was filled with a glowing moss. She craned her neck to get a better look as she walked through the opening.

The air was warm in the cave. Moss covered the cave walls. Marla reached out and touched it. The moss tickled her fingers, soft and giving under her hand. How was it here? Shouldn't the cave be wet for it to grow or something?

Marla dropped her hand back to her side and focused ahead. The path slowly dropped and curved around. It was dark, but for the soft glow of the moss. She couldn't even see the stepping stones under her feet anymore, just dark patches where there was no moss. Tialla was barely a shadow in front of her.

They rounded another corner. Marla gasped. The cavern ahead was large. Was it a cavern? The rock nearly closed over their heads, but a small part was still open to the sky. Stalagmites and stalactites scattered around everywhere but near the middle, old, dry, and covered in the same moss.

Issa wrapped an arm around her and guided her near the wall. She pointed to a spot, and Marla nodded. The others gathered in the middle. Four massive pillars of rock surrounded a stone altar in the middle. Stones paved the space between the pillars like a natural patio.

Kria walked to the altar. The others moved between the pillars and stopped, watching her. They raised their hands to the sky. Kria took a crown woven of grass from her pack and set it on the altar. She placed the fruit Marla got inside it.

She chanted, something soft and old, words Marla didn't understand. The stone patio glowed. Symbols on the pillars shone brightly, in reds and yellows and greens and blues. Her voice didn't echo, despite being surrounded by rock.

A pillar of golden light shone down through the opening above and covered Kria and the altar in a soft beam. She raised both hands and looked up as she chanted, her voice growing softer. The moss around the cavern brightened as well. When it got so bright that the whole cavern was illuminated, just when Marla was about to close her eyes, the light from above faded.

"It is done." Kria lowered her hands.

Issa left the circle and joined Marla by the wall.

"What was that?" Marla pointed vaguely at the circle and the opening above, before gesturing at the pillars.

"This is a point of power. A minor one, admittedly, but still important. Creative magic flows through all of nature, but in some places, it seems to gather and mingle before going out again. Lines of power connect these points, like rivers moving between lakes. We bless and care for these points, so the power always runs smoothly." Issa gestured at the altar behind her.

"The books didn't describe this. What happens to nature if you don't do this?" Marla walked with Issa as the woman steered her back into the tunnel.

"Nothing happens to nature. It'll continue on as it always has, though it will feel wilder. People, however, they'll notice." Adris stepped up behind her.

"Wilder? How will they notice?" She glanced back over her shoulder at Adris.

"We are planet-touched. We are part of nature in a way most of humanity isn't. We can ask nature directly for rain, or protection from storms, or even to keep predators away. We can do this for all humanity. Without us, people would have to deal with the worst of what nature can do. Storms grow wilder and destroy crops."

"What about the Light Chargers?" Marla looked up at Issa.

"They tap into and use the power of storms, draining it away. That's why the city has such mild weather. Without giving back, though, they can drain the area and suffer through droughts and ground-shakes. We go in and tend to nature to prevent this." Issa stopped at the narrow gap in the rock. "We keep the balance."

"Why don't we work together, then?" Marla squeezed through the gap, grateful she was smaller than Dornir, who had to turn sideways.

Tialla scoffed. "We used to, many centuries ago. It all started with a lovers' spat, and the next thing you know, the entire world is involved. This is why people shouldn't get married too young."

Adris snorted and hid their smile behind their hand. Kria's cheeks reddened, her mouth dropping open as she stepped through the gap. Dornir laughed as he followed, the sound still dampened by the moss. Issa grinned.

"Well, she's not wrong." Adris linked arms with Marla and moved her away from the opening. "We used to live together, with the Light Chargers. As the old tales go, anyway. Their powers are different, but complimentary. We're closer to nature, though. We call the seeds and heal and help life thrive. They can shape the world with more ease."

Marla blinked in the bright sun. After the dim cave, the sunlight hurt. It beamed in her eyes as it set low over the horizon. She brought her hand up to block the worst of the light.

"We'll walk for a bit before we camp. You need to get back to the city, where you're safe. There, you can learn to use your skills and defend yourself without the threat of being taken." Kria rested her hand on Marla's shoulder and squeezed lightly.

Tialla pointed off into the trees. "Light Chargers, and one of us."

Kria frowned. "How many? Can we do a rescue? We need to get her back."

"Two of them, and some powerless. Shouldn't we at least check it out? If I get closer, I can tell you more." Tialla crossed her arms over her chest. "This might be our only chance, and an excellent opportunity." She glanced at Marla.

"You want to use her as bait?" Issa clenched her fists.

Tialla took Issa's hands and held them. "If they see her and think she's alone, they'll be so focused they won't notice the rest of us. You can stay close and protect her. We'll move in unseen, and nothing will happen to her. I won't let them take her."

"Wait, what?" Marla rubbed her temples. "Can someone explain?"

"If there are two of them and only one of our people, they'll jump at the chance to grab you as well." Dornir nudged her lightly. "Being young and not fully trained, you would normally be incredibly vulnerable. They'll never expect that we already found you and are protecting you, so they won't be looking for us. We can sneak in and take them out, rescuing her."

Marla braced her chin against her hand. She'll never forget the look in Mia's eyes when they were caring for her, not if she lived a hundred lifetimes. Mia was so relieved, yet it seemed like she couldn't believe it either. The woman before that looked so hollow.

"I'll do it." Her legs wobbled. Was she out of her mind? No, if she were that woman, she'd want someone to help her.

"What skills do you already have? Anything you can get their attention with?" Kria held Marla's gaze.

"So far, I can call to plants in the soil a bit. I can feel the wind and the power in the land. That's about it." Marla shrugged.

"That's enough." Adris hugged her. "Just use your powers. Call to the seeds. It'll get their attention if they can feel you. If you're feeling daring, try to move the wind. They'll definitely feel that. Don't worry if you can't, though. They like the untrained ones."

"First, we get closer and look around. If they have too many servant guards, we send word for a rescue team instead." Kria spun on her heel and marched off in the direction Tialla pointed.

Issa stayed beside Marla as they followed. Tialla rushed up beside Kria. Dornir and Adris stayed behind her. The sun dropped below the treeline, leaving long shadows among the dim light. The trees were thick enough she could barely see the moon. Marla stumbled on a tree root.

"Here." Issa pulled her to a stop. "Close your eyes."

Marla stood before her, her eyes closed. Issa rested a hand over her eyes. Warmth flowed over her, surrounding her eyes. When Issa moved her hand away, Marla blinked. Her surroundings glowed faintly, like at the point of power, but much weaker. She could see every leaf and root, though.

"Thanks," Marla whispered.

Issa nodded. "You'll learn your own way soon. They use light spells, but they can't blind you now, either. You'll see the life energy around you, no matter how bright or dim things around you are. They can't overwhelm it. Just don't stare directly into a light spell." She smiled at Marla. Her muscles were tense.

They snuck through the bushes, Tialla leading. The sun set fully, and it was dark. Marla marvelled at seeing the trees and forest in this new way, each living plant or animal showing with a faint glow. Tialla finally stopped and kneeled.

Kria kneeled beside her. "What's their strength?"

Tialla picked up a stick and drew some lines in the dirt. The lines glowed a soft red. "There are the two of them, and she's here." The old woman pressed the stick tip into the ground, leaving glowing dots on her little map. "There are three guard servants. They all have training in non-magical fighting. Do not engage with them." She stared at Marla, holding her gaze. "We'll draw them away. You just need to keep the Light Chargers' attention."

Marla nodded. Her heart pounded in her chest. Could she? How? She'd find a way for Mia and everyone like her. The ledger haunted her, all those names listed as drained. She'd want to be rescued, too. Of course, if she messed up, she might be in their place. She stuffed her shaking hands in her pockets.

"I'll be close to you. They'll be so focused on you, I can use a sleep spell before they know what happened." Issa held Marla's hand. "Tialla won't be far, either. The others can take care of the guards."

"They'll have wards around their camp. You might feel them as patches of energy that don't feel quite right. Don't step in one, no matter what." Adris winked at her.

"Okay." Marla nodded.

Dornir hugged Marla. "We can use our powers and make it look like it's coming from you. If something happens, don't be surprised if they turn to you. They'll think you're having a magical outbreak, making you even more tempting." He took her hand from Issa and her palm tingled.

The others all held her hand, one at a time, leaving a surge of energy in her left hand.

Kria rested a hand on Marla's head. "We are with you. Whatever happens, look to Issa. She's your protector. Don't just run."

Marla nodded again. Her throat was tight. Words wouldn't come. What if she failed? She was mad. She must be. Ava said to get to the city. What was she doing?

"It's normal to be scared on your first rescue. We've got you." Issa pulled her close.

Marla relaxed into the hug and rested her head on Issa's shoulder. She took a deep breath. She could do this. They thought so, anyway.

"Let's get into position. Issa, you know what to do." Kria nodded at the group.

They headed through the trees, towards whatever Tialla sensed. Wait, was that them? Marla sensed something and tilted her head. The glow of a campfire caught her attention, pulling her from her magical senses. The crackle of flames confirmed it. They were camped just ahead.

Issa led her closer as the others moved away, spreading out. A Light Charger paced the edge of camp, visible in the firelight. Issa took her wide around the camp, circling behind the tent. They eased through the bushes without a sound. Was that snoring? Horses chewed the grass near the edge of camp.

They stopped at the far side of camp, facing the tent front. Issa nodded to her and released her hand. Marla nodded back. There was a single thick bush between her and the camp now. Issa melted into the bushes behind her, but Marla felt her there all the same. Something connected them now, through the magic in her hand.

She glanced back. Issa tucked herself among some nearby bushes. The woman pressed a finger to her lips. Marla nodded. She pointed to a spot near the edge of camp and Issa nodded. Even from here, she sensed the energy patches Adris warned about.

Setting her palm to the ground, Marla felt through the soil towards the spot. It vibrated much faster than anything natural. Now she felt three others just like it, lined around the campsite.

The Light Charger came around the tent, still walking slowly. He stopped and stared into the dark. Three men slept in bedrolls on the ground near the fire. A man in ornate Light Charger robes sat at the fire, a lap desk on his knees. He wrote on paper, his attention on his work. A woman sat beside him, still and lifeless. Her shiny black collar reflected firelight.

A stiff breeze blew through the camp, sending his papers scattering in the wind. The horses spooked and stomped as the pages blew among them, pulling at their tethers. Two pulled free and tore off into the bushes. Blankets rustled, and the tent flapped.

"Find her." The man set his lap desk down and ran for the horses.

The last horse screamed and circled their tether. Others crashed through the bush, getting farther away with each moment. The sleeping men rolled to their feet, blinking in the light as they looked around. They ran to the edge of the firelight and peered into the darkness. The woman sat, not reacting to anything around her.

Marla pressed low into the bush as a man stopped close to her. Footsteps pounded the soil as they charged about. She peeked out. They grabbed torches and lit them at the fire. The men charged into the bushes, scattering in all directions.

A melodic whistle called from beyond the camp, moving away.

"This way." One man waved at the others to follow.

The men charged off. The last Light Charger stood over her, his robes swirling as he spun. He called a ball of light and it hovered over his shoulder.

The ground under her warmed. Marla leapt to her feet and stepped towards him, her hands outstretched. She called to the plants below his feet. Moss grew up over his boots, fixing his feet to the ground as more plants surged to life. No, it needs to be thicker. At least it worked at all.

She dodged the fireball and rolled behind a tree. A cage of flames stood where she was moments ago. Marla stood and smiled, her heart pounding. His attention was on her completely. She swore as another fireball sped towards her. It dissolved as Issa touched the Light Charger, dropping him to the ground. Was he asleep? No, she realized, as she touched his energy. He was hibernating.

Marla walked over to the remaining horse. She reached for the massive stallion with her energy, putting as much calming into it as she could. Was she doing this right? "Easy, fella. You're safe."

He stomped, but stopped circling. Marla touched his shoulder, rubbing him slowly and gently. His sides heaved with each breath. He lowered his head and touched her chest over her heart with his nose.

"That's it, fella. You're okay." She stroked the sleek nose.

"Let's get that off you." Issa kneeled beside the woman.

Marla wandered over and kneeled by the fire. Issa touched the collar, and the metal rusted, crumbling as the lock fell away. She grasped either side and pulled it away from the woman's neck. The instant the collar was off, the woman turned her head and smiled at Issa. She moved so stiffly, though.

"Let him go free. We need to get out of here." Issa nodded at the stallion. She wrapped an arm around the woman and helped her up.

CHAPTER 11

A dris stepped from the bushes and walked over, helping Issa with the stumbling woman. She was already getting the colour back in her pale cheeks. Marla slipped the stallion's halter off and patted his shoulder. He snorted and tore off into the bushes after the others.

Marla darted after them, slipping into the bushes with ease. The woman walked steadier with each step she took. Kria appeared between two bushes and waved the group over. Kria led them among some thick trees. She pulled some branches aside, revealing a gap between some boulders. Adris slipped inside first. Issa and the woman followed. Kria nodded at Marla, and Marla eased through the gap.

She dropped into a sloping tunnel. Marla stayed close to Issa as they descended into a cavern. Issa took the woman over to a chair in a corner as Adris grabbed a canteen from a shelf. They offered her some water, which the woman sipped with help.

"Will Dornir be okay? Tialla?" Marla stopped near the chamber entrance. She looked back up the tunnel, which was empty except for Kria.

Adris laughed. "He'll be fine. He does this all the time. They're looking for you, a girl, and not him. Tialla will be here any moment."

Kria linked arms with Marla and guided her into the cavern. "They'll also be more worried about the missing horses and her." She nodded to the woman in the corner. "Dornir's smart and knows these woods. He'll be fine."

"How are you? Do you need some more?" Adris stroked the woman's hair as she lowered the empty canteen.

The woman smiled. "I feel it coming back. My power. Thank you." Her voice shook. Had she not spoken in a while?

"Don't thank us yet. We still need to get you to safety. This is just a brief stop on the way." Issa took crackers from a box. "Here." She offered them to the woman first, and everyone else after.

Marla took the dry crackers. "What does it feel like?"

"She's newly awakened," Adris explained.

"It's like getting my life back. Like waking up warm after a cold sleep in the winter. When they first put the collar on, I could feel them draining my power away. He pulled so much, and I couldn't resist. I was so tired. Unending tired. Now, though, now I feel alive." She smiled as she bit into a cracker.

"How do the collars work? Can we break them somehow? Can we stop them from working?" Marla looked up at Kria.

"We've been trying to learn more. Once we break one off, it loses all power. The enchantment drains away. Before use, they're just as empty of power. The only way to know might be for someone to go in and allow one to be put on, and that's too risky." Kria scowled and folded her arms over her chest.

"Don't let that happen. He put that on, and in a flash of light, my power was gone." The woman wept. She dropped her crackers and covered her face with her hands.

Tialla came in and marched right over to the woman. She kneeled beside her and rubbed her back. Adris handed Tialla a small bottle from a cupboard full of medicine. Tialla held the opened bottle to the woman's lips and helped her drink it.

Adris kneeled on her other side. "Breathe slow and deep. You're safe for now. You can rest."

Tialla took the woman's hands. Marla watched as the woman's hair lost the streaks of grey. It darkened through shades of brown until it was almost black. Her hollow cheeks filled, and her lips grew pink again.

"What?" Marla blinked.

Tialla gave the woman's hand a squeeze. "The energy draining will prematurely age someone. We'll be able to restore her fully once we get her back to the city. With some care, she'll recover completely."

Marla hugged herself tightly. "How long were you with them?"

A tear rolled down her cheek. "I was your age when they got me. I didn't listen and strayed too far from my group. It's been a dozen summers, maybe? I don't know anymore." She sobbed into Adris' shoulder. "I was almost dead. Another year at most."

Adris hugged her. Tialla rested a hand on her back and sent soothing magic into her.

"I knew you would come eventually," she whispered.

Marla raised an eyebrow and looked at Kria.

"We have to wait until they leave the city before we can rescue them. Getting into their stronghold is nearly impossible without inside help. Once they're in the wild, though," Kria grinned, "we can use our full powers to rescue them."

"Unfortunately, once someone gets taken, the Light Charger who has them will usually remain in the citadel and focus on mastering their new available powers. It can be years or tens of years before they leave. They know we're out here, waiting." Issa handed Marla some dried fruit. "Eat something."

"They're far enough away. We can take her to the nearest refuge." Tialla cradled the woman's cheek in her hand. "Our friends will take you to the city. We'll get word to your family that you're safe. You have all the time you need to recover."

"Thank you." The woman gripped Tialla's wrist with her bony hand. "You're sure it's safe?"

Tialla kissed her forehead. "Oh, dear child. I'm certain."

Dornir stepped into the cavern. "Maybe we should rest here first. They're heading back to the city but could turn at any time. We're well hidden and protected."

Kria nodded. "Marla, get some sleep, too. If you can't rest, let us know. Issa can help."

Issa pulled bedrolls from the corner bin and handed them out. Marla set hers up near a wall and curled up in the warmth. This wasn't what she thought her life would be like. The others are so practiced and just know what to do. Would she one day, too? What was the city like? Where was it? She knew maps and had seen nothing like one before. What would she learn there? Would she even make it to the city?

She focused on the room again. Tialla was resting with her back to the wall. The woman sat beside her, leaning against her. Someone draped a blanket around them. Issa was nearby like always, unrolling her own bedroll. Dornir sat near the entrance with his eyes closed. The others scattered around, settling down for some sleep.

She closed her eyes. Marla smiled. Was Adris snoring already? It was a soft sound, steady and rhythmic, soothing in a way. Her first mission and she not only survived, she helped. Sure, her body was tired, and her legs felt like wood, but she helped.

***

"Alright, everyone up."

The voice pulled her from sleep. Her skin was damp with sweat and her legs ached again. The running dream? The sun streamed down the passageway. How long had they slept? She sat and rubbed her eyes. Marla blinked a few times as she looked around.

The woman sat in the chair, eating more crackers. Her hair was limp and needed a good wash, but every trace of grey was gone. Her skin was darker. Could being drained really affect a person that much? Did it take her life energy as well?

"Everyone needs to eat before we go. We'll stop at the refuge before heading on our way. There's one more point of power between us and home." Kria handed canteens out to everyone.

Marla took the canteen and nodded. She unscrewed the cap and sipped. Dornir and Adris handed out day-old pastries from their packs. Marla nibbled hers. She smiled. Cheese and herbs, her favourite.

Once they'd all eaten, she helped Issa fold up all the bedrolls. The others cleaned up from breakfast and set used canteens in a box. Tialla checked the woman over again and nodded. Dornir walked over and offered her his arm.

"We'll take the time we need, but head directly there. Adris, take the lead." Kria gestured to the tunnel.

Marla followed the group behind Dornir and the woman. Adris snuck through the entrance. Marla crouched on the tunnel floor until their hand poked down and waved everyone up. The group eased from their hiding place and stepped out among the trees.

115

The forest was quiet, though Marla felt life around her. A fox slunk among the bushes, hunting. Mice scampered around in the undergrowth, hiding from him. Birds flew overhead, singing to each other. There was no sign of any people anywhere.

Where was this refuge? Was it close? If so, why didn't they go there sooner? If not, how were they going to get there safely? Marla swallowed her questions and stayed close to the others. Issa was nearby, as always, watching over her. Who was she, though? Where was she from, and how did she end up out here?

They walked for hours, seeing no one at all. The trees gradually thinned. Near the edge of the woods, among the thinner trees, a cabin and some outbuildings stood back from a road. Was this it? Smoke rose from the chimney. She sniffed the air. Burning wood, sure, but were those herbs in the smoke?

Issa smiled at her. "Yes, remember that smell."

"What is it?"

"All our safe houses burn that blend of herbs. If you smell that, you know you're near a refuge with people who can help you."

Marla inhaled deeply, letting the scent linger in her nose. If this was safety, she never wanted to forget.

Kria walked up to the cabin door and knocked. She used a rhythmic pattern of short, sharp knocks and softer hits against the door.

The door opened a crack. "Yes?" A woman stood behind the door, mostly hidden from view.

"One traveller, looking to go home." Kria touched her own forehead, before lowering her hand to her heart.

The door swung wide open, and the woman stepped back. "Welcome. Come in." She was older and dressed in typical work clothing, though her hair was neatly braided around her head.

Kria stepped inside, followed by Dornir and the woman. Marla followed, but Issa wrapped a hand around her arm.

"They'll only be moments. Come see the garden." Issa tugged lightly on her arm.

Marla followed her around the side of the cabin. "Oh, wow."

An herb garden to rival Ava's stretched along the side of the cabin. Some grew in pots they overflowed, and others were growing in neatly tended beds. Some flowered already while others were just emerging from the soil. A border of energy protected the tender plants from deer and other animals.

"I've never seen some of these before." Marla kneeled beside a plant with tiny orange flowers.

"That's another way to locate tended safe houses. They all have a full medicinal garden. Most also grow vegetables. Someone inside the safe house will have the skill to use all these, too. They can help you with nearly any injury."

Kria appeared around the corner of the cabin. "She's settled. Let's go."

They rejoined the others near the cabin door.

"Are you ready to try helping at the next point of power?" Kria held her gaze. She smiled.

"What, really?" Marla tapped her lips with her finger. "Sure? I don't know how, but I'll do my best."

Issa rested a hand on Marla's shoulder. "We'll teach you. It's better to start with the minor points of power. If something goes wrong, there's less energy to worry about."

"If you make a mistake, I'll be right there to help." Adris draped an arm over her shoulders.

"Do people make mistakes often?" Marla twisted her fingers together.

"When learning, yes. Don't be concerned. You'll do great." Tialla winked at her before turning and walking off.

The group followed, heading back into the trees. Marla glanced up at the sun. They still travelled south, mostly, and slightly east as well. The forest was thinner here, letting more light down to the smaller plants. Wildflowers grew all around now, little bursts of colour to brighten the forest.

Their stop for lunch was brief. The day was warm, and the sun felt good, so Marla tucked her cloak in her backpack. They stopped again at a fast stream. Adris kneeled beside the water and held their hand over it. After a long moment, they nodded. Everyone refilled their canteens.

"They'll teach you to do that, too. Adris is our expert in all things water." Issa tightened the cap on her canteen.

"I'm still learning," Adris protested.

"We all are, love." Tialla smiled at them. "Even me."

"Does everyone have a specialty?" Marla looked around at everyone.

They nodded.

Marla pointed at Tialla. "Shields, right?"

Tialla grinned. "Best around."

"You do a lot of diversions, so hiding, or camouflage?" She pointed at Dornir.

"You got it." He thumped his chest.

"You dropped him asleep easily. Is that your strength?" She tilted her head towards Issa.

"Sleeping and waking." Issa nodded. "Whether it's calling to new life or putting people into a state of resting, I do both with ease."

Marla turned to Kria. She raised an eyebrow.

"I'm sensitive to the flow of power. I can feel the state of the land around us and manipulate that to keep us safe. I'm a channeler. We're close. We'll be there soon." Kria led them away, close to where they headed earlier, but not quite the same way.

A specialty, huh? What was hers, Marla wondered. Did anything come easily to her? She was too new. How was she to even know?

By midafternoon, they stopped at the edge of the trees. Fields sprawled across the land before them as far as she could see. Farmhouses dotted the land, spread among the fields, with clusters of houses in some areas.

"This is it. The centre of all our activity in this country." Kria gestured at the fields.

Marla leaned against a tree as she stared out at the land. Grain crops were emerging from the soil. Orchards surrounded by stone walls grew close to the houses. Some fields looked like massive vegetable patches.

Adris lay their hand on her shoulder. "This is the heart of the agricultural district. Most food in the country is grown here. Much of it is traded in the city and surrounding towns. Close your eyes and feel for it. Breathe. Tell me what you sense."

Marla straightened up and closed her eyes. She took a deep breath in, held it for a moment, and let it out. The deep pulsing reached her immediately as energy flowed up through her legs. She let it flow out and followed it, sensing the hum of the crops and tingle of all the plants. Was it somehow easier, since being at the first point of power?

"That's unbelievable. The plants are happy, I guess? I don't know what I'm feeling, but it's a good feeling."

"Good. Feel the soil."

She sank down into the soil. The top bit felt damp, warm, and welcoming. She dropped farther down. Her skin itched. "It's dry down below?"

"Yes. They had good snowmelt from the spring, better than in many places, but not as much as they really should have. We focus a lot of our time and energy here because of how many people it feeds. There are more Wood Walkers here than any other part of the world." Adris squeezed her shoulder lightly.

Marla pulled her attention fully back into her body and opened her eyes.

"You need to pay attention and be aware when we're here. There are also more Light Chargers here than anywhere but their city." Kria folded her arms over her chest. "There are fewer natural areas to hide in. Here, your best chance is not being discovered. Hiding among the workers is your best bet. Try to avoid the raiding parties."

Marla hugged herself tightly. "Raiding parties? Like the people who chased me when I met you?"

CHAPTER 12

Issa pulled her close and hugged her. "As long as you stay with us, or with another group, we'll keep you safe. All groups have someone who can shield you and protect you. Tialla can feel Light Chargers from farther off than anyone I know."

Tialla winked. "I sneak up on them, not the other way around."

"Does that mean they can also feel us from a distance?" Marla winced at how shaky she sounded.

"A few. They're more likely to be here than in the forest. Once we've restored the point of power, we're leaving. With so many groups spread around here, it can confuse them, which helps. A good portion of the people in the fields are experienced Wood Walkers. You're still awakening, though, so you're easier to feel." Kria took Marla's hand and squeezed it. "The moment we're done, we're going to the city. You'll be safe there."

"We get the newly awakened through here as fast as we can, usually. Once you're in the city, they can't find you. This is the most dangerous area for the escort groups, though we're great at sneaking people past." Dornir grinned, showing teeth.

"The city with all the Light Chargers?"

Adris shook their head. "No, our city. Our refuge. Our home. Let's go. It's hidden away. You'll love it there. Everyone does."

"Ava called that a refuge, too. Sounds great. Where are we going here, then?" Marla straightened up. How close was this city? Would they be there soon? If safety was so close, why wouldn't they take her there first?

Dornir pointed to a spot where the forest curved around and jutted out into the field. "There. It's among the trees."

"We'll use the road. She can see us do a group blessing." Kria headed out along the edge of the treeline, towards a road not far away.

Marla stayed close behind her. The soil was soft and springy, making each step comfortable and quiet. They turned onto the road. It headed straight through the fields towards a cluster of buildings in the distance.

Kria stretched her hand out, keeping it low, her palm facing the field to her right. Issa stretched her hand down and to the left, to the fields on the other side. She glanced back over her shoulder and noticed the others also reaching for the fields.

"Feel," Adris instructed, their voice hushed. "We'll teach you soon."

Marla opened herself to the world around her. It got easier each time she tried, and she was getting a lot of practice on this journey. She felt the pulse of life around her immediately. Thin ribbons of power flowed from her friends and stretched out across the land. It was fuzzy, but she sensed the surrounding land absorbing the energy.

Tialla hummed a simple tune. Adris joined, singing softly. Soon the others were also singing, so quietly Marla almost couldn't make out the words. The energy grew stronger as they sang. It sank into the soil. They didn't stop until they reached the trees.

"I only felt the power reach out a few fields. Was it going farther, and I just couldn't tell, or what happens to the other fields?" Marla glanced back as she stepped among the trees.

"Others will tend to those. Remember, Wood Walkers are here all the time. Many live here and work in the fields daily. They knew we were coming, so they left this part for us." Kria smiled and tilted her head towards the thick bushes among the trees. "After you."

Adris took Marla's hand and pulled her between two huge bushes. Marla closed her eyes and held her hand up to guard against the branches as they walked through. Her foot caught in a low bush. She almost tumbled out as they emerged from between the bushes on the other side. Adris caught her as she dropped to her knees.

Marla opened her eyes. A path stretched before them, heading deeper among the trees. It was overgrown with grass, but the bushes didn't grow too close to it. The dirt tingled under her feet when she sensed it. She looked back but couldn't see the fields.

Adris pulled her out of the way. The others came through. They pulled her along the path through the thickening trees. The grass thinned and soon she was walking on a dirt path instead. Adris followed the path, weaving among the dense trees, pulling Marla along with them.

They stopped at a wall of trees, though the dirt path continued on through them. Adris stretched their hand out, and the trees shivered. Marla watched, open-mouthed, as the trees leaned away from the path. Stone slabs lined the path beyond the trees.

She stepped through the opening and onto the stone path. The canopy above her was so thick she couldn't see the sky, except for tiny slivers of blue caught as the leaves fluttered in a breeze she didn't feel.

They rounded the corner. A stone arch stood ahead. Marla let Adris pull her along as she stared at the arch. Who put it here? How did the moss that was covering the runes glow like that? She stared up at it as Adris dragged her through.

Just beyond the arch was an open area, fully encircled by thick trees and bushes. Standing stones formed a circle inside, with one massive stone in the middle. Marla recognised many of the runes from the other site, carved into the standing stones on all sides.

Kria walked over to the largest standing stone and rested her palm against it. "All you have to do is stand where we show you and let the power flow through you. We'll direct it for now. Consider this as a prayer. We're asking for people to live in harmony with nature. Not just us, but everyone." She traced a rune with her finger.

Issa draped an arm around her shoulders. "We work as nature's partners. I know you love the land, and you want it to be healthy. Let that fill you as you do this."

"I can do that." Marla smiled. She touched the little pendant through her shirt, tracing the wire-wrapped bird. It reminded her of Ava and being in the gardens. Her chest got tight, her heart beating fast. Home. Would she see it again?

Adris cradled Marla's cheek in their hand. "You can do this. I'll be right behind you, ready to help if you need. You won't need."

"Why me, though?" She held Adris' gaze.

"We all grow and age with the cycle of life. Time passes. One day we will pass with it, and you will step up. It's better if you're involved now, so you feel completely comfortable and confident. Besides, having Wood Walkers from all stages of life makes the prayer stronger." Kria gestured at the circle.

"It does?" Marla turned to Kria.

"Of course. Blending the wisdom of those who have been here a while with your youthful energy strengthens the magic. The circle goes ever on." Kria nodded to the group. "When you all are ready, we'll begin."

"Come stand here." Adris pulled her to the south, between two of the standing stones. "Can you feel it?"

Marla looked down at her feet. She shuffled around a little. "It's kind of like a static shock, but doesn't hurt?"

"Yeah, that's it. Move slowly until you find where it's strongest. That's where you should stand." Adris stepped behind her, closer to the wall of trees.

She shifted and took small steps, feeling the spot where the energy was strongest. She looked up at the others, spaced out around the circle between the stones. Kria set another woven crown on the nearest stone, along with some fruit, all balanced on the flat top. She began chanting.

The power under Marla flowed and shifted, moving up through her and back down again.

"Focus on your love of nature," Adris whispered.

Marla closed her eyes and thought of her time in the gardens, both tending plants and making pottery. She remembered the way the sun felt on her skin and how lovely a cooling breeze was. Marla opened her eyes.

Her chest warmed as the power flowed through her with ease now. It pulsed in bursts with the rhythm, growing and ebbing like the tide. Kria's voice was steady, though it echoed with the same emotions Marla felt.

The standing stones glowed, connected by the rings of power beneath her feet. Energy flowed freely through the circle, connecting the stones. The air crackled with more energy. Speckles of light floated around her as the circle glowed green under her feet.

"It is done." Kria lowered her hands.

The energy faded, leaving an echo in Marla's body.

Adris wrapped her in a hug. "You did great. You're strong."

Marla twisted in their grip. She hugged Adris back. "That was amazing."

Kria walked over. She lay her hand on Marla's shoulder. "You have a lot of power and love in you. One day, you will make a fabulous caretaker. I would like you to be my apprentice."

"A—apprentice?" Marla blinked. "Like, one day I do what you did?" She stared at the northern spot in the circle.

"Exactly. I believe you have what it takes to withstand the power the others can channel. You can learn to focus it. It'll take decades of training, and you'll still need to learn the other roles first. I think nature will be better off if you agree, though." Kria held her gaze.

Marla opened her mouth for a moment before closing it again. She blinked. "Uh, okay?" Wait, if she did that, would she travel around every year? Would she have a home anymore? Marla rested a hand over her heart. The warmth from the energy still infused her. Maybe it would be worth it?

"It's a great honour and comes with real responsibility. We'll teach you." Issa rubbed her back. "You have plenty of time."

She looked around the circle. A thin thread of glowing green light still connected the stones. The power hummed beneath her feet. "That was—I don't even know how to describe it."

Kria smiled. "You touched the source and made your first offering. You're fully one of us now. Some much-needed rain will arrive within days, now that we're finished here. Come." She turned and headed back through the arch.

"How many sites are there?" Marla followed with the others.

"Thousands of small sites like this. Wood Walkers from all over the world visit them and recharge them. There are only three massive sites, though. We're heading to the largest and most important one." Adris squeezed through the gap behind her.

"You can help me with that one." Kria stopped and turned to Marla. "We haven't been able to fully charge it for a few years. That's partly why the rains have been sparse, and why the weather is so unpredictable. For a full recharge, the strongest caretakers and their apprentices gather and connect with nature. I hadn't found an apprentice strong enough, and another's intended apprentice was taken. With your help, we'll be able to do the ritual once we rescue her."

"I thought you had to wait for them to leave the city?" Marla caught up as Kria started walking. She stepped over a fallen log.

"We do, but with the lack of rain, they've been coming out to find a solution. We've rescued more people in the last two annual cycles than in the ten before that." Kria grinned. "Our source inside the city tells me she'll be coming our way soon."

"One of them is working for you?" Marla stumbled and caught herself against a tree, her palms flat on the rough trunk.

Issa laughed. "There's more than just Light Chargers in that place. They aren't careful who they talk around for most projects and missions. It's amazing the things they'll say around a servant."

Marla looked out as they approached the vast fields. So many people, all tending the plants. What would it be like, working here, knowing your nemesis was so close? She hugged herself. Adris slung an arm around her and guided her as Kria walked along the treeline, back in the shadows.

They followed the edge of the fields for a while before turning deeper into the woods again, past the boulders and rocks that blocked their path earlier.

"Issa, now is a good time." Kria waved her up.

"Good time for what?" Marla glanced between the women.

"A lesson in magic, and how to help the forest. They'll wait here. Come with me." Issa headed away from everyone, deeper into the forest.

Marla followed. She glanced back. Dornir smiled, and Adris waved. She turned and walked with Issa. When they could no longer see the others, Issa stopped. They were in a small clearing with a few trees laying across the ground, the stumps partly rotted. One massive tree was blackened and splintered.

"This is perfect." Issa touched the broken stump. The blackened bark flaked off. "The tree was felled by lightning. You can tell by the char pattern and the way it shattered. Trees this large normally take a long time to decompose. I'm going to teach you how to return it to the soil faster."

Marla stared at the massive trunk, nearly as big around as her arms would reach if she tried to hug it. "The whole thing?"

Issa laughed. "No, not yet. There's no way you'd be strong enough. We're using it because if your powers go astray, this tree can hold it all and more. You won't harm a living tree by mistake. Or me. Especially not me."

Her cheeks burned. The warmth spread down her neck. "Why would we do this?"

"See how the sunlight now reaches the forest floor?" Issa pointed up at the patch of blue sky. "All that extra sun will help the new tree grow strong."

Marla touched the black bark, and it flaked away, leaving a dark reddish wood underneath. "That makes sense."

"Also, this tree will decompose and become fertilizer for the future tree and ground plants. Like your compost piles for a garden, but much bigger. If we break them down faster, we can also spread it a bit." Issa leaned against another tree. "Ready to try?"

"What do I do?"

Issa moved closer and set both her hands against the fallen tree. "All you have to do is call to the tiny organisms and insects. Channel some energy to them. They'll work faster." She pulled a circle of glass from her pocket and held it over where the bark was gone. "See?"

Marla peered down at the glass. Everything under it looked so much bigger now. Tiny insects scurried around, visible now. "Those were there this whole time?"

The woman smiled. "Once you learn to use your powers, you'll feel them and all life. From the giant trees to the tiny decomposers too small for this glass, even, you'll know them all. Now, focus on the tree crumbling and breaking down. Take a sliver of energy and give it to those creatures. See if you can break down a patch as big as your palm here." She tapped the trunk.

Marla lay her hands lightly over the tree and closed her eyes. Breathe slowly and open myself. I got this. The energy flowed beneath her feet and up through her. She called to the little creatures as she imagined the tree crumbling before her.

The wood vibrated under her hands. Pieces flaked away, falling around her boots and landing on the moss. Lichen spread under her fingers. Marla opened her eyes. Her heart sank as she saw how little had changed, though one spot had crumbled completely.

"For your first time, that was actually quite good. Your focus kept it incredibly concentrated. With practice, you'll be able to do more. Give it time. Once you're practiced, you can do things like this."

Issa collected a pile of fallen branches. She held her hand over them. The woman glowed faintly. The branches crumbled and formed a pile at her feet. Marla kneeled down and picked up a handful of the new soil and looked closer.

"It's actually soil. I could grow vegetables in this." Marla poked at the soil with a finger.

"That's the point." Issa chuckled. "This is why farmers like us so much. We go around every spring and fall and help with their fields. Often, we bring some of this new fertile soil to mix into their plots. Sometimes we give advice instead, like for them to rotate the crops differently, or when to leave a field fallow."

"No wonder Ava's garden always thrived. It didn't matter how wet or dry the year was, or what." Marla tipped the soil back into the pile.

129

"Once we finish the ritual properly and recharge the main point of power, the rains will return." Issa rested a hand on her shoulder.

"How long will it take to learn everything?" Marla spread some new soil with her toe. "You did that so fast."

Issa draped an arm over her shoulder. "By next spring, you'll know how to do everything you need to work as one of us fully. Each year, you'll get faster and more powerful. Even as we grow old, our powers keep growing, as long as you use them. People Ava and Tialla's age have powers we can only dream of, honed over a lifetime of use."

"How well can you do this?" Marla gestured at the massive log.

Issa raised her hand towards the tree. A section as long as Marla's arm broke down and crumbled into a pile in the gap. "Tialla could do half the tree in that time if she wanted."

Marla stared at the tree. How much practice would it take? Was it just practice, or is it also the strength of her connection to the forest? She sighed. The answers were probably in Ava's library. A library she may never see again.

"Let's go back." Issa steered her towards the others.

They wandered back through the trees. The leaves rustled in the gentle breeze. The sun peeked through the canopy in slivers, turning the leaves above her a bright green. She inhaled the slightly damp aroma of plants around her.

Issa stiffened and looked back. "We need to go. Nice and quiet," she whispered.

"How close?" Marla tucked in against her.

CHAPTER 13

"Not very, but don't linger."

She led Marla into the thicker bushes. They passed silently, despite brushing up against branches and leaves. It was like they were spirits. Marla stared at the bushes ahead with wide eyes. There was no way they'd pass through those.

The branches parted as Issa approached and they squeezed through with space to spare. She led Marla to a nearby stream. A fallen tree lay over the water. Issa leapt onto it and nimbly dashed across, pulling Marla with her. They dropped back to the soil, where Issa crouched. Marla tucked in against the tree beside her.

"Water helps. It confuses their powers sometimes. If you're ever in real trouble, get near water. Get in it if you can. They won't sense you as easily." Issa peered over the fallen tree, back to where they came from. "I don't think he knows where we went."

"I didn't feel a thing," Marla whispered. "How can I avoid them if I don't know where they are?"

Issa squeezed her hand gently. "You depend on us for now, and we won't let you down. Never go off alone. Not far. Soon your powers will settle, and we'll teach you how to sense them. Get a drink while you can." She eased down beside the water and scooped some up, drinking from her hand.

Marla crouched beside her and dipped her hand in the cold water. She shivered as she drank, the water numbing her hand. Once she dried her hand off, Issa led her back to the group.

Kria turned to Dornir. "We need to find a campsite or shelter. With them that close, I'd prefer a shelter."

He pointed into the woods, away from where the Light Charger was. "There are several of them between us and the site. How far do you want to go?"

Kria shielded her eyes with her hand as she looked up at the sun. It was dropping fast, nearly at the treetops now.

"It'll get dark soon. Maybe a closer one is better." Tialla tilted her head and raised an eyebrow.

After a long moment of silence, Kria nodded. "Find one close enough we can get there before full dark."

Dornir set off through the trees. Marla followed with the group. She wiggled her fingers, trying to get some feeling back in the icy hand. When that didn't work, she wrapped the edge of her cloak around it.

"Wait." Tialla stopped and turned. "That's her. This might be our chance." She stared off back the way they came.

"Her?" Marla whispered.

"The intended apprentice I mentioned earlier. They took her a few years ago, before we could get to her and train her. If we can get her back, she has more time to recover before we need to charge the great point of power." Issa rested a hand on Marla's shoulder.

"How many with her?" Kria crossed her arms over her chest.

"Just him. He must have servant guards with him, though. There's no way he'd travel through here alone with her." Tialla frowned. "Not unless—"

"Unless what?" Marla hugged herself, pulling her cloak tight around herself.

"It could be the young man." Tialla rubbed her chin.

Kria scowled. "If it is, we should call for backup and wait. He'd need to be incredibly distracted for us to succeed."

"Why?" Marla cringed at how small her voice sounded, how quiet that one word came out.

Adris' mouth hung open. Dornir tensed. Issa frowned so deeply her face creased.

"He's powerful. Normally we can take on any of them, even a small group of Light Chargers is nothing to us if we're careful. His elemental powers are strong. He's also drawing power from one of our strongest apprentice candidates, so he has access to her energy as well. Nobody gets onto the council at his age without being amazing at magic, and his strength is shaping rock. Usually by blasting it, Marla." Kria shook her head.

"Wait." Adris paced a tiny circle. "Maybe we can still do this safely. We know he's in the area, because we saw him in town. He spoke to Marla and wanted to see her again. He's young, and he travels with a younger taken one, right?"

Tialla nodded.

"I'm sure it's him. I bet he'd be really distracted if Marla showed up. Distracted enough to let his guard down, even." They grinned. "I only need a moment, and with Dornir for backup and Tialla to shield us, we got this. You two can grab her as we take care of him."

Issa wrapped an arm around Marla and pulled her close. "It's too risky."

Marla squirmed. "We need her, though, right? Can he really guard her and take me as well?" She stuffed her shaking hands in her pockets and held

Issa's gaze. No, she was insane thinking of helping. Safety was so close now. Though, wouldn't she want to be rescued?

"We'll get closer and see what we're dealing with. Issa, get her to the hideout. She needs rest before we try anything. Make sure she has a snack. I don't want to be too late and strike while he's sleeping. I want Marla able to talk to him." Kria sighed. "Be careful."

Dornir gave Issa directions, and the woman nodded. She led Marla through the trees, away from danger, as the others walked towards it.

"Don't get cocky just because our other rescues went well." Issa kept her voice low as they walked. "The other Light Chargers were strong and skilled, but this one is on the Inner Council, much younger than most. Only the strongest and best are on the Inner Council, and that usually takes decades of training and practice. He could easily be stronger than the last group all by himself."

"I'll be careful. I have no intention of being taken." Marla tilted her head and stopped. "Wait."

Something pulled at her, like an echo of pain shooting through her body. Marla closed her eyes. Where was it? If only she knew what she was doing, this would be easier. There, off that way, energy moved in a tiny tornado.

Marla followed the sensation. It was close. She kneeled. The grass before her shifted. A small bird lay in the grass, one wing bent in the wrong spot.

"What happened, little fella?" Marla eased her hand under the bird.

He panted as he lay in her palm, his wing outstretched.

"Well, that's no good. How about we help you feel better?" she murmured. "Issa, show me how?"

Issa glanced around, her face tight and lined. "Fine, but we make it fast." She held her hand over the bird. "It's a simple break. Imagine you're sprouting seeds. You add energy like that, but instead of thinking of growth, think of mending. Once that's done, I'll show you the next step. He's tiny, so don't use a lot of energy. I'll guide you. Ready?"

Was she? Marla nodded.

"Okay, let your power flow and fill him, but don't flood him. I'll help you direct it, but you're going to heal him."

Marla opened herself to him and pulled energy up through her feet. It flowed into the bird as she focused, though something was holding most of it back.

"Too much. He's tiny, remember. Feel how much I'm letting through?"

She nodded. "Yeah."

"Control it if you can."

Marla took a moment to focus on the energy and thin it down into a smaller stream.

"There. Like that. Now we'll start directing it." Issa nudged her energy through the bird, to his wing. "Think of mending."

With Issa guiding, Marla felt for the bone. The edges were sharp and fit back together neatly. What does mending even look like? Marla poured her care into the bird, hoping it would work. She willed his little wing to heal. The bone fused in place. With how tiny he was, it took moments.

She opened her eyes and held her hand up. He sat on her hand, both wings outstretched. He flapped a few times, sending a little breeze over her skin. The little bird launched himself from her hand and flew off, perching in a nearby tree. Marla smiled as she watched him go.

"Light Wielder," Issa hissed. "Go."

Marla glanced where Issa pointed. She took off through the bushes. Issa gripped her cloak and guided her in the growing dark.

"I just want to talk," he called after her.

She ran, her lungs burning. They sprinted through the trees, towards the safety Issa knew about. Underground. They need to get underground. She risked glancing back. He wasn't following. No magic chased them. How did he sneak so close? Why didn't Issa detect him?

Issa stopped and peered into the darkness behind them. "It's safe, I think. In." She pulled a bush back, revealing a cave.

Marla darted inside and scooted down the tunnel. She didn't stop until it was too dark to see. Issa caught up. She held her palm up and a ball of light floated over her hand. They followed the tunnel to the cavern inside. Marla collapsed in a chair in the corner.

Issa took a couple bottles of water from a box and handed one to Marla. "They never just want to talk. Some youngsters fall for that. Make sure you're not one of them. Sometimes a hunting party will send someone young and cute in first to lure you out. They'll act helpful and like they care. It's a trick."

"He wasn't that young." Marla rubbed her chin.

Issa laughed. "Oh, the young are so adorable. No, but he was younger than most. Too young to have her as a power source, usually. Was he the one from the marketplace?"

"I didn't actually see him," Marla admitted. "I kept my gaze down, so I don't know what he looks like. It sounded like him, though. It sounded exactly like him." Her hand shook as she lifted the water bottle to her lips. "Why didn't he chase us?"

Kria stepped into the cavern, the others behind her. She stared at Issa, her eyebrow raised. "Using magic with one of them so close? Did you think he wouldn't notice?"

"There was an injured bird." Issa shrugged. "Marla wanted to help, and it needed healing. Are we supposed to ignore those in need? He snuck up on us, Kria. I didn't feel him at all."

Tialla frowned and crossed her arms over her chest. "I got close enough to sense her better. It is her. He hasn't drained her as badly as the others. Her power is still decent. Once we get the collar off, she might even have the strength to help us."

Kria narrowed her eyes.

"If I didn't know better, I'd even say she was newly taken, though she's not." Tialla walked to the table and sat. The chair creaked as she shifted. "We know she's been gone about three years, but I can't explain why she's not been drained more. She won't need much recovery time before we visit the site."

"Can we actually rescue her?" Adris turned a leaf over in their hands. "If he hasn't drawn on her, is he that powerful? Or is he so powerful he doesn't need to draw on her much?"

Dornir paced slowly around the table. "It'll be dangerous. He wouldn't be out here alone if he couldn't defend himself. He wouldn't risk it. If he got that close to Issa undetected, we may not fare much better. He might feel us first."

Tialla cracked her knuckles. "He won't be far from her. He cared for her well. I think he didn't chase you because he didn't want to leave her too long. We can use that against him."

"Tialla?" Kria turned to her.

"I say we go for it. There's no guarantee we'll ever get another chance. If she's that powerful, he could do a lot of damage draining her, to her and a rescue team. He wants Marla, though. He's distracted. We might even change the balance of their power, keeping them all busy for a while, if he loses her."

"Dornir?" Kria turned her gaze on him.

He stopped pacing. "If Marla can distract him, we have a chance. If we work together, we can do this. I say we try." Dornir took a water bottle and opened it.

"Adris?"

They glanced at Marla. "I'm willing to risk it, but what about Marla? What if we rescue her, and things go wrong, and he takes Marla instead?"

"That's my concern, too." Issa rested a hand on Marla's shoulder. "I think we can do it, but who keeps her safe if something goes wrong?"

"I will. He won't touch her." Tialla raised her water bottle. "If you get her collar off, I am his match."

Kria nodded. "It's settled. We do this. Besides, we have one significant advantage."

"Oh?" Issa raised her eyebrow.

"We have something he wants, too." Kria smiled at Marla. "You don't need to be afraid. We'll keep you safe. It will be dangerous, but we can save one of our sisters. Are you willing?"

Marla gripped the armrests. How dangerous were they talking? "What do I need to do?"

"Dornir, she'll need a shield spell. Everyone else, we plan here."

"Let's go, kid." Dornir waved for her to join him.

"Kid?" She stood and followed him to the tunnel.

"You're still untrained. In Wood Walker terms, you're a child still. It's not personal." He shrugged, glancing back as he climbed the tunnel. "Just a little farther."

They went halfway down the tunnel, still covered by a few feet of soil over their heads. He stopped and closed his eyes. Marla sensed his power flowing around them.

"Good. I think they're far enough away. He shouldn't feel us, either." Dornir sat on the sloping tunnel floor. "The easiest shield spell is simple, but you need to focus." He gestured at the ground beside him.

She sank to the packed dirt floor. "Okay?"

He smiled. "All you have to do is pull power up around you. Let it circle you and ask for protection."

Marla closed her eyes. The power flowed into her the moment she opened herself to it. She imagined a bubble around herself, and the power flowed into shape.

"Excellent. Now, can you do that while someone is throwing spells at you? You need to ignore everything around you and focus on that shield, no matter what. The moment you think about the incoming spell, your shield might drop."

"Oh." Her shield slipped and fell as she listened. "What if I can't do this?"

He draped an arm over her shoulders. "Just do your best. If things get bad, focus on the shield. Curl up in the grass with your eyes closed if you need. We're there, too. We can all go after him at once and he will have to choose where to focus. Our working together is a strength. He has to defend her, too, and she won't help him."

Marla closed her eyes again and pulled the shield up. It was easier that time. She let it drop and pulled it up again a few more times.

"You learn fast." Adris smiled at her. They leaned against the tunnel wall, waiting, as Marla opened her eyes and looked at them. "I think you're ready. Our plan is done. Standard diversion four."

"Huh?" Marla stood and brushed dust from her clothes.

139

"You're the diversion. You just keep him talking to you. We take care of the rest." Adris grinned and dashed back down the tunnel.

"Come on. We can do this, and we got your back." Dornir led her back to the group.

Marla stopped in the cavern and pulled her cloak out. She pulled it tighter around herself. Issa took a thicker cloak from a box and draped it over Marla's shoulders. Marla smiled at her as she fumbled with the clasp, her fingers trembling.

"Are you sure about this?" Issa fastened the clasp for her.

She nodded. "I'm sure." Well, no, I'm most definitely not sure. She wrapped an arm around her belly. It's a good thing she hasn't eaten recently.

"All you have to do is keep him facing away from her. If you can draw him away from the tent, even better. We'll sneak in through the back wall if we need to, but we need time to get the collar off her. Once that's done, his power will still be strong, but he won't have the advantage anymore. Understand?" Kria held her gaze.

Marla nodded again.

"Stay safe, everyone. Let's go." Kria marched up the tunnel.

Dornir followed, Tialla right behind him. Issa linked arms with Marla and guided her along next. They stopped at the entrance until Tialla nodded. Marla sighed as she slipped back among the trees. The dark was deep, and she had so many shadows to hide in.

They snuck through the trees, towards the light and smoke from the campfire. The trees were thick enough that she heard the fire before she saw it. As they got closer, she saw the reflected light shining against the trees. A few more steps and she could see his camp through the trees.

"We're with you. You're safe," Tialla whispered. She touched Marla's hand and energy flowed into the girl. "Watch for traps."

Marla nodded. She stepped between the trees, weaving her way closer to the camp. After a few steps, she stopped and felt for traps. Was he powerful enough she wouldn't feel them? She took a deep breath and let her senses out. A trap shone like a beacon, not more than a few steps from her. Other traps were sprinkled around the campsite. She approached the camp, moving around the traps with ease.

She took another step and energy shot up her leg, tingling like lightning, making her muscles twitch. Marla froze. Hidden traps? Did he know she was coming? Would he come and check? She gripped her cloak as she leapt off the spot.

He stepped from the tent and looked out at the surrounding darkness. Could he not see her in the campfire's light? Maybe not, as it was between them. She kneeled and touched the soil. Was that him? Something felt odd about the energy in camp, something more than what she usually felt from the Light Chargers. Was his energy different somehow?

Calling to the life in the seeds, Marla sent a burst of power into the soil. He walked around the fire and stopped at the edge of his camp. She backed up behind a tree, careful of the unseen trap, and sent another burst out.

He glanced back at his tent before he strode into the forest after her. Marla dashed back a bit, sending more energy out. She stopped beside a fallen log and waited.

The man stopped close to her. He called a ball of light, and it hovered over his palm, casting a harsh glow between them. "It is you. I thought that felt familiar."

She shifted from foot to foot. Keep him busy? How?

CHAPTER 14

"Have you changed your mind about joining me for tea?" He waved his hand vaguely towards his tent.

"Maybe. I was curious why you want tea with me. You're a man of power, and I'm just a farm girl." She clasped her hands behind her back, twisting her fingers together.

"We both know you're more than that." He laughed. "What would you like to ask me? I know the look of curiosity when I see it."

She took a slow breath. So many questions, and he was offering to answer them?

He smiled widely. "Seriously, ask anything."

"I've never seen a camp like that," she blurted out.

The man chuckled. "Would you like to come see it? Ever see how nice it is in one of our tents?"

Oh, drat, no. I need to keep him away, not get closer to his camp! "It wouldn't be proper, me going with a strange man into a tent alone."

"We can make it proper. If you come and work with me, nobody will think anything of it." He held his hand out to her. "You can be my research assistant."

This is not where I expected our conversation to go. What now? Marla bowed her head slightly and took a half-step back. "I don't—I mean, I can't—"

"Take a breath." He took a step closer. "I won't hurt you. Just relax."

Energy flowed towards her, not from below, but from him. She called the shield up, wrapping the power from below around her like vines. His energy hit hers and stopped. He frowned and his brow wrinkled. He looked at his outstretched hand.

Had she distracted him long enough? Could she flee now? Every instinct screamed to run, though there was something different about him, too. She took another half-step back and backed into a tree. "You hurt them," she stammered.

"Hurt who?" he held his hand out again.

"The women."

He shook his head. "No. We care for them, and they live in luxury. Most people only dream of living as well as they do."

"They're almost dead inside. Doesn't that bother you?" She hugged her cloak tightly around herself.

He was silent for a long moment as he watched her without moving. "They're our partners. With their help, we let people live better lives. Everyone benefits."

Marla stamped her foot. "Not them, though. They don't get anything from this partnership, as you call it."

"You're mistaken, and I can prove it. Come with me back to the Citadel and I can show you how—" He dropped to the ground, his eyes closed.

Dornir stood over him with a thick stick in his hand. "Ready to go?"

Blood oozed from the back of the Light Charger's head. Marla nodded. Dornir strode over and took her hand. Marla ran with him into the trees.

"We got her away. You did great." Dornir glanced down and smiled at her.

Her hand shook. She gripped his hand tighter as they ran. Marla glanced back. Tialla kneeled over the Light Charger. Her hand glowed green. Dornir guided Marla between thicker trees, and she lost sight of the camp.

"She'll be okay?"

Dornir laughed. "She'll be fine. We need to get her back to the city where she can rest fully."

Her legs burned as she dashed along beside him. Where were they? She didn't dare close her eyes and feel. Would she be able to feel around while running one day? Tialla sure seemed to.

They rounded a thick cluster of trees. Dornir slowed. He stepped through a small gap, pulling her behind him. He kneeled and dropped into a hole. Marla dropped to her knees and eased her way down. She scampered down the tunnel behind him, towards the lantern light at the far end.

Issa and Adris kneeled beside the woman in the corner, a thick mattress cushioning them from the ground. The woman's eyes were closed as she lay on her back. Issa held her hand over the woman's heart. The air hummed with healing magic.

"She'll be fine." Kria handed Marla a water bottle. "Once she's up and walking, we'll get her home."

"Home? You know where she's from?" Marla took the bottle and opened it. She took a long sip.

"No, child. Home. Our city. You'll get to see it, too." Kria lay her hand on Marla's shoulder and squeezed lightly.

Adris retrieved a water bottle and took it over to the woman. They dropped some herbal tablets inside and shook it. "Here. This will help you feel better."

Issa eased the woman up until she sat and kept an arm around her in support. Adris held the bottle to her lips. The woman wrapped her hand around the bottle and took a sip. A moment later, she downed the rest in a few massive swallows.

Tialla strode into the room, her cloak billowing around her. "There. He won't be coming after us any time quickly." She brushed her hands together. "Though he'll wake faster than most."

Marla pressed her hands to her cheeks. What did they do to him? Did she care?

Tialla laughed. "Nothing like that. I wrapped him in some vines after healing his head. When the sleep spell wears off, he'll need to free himself before he can do anything else. We'll be long gone by then." She walked over and kneeled beside the woman. "Let's get you healed before then."

Marla looked around. The room looked carved from dirt. It was smaller than the other caverns, but better stocked with boxes and supplies. There were spare blankets and bottles of healing herbs. She looked over at the group and froze.

The collar sat on the dirt floor, tossed aside when they removed it, the clasp shattered. The metal was dark and dull now, no longer the shiny black when she wore it.

Dornir rubbed her back. "Breathe. It can't hurt you." He leaned down and picked it up. "They're good once. After we remove them, they never work again. This is scrap metal now." He held it up for her. "You can touch it. It won't affect you."

The metal was thin and slightly flexible. It thickened near the crumbling clasp, which flaked away more when he touched it.

"How do they work?" Her voice trembled and was so quiet it was almost a whisper.

He shrugged. "We're not fully sure. It's powered by their magic, not ours. We support life. We don't steal it, except in extreme circumstances." He tossed the collar into the corner.

"Are you ready, Love?" Tialla held the woman's hand.

The woman nodded. Tialla and Issa supported her as she stood.

She was shaky for a moment, but straightened up and smiled. "I feel like myself again. I can touch nature."

"What's your name, child?" Tialla kept an arm around her as they took a few steps together.

"Lissana."

Kria grinned. "Lissana Norrithan?"

The woman nodded.

"I knew it was you. We've been looking for you since they took you, and tonight was our first real chance. We need to get you home. It's not far. Are you ready?"

Lissana nodded. "I knew you'd come, eventually."

Marla glanced up at Dornir as Tialla helped Lissana to the tunnel.

"Her story is much like yours," Dornir explained, his voice low. "Like you, she was powerful and headed to be an apprentice. So powerful, her local Wood Walker didn't start her training yet. It was too risky. An escort team was sent, but they found her before our people got there. In a way, that's a blessing, at least."

Marla walked with him behind the others, heading up the tunnel. "A blessing?"

"They drain our powers away with those collars. It can blast open our energy channels if they're not open yet, but can't make full use of the wilder powers of the untrained. Their ultimate prize would be someone like Tialla, but the risks of taking her would be so great, they prefer to make do with the untrained. They can snatch you in seconds with little risk to them."

She shook her head as she followed Issa. Would she be taken, too, or could she last long enough to learn? Her thoughts wandered back to her childhood as she stepped out into the forest. Back then, she didn't know the people who freely handed out books were kidnapping people and draining them of life. How can people value knowledge, but treat others like that? What happened to working for everyone's benefit?

Tialla guided the group through the forest. Issa and Adris stayed with Lissana, though the woman walked on her own. They changed their path a few times, but always headed southeast. They walked until the sun peeked up over the trees.

Kria looked around, the forest streaked with the purples and reds of sunrise. "This way."

She led them down into another tunnel, this one hidden between boulders. This one led to a room large enough for everyone to lie down. Adris and Dornir passed bedrolls around, taken from a stack in the corner. Kria handed Marla and Lissana an extra blanket.

Marla curled up in her bedroll near the wall. Once everyone settled, Kria turned the lantern off, leaving the cavern dark. She lay quietly and listened to her friends settle, their breathing slowing, and the rustling stopped. Adris let out a soft snore within minutes.

How many people like her awakened each year? How many had their lives uprooted, having to run for some place they'd never been? How did those in the farthest reaches of the country make it without being taken?

"Get some sleep. Things always seem scarier when we're tired." Tialla rested a hand on Marla's shoulder.

She rolled and looked at Tialla.

"Sleep. You really will feel better." Tialla rubbed her shoulder.

Marla rolled back over and closed her eyes.

***

Her legs burned. She ran faster, pushing herself on. Someone crashed through the bushes behind her, catching up. Don't look back. She dodged a tree and headed deeper into the forest. Their footsteps pounded behind her. Fingertips reached for her back.

The ground dropped away. Marla plunged towards the gully floor. She hit the ground and her arm snapped. Her breath fled from her lungs. The world spun around her. Someone was laughing. Who? Where? Marla looked up and tried to focus, but everything was a blur.

The Light Charger stood there, pointing at her. "You're useless. I'm special, and you're nothing." Wait, that wasn't his voice. Why did he sound like a boy?

"Up you get. Come on. We'll be there in a few hours." A hand shook her shoulder, yanking her from sleep.

Marla batted at the hand and curled up tighter. Her body ached, and she was sweaty and gross. When would she ever see a hot bath again?

"None of that. Get up. We're going home today." Issa kicked Marla's boot lightly.

"Home?" She rubbed her eyes and sat up.

"Imagine a place where you'll never be chased. Somewhere where the food is plentiful and fresh, and nature is all around you. You'll love it." Issa offered her a hand. "We also have an amazing library."

Marla perked up. Library? She took Issa's hand and stood. Lissana was sitting with Tialla in the corner, eating dried fruits from tins. Dornir handed Marla a package of fruit wrapped in waxed paper.

"Thanks." Marla popped a dried apple slice into her mouth.

"When we get home, we can feast." Adris danced across the floor and took a water bottle.

Lissana took the offered water bottle and sipped from it. She smiled. "I can't wait." She still sounded weak, like she hadn't spoken in a long time. "It feels like forever. How long has it been?"

"You'll be welcomed most warmly." Kria unwrapped a biscuit and nibbled on it. "You can rest and recover fully once we're back. It's been almost three years."

"Three years." Lissana stared at the floor by her feet. "It felt so much longer. Have you seen it?" She looked up at Marla.

"No, I'm new." Marla shook her head.

"We'll get you both there safely." Tialla squeezed Lissana's hand. "It's not far now, and we know the way well."

The room fell silent as everyone focused on eating. Finally, Marla would see the city Ava wanted her to get to. She could be safe. Her family and few friends were far away, though. Could it be home without them? She had new friends now, though. Would they stay in contact, or would she be on her own? The library, though. She could live there alone forever and be fine, diving into everything she could learn.

They tidied their wrappers and folded the blankets. Kria circled the room and nodded. Issa extinguished the lantern as they headed up the tunnel.

Adris and Dornir stayed beside Lissana while Tialla took the lead. Issa kept Marla company. The others walked behind them.

How could Light Chargers get away with taking people and using them? Did the people really not know? She didn't, and she was as well read as anyone else. Ava had a secret library, and she knew. Were the Light Chargers keeping it from ordinary people? How did they explain it when they travelled?

Her foot skidded as the rock rolled away under it. The hillside was uneven, and she watched her feet now. There was gravel everywhere among the thinning grasses. They skirted around boulders as they walked, the trees growing around and sometimes among them.

He claimed the girls weren't harmed. How could he not know what they were doing? He was part of it. Does that mean everything he told her was a lie? Did they actually live in luxury? How could that be a fair trade? Sure, they'd be comfortable, just empty inside. No, that wasn't a fair trade at all. The women were always so happy to be freed. If it was so wonderful, wouldn't people volunteer?

Marla perked up and focused ahead. What was that noise? A crashing, or a roar of some kind? She opened herself and felt the ground vibrating slightly.

CHAPTER 15

"I t's the waterfall. Come." Issa smiled and took her hand.

"Waterfall?" Marla peered around the others, but couldn't see it yet. She'd never seen one big enough to sound like that.

"You'll see in a moment."

The roaring got louder as they came around a rocky outcropping. Marla gasped. A massive wall of water fell from above, spraying a fine mist into the air. It landed in a pool below, carved from the rock with time and persistence. She'd read about them, but nobody ever mentioned how loud a waterfall was, or how it almost shook the ground.

"The path is narrower here. Marla, you're smaller. Walk with Adris and Lissana. Follow me." Kria raised her voice to be heard. She set off along the rocky ledge.

Marla moved up beside Lissana, between her and the rock wall. Adris stayed closer to the pool. The rock was rough where she brushed her fingers over it, though it was also warm and damp. She stared up at the top of the waterfall. Her neck ached.

Her boot slipped but caught on the rough rock beneath her feet. The mist coated everything, landing on her skin and cloak as well. Lissana slipped. Marla held her tighter, one hand on the rock beside her for balance. Adris kept Lissana from falling, their arm around her keeping her up.

Kria kept walking, her steps confident and steady. She passed among the vines, disappearing into the rock face. Marla reached for the vines. They shifted in the breeze. She pressed through as the vines swallowed them.

Lanterns illuminated the tunnel. It was twice as wide as the path outside. The river ran through the tunnel beside them, filling the space with the sound of rushing water. They followed the tunnel, gently sloping down.

The rock was damp, but the air was warm, like the rock gave off heat instead of the sun. They curved around, following the water. They rounded a last corner and Marla saw daylight ahead. She glanced over. Adris grinned at her. Marla glanced back. Tialla was nearly skipping. Dornir fidgeted. Issa also had a spring in her step.

They stepped into the sunlight. The rock below her pulsed with energy, and she hadn't even opened herself to it. Runes carved into the entryway glowed. She shielded her eyes as they adjusted to the bright light.

Marla gasped. The river rushed on, carving its way across the land and into a city. The entire area was full of plants of all kinds. Deer wandered past, ignoring them completely. Birds flew about, singing to each other. The space was open to the rich blue sky, though high rock walls surrounded the entire area as far as she could see.

A wide path of slate slabs stretched from the tunnel to the city. Marla couldn't take her eyes off it as they approached. Wooden buildings with brightly painted designs spread before her, some tall and grand with pillars, and others small, like family homes.

"Welcome to the city." Kria gestured ahead. "Come. We need to get Lissana cared for, and you need a family."

"She stays with me." Issa stepped beside Marla and wrapped her arm around her.

Kria bowed her head. "Of course."

"Thanks," Marla whispered.

Issa hugged her as Dornir moved beside Lissana again. "I found you. I get to keep you."

Marla laughed. "I'm not a lost shoe or something."

"No, you're more like a long-lost daughter. Would you like to meet the rest of the family?"

Marla nodded. "What happens to her?"

With an arm still around her, Issa guided Marla down the slate path behind the others. "She'll go to the healers first. Once she's ready, she'll join a family and settle in as well."

They walked through a massive arch formed by two trees that bent towards each other, their branches intertwining. People gathered on the wide streets on either side, waving at Marla's group, and her specifically. More people sat on patios, sipping from steaming mugs as they talked with friends. Others worked together, weaving and embroidering, or making furniture and things from wood. She could even see people gathered around easels with paints beside them.

"Our home is this way." Issa led her down a side street half as large as the one going straight through the city. "That's the bathhouse." She pointed to the right. "Anyone can go there. Would you like to see it?"

"Sure. A bathhouse? One place just to take a bath?"

Issa led her up the steps. The outer doors were open, slid back in their tracks. Issa slid an inner door open enough to walk through and closed it behind them. The air was humid. They walked around a wooden screen and through an archway. A woman stood at the arch, a sword hanging from her belt. She nodded to them. Marla nodded back.

They passed through a short hall and rounded a corner. Marla's jaw dropped. The walls were high, and the roof was open in the middle, letting some of the humidity out. She could breathe easier in here. The middle was an immense pool of water with fountains and waterspouts. The space around the pool was all stone tile, with a roof over it held up by pillars.

Women rested in the water with friends or reclined on stone benches under the partial roof. Nobody was alone here. A group of young women laughed and splashed each other, their hair piled up on their heads and clipped in place. One of them was talking, like she was telling a story or something, and the others were laughing as they listened.

Marla looked over at the wall. A mix of younger and older women gathered there, some sitting on the edge of the pool, others just in the water on a built-in bench. A thin and pale woman was in the middle, being held and hugged by the others. A young woman braided her hair as an older woman rubbed her back.

"They recently rescued her," Issa explained. She led Marla around the edge of the room.

She followed Issa into a small garden with a high wall around it. Marla glanced back at the pale woman. She had the same dark circles around her eyes, laying quietly as the others supported her. "Is she okay?"

"She will be. We're not sure why, but they need to be careful if they're going to take our power. They touch the taken as little as possible, and in limited ways. The taken mostly live in seclusion in their captor's rooms, coming out only when he needs her. The more powerful he is, the more she goes out. Some of them live most of their lives in one room, with only him for company. They're deprived of touch and community. The Light Chargers learned early on that forcing attention on us shuts down our magic completely."

Marla braced against the wall. "How could she stand it?" She peered through the doorway. Marla might have mostly kept to herself back home, but she had Ava and her family, and a couple of close friends. She was never so alone as that.

The pale woman eased onto a towel at the edge of the pool. The women with her poured an oil onto their hands and rubbed it into her skin. She opened her eyes and met Marla's gaze. Was that a smile? Marla's heart warmed. Maybe there was hope for a complete recovery.

"Something about the collars drains them of the strength to care. The first thing we do is surround them with others who care for them. The taken don't even get to talk to each other until we free them. The only reason they're touched at all is if they need medical care, and the Light Chargers can't heal as easily as we can. It's an incredibly lonely existence." Issa brushed her fingers over a flowering vine covering the wall. "Anyway, we'll come here soon for a relaxing bath. There are more things to see."

They passed back to the main door, nodding to the guard as they left. This time, Marla noticed the painted murals on the walls. Shelves with folded towels were spaced around the room, with hooks for clothing under them. A changing room?

Issa led her down the street. "That's the library. Anyone can go in there, too." She pointed to a building close to the bathhouse.

Marla straightened up and grinned.

"Let's go see." Issa linked arms with her and pulled her up the stone steps. "We have time before our meal is ready."

They stopped at the closed double doors. Marla touched the carved book mounted as a handle. It opened with a light pull. She stepped into an entry much like the bathhouse, but this one didn't have an armed guard. Someone was sitting at a desk, reading. They looked up as Issa led Marla through.

Marla stared with an open mouth. It was massive, like the bathhouse, but the ceiling had a full roof. There was a balcony around the room, and shelves lined every available space, even around the pillars. A few areas had tables, and chairs were scattered around the shelves. A wide staircase led to the upper balcony.

How long did it take to collect all these? Were they able to make books here? Despite holding onto every book she ever got, Marla's collection wouldn't fill one whole shelf unit here. How many hours would it take to learn where everything was? Time well spent, as far as she was concerned.

"Once you're settled in, we'll come back. I'll show you around properly. You can get lesson books and even personal books here, too. Your room has plenty of shelf space at home. This library has the best collection of healing and medical books. The central library has the greatest collection of scientific texts ever assembled. It's even better than the Light Charger's library, so I've been told." Issa grinned.

A bell rang in the distance. Marla heard it clearly, despite being indoors.

"Are you hungry? Everyone will be excited to meet you." Issa took a gentle hold of her arm and guided Marla back outside.

With a last glance back, Marla followed her out. They walked down two more streets, mostly lined with smaller buildings that looked like houses. People were all walking in small groups, all heading into these buildings surrounded by low hedges.

Issa stopped at a path and turned down it. They walked up the path to a larger house, far larger than any house in her town. The door was open, and she heard voices. Issa didn't slow, she marched right in, so Marla followed.

The front room was as big as her parents' house was. Padded chairs and benches spread around the space, along with small tables, most with books piled on them. Issa walked past this room to an archway, where the voices were coming from.

"Hey, everyone. I'd like you to meet Marla." Issa pulled her through and stood her before a table, where a few people were placing plates and bowls of food.

Dornir waved and patted a cushioned chair beside him. "Come and sit. We'll help you settle, no judgement here."

Marla smiled as she sat on the chair. "Hi, everyone."

An older woman walked over and rested a hand on her shoulder. She had a weathered face and strong smile lines. "Welcome to the family. I'm Clarissa."

"Thank you. It's a pleasure to meet you." Marla smiled back at her.

"Come. I'll show you your room while they finish setting the table." Clarissa took Marla's hand in her iron grip. She steered her from the chair and down a hallway. "I'm not sure what you're used to, but it's warm and dry, and we're close if you need anything."

"I'm sure it'll be great." Marla allowed herself to be pulled into a room halfway down the hall, not that she could free herself if she wanted to.

The room was twice the size of her former bedroom. A bed with thick blankets took up one corner. One wall was full of bookshelves from floor to ceiling. Most shelves were empty, but there were a few books waiting for her. A desk and padded chair were near the window, which looked out into a garden. The wardrobe stood near the door.

"It's wonderful." Marla nodded to Clarissa. She walked over to the shelves and examined the books.

"Issa will help you fill those shelves and get you some clothing." Clarissa strolled to the window and looked out. "We share the garden with the neighbours. You've met some of them already."

Marla stepped beside her and looked out. Four houses bordered the garden, including hers. Marla waved at Adris and Tialla, who were crossing the garden. They waved back before splitting and going into different houses.

"They're our neighbours?" Marla couldn't help smiling. Her new friends were close.

Clarissa chuckled. "Teams are kept close together, though often live apart like this. Kria lives with Tialla as well. Now, let's go eat."

They returned to the massive table in the kitchen, where everyone gathered. She settled between Dornir and Clarissa. A young woman smiled at her from across the table. Issa said a blessing before sitting, and everyone started taking food.

"Help yourself to whatever you like." Dornir passed her a bowl of vegetables.

She nodded and took the bowl, setting a huge scoop of veggies on her plate.

"Clarissa, can you take Rinnia and get Marla enough clothing for a few days after lunch? We'll get her fit properly soon, but Kria wants to meet with us. She'll need lounge clothing, night clothing, and something to run around the city in." Issa handed Marla a basket of pastries.

"Certainly. The young one can pick the styles, and I'll get the size and colour right." Clarissa narrowed her eyes at Marla as she looked her over. "Favourite colours? Let me guess, green and blue, right?"

Marla raised an eyebrow. "How did you—oh." She looked down at herself.

Clarissa winked. "You look like a forest girl."

Marla looked over at Issa as she bit into a pastry.

Issa shrugged. "We all have parts of nature we're closer to. With you it's the plants. Dornir loves the sky. Adris is a water lover like Clarissa. I prefer the soil."

She took a scoop of rice and lentils and inhaled the sweet spices. "If I ever need a snack or something to drink, do I just help myself, or ask, or how do you do that here?"

"Help yourself here." Issa pointed to a cupboard. "The glasses are in there, and the plates are in the next one over. If the food doesn't have a red string around the container, you can help yourself. The red string means we're saving it for a special purpose."

"Don't spoil your meals, though, as we eat as a family." Clarissa held her gaze. "We'll make sure you know when meals and family activities are."

Marla looked around as she ate. The others began talking about people and things she didn't know, so she looked around again. Two massive brick ovens took up one wall. One had a grill section, and the other had a stone heating slab instead. Partly open windows stood on either side of them, letting the heat out and a cooling breeze flowed in from the open front door. The cupboards had a counter, and a worktable stood near them.

"The end cupboard over the counter is full of teas. You can make some any time. All other drinks, including juices, are in the cold box. We'll show you where the pots and utensils are later, and don't be afraid to poke around and find things, either." Issa gestured at the wall of cupboards.

Dornir poured juice into her glass. "Try this one."

Marla took a sip and smiled. There was a touch of something almost sour, but a sweetness to balance that out.

"We grow those fruits in our garden." Rinnia filled her own glass. "They only grow here in the city. There's plenty, so you can always enjoy some."

She finished her pastry, licking the crumbs from her fingers. "This was Ava's recipe, wasn't it?"

Issa chuckled. "It's a popular recipe here, and she took it with her when she left. It goes many generations back."

"Does everyone live like this? In groups, in these kinds of houses?" Marla scooped up the last of her veggies and stuffed them into her mouth.

"Yeah, pretty much." Dornir drank the last of his juice. "The only difference in the houses is how close they are to the libraries and other shared buildings. Oh, some are larger, and hold bigger families like ours."

"Don't worry about cleaning up today." Issa gestured at Marla's plate. "Kria will be here any moment for you."

Someone knocked on the door. Marla whipped her head around and stared in that direction. She couldn't quite see the door just through the archway from here.

Dornir smiled. "That'll be her. Nearly anyone else would use the other door." He slid from his chair and walked over.

Issa met Marla's gaze and tilted her head towards the door. "Go on."

Marla stood and followed. The first door down the hall was open, leading her into a mudroom with hooks for cloaks and benches to sit on. Boots were lined up along a wall, sitting neatly on mats of different colours.

Kria waved her closer. "How are you settling in?"

Marla crossed the mudroom and stopped beside Dornir. "I'm doing well. They were just telling me more about the city."

"We're about to see more of it. Come." Kria opened the door and stepped out into the garden.

Dornir draped a cloak over Marla's shoulders and nudged her out the door. Kria set off down the garden path, towards the gate between two of the houses. Marla dashed behind her, catching up at the gate.

"How many people live in the city?" She looked down the street both ways. There were houses as far as she could see. There were so many people.

"How many people lived in your town?" Kria glanced over at her.

Marla shrugged. "Maybe a hundred?"

"This place is probably ten times as big. All Wood Walkers who aren't out doing our work call it home. Every continent has a city like this, though not all are hidden." Kria headed back towards the wide road that ran through the city.

"There are more people like us around the world? How many?" Marla looked up at the stone pillars supporting the wooden arch they passed under.

"Many thousands around the world. We're a small group, but important. There are about as many Light Chargers as well, though. Always be careful out there. Many Light Chargers are harmless, too new or weak to do anything to us, but many are a threat."

Kria draped an arm around Marla's shoulders as she turned on the main road. There was a massive building ahead, with wide steps leading up to it. Marla stumbled against Kria as she stared at this new place. It looked like the other shared buildings but was easily twice as large. An enormous waterfall cascaded down the cliff face behind it. Where did the water go? Some flowed around the city, but what about the rest?

"That's the central library. Our council also meets there. You'll also find some research labs in the back, close to the library. They study advanced healing and farming techniques there." Kria nodded at the building.

The closer they got to the building, the bigger it seemed. It towered over her. Just when Marla thought she'd be climbing those steps, Kria pulled her down a side path around the building. They approached a cluster of boulders around the side. This path was made of black stone and had vibrant green moss growing between the slabs.

The path curved and led straight to the boulders. As she rounded the curve, Marla saw a cave entrance blocked with a gate. Two people stood watch on either side. They had swords at their belts, though Marla could sense power running through them as well. Their tunics had a tree symbol embroidered on the front. The same tree symbol glittered on banners on either side of the entrance.

Kria nodded to them as she approached. They nodded back, watching, but not moving otherwise. She opened the gate and stepped aside. Marla stepped through, and Kria closed the gate behind them again.

Torches burning with the magic light glowed on the walls, spaced close enough there were no deep shadows. The flames danced and flickered, even crackling softly. The path sloped down and curved around, hiding their destination from her. Kria walked steadily on the smooth path, following the tunnel as it curved back and forth. They rounded a tighter corner, and the tunnel opened up.

Marla stood there with her mouth open. The cavern was large. Water flowed down the back wall into a pool that took up most of the chamber. There was a low stone wall between the floor and the water, just high enough a kneeling person could reach over and into the water. Soft moss cushioned her feet and covered most of the rock in the cavern.

"What is this place?" Marla whispered. Somehow, it didn't feel like a place you should make a noise in.

"This is the Sacred Pool." Kria walked to the low wall and kneeled on the moss.

Marla followed, taking slow steps. She kneeled beside Kria. Despite the water everywhere, it smelled fresh and sweet. The rock was dry.

"Sit quietly for a moment. Think of nature, and how you're a part of it." Kria leaned her elbows on the low wall.

She closed her eyes. It wasn't hard to imagine how it felt to walk through the woods near her town. She knew all the birds that sang there. The mountains nearby directed wind their way, giving them a cooling breeze in the heat of summer. Marla could even feel the heat of the sunlight as it hit her face and arms when she worked in the garden.

The rock beneath her knees warmed. Marla opened her eyes. The pool of water shimmered with sunlight. It glowed so brightly she shielded her eyes. Marla looked up, but only saw rock above her. Where was the light coming from?

"This explains a lot." Kria rubbed her cheek. "That light is coming from inside you."

"Inside me?" Marla reached down and touched the water. She clenched her teeth at the cold. She pulled her hand out and shook the water off.

"Allow me." Kria nodded towards the wall.

Marla scooted back. Kria stretched her hands out towards the water. The pool surface went completely still near her, the ripples from Marla gone. A few flecks of light danced across the surface right near Kria, but the water was dark otherwise.

"Think of a line." Kria dipped a finger in the water and drew a line across the top of the wall with it. "At one end is creation magic, and the other is destruction magic. It's not that simple, but it works for this explanation." She dipped her finger in the water again. "Some people have a lot of either type." She dabbed water at both ends of the line.

Marla came closer and kneeled again. "Okay."

"I have mostly creation magic." Kria placed a drop of water near one end of the line. "I only have limited access to destruction magic. Only a tiny glimmer of light shows up for me. You, however, you are full of both. Creation magic is still dominant in you, but you have more access to destruction magic than is usual."

CHAPTER 16

M arla gripped her cloak. "Is that a problem?"

Kria smiled. "No, the two magics should work together. We used to partner with the Light Chargers, back when they were the Light Wardens. Destruction isn't always bad. When the two are used together, everyone benefits."

"Why don't they work with us, then?" She leaned on the wall and stared down into the water. How deep was it? She couldn't tell.

Kria shook her head. "They would need to see us as equals. We move in the wild places, where the soil is damp, and the sun warms us through. They prefer their towers and cushions, their white robes, and people adoring them. With their power, people look to them for solutions, and they like that."

"We want different things," Marla muttered. She dipped her fingers in the cool water and sent ripples across the pool.

"We do, indeed." Kria snorted. "Can you imagine them setting aside their comforts to walk knee-deep in mud with us? Them, bent over in a field, soil up to the elbow, as they plant and tend crops? They'd need to abandon their egos to see us as equals."

"I don't understand them," Marla whispered.

Kria wrapped an arm around her and hugged her. "And you won't. We can't thrive so disconnected from nature. We used to keep them grounded and connected, so their magic could flourish for everyone's benefit. Now that we work separately, neither side is as strong."

"Is there anything we can do?" Marla straightened up and leaned into the hug, Kria's strong arms around her.

Kria nodded. "Sometimes we get Wood Walkers like you, who have more light inside than most of us. It helps balance things out. They are more likely to feel you when we leave the city, though. Don't go without someone like Tialla to help shield you."

Marla watched the water sliding down the far wall, slipping into the pool with a gentle trickling sound. "I'm sorry."

"What for?" Kria shook her head.

She sighed. "I didn't mean for any of this to happen. I didn't want to put others in danger or anything. My life was supposed to be ordinary. I thought I'd live and die in my town."

"Don't be sorry for being who you are. Sure, you need more help now, but once you settle and learn, you'll be able to do things many of us can't. Now that I know how much shielding you need, we can protect you better." Kria hugged her tighter.

She surrendered to the hug and rested her head on Kria's shoulder. The moss under her warmed and energy flowed up into her. Was the planet giving her a hug, too?

She soaked in the care for a few long moments before straightening up again. "Does everyone come here?" Marla leaned over the water again.

Kria shook her head. "No, only those we suspect have more light, like you. Come." She stood.

Marla got up and followed her from the cave. What did this mean for her? She has both light and dark. Both can be good. Was that how the man sensed her? Was he just that powerful, or did he have some dark in him as well?

The city was quieter on the walk back to their little garden, though Marla dwelled in her thoughts. She replayed every interaction with him in her mind, looking for something, but what? Kria wrapped an arm around her and guided her down the right street, when Marla almost missed it.

"Supper will be ready in a while. You have a lot to think about, so why don't you relax and maybe meditate? Issa can also help you sort through your thoughts. Get some rest." Kria opened the garden gate and led her through.

"Thank you." Marla bowed her head slightly.

Kria smiled. "Go. We have plenty of time to talk later. You still need to settle in."

Marla followed the path to her door. Plants reached from their beds out into the path, brushing against her ankles. Each touch left a trace of warmth on her. The gentle breeze caressed her skin as it passed. Marla took a deep breath as she walked up the couple of steps.

Issa leaned on the archway frame as Marla came in. "Good. You're back. There's some clothing on your bed for you to try on. If anything doesn't fit or is in colours you don't like, set it aside. We'll get you more soon, but this'll do you for a few days."

"Thanks." Marla took her borrowed cloak off. Where was it supposed to go?

"Third hook from the door." Issa waved as she disappeared back into the kitchen.

She wandered down the hall, looking into the open rooms as she passed. The room beside hers looked much like hers, but had little clockwork toys and objects on the desk and many shelves. She longed to linger and see them. Later she would ask whose room it was, and if she could, maybe.

The clothes were stacked neatly in a few piles on her bed. Everything was a colour she liked, from vivid blues and greens to some light greys, and even a few the colour of light sand. Marla closed her door. Taking one thing at a time, she tried it all on.

The tunics were light and flowed around her body as she moved. Some were woven from such an incredibly fine thread it felt like she was naked. Others were a soft wool that was perfect for cool nights. Some tunics left her arms completely bare, and others were like what she was used to, stopping at her wrist or past her elbow. The leggings and pants were a mix of tough fibres for working in gardens and the same light fabric for relaxing in. It all fit well enough.

There was a soft knock on her door, and it opened a crack. "How does it all fit?"

Marla opened her door for Clarissa. She smiled and let the woman see the light outfit she still wore in a shiny emerald. "It feels good. I've never seen this fabric before." She touched the hem of her tunic.

"I'm not surprised. That's a fabric we make here, and we don't trade it. You'll only find it in this city. It's perfect for summer days and warm nights. It's not our only protected craft, either." Clarissa grinned and winked.

"How did you guess my size so well?" Marla brushed her fingers over her belly, the smooth fabric letting her hand slide with ease.

Clarissa laughed. "Many Wood Walkers finish their training and go out into the world for a while, helping people out there. I've spent nearly my entire life here, healing people and helping newcomers settle in. I can glance at someone and know, no matter how baggy their clothing is."

"You never leave?" Marla tilted her head and regarded the woman.

"Not often. If someone needs advanced healing and can't come here, I will go to them. Mostly I help our rescued kin and bring them back to full life." Clarissa glanced at the messy pile of clothing now on Marla's bed. "Once you put things away, you have time for a nap before supper if you need, or a bath here."

Marla looked back at her bed, where she tossed everything after trying it on. Her cheeks warmed. "I think I might have a bath. It's been longer than I like."

"Our plumbing is the same as what you're used to, but the water is naturally fresh. Enjoy. It's that door." Clarissa pointed across the hall and down a little, to the first door on her right.

"Thanks."

She pulled her new house robe over her arm and headed for the bathroom. The tiles were warm under her feet. Marla stepped onto the soft, woven bathmat. The bathtub was far larger than she was used to. She reached for the taps and turned them. Water flowed into the tub with a splash, running far faster than she was used to. Even with the tub this large, she could fill it in moments. She smiled and shook her head.

With the tub full and her dirty clothing tossed in the corner, Marla slipped into the warm water. She leaned against the sloped back of the tub and closed her eyes. The light scent of flowers mixed with soap made her smile. This was much better. If she left here, how often would she get a proper bath? Scrubbing with a cloth was fine, even a quick wash in a basin worked, but this was definitely the way to go.

***

Marla looked up through the window. The moon shone down on her, illuminating the book in her lap. Her desk lantern glowed, casting a golden light around her room. She thought about the last day now, her first full day here since she arrived.

They ate supper last night as a family. Clarissa said the blessing, which was her right as the oldest. Dornir made sure she tried everything, from the stew to the roast vegetables and cooked grains. Even coming from a farming town, she'd never seen such variety in her life. After that, she spent the evening in her reading chair, curled up in the corner.

She slept so soundly last night, snuggled in among the warm blankets and the soft mattress. They got her up with the sunrise, but she was so rested, she didn't complain. Choosing clothing of so many colours and styles was a treat, and she didn't even have much yet. She needed help to know how warm to dress and had to change for the afternoon when it warmed up.

Her legs were still tired after the morning tour. They showed her much of the city, at least the closer parts and the buildings she'd need the most. Marla met her study group as well, all people close to her own age, and most newly awakened or in their first year. They spent the afternoon in the gardens and libraries where the newly awakened trained their powers.

Now she was curled up again in her reading chair, waiting. Her new books were sorted on her shelves, with plenty of space for more books later. The book on moon enchantments was open on her lap. The ink shimmered as the moonlight hit it.

"Ready?" Issa stood in the doorway, leaning against the frame.

Marla looked away from the window, to where Issa waited. "Yeah. Where are we going?" She set her bookmark and closed her book.

"Bring your cloak. We're going to a garden. I'll wait outside." Issa turned and walked away.

She set her book on her desk and followed. Marla stopped in the mudroom and grabbed her light cloak, swinging it around over her shoulders. She stuffed her feet in her boots and stumbled towards the door, her fingers still fumbling with her cloak clasp.

"Goodness, child. She would have waited. You'll kill yourself doing that." Clarissa met her at the edge of the garden, shaking her head. She reached over and fixed the clasp.

Issa smiled. "Take a moment and straighten yourself up."

Once her cloak was on, Marla crouched and pulled her sock up before adjusting her boot. Her fingers shook. She was about to do her first group lesson. Wasn't she allowed to be nervous? With her boots fixed, Marla stood.

Issa wrapped an arm around her. "Don't worry. Most of them you met earlier. They'll be as curious about you as you are about them. They'll want to be your friend."

Friends her own age? Her town was too small for that, mostly. "How long have they been here?" Marla walked with Issa down the path, turning to wave at Clarissa at the gate. They headed down the street towards the edge of the city.

"Most are still new, like you, and have been here less than a month. We're still teaching them beginner magic. A few of them will have been born here. Nearly everyone comes from outside, though, brought in by the escort teams."

"Is our team an escort team?" Marla looked down the quiet side streets as they walked.

Issa shook her head. "No. We just found you first. Kria saw your potential and chose to add you to our team. Normally, you would have been brought here and stayed for all your early training. We can keep your training up when we're in the field, though."

Marla stared at the ornate metal fence ahead, more decorative than functional. Other young people walked through. "What are we if not an escort team?" She marvelled at the garden inside, illuminated by the moon and by lanterns hung on carved posts.

"We're one of the Dozen. The Dozen are groups that visit the most important sites and offer blessings and prayers. We look after humanity's connection to nature." Issa led her through the gates. "It mostly means we travel a lot at this time of year. You'll come with us."

A group of young people gathered beside a fountain. Marla took a slow breath as Issa led her over. Most were like her, young, and a few were Issa's age. There were maybe twenty people here, gathered together, including a young man.

A woman clapped her hands together once. "Now that we're all here, let's begin."

The lanterns around them brightened. The students split into groups of eight, each with an older woman to lead them. They spread around the garden. Marla listened closely as Issa explained the first protective enchantment to her group.

"Remember to feel for the energy around you. Don't hesitate to borrow some from the moonlight. It's gentler than the energy from the sun, since it's reflected. On a moonlit night, we have an almost unlimited source of energy, if you remember your own limits." Issa held her hands up. "Now, spread a bit more and try it a few times. I'll come around and make sure everyone gets it. Keep practicing while you wait. This can save you."

Marla moved along the fence a bit into a quieter corner, where she was surrounded by plants. She closed her eyes and opened herself to the energy around her. It rushed up into her, familiar and warm. Focusing on the enchantment, she raised her hand. Moving her fingers as Issa showed her, Marla traced lines in the air.

Her power grew, focused and strong. Marla opened her eyes and pointed down, rooting herself to the soil as the enchantment settled over her. Her body had a faint glow around it. It tingled slightly as it covered her like a second skin.

"Excellent, Marla," Issa called from nearby. "Rest a few moments and try again. You want this one to be second nature, so you can call it in an instant."

Marla smiled back at Issa, though her smile faltered at the sad look on the girl's face.

Issa patted the girl's shoulder. "You're doing fine. It takes practice for most of us. When I first learned, I took the whole evening."

"Really?" Her lip trembled.

"Really. Besides, I can feel your strength is in calling new seeds to life. If we partner you with someone strong in protective enchantments, think of all the good you could do together."

The girl smiled widely. Marla nodded to her, smiling back. As the girl tried again, Marla looked around the garden with her senses. The plants practically hummed with energy. There were many enchantments in the garden. A couple she recognized as protective enchantments, but most she'd never seen before.

Marla tried the shield a few more times, each time getting faster. Each time she rested, she opened herself and explored the plants. Many in here she'd never seen before. She also watched the others. Some got it on their first few tries, like her. Others needed more help. Marla called another barrier and held it for a few moments longer before letting it dissolve.

As the group all got the first enchantment, Issa taught two more, each more complex than the last. Marla found moving the energy and shaping it easy, so she had plenty of chances to practice as some others took longer. She cycled between the three, sorting their patterns in her mind as she called them around her.

"Hi." A tall and thick young woman approached. Her hands lacked any callouses, and she wasn't well-muscled.

"Hi." Marla gave a small wave. How were you supposed to greet other new young people?

"Issa is your teacher? You live with her?" She tucked her long black hair over her shoulder.

Marla nodded. "She's teaching you, too?"

"Yes, I'm in her study group. My friend as well, until you showed up. She got told this morning." The young woman stared at her as she toyed with the end of her braid.

"I'm sorry. I didn't know that could happen," Marla stammered.

She shrugged. "She was sad until they told her she was going to a group in the medicinal gardens. Only the best get to work in there, because the herbs are so important. I'm Teela." She stuck her hand out at Marla.

Marla reached out and touched palms. Good, a familiar greeting. "I'm Marla."

"It's nice to meet you, Marla. I can help show you around a bit, if you like. You can meet Marianna, too. She won't be mad you took her spot."

Issa walked past. "Feeling good about all three? I want to see them now." She stopped and faced the girls.

Teela snapped to attention and did all three spells, one after the other.

"Good. The Moon Sigil Protection will be even stronger if you curl your fingers more, like this." Issa demonstrated. "Marla?"

Marla tapped into the surrounding power. It filled her immediately. Marla channeled the enchantments, one by one, letting them fill her first. Each snapped into place, gleaming in the moonlight.

"Excellent. Alright, everyone, that's enough for one night." Issa clapped her hands, and everyone scattered. "Come, Marla. You need to sleep. Are you tired, or will you want a tea to help you settle?"

Marla walked with her from the garden. "Honestly, I could drop right here."

Issa chuckled. "When we get back, wash up and go right to bed. Get as much sleep as you can. You'll need it."

CHAPTER 17

"Once we've eaten, we go. I'm sorry. Normally we let new people stay longer to settle in, but with us being short right now, they need us at another site." Issa set a bowl of steaming oatmeal in front of Marla.

"I'll be okay." Marla scooped some cream and added it to her bowl. She spooned some apple pieces in as well.

"I visited Lissana last night, before your lessons. She's recovering well, and her powers are coming back faster than expected." Issa poured herself a cup of tea. She sat across from Marla.

"How's she doing? She was in better shape than most we rescue." Dornir grabbed a basket of fresh buns and brought them over to the table.

"She's strong. Resilient. Ready to get out there and help." Issa smiled. "She's got a lot of fight in her. It's a wonder. Most rescues take a while to get that spirit back."

"Why her and not the others?" Marla gripped her spoon tighter.

Issa shrugged. "There are many possibilities. Short of sending someone in deliberately, we'll never know. It's possible her captor was careful how much he pulled from her at once. Maybe she was resistant to being drained somehow. We don't really know how the collars work."

Dornir took a bun and handed it to Marla. "We get the collars off fast during a rescue. They can track people wearing them. We've never been able to study one properly." He took his own bun and spread butter inside.

"Can't the rescued tell you more?" Marla took the offered butter knife.

"None of them can describe what happens with any detail. They just experience a flash of light and feel drained. Our magic and the Light Chargers don't quite work the same, so we can't charge a collar, not that we have a new one to try. Most of us can't feel the light well enough, and many of them can't feel us, either. Some can, though." Dornir looked up at the archway and froze.

Marla followed his gaze. Clarissa stood in the archway, braced against the frame. Tears rolled down her cheeks. Her body shook.

Dornir got up and went to her, pulling her into a hug. "Come with me. You can have breakfast in bed today. There's even some Tulla fruit for you." He guided her down the hall and out of sight.

Issa stood and went to the cupboards. She collected a plate and filled it with food before setting it on a tray. Taking a bright red fruit from the cold box, she cut it and set it in a small dish. She took a tray from a cupboard and placed the meal on it.

"I'll be right back."

Marla ate quietly as she waited. Another sacred site? Was it close? How much of the country would she get to see? Would she ever go farther? Was it safe, though? She picked up a piece of toast from the plate, with butter already spread on it. As a small-town girl, she never expected to leave at all.

Issa and Dornir came back as she started on her second piece of toast.

"Where's Rinnia?" Marla set her toast down and reached for her juice glass.

"She's staying with Clarissa for a while. Clarissa finds goodbyes hard, especially when someone young leaves. She's so afraid they'll take one of us." Issa poured herself a cup of tea.

Marla inhaled, sniffing the fruity aroma. She stared at the teacups for a long moment. If she was travelling, did she really want a cup? Marla shook her head and sipped from her juice glass.

"I've already packed a bag for you, so you could sleep longer. It's by the door." Issa collected the empty plates and carried them to the sink. "Your new travelling clothes fit you well."

Dornir filled the sink with water. He rolled his sleeves up.

Marla smiled as she looked down at herself. Her soft and clean clothing moved like a second skin, with enough room she could jump or crouch without worry. Now she looked like them, like she belonged with the group. Besides, she had so many pockets in both her shirt and trousers.

"This time we're passing as a science team, not as merchants. If anyone challenges us, Adris will do the talking. They're an entomologist doing advanced studies on water insects, and Tialla is passing as their advisor. You're simply another student helping out. Dornir and I are hired guides."

"Okay, I'll have to be quiet. I don't know much about insects yet. I was more a geology girl, myself." Marla picked up her toast and finished it.

"Excellent. We often pass as science teams, as they are common, and we can go anywhere like that. Nobody thinks twice about a science team wandering through the bushes. We can stay at inns. The more remote the better, and it's considered normal." Issa took her now empty plate.

"Hey, we even had one in our town once." Marla paused, her mind spinning. "I was young and don't remember it well. They were studying—our fertilizers, I think?" She rubbed her chin. "Wait, they spent a lot of time with Ava. Were they Wood Walkers?"

Issa laughed. "Yes, but they really were a science team. We do a lot of studies. The Light Chargers also have science teams, and so does every school of any size. They're all independent of each other, though everyone shares results, so we all benefit. How else do you think we survive things like drought and such?"

"They'll be waiting." Dornir nodded towards the shared garden. He set the last dish in the rack to dry.

"Right. Let's go." Issa ushered Marla from her seat and to the door. "We have new boots for you, too. They're more suited for being a student. They're already softened, so you shouldn't get blisters."

Marla crossed the mudroom and stopped at her boots. A second pair sat right beside them, along with a backpack full of gear. She pulled her socks up and slid her new boots on. They fit well, with plenty of room to wiggle her toes, though not so big she'd trip or slide around. She followed them out and down the street.

Kria and the others were at the front gate, close to the waterfall. Everyone had clothing like hers, though the colours and styles varied slightly. Adris stuffed their pockets with little notebooks and magnifying glasses and marking pens.

"If everyone is ready, we'll head out." Adris waved them on as they turned down the path, away from the city.

Marla walked near the middle of the group. How was Adris so awake when they struggled so much on the last trip? The mist was cool against her skin as they got closer to the roaring waterfall. She felt the rumble through her boots.

They stepped from the tunnel and into the sunlight. A strong tingling covered Marla. She glanced back at Tialla. The old woman smiled and waved.

Her clothing and skin stayed dry as she passed the waterfall. Her boots gripped the wet rock with ease. Marla glanced up. Water beaded on an invisible dome over them. It rolled down past her and dropped to the rock at her feet. As they left the waterfall behind, the dome faded.

"It's better to start the day warm and dry." Kria gestured back at the waterfall. "We can request a shield when we leave on a mission like this."

Marla glanced back down the path. A woman she didn't recognize walked back towards the city. Mist formed around the woman in the shape of a smaller dome. She walked back into the tunnel and out of sight. Marla turned and focused ahead.

The group followed the path into the forest, leaving the roar of the waterfall behind. Birdsong replaced it, along with the rustle of leaves in the breeze. Marla looked up and around and smiled. She took a deep breath in and sighed.

"This site isn't far. It's a couple of days' walk." Issa pulled a map from her pocket and held it out to Marla. "Pull a little magic up and touch it."

Magic? Marla shrugged and took the map. She called the energy up through her, filling herself with nature. Unfolding it until she saw where they were, Marla touched her fingertip to the map. Symbols glowed on the page.

"What?" Marla blinked and looked closer.

When she moved her finger over a symbol near them on the map, an image rushed into her mind. She saw a cave entrance partially covered by bushes and moss. The sun streamed down on it, the slanted early rays of morning. Somehow, she just knew how deep the cave was, where all the branching paths went, and even where the standing stones were deep inside.

"What was that? What did I see?" She held the map out towards Issa, her hands shaking.

Issa smiled at her and took the map. She folded it and put it back in her pocket. "Your powers have developed enough to bring our maps to life. You can see the basic information right now."

Marla raised her eyebrow. "That was basic? What's the highest level like?"

Tialla linked arms with her and guided her along again. "When I touch the maps, I can see the sites at any time of day, not just the moment I touch it. I also get a complete history, including who was part of each team to charge the site as far back as I want. I can also see markers you cannot."

"That's—" Marla pointed at Issa's pocket. "How? That's incredible."

"We'll have a lesson all about them soon for you. There's one in your pack as well. If anyone without our powers touches them, they'll look like an ordinary map. It takes a touch of your powers to activate the maps. Blue markers are sacred sites. Red markers are all safe houses and refuges. If anything happens, head for a red marker. Larger red markers even have people there who can help you." Tialla let go of her arm and kept pace beside her.

"Oh, uh, great." Marla tried to recall the cave image and the information, but it was slipping away. "It's not permanent?"

"Only when you touch it while at the site. Otherwise, it slides from your mind." Tialla smiled at her. "Feels weird, huh?"

"Yeah." Marla stopped and rubbed her chin. "So, the more places I go, the more I'll remember?"

Dornir sidestepped her, his hands on her shoulders. "Careful now. Yes, if you take a moment and touch the map every time we go somewhere, you'll learn so much. I've been in nearly every safe house in the south and know them all well. Close to the city, I don't carry a map at all anymore."

Adris patted their pocket. "I still have mine and use it regularly. I'm still learning."

Marla looked up at Tialla as she began walking again.

Tialla winked at her. "I stopped carrying mine decades ago. These boots have seen many a place in my time."

Marla shook her head slowly. What powered a map of magic? She knew all about regular maps, learned to read them from her geography books, but this was never mentioned. Did the Light Chargers have their own maps, too? Wait, could she use those, if she had some light magic in her?

She tilted her head and looked down at her feet as she walked. "Are we on some kind of path or something here? The ground feels different under my feet."

Dornir slid his arm around her shoulders, careful of her pack. "You got it. I think we have another pathfinder here." He nudged her lightly. "If you ever get lost and can't find your map, feel for these paths. Follow them. They'll bring you home."

"She's not a pathfinder. She's a channeler."

Dornir stopped, his arm falling away from her. His jaw dropped. Adris stared at Marla and pointed at her. Issa and Tialla didn't react, though.

"Really?" Adris threw their arms around Marla and hugged her tight. "That's great."

Marla took a gasping breath. "What's a channeler?" she wheezed. Why was everyone staring?

Issa pulled Adris away. "You'll suffocate her."

"Sorry." Adris grinned sheepishly and stepped back.

"A channeler can touch the lines of power and change how the power flows. You won't just tap into it; you can alter it. You know how Tialla can call on the power and heal people with it as easily as she breathes?"

Marla nodded.

"You can do that for nature. You can get the power flowing properly after it's been disrupted." Issa took her hand and headed down the path Marla could feel, but not see.

"I can't. I don't know how. I'm just me—"

Tialla chuckled. "Of course you can't—yet. We need to teach you. It's why calling seeds awake is so easy for you. You're bringing them power right from the land. Most seed callers touch the seeds and awaken them. You channel power into them instead. Same effect, different reason."

Marla stumbled over a root. Issa steadied her as she regained her footing. She took a slow breath.

"Alright, what's so exciting about being a channeler?"

Dornir winked at her. "When you learn how, you can channel energy for us, or blend our energies together. You can lead the charging of a sacred site one day. All group leaders are channelers."

Marla stared at Kria.

"Yes, I'm a channeler, though my side powers are a unique blend compared to yours." Kria shrugged. "People are complex. We're never just one thing. We need to get going."

Adris bounced up beside her and walked with her. They told Marla stories of a friend who was a channeler. Marla listened to every word. Adris had so many stories, Marla didn't feel the time pass until Kria called for a lunch break.

"Already?" Marla's stomach growled, and she looked down at herself. "I guess so."

Everyone settled near the stream, choosing fallen logs or large rocks as chairs. Marla found a sun-warmed rock, though the sunbeam had moved on already.

"Food is in your pack." Issa nodded to Marla's backpack, which rested on the ground at her feet. "Side pouches. Take one labelled bread pocket for now."

She found the paper-wrapped packages and rustled through them, reading the labels. Adris showed her how to tear it open so she could hold it without a mess. There was a delightfully sweet onion sauce inside, and the waxed wrapper kept her clean.

"These are the best. So tasty, and full of energy." Adris bit into a pastry wrapped around vegetables and grains.

Marla took a bite of her bread pocket. "Mm." She pointed at her food as she closed her eyes and let the sauce coat her tongue. Was that just a little honey? Fruit? Either way, it gave just the right sweetness.

"They feed us well when we leave a staffed outpost." Dornir bit into his wrap, going silent as he smiled and chewed.

Marla took her time, enjoying the mix of flavours. Who made these sauces? She'd never had it before, but she'd eat it again and again if she could. There was even a spice in there she didn't recognize at all.

Once everyone was done, Issa held her hand out. "I'll take the wrapper."

She handed her wrapper over. Issa crumpled the wrappers in her palm. Marla watched as the paper crumbled into fragments, breaking down before her eyes. Issa opened her fingers and let the ashes fall.

"Let's get moving. I want to leave this area before nightfall." Kria pulled her pack on and snugged the straps again.

With garbage taken care of and full bellies, the group headed through the trees, still marching north. Nobody spoke. Marla listened to the birds as they walked. Even though they walked for hours, there was always something to grab her attention, from small animals to rocks she could identify from her geology books.

Tialla stopped. "A hunting party. This way." She turned slightly left and strode off.

"Are we in danger?" Marla whispered to Issa.

Tialla shook her head. Issa stayed close. Adris looked pale. Dornir clenched his jaw. Kria was frowning deeply. They slipped through the trees, away from the path she could feel in the soil.

"They're chasing someone." Tialla stopped and stared between the bushes.

Marla strained to see or hear anything.

"Do we help, or hope someone is close?" Dornir crossed his arms over his chest.

Kria shook her head. "We need everyone for the point of power. Can you two help without being taken or getting chased off? You won't have backup." She ran her fingers through her hair and sighed. "Why now? Issa, Tialla, get Marla to the nearest refuge. I'm right behind you."

Tialla grabbed Marla's hand and darted into the bushes. Issa was behind them. Marla stumbled and scrabbled to get up again. Issa wrapped her arm around the girl and hauled her up. They rushed towards safety.

"They're on horses," Tialla muttered. "They've split into two groups. Hurry."

The ground shook with the pounding hooves. A bright flash to their right blinded her for a moment. Thunder cracked, and the shockwave shoved her. She clung to Tialla as she ran.

Tialla pulled her down under the cover of thick bushes. Magic rolled over them like a dome, a powerful shield that overwhelmed her senses. Marla glanced back. Where was Issa? Another lightning flash made her vision go white again. She blinked rapidly as her eyes watered. Tialla held her close as the thunder rolled over their barrier.

The barrier dissolved. Tialla hauled her up and pulled her to another cluster of bushes. Dirt sprayed her as another lightning bolt struck nearby.

"There they are."

CHAPTER 18

Tialla sprinted for the ravine, pulling Marla with her. Issa? Where was she? A fireball rolled past, spattering against a tree where it dissolved. The heat blast against her for an instant.

"I've got them."

"She's mine. I marked her."

Pounding hooves drowned out the shouting. Her vision was clearing. They were sprinting for the ravine. Why? Was she going to jump? Tialla wasn't slowing. Her focus was fully ahead. Marla tensed. Her palms sweat, loosening Tialla's grip.

A fireball sped at them from the left. Tialla leapt one and pulled her down as another passed. Marla ran with all her might, her heart pounding. She ducked another fireball. The ravine was close now. Marla shook. Her complete attention was on the steep drop ahead. Her arm ached.

"Now." Tialla leapt.

Marla threw herself forward with the old woman. A massive blast of wind smacked her from the side, ripping her sweaty hand free of Tialla's. She spun and tumbled, smacking the ground hard. Air rushed from her lungs. She grunted. Marla curled as she rolled. She crashed into the bushes, stopping against the thick branches.

Pain shot through her. She pulled a slow breath in. Her ribs ached. Every movement hurt. Air hurt against her scraped and raw skin. The world spun around her. She took another shaky breath and closed her eyes. Where was safety?

No time to stop. She staggered to her feet and braced against a tree. Which way? Marla abandoned her pack under the bush and scrambled towards the thicker brush, away from the steep drop she couldn't save herself from.

"There she is. Get her."

Marla took off away from the voices. Her legs shook, but she forced herself to keep going. Where were the others? Horses galloped, their feet shaking the ground. Nature, give me somewhere to hide. Please?

A ball of light shot past and hit a tree ahead of her. The tree exploded.

"No! She's mine. I have rights."

Something smacked her back, sending her to the ground. Lightning danced over her skin. Her body twitched. She couldn't draw a breath. Marla lay on the soil, her scraped skin sending stabbing pain through her as she shook.

The lightning stopped. Marla went floppy, too tired to move as she tried to draw a breath in. Footsteps sounded all around her. She rolled to her side, off the burning skin on her back, and looked up. Men on horses stood nearby, while other men surrounded her.

The world around her went fuzzy as her eyes partly closed. White boots approached, one slow step at a time. She forced her eyes open fully for a moment and saw the white leggings and robes, too. Marla sucked in a breath. She held her arm to her chest, cradling the scarred limb.

He kneeled beside her. His hand burned against her forehead. "Breathe through it. I'll have you back in no time." He stood and walked back to his horse. She knew that voice. It wasn't the voice of her dreams and fragmented memories. No, it was far more recent.

Two men in plain cream robes walked over and set something beside her. They rolled her onto it. Pain shot through her as she lay on her damaged back. Marla whimpered and tried to curl. A man held her down as the other man fastened leather straps over her. Once they immobilized her, they stood, lifting her on the canvas stretched between two poles.

Her body throbbed and burned. Everything hurt, stabbing pains from the lightning. She was vaguely aware of the man riding his horse near her as they carried her away. Marla struggled to breathe. The world around her went dark.

***

Pain dragged her from the bliss of unconsciousness. Her skin still ached. Sweat beaded on her forehead. Marla bit the rough wool blanket covering her, clenching her teeth on it. Tears leaked from her eyes. She tried to pry her eyes open.

Tall buildings lined both sides of the road. Crowd noises overwhelmed her. Blurry shapes moved around her. Her heartbeat pounded, drowning out most noises around her. The wagon jostled her, and pain shot through her again. The world around her faded.

***

Pain pulled her awake once again. She rolled to her side. Tears slid from her eyes and landed on the mattress. The light blanket covering her was softer this time, though still not comfortable on the skin. Most of her skin no longer hurt, just her back where the spell hit her.

How was she supposed to convince the planet that people deserved its abundance when they treated each other so badly? Maybe it would be better if humanity were gone. Did she really believe that, though? Her back twinged and pain sparked up and down her spine.

A door opened behind her. Someone approached. They walked around and kneeled in front of her on the stone floor, beside the mattress she lay on. Marla opened her eyes and met his gaze.

"You're awake. Good. Lay still. I'll treat that wound. It's time for more ointment."

He held a jar in one hand. This man was younger than the others, though not as young as her. His hand was gentle as he touched her shoulder. His robes were a pale blue instead of white. He eased the blanket off her back, though he let her clutch it to her chest.

"Breathe slow and steady. This might be uncomfortable still." His cool fingers touched her bare upper back. He moved around and kneeled behind her.

Marla cried out and tensed, pulling away as he smoothed the ointment on her hot skin. His hand clamped on her shoulder kept her in place.

"Breathe. It'll be over soon."

Of course, he was calm. He wasn't the one in agony, hurt by people who kidnapped him, was he? She hissed through clenched teeth.

"There. That's it for now. When you're ready, I have tea for you." He closed the jar and wiped his hand on a cloth. The man came and kneeled beside her head again.

Marla shook her head. She wanted nothing from him.

"If it's nausea, I have something for that, too." He rubbed her shoulder lightly. "Most people with injuries like yours feel sick."

"How many injured people have you seen?" Her voice trembled. Marla blinked back more tears.

"Like you? At least one every spring, and a few each year. Most people who come in resisted and need some care." He tucked the blanket up over her shoulder fully again.

Marla held his gaze. He had the most complex eyes she'd ever seen, with flecks of blue and gold, and a little green that glowed mixed in.

"Rest. He won't come for you until you've recovered more."

"Come for me?"

"You're in the health care section right now. We'll get you ready for your new life here, so you can serve him right away. Just think of how many people will lead better lives because you're helping." He smiled at her.

Serve him? Health care section? Her stomach lurched.

"You need rest. If you need anything, call for me. Sleep now. Your body needs to heal." He stood. His robes flowed around him as he walked away, his steps quiet and graceful.

She heard the door close. Marla shifted. Her muscles protested and her skin ached. She went still, and the discomfort stopped. How could she get out of here? She couldn't become like the others, hollowed out shells of women. What was it like to feel so dull and lifeless? How can she prevent it, though? She had to get out, but go where? Where was she?

Could she really keep helping, keep charging the points of power? How could she plead for humanity after this? Her heart ached as memories of the pain made her squeeze her eyes shut. No, they don't deserve nature's blessing.

A flash of a memory ran through her mind, her as a child running barefoot through the garden. The wind rustled her hair. She laughed as she ran. How many little girls were just like her, enjoying the fresh peas right from the pod? How many little faces were stained with berry juice after picking a bush clean? Could she deny them?

189

Her body still felt cold. Was that the room, or just a side effect of her recent injuries? She stared blankly ahead at the corner. Wait, that was green. She reached out, ignoring the discomfort, and touched the stone floor beside her mattress.

Moss? Even here? It was soft and warm, and when she touched it, a tiny surge of power rushed through her. Marla smiled. A piece of her world was here.

"I won't give up," she whispered.

Energy surged up through her. Her fingertip glowed as nature flooded her body. Her finger warmed. The warmth grew, spreading up her arm and into her chest. The power surged with each beat of her heart. By the time the warmth reached her toes, the ache had eased. Marla wrapped the blanket around herself better and sat.

Where was her clothing? The blanket was large enough to fully wrap around her. The mattress was thick and soft, and protected her from the cool stone floor. The room was small, barely wide enough to stretch across and just over twice as long. There was a bucket in the far corner that smelled. A small table was in the corner near her, with some bottled water and a metal cup. Other than her little patch of moss almost hidden under the mattress, the room was empty of all life but her.

The room spun around her, and she lay on her side again, her fingers stretched out to the moss. Could she remember the spell? Was the moon out? The spell was stronger with the moon up, but there weren't any windows.

Focusing on her connection to the moss, Marla grit her teeth and called to the magic. What was step one? Let it fill her. She opened herself and the power flowed up into her. The world stopped spinning. Her jaw relaxed as the pain eased again. Their healers mustn't be as good. Could their magic be used to heal, or did they rely on herbs and medicines?

The magic filled and flowed through her now. What was step two?

The door opened. Marla sat, pulling the blanket tighter around herself. The healer walked in with another man behind him. She scowled at him and his white robes. He got her to come with him after all, just not willingly.

He walked over and kneeled beside her, ignoring how his white robes brushed on the floor. "How are you feeling?"

She raised an eyebrow at him. Another wave of nausea rolled through her. Marla doubled over and dropped her head to the mattress.

He rested his hand on her shoulder. "Hasn't she been treated?"

"She wouldn't accept anything for this," the man in blue explained. "I'll get an elixir for her now."

She heard the door open and close again. Her stomach rolled, and she whimpered.

"Slow and deep breaths. It'll help. He'll be back in moments." His voice was soft and calm.

This was all his fault. Why couldn't he leave her be? What did he want from her specifically? How could she get away? Her mind settled with the memory of Issa's class in the garden. A protection spell, one she was good at, but would it work here?

The door opened. The man in blue came over, bottles clinking together in his hand. "She needs both. The green one is for pain, and the pale one is for nausea." He kneeled near her. "Come, miss. Sit or you'll choke." He pulled her up with his hands on her arms, away from the burns.

The blanket moved over her raw skin, and she whimpered. Marla gripped the blanket, her fingers nearly white.

"You'll feel better if you take this." The man in blue uncapped the bottle and held it to her lips.

191

Tears rolled down her cheeks as she met his gaze. She let her mouth drop open a sliver, and the liquid trickled inside. The bitter medicine coated her tongue and throat. She coughed. He held the bottle away for a moment and let her catch her breath. The pain was easing already. Was it worth taking the rest?

"It'll work immediately," he soothed, as he set the bottle back against her lips. "You need to take it all, though."

She managed to get the thick medicine down. He was right. The pain was half already, and the blanket no longer was so rough against her burns. He set the bottle aside and wiped her mouth with a soft cloth.

"There. Now the second one." He uncapped the other bottle. "Slow and easy, just like the last one."

She wrinkled her nose at the sharp taste. Her mouth tingled as she took the medicine. Was this supposed to cure nausea, or cause it? Whatever happened to a nice pot of tea, or those candied roots Ava made?

Her stomach calmed. Her eyelids felt immensely heavy. Marla leaned against his hand for balance.

"That will probably make her sleep for a while. I'll let you know when she's awake again." The man in blue eased her back down to the mattress on her side.

"Alright, I'll get her something to wear. Tell me right away when she wakes."

Someone tucked the blanket fully around her again, pulling it down over her feet as well.

***

Light filtered through her eyelids. She opened her eyes and slammed them closed again, her arm over her face. Right, the bare room and the bright balls of light over her head. What happened to Tialla and Issa? Did they get away? The others? How could Tialla survive the fall into the ravine? Might she have died? Was it Marla's fault for not knowing enough?

The door opened. Marla moved her arm and looked over. The man in blue stepped into the room with the Light Charger. She scrambled up to sit, pulling the blanket around her like a flimsy shield. Marla staggered to her feet and braced against the wall with her hand.

"She's ready for her neckband." The man in blue bowed and stepped to the side.

"Excellent." The Light Charger stepped closer. "I brought you something to wear." He stretched his hand toward her. He held a shiny cloth in a pale cream.

Marla narrowed her eyes. Clothing would be nice. Hiding under the blanket wasn't fun and meant she couldn't use her hands to defend herself. "Thank you." She clenched her jaw as she reached for the clothing.

"The silk will be soft against your healing skin."

She held the blanket up with her arms as she took the cloth and unfolded it. The fabric was soft and light, much finer than the cotton she loved.

"How are you feeling?" He smiled at her.

Marla looked up at him and raised an eyebrow. "I feel okay, considering you attacked and burned me."

His smile faltered. "My apologies. I didn't know he was going to break the rules like that. He had no right to attack you."

Rules? Marla shook her head.

"Rest. I'll be back after supper to bring you home."

The man in blue stepped forward. "Do you need help to dress, miss?"

Marla shook her head. She turned away, staring down at the light cloth in her hands.

"Call if you need anything." The man in blue led the Light Charger out.

She sank to her knees on the mattress. So, this is what silk feels like. Would it be warm enough? The room seemed so cold and bare. How would this feel against her skin? It was better than not wearing clothing, but did she want anything from him? Her own clothing was gone, probably destroyed. What choice did she have?

Marla eased the dress over her head and let the shiny fabric slide down her body. It was smooth and light, airy even, and didn't irritate her fresh healing burns. She was going home soon, but not her home. His home. How long before he leaves the city, and she could be rescued?

There must be some way out. Marla stood and walked around the room, pacing slowly. There were no windows. It was just the one door. Her feet grew cold against the stone floor. She shivered. The light above her gave off no heat at all, unlike the warming lanterns her people used. It burned brighter than the lamps back in her village.

She shivered again. By the time they came back, she'd either be tired from pacing, or cold. She glanced at the blanket on her mattress. It smelled of ointment now, and it made her nose burn when she was close. Was that their plan?

The door was metal, cold, and unyielding. She rested a hand flat against it. The handle turned part way, but the door wouldn't budge. Locked, of course. The frame was also metal. Could she touch it? Marla took a slow breath. The metal under her hand was cool and lifeless. No energy flowed through it.

She brushed her fingers over the smooth stone wall as she walked back to the mattress. Ointment smell or not, the room was chilly. She dropped to her knees again and huddled under the blanket. Stretching her hand out, she touched the soft moss.

Wait, was the moss connected to nature in a bigger way? How else would it get here? She touched the moss with her magic. Maybe, if the moss was connected through soil between the stone blocks, maybe she could contact her people somehow? How, though? Marla lay on her side again, her feet tucked up under the blanket.

Some time later, many daydreams at least, the door opened. The man in blue brought a tray in. He set it on the floor beside her mattress. "Here, miss. Eat. You need your strength to settle in and take your place here."

Marla stared at the tray as he left quietly. Was this supper? Would they move her as soon as she was done? Maybe it was lunch, and she'd die of boredom in the meantime? Marla felt for the sun. Her senses stopped at the stone walls. The sun was lost to her.

A bowl of mushy grains with finely chopped vegetables sat on the tray. A plate of wilted greens kept it company. They expected her to eat this? Marla took her spoon and pushed the greens around. Nope, not happening. She dropped the spoon in the bowl and pushed the tray into the corner. With nothing else to do, Marla curled up under the blanket and waited.

CHAPTER 19

The door opened. The Light Charger walked in. He held something shiny in his hand. The black metallic surface reflected the light. Her heart hammered. No, not a collar! She scrambled to her feet and backed into the corner.

"Just stand still. This will be over in moments." He walked towards her with slow and steady steps.

"No. I refuse." She brought her hands up.

The man in blue was still in front of the door. Could she get past him?

"You can't refuse. You don't leave this room until you're wearing this." He took another step.

"Then I'll die here." Marla narrowed her eyes at him.

"Don't be dramatic, miss." The healer held his hand out to her. "Master Kienan can have that on in moments. No harm done."

"I'll be dramatic if I want. Go away."

He took another step. If he reached out, he could grab her. The room was too small. Marla cursed. She darted past him. Marla kicked out, her bare foot colliding with his shin and catching in his robes. She dropped and rolled, heading for the door.

Arms wrapped around her. She scrambled and slammed her elbow back. The arms loosened. Kienan grabbed her wrist as she aimed again, pulling her arm straight out and away from him.

The man in blue dashed closer and pinned her to the mat. She thrashed and fought, sweat coating her skin and making her slippery. Marla bit at the hand reaching for her neck. The skin on her back sent stabbing pains through her.

Kienan moved her arms over her head and the man in blue held her there. He pinned her legs down and kneeled over them. "You'll feel better in a moment."

She screamed as she fought. Marla tucked her chin and scrunched her shoulders. Kienan dodged her snapping teeth and gripped her chin in one hand. He eased the collar under her neck and brought it around, using his arm under her chin as he grabbed both ends. The latch snapped into place. Something glowed a pale yellow. A flash of light filled the room, overwhelming her vision.

Her energy flowed up her body to the collar against her skin. Her limbs got heavy, and her thrashing slowed.

"That's it. Give it a moment. You'll feel peace. Just a moment more." He held her chin again, his fingers against her cheek.

This isn't peace. This is emptiness. Her power flowed from her and into the collar. No. Fight. I have to fight.

"I can feel her already." He lifted his free hand and called a ball of light over his palm.

The light glowed brightly, irritating her already pained eyes. It glowed with every colour she could imagine. Marla closed her eyes and saw the lights inside her eyelids instead.

"She's powerful. She'll last a long time with care." The man in blue relaxed his grip on her arms.

Something inside her stirred. Wait, I know that energy. That's my light. She focused on the light inside, growing brighter as her creative energy pulled away. Help me, please. Destroy the collar, she pleaded. Her light moved inside her, up her belly and to her neck.

"I'll be back in two bells. That'll give the collar time to draw excess energy away and calm her." Kienan stood, releasing her. He stepped back, away from the mattress.

Marla lay quietly, focused inside herself as she guided her light higher towards the collar. His voice sounded distant. She pushed it away and kept encouraging her inner light.

"I'll get her cleaned up." The man in blue stood and stepped back.

The light was almost to her neck now. She barely registered the sound of the door. No, just a little more, now. It resisted going near the collar. No, you'll do as I say. She pressed her power up until the light was against the collar.

Her creative energy swirled up against the protective band of light she made, but it didn't leak out or past her new barrier. Something connected her to him, but the connection was stable now. Her thoughts cleared. Her body still felt sluggish, like she badly needed a nap, but she could move with more ease again.

Wait, I have to act the part until I can escape, she realized. How were they? She'd seen enough to get some idea, at least. While his last captive was livelier than most, even she was subdued. Marla, you can do this, she encouraged herself.

Marla lay on the mat and didn't move. She looked up at the door. The man in blue stood watching her.

"There. That's it. There's no need to fight us. You'll be well cared for." He smiled at her.

He didn't react to her meeting his gaze. Maybe they expected this to take a little time? Better learn fast, though. One wrong move might give her away. Unless she convinced them she was harmless now, maybe?

The man in blue took a cloth and a bottle of water. He kneeled beside her. "Look at you, getting all sweaty like that. Roll onto your belly and I'll check your back."

Marla froze. What now? Should she listen? What if she didn't? Would they know she blocked the transfer of energy somehow?

His hands guided her onto her side. She let him move her. He set the blanket over her legs and hips before easing her dress up.

"That looks sore, but you didn't make it worse." He poured water into the metal cup and dipped the cloth in it.

She flinched as he wiped her back, the cloth soft against her raw skin. The dress was already drying from her sweat. What was this silk made from? Plant fibres took a lot longer to dry, usually. Marla lay still as he cleaned her lower back as well. Once she was covered again, he moved the blanket and washed her legs.

"Roll over."

What? Marla froze. Wait, what would the others do right now? Her mind was blank.

The women are only touched for health and hygiene reasons. Issa's words flowed through her mind. Well, that was something, at least. Marla allowed him to roll her without resisting.

He washed her arms first, before wiping down her belly. He always kept her mostly covered, using the blanket to help. Marla closed her eyes and thought of the massive tree they hung a swing from back home. They'd take turns swinging so high the branch would creak or run around the trunk playing chasing games.

"There you go, miss. Rest. He'll be back soon enough."

Marla opened her eyes and watched him walk away, the cup and cloth in his hand. He dumped the dirty water in the bucket in the far corner.

Her tears flowed freely. Something was missing within her. The energy he had already taken left an empty spot inside. She pressed one hand to her heart, and the other over her lower belly. Would it come back, or was it gone for good? No, she met people who were freed. It took a while, but they recovered. Some of them were thriving, even. She just needed to survive until she could be rescued.

He walked back over and kneeled beside her. "Don't worry, miss. The big feelings will ease soon. Embrace the peace."

Peace? That void in her energy, like it was much too thin, that wasn't peace. No, but if I have to swallow the big feelings to hide what I've done, I will. I'll hold my anger until I can use it. Then I'll burn this place to the ground, stone and all.

Marla took slow and steady breaths. She reached out and touched the moss, hiding her movement like she was stretching. There. Nature is still there. I can't draw more power in, but I can sense its heartbeat. She hasn't forgotten me. Marla almost smiled.

"That's it. Let go."

Oh, he's pleased when I show hints of emotion? Marla let a shadow of a frown cross her face before relaxing her expression again. He watched her and waited, not reacting. So, traces of emotion are okay, at least for now.

What else? Right, the women never looked at anyone as long as they wore the collars. Was that because of their low energy, or something else? Should I avoid meeting anyone's gaze? I never want to look at Kienan again, so that won't be hard. How can I look around and find my way out if I'm always staring at my feet?

Marla closed her eyes and sank inside herself. Her thinner energy flowed around, circulating like normal. It bounced off the barrier she made at the collar and stayed inside her. Was it enough? Could she still use it if she needed, or did she risk giving him anything she tried to use? What would she do in this stone city devoid of nature? Marla settled her thoughts and flowed with her power. She needed to know more.

The door opened. Kienan stepped inside the room and stayed at the door. "She feels calmer inside."

Marla opened her eyes and stared at the wall. He could feel her emotions?

"Huh, still some fear. Well, that should pass quickly, too. If she's ready, I'll take her now."

The healer took her hand. "Come, miss. Time to settle in."

She hesitated a moment before standing. Marla kept her gaze down. Her legs wobbled for a moment. She was just as strong as ever physically, but her drained energy was definitely affecting her control over her body. Marla gripped his hand as she steadied herself.

"She will need more time to rest." The man in blue walked her slowly over to Kienan. "She also hasn't eaten yet. Make sure she has something before she sleeps. With how strong she is, don't be surprised if it takes a few days for her to settle fully."

"I will." Kienan took her hand and pulled lightly, guiding her through the door.

Interesting. Does that mean the collar doesn't work right away, not completely? I might have a few days to figure this out before they realize what I've done. Unless the collar is working, and I only slowed the transfer. Maybe I'm the one being fooled. No, the flow between us has stopped. Now it's like the energy he took is circulating between us instead.

She let him lead her from the room. The halls were a mottled white marble. Her bare feet were silent on the floor, though his boots left a faint echo in the empty hall. The first few halls were deserted. The air was cooler, and she suppressed a shiver. She glanced at the colourful tapestries as they walked past.

Noise grew ahead of them. They turned a corner and walked through an archway. The hall she found herself in was massive, with multiple hallways leading off, and an enormous staircase leading up to a higher floor. Many people in white robes like Kienan wore stopped to look at her as she passed, the silver trim flashing in the lamplight. Crystals hung on ceilings and walls, giving off that cold white light.

He took her to the stairs. She climbed the steps beside him, reaching her short legs higher. He slowed for her. This place was not made for her. Even the stone benches were higher and wider than she was used to.

At the top, he guided her down a hallway and through another archway. Two men in armour stood on either side of the archway, both with swords hanging from their belts. He didn't acknowledge them as he passed. They stood at attention, glancing at her as she walked by.

They passed many ornate doors before he stopped partway down the hall. He placed his hand on the door and the wood glowed. The lock clicked, and the door swung open. He guided her inside.

"Welcome home." He pulled the door closed behind her and the lock clicked.

Marla stared at the room, her mouth open. One side of the room had a sitting area with a sofa and some chairs. Bookshelves packed with books lined the walls over there. There was also a low table with scrolls and books stacked all over it. The other side had a carved wooden desk. Behind that, she noticed a padded bench, a small table, and a large cushion on the floor.

He led her to that corner. "I made sure everything was padded and soft for you. This corner will be your space. You should be comfortable here."

Marla frowned. Was she supposed to be grateful?

Her gaze fell on the immense windows along this wall, including above her corner. She stared out into the fading sunlight. The windows looked slightly foggy, like the glass was slightly rippled. She could still see through well enough, though. Long shadows crossed the city below the hill this building sat on.

"We're looking out over the Merchants' Quarter." He stood beside her, close enough to wrap an arm around her shoulder, but he let go of her hand instead. "During the day, you can watch the markets fill with people. Everyone comes from all over to trade here."

Lanterns waved as people below carried them. Occasionally, the light would reflect off something. A sword, maybe? Did the city have a watch like her small town did?

"Get settled. I'll have food brought." He walked to his desk.

Marla turned and looked around again. There were two other doors here, both on the back wall. One had a light glowing inside. She could see a bed and dresser, both as fancy as his desk. The other room was dark. Neither seemed like a possible escape route.

She clenched her jaw. He was still watching her as he pulled his desk chair out. She slumped onto her cushion and leaned against the wall. The desk blocked her view of most of the room now. Was she supposed to spend most of her time here?

He sat and turned his attention to his desk. Kienan picked up a slender stylus and wrote on something on his desk. "There. Food is coming. Rest."

He glanced back at her before turning back to his desk. She lay back on her cushion and stared up at the sky through the sliver of window she could see. Papers rustled. She ignored it and focused on the stars beginning to appear in the sky. Did she recognize them? Marla shifted a little so she could see more of the sky.

Someone knocked on the door.

"Stay there." Kienan stood.

He walked to the door and opened it. She couldn't see around the door from her place in the corner. He took a tray from someone and pushed the door closed with his foot. Kienan carried the tray over.

"Here. You need to keep your strength up." He set the tray on the floor beside her. "I'll set the locks for the night. Don't try to leave. The spells with react to your neckband and you'll get a nasty shock if you touch the door."

She watched him walk to the door. He set his hand against it and muttered something she couldn't make out. The frame glowed brightly for an instant.

"Eat." He pointed at her tray as he walked to the bedroom.

Marla picked up her spoon and examined the food. The bowl was grains and vegetables, but this time, there were spices mixed in. She inhaled deeply. The vegetables were in larger pieces, though still bite sized, and had their bright colour. They weren't overcooked. This was definitely an improvement over the bland mush the man in blue tried to give her.

Did she want it, though? Her spoon hovered over the bowl. Not eating would be one way to protest. It would also make her weak, though. If she was going to get out of here, she'd need every advantage she could get. Maybe there was another way to resist that wouldn't weaken her?

Wait, had they drugged it? Could she tell? How? There wasn't any sign of the herbs she knew could affect her like that. Did they have anything else that would affect her, like a medication she didn't know about? Marla frowned and looked up at the bedroom door. He was leaning against the frame, watching her. His over robe was gone, and he wore a sleeveless shirt instead.

She picked up her bowl and held it close to her chin. Marla scooped up some food and ate, her gaze down at her tray, though she felt his presence.

He turned and went back into his room. So, she could still passively sense and he didn't seem to notice?

The flavoured oils coated her tongue and let the taste of herbs linger in her mouth. It was as good as anything she had back home, either home, and Marla finished every bite.

"That's better." He returned from the bedroom and walked over. Now he wore loose robes in a dark orange silk. "You can get water from that tap." Kienan gestured at a pipe extending through the wall over the table near her. "Use those cups."

Marla took a cup. It was a light and smooth metal with an almost mirror-like surface. She held it under the tap. How did it work? She frowned at the little pipe.

CHAPTER 20

H e kneeled beside her. "Touch it like this." Kienan placed his finger against the side of the pipe.

Water flowed into her cup in a gentle stream. When the water nearly filled the cup, he took his finger off the pipe. The water stopped again. She sipped from the cup. The water was clear and tasted like it should. She leaned closer to the tap and inspected it. Magic? Technology? Both?

"There's a valve inside. The sensor is magic, and it interacts with the valve, which is a normal metal valve. Wash up before you sleep." He nodded to the other dark room.

She nodded slightly as she sipped her water. Once her cup was half-empty, she set it on the table and stood. He walked ahead of her to the room. Kienan touched a metal wall plate, and the lights came on. It was the same glaring crystals as in the medical room, though these had a piece of extremely thin cloth stretched around them to diffuse the harshness a bit.

"Your towels and supplies are these." He pointed to a set of cream towels and a basket with soaps and bottles in it. "Mine are the white ones. You are familiar with everything else in here?" He gestured at the toilet and sink.

Marla nodded. It all looked like what she had back home, though far shinier and grander. The taps had handles in here, like she was used to.

He left. She swung the door closed. No lock? Marla frowned at the door. Taking her little basket of soaps and a facecloth, she went to the sink. The hot water came out hot right away. She yanked her finger back and turned the cold on, letting it soothe her skin.

She looked up in the oversized mirror over the sink. The shiny black collar made her frown. Marla touched it. The metal was light and warm, but unyielding. A tear rolled down her cheek as she filled the sink with warm water.

Were most women too tired to wash properly on their own here? Most of those she saw rescued needed help for the first few hours until their energy came back a bit. She rubbed the floral scented soap on her skin. Would she need that kind of help, or could she get away before that happened?

No, the woman they rescued from him had more energy than most. There was hope for Marla yet. She washed quickly and set her towels and cloth to dry. Once her little basket of soaps was back on the shelf, she opened the door and turned out the light.

What should she do now? He was sitting in one of the cushioned chairs, reading a thick book. Her attention wandered to the extensive bookshelves behind him. After a long moment, she wandered back to her cushion. He watched her until she settled again.

Were they already looking for her? She lay back and stared up at the sliver of sky. They'll need to wait until she leaves the city. How long will that take?

A flash of light flared in the corner. She looked over. He held his hand out, a ball of fire floating over his palm. Her power flared inside her, but her light kept the rest of her magic from leaking out. Did he know? Was he testing their connection?

He frowned and closed his hand into a fist. The fire disappeared. "Get some sleep. Remember, don't try and leave. You won't like the result."

Kienan closed his book and set it on the little table by the chair. He stood and walked to his room.

With nothing else to do, she curled up and pulled the blanket over herself. The lights went out when he snapped his fingers. She huddled under the blankets and closed her eyes. His boots clicked softly against the stone as he moved around in his bedroom. Cloth rustled, and everything went quiet.

She rolled onto her back and stared at the stars. Was this her chance? He'd be expecting her to try, wouldn't he? Should she be too tired to try? He must know there's something wrong with the link by now, though. His frown was too deep.

Does he know? If he's not had a lot of experience, maybe he isn't sure? Does he actually know that much more than I do? Maybe it's different each time, and he has no idea what's normal or not, either. She'd been with him for a few years. Maybe he forgot what it's like.

A sliver of the largest moon was over her now. How long has it been? Her eyes had fully adjusted to the dark. Marla saw enough detail to move around safely. Easing from under her blankets, she placed a bare foot on the floor. Taking her time, Marla stood.

Her feet were still on warm stone, but she shivered and wrapped her arms around herself. From the waist up, the room was chilly. She took a couple of steps. The stone turned cold underfoot, and a breeze hit her bare shins.

Dragging her toes along the floor, she found where the warmth stopped, and the cold began. Marla stepped back onto the warm stone and crouched. Warm air surrounded her. Interesting. She had a space large enough to sleep and sit up, even get some water, and still be warm all night. Was this another way he'd try to keep her quiet at night?

Was there radiant in-floor heating around her space? She'd read about it once, but always wondered what it would be like. No, the tiles would get cooler gradually away from her space, not suddenly like that. Magic? They controlled fire and lightning the way she influenced nature, so maybe?

Wrapping her blanket around herself, Marla stood and crept away from her corner. Her steps were silent as she crept from her cushion. She approached the door. Marla was almost arms-length away when she stopped and backed up a few hasty steps. She curled her toes. The floor close to the door was freezing.

Marla stumbled back to her pad and tucked her feet under her blanket. It had to be magic, of course. She rubbed her feet carefully until the skin warmed again. Was anything else protected? She looked at his desk. Maybe he had papers that could help her somehow? Would she even know what was useful?

Curling up tighter on her cushion, Marla stared at his bedroom doorway. There wasn't any sound, no breathing or snores, nothing to show he was still alive. She shivered. He could be standing in the shadows, watching her, and she'd never know.

She rolled to the wall and pulled the covers up, only her nose and mouth poking from the blanket. Marla closed her eyes.

***

A page rustled. Marla lay still for a long moment before opening her eyes. The stone wall greeted her. Right, her corner. She listened. Metal scratched on paper. His chair squeaked. She rolled, keeping the blanket tight around herself.

Kienan sat at the desk, his stylus in his hand. He turned in his chair. "Wash up. You can eat after that." He pointed at her breakfast, a still steaming bowl on a tray on her table.

Marla eased her blanket free and shoved it on her cushion. She placed her feet on the warm floor and hissed. Marla fell back as she stood, shooting pains running through her feet.

Kienan took a tin from his desk drawer and stood. He walked over and kneeled beside her. "I told you; you wouldn't like it." He lifted her foot and inspected her sole.

He sat quietly as he let go of her and opened the tin. Kienan scooped some ointment up and rubbed it on her foot. She squirmed and twitched, gripping her cushion in her fists. He didn't let go until the ointment was rubbed in.

The ache stopped, and the tingling eased. She stayed quiet as he treated her other foot, still squirming a bit, but resisting less. Once he released her foot, he wiped his hand on a soft cloth from his pocket.

"There. Now you know better from experience, so you won't try again, will you?" He held her gaze.

Marla stared, but didn't reply. She curled her feet up away from him.

"Don't stand for a quarter bell. Let the ointment work. I'll tell you when you can wash and eat. Perhaps a cold breakfast will help you remember to listen." He capped the tin and returned to his desk.

Marla reached for her tea. He didn't forbid her from drinking. Her fingers wrapped around the warm cup, and she picked it up. He glanced back, but said nothing. She slowly sipped her tea, willing the time to pass faster.

She brushed her thumb over the raised pattern on the now-empty cup. Who knew boredom was so tedious? She sure didn't. Maybe she'd die of boredom before they rescued her.

He glanced over. "Go wash. There's clean clothing for you in there."

The metal cup clinked softly as she set it back on the tray. Marla stood and stretched. The cold air was gone. The stone was warm against her feet as she walked across the room. It had to be magic. With a last look back, Marla snuck inside and closed the door. He met her gaze before turning back to his paperwork.

May as well take my time. The food is already cold. Marla took her little basket of soaps and a small towel to the sink. If this was the only privacy she was going to get, she'd make the most of it. If she closed her eyes, she could imagine she was back at either home. If only the soap smelled of herbs like she was used to.

Once she washed and got ready, with brushed and braided hair, Marla put her clean dress on. She opened the door and stepped out. The room looked even bigger, with the sunlight streaming through the windows like that. The massive bookshelves grabbed her attention again. So many books, it almost rivalled Ava's basement collection. The shelves were so tall they had ladders on wheels attached to them.

"Eat first. If you finish everything on your tray, you can read while I work."

Marla turned her attention to him. He'd let her read? He was watching her again, that calm expression on his face. What was he thinking? What would happen if she didn't listen? What would he do? Dare she try to find out? No, she'd probably learn soon enough, anyway. No need to poke the bear. Besides, there were so many books.

She returned to her cushion and sat on the edge near the little table. She pulled the tray closer. What was that? Marla picked up a piece of bread. It was stiff. Someone had cooked it again? She bit into it. It crunched between her teeth. Something sticky was spread over one side, and it made the crumbs stick in her mouth. How was it actually colder than room temperature?

"It's better when it's still hot." He didn't turn, he just kept working, his stylus scratching on the paper.

Hot? Cold crumbs clung to her cheeks. The sticky spread was sweet, almost too sweet. Marla reached for her teacup. Oh, she already drank it. Why would people heat bread and make it stiff on purpose? She shook her head as she filled her cup with water.

The bowl held an odd mixture that could be grains soaked and cooked. Leaving her stiff bread on the small plate, she dipped her spoon in the bowl. Marla scooped some up and lifted it. She touched her tongue to the glob on her spoon. There was a spice in there that made her tongue tingle lightly, but not in a bad way.

"You'll get to experience everything this country offers, as you live with me. That's spiced with Rinnaw, from the north. The fruit spread is from the northeast. It's a real delicacy, and we get a first chance at trading for it. If you behave when we travel, I'll make sure you get to try the best things from every region. Have you ever soaked in the hot springs in the west?"

Marla shook her head. She stuffed the spoon in her mouth. The grains were gummy, but not bad. Much better than the stiff bread. That bread tried to choke her with each bite. With the lure of books encouraging her, Marla looked at her tray again.

She picked up the odd yellow fruit from the tray. It was almost a sphere, but not quite. Marla lightly squeezed it. The skin gave under her fingers slightly, but the fruit resisted the pressure. She dug her fingernail into the skin. It left an indent but remained intact. What is this? Is she supposed to eat the skin as well?

He kneeled beside her. Marla jumped back, bumping against the wall. How did he move so quietly? Shouldn't his boots have given him away?

Kienan took the fruit. "You peel it like this." He twisted the stem. The skin split neatly. He pulled the skin apart. "Now you eat the insides. Even the seeds are nutritious."

She nodded and accepted the fruit, cradling it in her hand like he had. The inside was in segments, each with a seed inside. Marla eased a piece from the skin and held it up. The flesh was pale. She bit into it. It was sweet, like most fruit. Juicy. Finally, something delicious was on her tray. Marla took her time, savouring the sweet, her eyes closed as she focused on the flavour. It was watery in a good way. Less, and it would be too sweet.

Abandoning the empty peel on her tray, Marla picked up her bowl again. It was still half full. Most of the stiff bread waited for her as well. Marla looked over at the bookshelves. Was it worth it? If she ate the grains but couldn't choke down the bread, would he still let her read? If he didn't, she'd have eaten the mushy cold grains for nothing.

"If you don't want to finish, sit quietly while I work." He didn't even turn to look at her, he just kept writing.

Marla sighed. She abandoned the bowl on the tray and flopped back on her cushion. The sliver of sky was blue and bright. What a gorgeous day to be outside. She glanced at the clock on the wall. It had extra markers on it. What did they mean? She told time mostly by the sun, since she was outside so much. What were those extra symbols for?

Maybe she could figure it out if she paid attention. It's not like she had anything better to do. One counted the bells, and another divided the time smaller. What were the last two for? They moved in much smaller circles set into the larger clock. One didn't have symbols at all. Time marched on, but she was no closer to figuring it out when the first bell neared.

He set his stylus down and turned in his chair. "We're going to a meeting soon. I expect you to sit quietly beside me. Listen and behave, and we can see a garden after midday. Don't listen, and you'll practice sitting until you get it right. Understand?"

Marla sat up. She opened her mouth, but the words caught in her throat. Was the band silencing her? She nodded, tears gathering in her eyes. She wiped her eyes with her hand. He frowned, his attention still fully on her.

No, pretend I'm one of them. She looked down at her knees. No emotions. Just empty. I can pretend to be empty. I must. With a few slow breaths, Marla's emotions calmed.

"When we go, you will walk quietly beside me. Stay close and keep up. If you wander or try to run, there will be consequences."

Marla nodded, her gaze still on her knees. She needed time to learn her way around, or she'd never make it far, anyway. She didn't have to escape today. How long will her magic hold out, though? Will it start draining again at some point? It felt solid and steady so far, her protection still in place. Would it last?

"Come." He stood. Kienan folded his arms over his chest and waited.

Did she even want to? Marla debated a long moment as his frown got deeper. She unfolded her legs and eased to her feet. Marla walked over to him. He nodded and headed for the door. She matched his pace, nearly jogging to keep up. Why did they all have to walk so fast?

He slowed as they left the room. The latch clicked behind them. He led her down the hall, this time at a pace she could manage without running. They passed the guards at the archway and turned down the stairs.

There were so many side halls. How would she ever learn her way around? How long would this take? Her heart sank as she glanced down another side hall.

Kienan cleared his throat, pulling her attention back. Marla looked up. He was already at the next intersection, arms crossed again. Marla walked over, her gaze down. She needed to focus and pay attention. How would he react if she didn't listen around others?

They approached a wide hallway. There were so many Light Chargers ahead. How could so many be in one place like that? Those headed for the double doors at the end all had someone like her following, each wearing clothing like hers, too.

He followed the others, moving beside an old man in Light Charger robes. "Good morning." Kienan bowed his head to the man.

"Morning. How's it settling in?" The man glanced at her. "Must be full of energy still to be so attentive."

Kienan nodded. "She's settling fine. This is her first meeting, so we'll see how it goes."

Marla wrinkled her nose as she stared at her feet. It? She glanced out the massive wall of windows as they neared the doors, her attention just on Kienan enough to stay with him.

"I find a few nights of being cold and hungry takes the fight from them."

Marla tightened her hands into fists.

Kienan chuckled. "We all have our own ways." He shrugged.

CHAPTER 21

They passed through the double doors. Marla snuck a look around. The walls were lined with shelves, though a few maps hung in frames protected with glass. Globes and tools sat on some shelves. She recognized one from a book on navigation. Another was a telescope. Many more she couldn't hope to identify, despite all her reading.

He walked right over to some padded chairs set in a circle near the middle of the room. Some men already sat. Some were older, with greying beards. Others were more middle-aged. Each had someone beside them. There was even a young man sitting on a cushion beside a chair.

Kienan stopped at a chair. He pointed at the cushion. "Sit here. Stay quiet. Don't fidget or draw attention to yourself." He raised a hand to her shoulder but stopped short. After a moment, he lowered his hand again.

Marla sat on the cushion, curling her legs up. How long would they be here? She snuck glances at the other people like her. All were older, even the young man. Most were more than a decade older, at least, or so it looked. They all sat with their hands folded in their lap. Nobody looked over at her. Nobody looked up at all.

The Light Chargers all moved to their chairs and greeted each other. Marla listened long enough to hear something about a project someone was overseeing, some kind of infrastructure in a region to the north. There was an unstable hill, and they had some kind of building at the bottom. Irrigation control? Yeah, she could see how that was important. Why put

216

it somewhere at risk, though? Wasn't it better to work with the land than fight it?

"I said at the time the site wasn't our best choice." An older man tapped his fingers against the arm of his chair.

"No, you wanted to put it somewhere inaccessible instead. We can stabilize the hill, and everything will be fine. Between magic and technology, we can make the current site safe. Now we just need to ship fertilizer in, so the crops don't die." Another man shifted in his chair, crossing one knee over the other.

What? Were they trying to grow food somewhere without enough water or nutrients? What madness were these people up to? Marla suppressed the urge to shake her head. Any farmer could list their mistakes. Some land was meant to be pasture, and other parts should remain wild. These people were running things?

"We have a few different options on how to stabilize it, depending on how fast we need to work, and how long we want the fix to last." Kienan briefly explained a few options, getting up and pacing as he listed benefits and drawbacks of each. "Those are only the most obvious solutions. There are others as well."

Marla plucked at the little fibres on her cushion. Was she really supposed to just sit here as long as these people made questionable decisions? She almost shook her head. No, the first chance she got, she was out of here.

She glanced at a woman across from her. This woman was older, more like her own mother. Her skin was so pale. Even her lips looked almost white. The woman didn't look back at her, not even once. How long ago had she been brought here? Did her Light Charger never leave the city?

"So, the plan is set. Draw up the designs with your team. I'll have maps and information sent to your room and workshop so you can get started. Good meeting, everyone." The oldest man stood. He wore a wide silver neck chain over his robes, with precious stones set in each segment. "I'll update the Chancellor. Be ready for the full council meeting later."

Most of the Light Chargers stood and left. Kienan sat quietly. Marla risked a glance up at him. He tapped his chin as he stared out the window. A few others stayed as well.

"Are you hunting for a new source?" One man stopped beside another and looked down at the older woman.

The seated man nodded. "I have to. This one is nearly spent. After over three decades, who can be surprised?" He patted the woman's head. "I'll be going out later today. I can't wait any longer. The instant I don't have extra energy to tap, my apprentice will challenge me. He's been pushing in small ways already."

Marla looked up at the nearest map on the wall. It was a fine line drawing of her entire country, though it had marks for something other than towns and cities on it. What was it for? Her fingers curled on her cushion as she fought the urge to get up and look closer. She couldn't read the legend from here.

"Still new, huh?" Another man stopped beside Marla.

She met his gaze for a long moment, staring defiantly at him. Kienan tapped her shoulder. Marla turned her gaze down and glared at her cushion.

"Not even a full day so far. It's our first trip from my rooms." His hand lightly rested on her shoulder.

Marla bit her lip as he squeezed her shoulder for a long moment. He let go. She closed her eyes. Hold that anger. Use it later, she reminded herself.

"I take them to the post first, so they can see what happens if they're disobedient."

Her skin crawled. He was still looking at her. He had to be.

"Jornir will be there in a few minutes, actually. Escape attempt again. Might be good for that one to see."

Marla risked a glance up at Kienan. He was frowning at her, his jaw tight. She stared at her knees. If they were willing to fight nature, what hope did her people have? Just another resource to be used and discarded.

Kienan stood. After a long moment, he cleared his throat. She got to her feet. How was she supposed to know when to follow, and when he was just going to pace or something? Her cheeks burned. She had to get out of here.

He strode from the room. Marla jogged to keep up, though her legs tingled from sitting for so long in one position. She stumbled as he turned down a smaller side hall, catching herself on the wall. He slowed for a moment.

A woman cried out in pain. Her voice echoed off the stone. Where was it coming from? She spun, looking around. The cry came again. With the echo, Marla couldn't find the source.

"No. Walk quietly." He gripped her arm, his fingers digging into her skin.

She winced and pulled away, a muffled cry escaping her lips. Huh, the first sound from her since the collar, and it was one of pain. Fitting.

"We're going back. You need to calm down, and the neckband needs more time to work." He pulled her close and held her gaze.

She glared back at him. It didn't matter anymore; he knew something was wrong. Her energy was stable, though sleep was never far away. Marla allowed her anger to fill her completely.

His eyes narrowed. "Maybe it's too early for you to be out at all." He pulled her down the hall.

She fought tears as he dragged her towards the stairs. Her shoulder was screaming at her from the angle he held her at, but she couldn't help it.

Marla tripped and her knees hit the stone. Blood dripped down her shins. He pulled her up and kept going, though slower now.

He opened the door and pulled her into their rooms, kicking it shut behind them with his foot. She staggered along beside him to her corner. Kienan dropped her on the padded bench. She fell back. Her elbow smacked the wall, sending shooting pain up her arm.

Kienan stood over her, frowning down at her. "Sit still. I'll get something to clean that." He nodded at her bloody knees.

Once he left the room, she looked at her arm. Little purple bruises were forming where he grabbed her, though the pain went deeper. Her elbow still tingled and stung where she hit the wall. Her knees ached. This was supposed to be her life now? No. She was leaving.

He came back from the bathroom with a bottle and cloth in his hands. Kienan walked over and kneeled in front of her. "Stay still." His voice had lost the hardness from before.

She watched him get the cloth damp with the smelly liquid. Those weren't herbs. What was in that bottle? It made her nose sting.

Kienan touched her scrape with the cloth. Marla hissed and jerked away. Stabbing pains worse than her elbow shot through her leg.

"Stay still," he snapped. Kienan grabbed her ankle and pulled her leg back. "I'll be done soon if you stay still. You don't want an infection."

She cried as he cleaned her scrapes, tears flowing down her cheeks unchecked. Her knees throbbed worse from whatever that was than from falling earlier. Each time he touched the cloth to the wound, she twitched and squeezed her eyes shut.

"Almost done. Breathe," he murmured. What, he was being kind again?

Marla whimpered into her blanket as she collapsed, her face pressing against the cloth. The sharp stinging stopped, but her knees still ached. A light wool blanket settled over her.

"Rest. You'll be tired. Take every moment you need to rest."

She rolled to face the wall. His footsteps moved away. Could she heal herself? Marla closed her eyes. How did she do this again? Right, slow breaths, and focus. Marla reached up and rested her hand on the windowsill, feeling the warmth of the sun on her. It didn't replace what she lost, but she could feel it mingle with what she had left.

Focusing on where she ached, Marla called her healing. As her energy moved in her and worked, the sunlight flowed in and kept her energy stable. Okay, it's slower than when she could draw right from the land, but her healing still worked. What other powers could she still use?

Her skin was still a raw dark pink over her scrapes, but no longer stung. The bruises faded a bit, and the ache stopped. Her elbow was recovering without her help, though she used a touch of power to prevent a bruise from forming.

Marla rolled onto her back and looked around. He was sitting in one of the padded reading chairs across the room. His feet were up on a stool, and he held a thick book open in his lap. His brow wrinkled slightly as he met her gaze. Could he feel her using her magic, if he could feel emotions?

She rolled back to the wall, pulling the blanket around herself fully. What did she know? She was on a higher floor and didn't know her way down. There were guards regularly spaced through some halls. Nobody in her kind of clothing walked alone here. The odds were against her.

Tears gathered in her eyes. She wept silently. Marla listened as he moved around, taking books from shelves or writing things down, sometimes working at his desk and other times he paced around the room.

Thirsty finally, Marla sat and filled her little cup. She sipped the cool water slowly. Yesterday he was kind, at least. Today, it was like he didn't care if he hurt her. Which was really him? Both? No, she refused to live in fear of what he would be like next. Marla touched her healing skin, still darker than her healthy skin.

Her stomach growled. Using her magic stirred her appetite. She looked at the little basket on her table. Crackers? Marla took the wrapped package and looked closer.

"You can snack any time you need. I'll make sure you always have something. They're full of energy and nutrition." He was speaking softly to her again.

She opened the container and pulled some crackers out. Marla nibbled on the corner of one. Nuts, dried fruits, and seeds were baked into a grain base she wasn't familiar with. Her stomach calmed as she ate. She took her time eating. It wasn't like she had anything else to do, after all.

Marla leaned back against the wall and looked up at the clock. Some markers moved a lot, while others hadn't moved nearly so much. The sun hadn't moved far across the sky, either. Had so little time passed?

Those bookshelves looked so inviting. Marla stared across the room at them. How mad would he be if she just went over and grabbed a book? Surely it would be better than dying of boredom? Air filled her lungs as she took a deep breath. Easing from the cushion, Marla walked across the room, passing him working at the desk.

He didn't say anything as she walked by. Marla went to the nearest shelves and scanned the titles. Science books. She grinned with delight. He had books here she'd never seen before, not even on lists passed around to everyone. Could she read them by moonlight when he wasn't looking?

Her hand passed lightly over the spines of books, stopping over one near the end of a shelf. Her breath hitched. Magic transference? Was it about the collars? It had a small symbol on the spine that looked like the band she wore. Dare she pull it out and look at it?

Fingers wrapped over her shoulder. Marla leapt back, her hands up in front of her. Her heart raced.

Kienan frowned. "I didn't mean to startle you. If you want to read, you may read any books from those shelves." He pointed to the shelves near the reading corner, where the comfortable chairs waited. Was she even allowed to sit there?

Taking a deep breath, Marla lowered her hands. Her energy swirled around inside her, pressing against the barrier of light, threatening to push through. A few more deep breaths and she settled, the swell of magic calming in her belly again. Was the magic restless, trapped inside her like this, or was something else going on?

Reading was better than not reading. Marla went to the shelves and browsed for a few moments. Ah, there it was. She pulled the book on wetlands from the shelf and wandered back to her cushion. No point poking the bear to see if she could use the chairs. At least he allowed her to read.

By the time she settled on her cushion, he was back at work, his stylus moving swiftly over the page. He glanced over at her, the book in her lap, and tapped his chin for a moment. Surely, he knows something is wrong now. What can he feel? Somehow, she must get that book. She'll read by moonlight if she must.

Wetlands weren't common near her village. The nearest one was past all the fields and deep in a forest. She'd only been there once. Marla delved into the information. Page after page, she soaked in the knowledge.

The sun beamed down on her as she read. The warmth soothed her muscles. She couldn't tap into it like before. The sun that hit her skin still helped her ease her tight muscles from all the sitting. The band kept trying to pull her energy out, but her shield held firm. The balance was fragile, and as she just learned, possibly temporary. No wonder the rescued were so drained. This was no way to live.

He gathered some pages and stacked them before sliding them into a folder. Kienan stood and went to his room, returning with a colourful cloth in his hands. It shone in the sunlight like her dress. Silk?

"I have an important meeting to attend now." He draped the sash over himself.

Marla looked up. Was he leaving her? Was this her chance to escape? Could she take the book with her? Imagine what her people could do with information on the bands, though. She had to try.

"When we are there, I expect you to sit or kneel quietly beside me again. Don't fuss or fidget. Wait patiently while we discuss things. Obey and I'll reward you. Cause a disturbance and you will be reprimanded. Understood?"

She raised her eyebrow and frowned. Was this her life now? Following him around and kneeling, like she didn't have better things to do? Marla flopped back on the cushion and sighed.

He walked over and stood over her, his hands on his hips. "That would be causing a scene. Get up. We're going." Kienan smoothed his sash as he went to the door.

Would it be worth resisting just to see what he'd do? She remembered those cries of pain in the hallway. No, he might do whatever that was to her. Besides, she might learn something useful in these meetings, something her people could use against the Light Chargers.

He scowled and took a few steps towards her. Marla eased to her feet and walked over to his side. She stared at her feet; her hands curled in loose fists. No, take a breath, she reminded herself.

Kienan touched the band around her neck. "You still have so much energy, even now?" He frowned at her again.

The floor almost sparkled in the sunshine where the beams hit the floor. She refused to look at him.

"I'll get a new band enchanted for you today. In the meantime, behave. I'd rather treat you well, but that's up to you." He took her arm in his hand and steered her out the door. "Come. We don't want to be late."

CHAPTER 22

Marla hustled down the hall beside him. The floor was cold and unyielding under her feet. There were windows at the end of the corridor, but they didn't look like they opened. She kept her gaze down as they went, though she noted every side hall and passage she could. How could she get past the guards, though?

He led her through another guarded archway into a wide hall. She looked up. Windows in the ceiling?

"Come," he said softly.

She shook herself from her thoughts and hustled to his side.

"It is grand, isn't it?" he whispered to her.

Marla nodded.

"Behave and we'll take our time going back. You can have a proper look around then."

She glanced up at him for a moment. The corners of his lips turned up in a slight smile. Marla suppressed the urge to rub her temples. One moment he threatens her, the next he acts all friendly?

Guards stood on either side of the massive double doors. He marched through without slowing. Her feet ached as she nearly jogged to keep up. These stone floors were unforgiving on bare feet.

She wasn't sure what she expected their meeting rooms to look like, but this wasn't it. Marla nearly stopped in the doorway, but she caught herself and pushed on. Hopefully, nobody noticed that. She followed him to another of those thickly padded plush chairs.

Everyone watched as she settled on her cushion beside his chair. Don't mess up, please, she reminded herself. Marla curled up and kept her gaze down, only looking around the room near floor level. Her breath hitched again. The chairs were scattered around the room, some at tables and others with small side tables instead. Each chair had a cushion, and all were occupied.

"She's doing well for one so new," an older man commented.

His hand rested on her shoulder. "She'll be an excellent companion, and for many decades, too."

Marla froze. Decades? No, she did not sign up for that.

Another man walked over, his shoes clicking on the stone floor. Marla closed her eyes and wrapped her arms around herself as he kneeled before her.

"Don't touch. She's still adapting." His hand tightened on her shoulder, gentle in its firmness this time.

"I wouldn't dream. She's strong, though. Which hunting ground did you find her in?"

"I didn't. I ran across her somewhere unexpected."

"Mark the spot. I'll send my trackers to investigate. There may be more like her out there."

"To business, now that we are all here. I call order," another man announced, his voice carrying across the room with ease.

Marla wrinkled her nose as the man left. The overly sweet smell of flowery perfume lingered around her. As much as she wanted to rub her burning nose, she didn't dare. With everyone's attention off her, Marla looked around the room instead, taking it in with momentary glances before looking down.

All the Light Chargers wore a sash like he did, though the colours varied. The people on the cushions, all women except that young man, they all had dark circles under their eyes except a few. Some she could barely see because of the tables in the way.

Like the other room, this one was lined with shelves full of books and tools. There were more maps on the walls as well. One near her showed the southern region, and even had a small dot where her town was, nestled in among the golden fields painted on the paper.

"The rainfall this year is inadequate again, and it looks like another lean year. I need solutions, people. If we can't help them, who will?" The older man with gold jewellery around his neck paced in front of some massive windows.

"Put a travel ban out between regions. Only allow our supply wagons to trade beyond regions. We can draw more food from the outer regions to feed the city, and nobody will know how widespread the issue is. City people will still have enough, and we'll prevent riots."

Marla looked over. A woman Light Charger? A younger woman sat beside her on the cushion, staring at the floor. She was so slender a light breeze might knock her over. The Light Charger wore the same robes as the men. Her hair was tied up and tucked in. At a distance, she could be mistaken for any of the others.

"That might work for a year, but we don't know how long the weather will be an issue. It's not the farmers doing anything wrong. We control the elements, but we don't control nature." The older man shook his head. "We need rain, and we need a lot of it."

"We can use our powers to blast irrigation ditches. Not only would that bring water right where it's needed, but we'd be visibly doing something."

The old man turned to the speaker. "That would take an unmeasurable amount of power. We barely have the resources to maintain the system as it is. Where do you propose we get the additional resources?" He looked right at Marla.

She dropped her gaze to the floor. Did they mean her people? No. No way. That was madness.

"No, wait. We just might use this to our advantage yet. Just think, if we build an irrigation system in one area and prove it works well, people might bring us their daughters instead of hiding them. It's for the greater good." The speaker gestured at the map. "The highborn already offer their daughters freely, but we've never been able to convince the lower classes to see how it benefits them. Maybe this is how we do it."

Marla's cheeks burned. She gripped her cushion right near her legs. Kienan's hand dropped to her shoulder, squeezing firmly but not hard or painfully. Marla took a breath and relaxed her hands. He moved his hand away again.

"This could be revolutionary for us," another man agreed. "The highborn only produce a couple a year for us, if any at all. It would consolidate our power if we prove we can solve all of society's problems, and all they have to do is give us a steady supply of power to tap into."

Kienan shifted in his chair. "For that to work, you'd have to prove you won't mistreat the resources, or drain them beyond recovery. The highborn give us their daughters because the girls are treated well and live in luxury, even as they serve us. If the lowborn are used and discarded, their families will eventually make trouble. It could take decades before they revolt, but what's the point if we don't think long term?"

The old man stroked his beard. "We'll test this on a small project, maybe one county. We can show the farmers how it will benefit them, and those girls will be treated like the highborn are. If that works, and more are brought in, we'll have to control public relations. Has anyone considered how it'll affect the balance of power inside these walls if more Light Chargers have access to their energy?"

The group fell silent. Wait, did that mean most Light Chargers didn't have someone like her to drain? She thought back to the hallways and all the Light Chargers who walked alone. Did only the most powerful get the captured? Only Light Chargers with gold trimmed robes had the captured with them. Did having someone like her affect someone's rank and status?

"This might be an opportunity there, too, though. We might gain their support by making resources more widely available. Access to that kind of power is out of most of their reach. If we control who gets the power, and how much, we still have the advantage. Right now, we hunt for resources. If they're brought for us and distributed among the lower ranks, we can keep the most powerful and pass down those who are almost drained, as well."

Marla balled her hands into fists and pressed them into her cushion. No. No way. She had to stop this somehow. How could she possibly prevent it? It might be easier to bring back the rain than stop them directly. She had to get free and tell Kria.

His hand gripped her shoulder and squeezed. Pain shot through her as a finger hit a tender spot. She shrunk back and curled up with her mouth open in a wordless cry. He let go immediately.

"On to more practical matters, then. If we're going to build irrigation ditches, how, where, and what do we need?"

Could she bring back the rain? She could touch nature, just like her people. If she got free and rejoined them, could they save both the crops and her people? Her legs cramped, but she remained still, her shoulder still aching.

What had Issa said about this? We used to work together until the two magic types split. There's an imbalance growing between us, and in nature. It's what's causing the drought. So, the Light Chargers are responsible?

Their solution will only make this imbalance worse. All they needed to do was stop using her people and work together instead.

Would they, though? Their entire way of life is built around status, prestige, and power. They want fine things and marble floors and comfort. Could she even prove they were the cause and somehow make them reconsider? How can she, when they stole her voice?

"That's it. We'll send a new team out under Drylor's command and get as many resources as we can. Kienan, before you go, I want you to mark anywhere you've even seen a hint of one, including where you got her. The country is a big place, and if they're hunting in new locations, anything to narrow it down will help." The older man gestured to a table by the wall.

Kienan nodded. "I'll work in my room when I'm done." He dropped his hand to her shoulder, but rested it lightly this time. "Sit quietly, eyes down, and wait. I'll only be a moment."

She remained in place, her fingers running along the hem of her dress. The stitches were fine and close together, almost too small to feel. She risked glancing towards the windows but couldn't see out from here.

A man walked close behind her, so close she could hear him breathe and smell his scent. She tensed. Should she move? Dare she not move?

Kienan looked over. "She's new. Don't interfere."

"I meant no offence. It's powerful. Where did you find it?" He stepped around her and walked over to the map.

I'm not a thing, she whispered in her mind. I don't belong to you. Not to anyone. Her fists tightened. Marla blinked back a tear. One day I'll tear this place to the ground. I promise, in the name of Wood Walkers everywhere. One day, we'll all be free.

Kienan stood in front of her, at the edge of her cushion. When did he come over? She looked up at him.

"Follow."

Marla suppressed her growl. If she didn't want to leave this room so bad, she'd make a fuss and destroy things. She shifted again and pins and needles sensations ran along her legs. Marla rubbed along her legs for a few moments. Instead of reprimanding her, he simply watched as she got to her feet on trembling legs.

She walked along beside him on her shaky legs. He walked slowly for her, not reacting when she grabbed his sleeve for balance for a moment. They strolled through the doors and out into the wide hallway. Once they turned a corner, he stopped at a bank of windows and stood, his hands lightly clasped behind his back.

Could she get used to this, the two sides of him? Marla ignored the fleeting question and looked out at the city, her hands braced against the windowsill. Buildings stretched as far as she could see. How would she ever find her way out? How could she hide in that mess?

"Come." His voice was soft and quiet. He turned and strolled down the hall.

Her legs had stopped aching already, so she matched his pace easily this time. Marla openly looked around, especially out the windows. A garden of sorts surrounded the building, but not the overgrown kind she was used to harvesting herbs from. It was grass and stone paths and some shrubs and such.

They turned another corner and walked down a hall. She stopped short at the next intersection. A woman lay on the floor below a stone pillar in one corner. The man in blue had her propped up against him and was holding a cup to her lips. Her eyes were partly closed. She didn't move. Her body lay limp against the man. Was she even breathing? Barely, but she was.

Kienan stopped for a moment. He nodded to the man in robes, who leaned against the wall with his arms crossed over his chest.

This man returned the nod before frowning down at the woman. He gestured at her. "Listen to him, or this could be you next."

Marla blinked up at this man, his face set in a deep scowl. What did they do to her? Marla couldn't see anything physically wrong with her, aside from her being almost dead. What had they done to her that wouldn't leave a mark like that?

The healer tilted the cup and a little liquid trickled into her mouth. "This one will need a month to recover, at least. You barely left her enough to survive on."

"Maybe she'll think about that next time, before she disobeys me." The man turned on his heel and marched off down a hall.

Kienan wrapped a hand around her arm and gently pulled Marla towards some stairs. She stumbled along behind before her brain caught up to the fact she was walking. The halls passed in a blur. Were they going to do something like that to her one day? What did the woman even do that was so horrible? Could she possibly have deserved that?

A door opened, and he led her through. Marla looked around, though she couldn't focus. Were they back? That was her cushion. Hers, but not really hers. When did they get back?

Kienan kneeled in front of her. He cradled her cheeks in his palms. "Look at me."

She blinked and tried to focus on him.

"No, really look at me. Try again."

The warmth of his hands pulled her attention from her thoughts. She looked up at his eyes, so close now. Different shades of brown looked back at her, a mix of golden honey and deep brown intermingled. His whiskers were just growing back in. This close, she could smell the light scent of the floral soap on his skin.

She opened her mouth. So many questions wanted to tumble out, but no sound made it. It stopped at that cold band, like it stole the very air from her lungs. Marla tried to glance at the door, but his hand stopped her.

"The most common punishment is to draw excess power from you until you don't have any energy to go against our wishes. We can store small amounts of it." He frowned. "If we pull too much, it'll only leak away. He only hurts himself by draining her that badly. The energy he gained will never last through her recovery. He'll be weak and vulnerable."

A tear rolled down her cheek and stopped at his fingers. Was he certain she'd recover? The only time Marla ever saw someone in that shape, a farmer had an accident, and his eyes looked like that before he stopped breathing.

Kienan stood and led her to her cushion. She curled up tightly on it. He draped her light blanket over her. His fingers brushed over her collar as he moved some strands of hair from her face. His brow furrowed, and he frowned.

Did he know? Could he sense the well of power inside her, rushing against the dam of light energy she made? Was he trying to draw power from her? Marla shuddered. Breathing was hard, as her chest muscles cramped. She pulled a slow breath in and let it out again. There, that was better.

"Rest. I'll have someone come and check on you."

Marla rolled to the wall. She had to get out of here. His desk chair scraped against the floor. A stylus scratched on the paper. His chair moved again, and his footsteps moved away. The door opened.

"Sir?" a quiet voice asked from just outside the room.

"Take this to Mannir."

"Yes, sir."

The door closed, and his footsteps approached again. Marla listened as he sat down and began writing again.

If she got away and they brought the rains back, would the Light Chargers abandon their plans? They wouldn't need to build such an extensive irrigation system if the rains were steady. Of course, that all depended on her getting away.

Was there another way to stop them? Marla sifted through everything she learned so far. The elite class willingly gave their children for this. Why, though? Did they know what was happening to them? Would anything change if they knew? A couple a year at most, if any, so it wasn't many. Still, she only saw so many of her people here. How quickly were they drained and discarded?

The knock on the door made her heart race. Marla gripped her blanket and pulled it tight around herself. Someone was coming here? Marla strained to listen as Kienan walked to the door.

"You requested my presence?" A light male voice came from just outside the door.

CHAPTER 23

"Yes, come in." Kienan stepped back, and the door closed. "I want you to check her band. I don't think it's working fully."

"Oh? Certainly, but what makes you think so?"

Their footsteps came closer. Marla curled up even tighter, her grip on the blanket making her fingers ache. Was this it for her?

"The transfer began normally enough. I felt the rush of energy. I can only pull a fraction of what I know she has, though. She also has more energy and curiosity than any others ever did at this stage." Kienan kneeled behind her, his robes rustling softly. He rested a hand on her side.

Marla twitched. She took a slow breath. If she acted quiet in front of this man, would he think she's more drained than she was?

Frigid fingers touched her neck. Marla flinched, fighting the urge to crawl away. Energy tingled around her neck.

"The band itself is working as it should. She seems docile enough. I can make a new band for her if you prefer, but it won't be ready until tomorrow."

Kienan's fingers briefly tightened on her side. "Do it. Is it possible she has so much energy the band can't handle it normally?"

"It's rare, but that has happened before. I can increase the flow capacity of the new one. You'll need to be careful about not draining her, though. I'll need to dig out the plans for the high-flow bands. Only a few have ever been made. Making a run for Chancellor?"

"No, I'd rather be out in the field working on projects. I'll be careful with her. If the new band works, will it calm her emotions?"

"It should. I'll get started. You have your own projects to work on as well. Perhaps resting here, away from the commotion downstairs, will also help. The calmer they stay when they settle, the faster the bands work. Adrenaline can also slow the transfer."

"It can?" His fingers twitched against her side again.

"Absolutely. You're young, and she's only your second. The calmer she stays, the faster she'll settle. Work here as much as you can, and only go to the workroom when you need. It'll help."

Cloth rustled as they moved away. The door opened and closed again. Adrenaline? Marla frowned. There's no way she could keep on heightened alert like that long enough to help, was there? It was bad for the body. No, time was passing. She needed to get out.

He came back, his boots making the soft clicking in the room's silence. He kneeled beside her, his hand resting on her shoulder. Kienan pulled her onto her back, rolling her until she looked up at him. "Is it scarier because you don't understand how the bands work, or what's happening, or because you don't know how much you can help people?"

Marla blinked rapidly. The tears rolled down her cheeks. She opened her mouth, but silence came out. She nodded. Her voice was as trapped as her magic.

He stood and walked over to the forbidden shelves. Kienan pulled a book beside the one on energy transference. This one was much thicker and larger. He brought it over and held it out for her.

"This book has true stories of partnerships like ours, and how they helped people around the country. Once your powers are stable and your band works properly, we can use our joined powers to do things few other mages can. You'll get to help me on all the projects I'm designing, things that'll help farmers all over the country. We can keep our workers safer, too. Wouldn't you like to help people like that?"

Marla sat up and took the book, her blanket still wrapped around her. She propped the book open on her knees. The first story had an ancient photograph of a man in white robes, with a man wearing a collar standing beside him. They were both smiling. She touched the image over the collared man's face. He looked so happy. What changed over the years?

Another knock on the door yanked her attention from the page.

"That's lunch. Sit. We'll set the book aside, and you can read it after." He stood and went to the door.

Marla flipped through the pages. Photos were newer and better quality later in the book until modern photographs graced the pages. That wasn't the only difference, though. She could point to the exact picture where the smiles stopped, and the kneeling began. She stopped at the last story. It was him. It was Kienan and the woman they rescued.

"Yes, the book is updated every few dozen cycles." He set her tray on the low table. "Here. Read when you're done." Kienan took the book from her lap and set it on the wide windowsill.

Marla nibbled on her lunch as she thought back to those early pictures. Were the relationships different back then, or were the collars? Her people were healthy and looked happy, despite being older. What changed? Were the answers in the book, or was it just stories told to make people happy and cooperative? Whatever changed, it happened about 150 annuals ago.

Kienan took her empty tray when she finished her meal. Marla snatched the book from the windowsill and opened it again. The introduction was all about how the partnerships benefitted everyone. Marla frowned.

Everyone was a stretch. The women she saw rescued, the woman on the floor here, none of them were better off.

She flipped to the first story. It had details about their lives, how they met, and how he willingly loaned his powers through the transfer band. They were childhood friends. She flipped a few more stories in, maybe a third of the way through, and looked at another story.

A special program had matched this pair. According to the book, she volunteered. She still stood with him, her arm linked with his, and she had a slight smile. Marla flipped to the last third, past whatever changed.

This time, the kneeling woman was listed as chosen. Chosen or hunted, though? It was maybe a hundred annuals ago, so she had no idea. The woman wasn't smiling, and she looked tired, even in the slightly grainy old picture.

There was another interesting difference, Marla noted. The types of projects the pairs tackled were different, too. Initially, it was a lot of smaller projects with other pairs. Now the lists were of grand public works, where one pair led the entire project. That had to be more draining for them. No wonder they looked so tired.

She flipped to the last story. His story. Marla read every detail. Who was this man she was stuck with? The woman looked as good in the picture as she did when they rescued her, and much better than most of the women for a good fifty years earlier. While she didn't smile, she did look at the camera.

Most of the others were involved with roadworks and grand stone construction, but Kienan specialized in water systems and aqueducts. It did say she was chosen, so that must be their code word for kidnapped. Marla closed the book and stared at the bookshelves opposite her. What was she to make of this?

Well, partnerships weren't always so one-sided. Could they share magic without a band? Ava must have a book on this topic. Her library included history books going back long before this book started, hundreds to thousands of annuals, maybe.

The smooth cover slid in her fingers and the heavy book landed on her shin. Marla winced and let out a gasp.

"Are you alright?" He was at her side in seconds, kneeling beside her.

Marla nodded. She rubbed her shin.

"I need to go to the workshop for a short while. You'll come with me. I'll be busy, but there's a cushion there for you to rest on. You can bring a book or read one there. All the books there are on public infrastructure, though."

She eased to her feet and wandered to the bookshelves. She found a book on wetland ecology and pulled it from the shelf. He had so many books on wetlands, a topic she never thought to read much about before. Kienan waited for her at the door. Once she was at his side, he held his hand out for the book. Marla passed it over and stood beside him.

He led her through quiet halls, down the opposite direction from the meeting rooms earlier. Some of these halls were barely wide enough to walk beside him. They went down one floor and through many smaller hallways.

Kienan stopped at a door halfway down a hall. She followed him inside and stood quietly as he closed the door again. Marla wrinkled her nose as she suppressed the urge to cough. A haze filled the room, coming from glass contraptions on desks. Each had a thin and flexible hose the workers sucked the smoke through as they drew on papers on their desks.

He took her across the room, to the far corner by the windows. One window right above her cushion was open, letting fresh air inside. He sat at the desk and gestured at the cushion. Once she was sitting, he gave her the book. Marla rubbed her nose. Down here below the window, the air was still thick and smoky. Her eyes watered as she opened the book. Her breaths were quick, and she coughed.

"Stay here. I need to check their work." Kienan stood and walked to the closest desk.

She curled up and pressed her head to the cold stone. Her stomach rolled and churned. Marla coughed again. The smoke tickled her throat, coating it. Tears streamed from her eyes as she coughed again. Whatever was in those, it was like breathing in a campfire with Connik powder mixed in, hot and spicy, and it burned.

"Coratar, take her to the balcony for some air." Kienan nodded to Marla.

A man in cream clothing moved from his place near the wall and walked over to her. He kneeled and took her arms in his hands, pulling her up. Marla leaned against him as she staggered towards the balcony doors. She gripped his arm. He opened the doors and guided her out into the fresh air.

Marla stretched her neck out and gulped in the clean air. Her lungs still burned in spots where the residue clung. She stepped to the stone railing and stared out at the city. Looking up over her shoulder, she could see the tower rising above her, reaching to the sky. Looking down, she was only a story above the grass. Not too high at all.

Coratar walked behind her, matching her slow pace as she wandered the balcony, leaving the smoky room behind. Each deep breath brought more energy back, clearing her lungs. Marla inched along towards the end.

The stone blocks were fitted tightly together. She'd never hold on. The ivy might do the trick, though. If she could make it to the very end, swing herself up and over, she had a chance. He wasn't far behind her, though. Marla would have to be quick.

Marla sprinted for the railing and pushed up over it. She grabbed for the ivy as she plunged down. Fingertips brushed against her back, sliding on the shiny fabric. The plants tore loose from their supports, but still clung with the tenacity of nature.

Her shoulders ached as she jolted to a stop. Her fingers slipped. Marla scrambled down, grabbing what she could as she fell. The air rushed from her lungs as she landed in the shrubs below. Marla gasped. The world around her lost focus for a moment.

"Stop." Kienan leaned over the railing, staring down at her.

Marla pressed herself up and took off down the stone path. How would she get over the wall? Her powers worked, at least a bit. What could she do fast before anyone caught up? She dodged between two small buildings and headed for the far corner.

No ivy, but there were trees inside. The branches were cut back until well above her reach, though. Still, they were trees. Could she touch them? Marla ran for a gigantic tree with wide-reaching branches. She called to it. Please, come down for me?

A massive branch lowered to her level. Marla leapt for it and shimmied up towards the trunk. She glanced back. Men in armour were racing towards her. She crawled faster, scraping her skin on the rough bark. The branch rose again, taking her with it.

A fireball whipped past her. She ducked and scrambled along the branch. Once she was close enough, she leapt to the wall.

"Don't. You'll hit the tree." Kienan grabbed another Light Charger's arm.

Marla scooted along the wall. There weren't any buildings or anything she could land on, just the wide street all along the wall. People were stopping and pointing. She gripped the edge of the wall and lowered herself as far as she could. Marla dropped and hit the stones.

Pain shot up her legs. Her ankles ached. She whimpered. Marla focused on her feet and healing them. The warmth flowed, though slower, with the collar on. The cracked bones mended.

"In here." A door opened just far enough for her to sneak through. A hand poked out and waved.

She darted across the street on unsteady legs. She'd need to fix those ligaments soon, but at least the cracks were gone. The arm pulled her inside, and the door closed behind her. She stood in the darkness. Where was she?

"That was brave, but foolish. Keep quiet." The hand released her, leaving her huddled by the door. "I'll be back when it's safe. Don't move. Don't speak. Mostly, don't answer the door or use your powers again." Fingers touched her collar. "What?"

The metal snapped, and the collar fell off. Marla wrapped her hands around her neck and felt the skin, an indent where the collar had been. Her skin was hot and sore.

Metal hinges creaked. Lantern light shone from within the cellar hatch. "In. You'll be safer underground." The man nodded to the stairs; his face half-illuminated by the distant light.

Marla scooted down the stairs, gripping the rope railing as she descended. Ava's warning echoed in her head. Stay underground. You're safer underground.

"Quiet now. I'll be back." The hatch closed above her. A metal latch clicked. She was alone.

She turned and looked around as she stepped onto the packed dirt floor. Stone walls surrounded her. Crates filled a corner, covered in dust. Shelves held jars of preserved foods, all labelled with a type of food and a date.

Marla walked to the wooden door opposite the stairs. It was solid and thick and old, but still sturdy. The metal latch held fast when she tried to turn it. It was warm, though, and a rune glowed on the door when she touched the latch. Wait, she knew that rune. Was he like Dornir, one of her people, or just one of their allies?

She touched the rune with her fingertips. A dark light flared under her hand, like normal light, but tinged with a deep purple. The lantern went out, plunging the room into darkness. Only the purple glow let her see at all. The latch clicked.

This time, the handle turned easily. Marla pushed the door open. She reached out and touched the tunnel walls. Timber beams supported the walls and ceiling. The tunnel was wide enough for her to stretch her arms nearly out. She stepped inside and closed the door.

Tiny balls of light formed as the door shut, illuminating the path. The soft light reflected on some moss, which glowed on the timber beams. Wait, that was the moss from the sacred sites. The tiny balls of light hovered around her, like little fireflies dancing over her head.

She set off down the tunnel, following it as it curved around. Sometimes it turned a corner and changed direction. The lights led her on, showing her the way. Now and then, the ceiling vibrated, like a heavy wagon rolled overhead or something. Dirt shook loose and floated down, coating her in a fine dust. Marla waved the dust from her face and kept going.

Opening her powers, she felt above her. Yes, it was a street, with flat stones over her head. She could feel the vibrations of footsteps and wagon wheels. She pulled her powers back and kept going.

Side tunnels now branched from the wider one she walked, each darker and narrower than the last. Where was she even going? Who made the tunnels and when? They all had the same supports as the hideouts and sanctuaries. It must be her people.

Following the pull of her city, Marla kept walking. The lights kept her company, never veering from the straight path. The tunnel began rising. The lights changed, glowing brighter and moving faster. Marla sped up, almost jogging now. The tunnel seemed to go on forever. How long had she been running?

The tunnel stopped at a ladder. Light flowed in through small gaps in the boards above her. Marla climbed the ladder and pressed up. Was it latched? If so, this was all for nothing.

"Get it open. Be ready." A muffled voice spoke above her, on the other side of the wooden hatch. Light Chargers? Her people?

Wood scraped against wood. More light flowed in. Old hinges creaked as the hatch lifted, swinging back over her head. She blinked up at the faces peering down at her, the light behind them blinding her.

CHAPTER 24

Hands reached down and took hers. They pulled her from the ladder and up onto the soft soil. Arms wrapped around her as she blinked. Trees surrounded her.

"Marla, you're okay." Issa crushed the girl in a tight hug.

"We were planning a rescue. How did you get away?" Adris rested a hand on Marla's head. "Let the girl breathe, Issa."

Issa relaxed her hug but didn't let go. Marla leaned against her, soaking in the warmth. She squinted against the sun, her eyes still adapted to the dim tunnel. Trees. She made it to the edge of the forest.

Tialla kneeled in front of Marla. She pressed her palms to Marla's cheeks. Warmth flowed into her, soothing her aches. "You're in better shape than most, especially mentally. Even after a day." She leaned forward and kissed Marla's forehead.

Kria stood over her, her arms crossed over her chest. "Can you tell me anything about those who remain? Who still needs to be rescued and where they are?"

Marla looked up at Kria, her head against Issa's shoulder. "I learned some. Maybe not enough, but I'll share what I can."

Kria nodded. "First, we get you back. The final ceremony is in two days, and we need you at your full strength. If we get this done, the rains will be restored. If we get this done, nobody goes hungry this winter. I'm not missing another year. Let's make it happen."

Marla met Issa's gaze and raised her eyebrow.

"We need people with the right blend of powers for the ceremony. Those we've already rescued are recovered enough to help, so as long as you're feeling up to it, this could be it. The first year in a while we can do the ceremony right." Issa hugged her firmly again.

"I'll do what I can." Marla hugged her back.

"I know." Issa relaxed her hug and helped Marla up.

Marla gripped Kria's sleeve. "They're planning something. I was in some meetings with the council and such. They're planning a massive project."

Kria shared a dark look with Tialla. Her eyes narrowed. "Tell me everything you can. Talk as we go back. We arranged a ride. It's waiting at the nearest safe house."

"How about some proper clothing first?" Adris held a bag up. "There's even boots in there for you."

She grinned. "That would be so great. Now that I'm not running, I'm cold."

Adris held a cloak up for her while Issa helped her change. Once she was done, Marla wrapped the warm wool cloak around herself.

Dornir jogged through the trees and stopped beside them. "Everything's ready. Oh, hey, it's great to see you. Can you walk, or do you need help?"

"I can make it." Marla coughed.

Tialla held her hands out. Marla slipped her hands over the old woman's. Her lungs cleared and she could breathe fully again.

"I don't know why they insist on using that brain-addling stuff," Tialla muttered. "It's addictive and horrible for you."

"That's exactly it," Dornir muttered. "The workers only get it while they're actively working, so they always go back, no matter what." He shook his head and smiled at Marla. "I don't know anyone who has ever escaped on their own before, especially not from the city like this."

Issa hugged Marla to her side and steered her through the trees. Dornir stayed close on her other side.

"I did learn more about the collars. My powers saved me." She explained all about the collar fastening around her neck, and how her powers reacted as they led her through the forest.

Lights in the distance flickered. The safe house? Marla smiled. It had to be. Her body was too weak to run again so soon. Even walking took everything she had.

"Yes, that's our ride home. You can sleep on the way. We'll take turns driving so we don't have to stop." Dornir gripped her shoulder lightly.

Marla tensed. Her heart raced. No, his touch wasn't a threat. He pulled his hand away and furrowed his brow. She took a slow breath and let it out. She was safe. He would never hurt her. Issa rubbed her back and Marla settled.

They walked towards a cabin. Kria headed for the cabin door, while Issa steered her towards the large shed or barn beside it. They rounded the corner. A snort greeted them. Two huge horses stood harnessed to a wagon full of crates, their heads down as they snuffled through piles of hay.

Dornir shifted a couple of crates at the back, revealing a large hiding space inside. With a boost from Adris, Marla scrambled in, crawling over the thick blankets spread out. She curled up in a front corner on another blanket. Issa, Adris, and Tialla joined her in the hiding space. The crates shifted back into place.

Tialla held her hand up and power surged around them. Barriers. Marla felt the warmth as the magic enclosed them fully. She really was safe. Maybe she just might make it back after all.

"Sleep. You've been through a lot." Issa draped a blanket over her and tucked it in.

Marla let sleep take her as the wagon started to roll.

***

She glanced over her shoulder at the waterfall. The city had been her refuge for a couple of days, a place she could rest and recover. After a long sleep and an enormous meal, Marla spent her time learning to tap into and charge the lines of power with Issa and Kria's help.

There was a second cave beside the sacred pool. Inside, several small lines of power joined and flowed to a larger line. They tended and charged it daily, and Marla learned how to help. With the practice she got there, she could call energy with ease now.

Marla focused on the forest ahead of her. Outside the city's magic, she wasn't safe. She stuffed her trembling hand in her pocket. How could she leave so soon? What if he was looking for her? Didn't he say he marked her somehow? Could he track her through it?

"Are you alright?" Kria linked arms with her. "I know you haven't fully healed mentally, or even begun to process what you went through. Issa told me about the nightmares. Once we're back, we have until next spring to heal it all. I'm sorry."

Marla shook her head. "No, I get it. I want things fixed, too. I can feel the changes in the power now. I know how important recharging our connection to the lines is."

"You are our most promising channeler in many annuals. Still, you could have stayed if you needed to." Issa stared at her boots as she walked.

"I have to do something. I can't just sit while things get worse. Besides," her voice shook, "I couldn't wander around and move freely in his city. I need to walk for a while. Feeling confined like that—I don't even know how to explain it."

"I think I know." Issa took her hand and squeezed lightly.

Marla walked between them in silence for a while, lost in her thoughts. Tialla and Dornir were on lookout duty, and she needed time to think. Issa and Kria probably had no idea her window was open a crack when they talked in the garden. They debated so long whether she should come that Marla fell asleep part way through.

"Will he come back?" Marla peered through the trees.

Kria nodded. "Probably. He found you here before. That's why we're heading to the nearest village to catch a ride. We're going a completely different route."

Dornir had led them more east this time. Maybe she would be safe. Where was she supposed to belong if the forest no longer felt safe? Did she have a place anymore? Is this what being adrift in an ocean feels like? Someone described it in a book once. She couldn't imagine the feeling at the time, but now?

The village was small, with only a few buildings and houses, but everyone smiled and greeted them. A sturdy pair of horses stood hitched to a cart packed with scientific equipment. Marla looked around at her group, all dressed in outdoor work clothing again. No hiding among crates this time.

"Come sit with us." Adris tossed their pack up in the back and leapt up into the cart. "The lead scientist sits with the driver."

Issa tossed her pack to Adris before walking up to the front. Marla leapt up and joined Adris on a side-facing bench. The wood was smooth from years of use and a fresh coat of paint. She looked around at the small village as the others joined them in the back.

"Everyone ready?" The driver heaved herself up onto the seat in front.

Issa looked back at the group, all settled on benches already. "We are." She smiled at Marla.

The woman picked up the reins, and the horses set off. They walked to the road, weaving through the small houses and fenced yards full of chickens. Once they were on the road and the village was behind, the horses picked up a trot. Marla watched the land roll by, travelling faster than she had yet.

"We can use these for travel when speed matters, but we have to be careful. Most science teams won't want the expense, though a few sure can." Adris gestured at the equipment packed in around them, in crates of straw or lashed to the frame of the wagon.

"Is it safe?" Marla gripped the side of the wagon.

"It's safe. You can gallop with these wagons, though it's better not to. The horses do better when travelling slower." Dornir grinned as he leaned back, his arms along the sides of the wagon.

"Boys and their love of speed and danger." Tialla smiled and shook her head. "It's a wonder any of you live to grow up."

"We're going to pass some of them soon. Stay calm. Keep talking to Adris. You can keep your head down and pull your hood up, but don't look like you're trying to hide." Dornir flicked his fingers towards the road ahead.

Marla glanced over Issa's shoulder. She saw a small group ahead, at least a couple on horses, and all wore white or cream. She turned back and stared at the wagon floor. So soon?

"Here, check this map out with me." Adris unfolded a map across their laps.

Marla took a side and helped stretch it out. Adris pointed out some markings on the map, explaining what some of them were. Wait, she recognized this area. An incredibly similar map was on the table in Kienan's rooms. He had a site marked on it where a project was being surveyed. No wonder he was nearby when she met him. Would he come back so soon?

They passed the men on horses and their servants. Marla kept her head down and focused on the map. She didn't see anyone with a collar, though. She resisted the urge to touch her own neck. At least her skin was healthy again, the red mark and indent gone.

"See, just like that." Dornir grinned at her. "Yes, we got that map from our source inside their council building. If we're on an official project, they're less likely to hold us long if we're stopped."

Marla let out a breath and dropped her head into her hands. Adris rubbed her back until the trembling eased. Once her hands were steady again, she turned back to the map.

Time passed, and she scrutinized the map. They folded it up and ate in the back, not stopping for a moment. Another group of Light Chargers passed them without incident. Adris kept her busy and calm, showing her one of the tools. They even passed another survey team, though this group was on foot with their gear on their backs.

"We'll arrive at sundown." Kria looked up at the sky. "We can charge the site before we rest for the night."

The cart stopped at another town. A survey team waited at the stop.

Dornir leapt down and helped Marla from the wagon. "It's how we caught a ride. The wagon was coming anyway," he whispered. "We were lucky."

Adris tossed Marla her pack. They handed Issa's down as well, before jumping off.

"They're here," Tialla muttered. "Not in town. They're in the forest. We'll have to slip past them if we want to get there tonight."

Kria scowled. "It'll be more powerful tonight. Why did they have to pick today?" She shook her head.

Adris rested a hand on her shoulder. "We can do this. The farmers need us."

She slung her arms through the straps and pulled her pack up. Adris helped her snug up the straps before adjusting their own pack. Marla pulled her hood lower over her head, blocking the setting sun from blinding her. The forest was close, just past a couple of fields. Close and thick.

Marla relaxed as she walked among the trees, even as she glanced around, watchful. The long shadows stretched, reaching deep among the trees. Birds sang and followed as they walked. Power built under her feet. Energy flowed along a line right nearby, leaking out into every living thing around, including her. It filled her completely and hummed with her heartbeat.

Tialla pointed off to one side. Marla strained to listen. A horse stomped their hoof. Her heart sped. Was it him? If it was, he wasn't looking for her. He was working, she reminded herself.

Kria pointed to Dornir and Adris before pointing off into the forest. They slipped away, heading towards the sound. Tialla and Issa moved closer to her. They kept their steady pace, following the power under their feet.

Could she use it? Marla opened herself and invited it up. Her legs tingled as the power flowed through her, rising to circulate around her. Sounds sharpened. The breeze caressed her skin, slight though it was. The smell of damp soil reached her from somewhere ahead.

There, the horse was ahead and to the right. It felt like a deer, but bigger and calmer. Just a hint of an animal in the wider forest around her. What was that, though? Marla turned. Tialla turned with her. The old woman raised her hands.

The bushes shook. A man in a white robe stepped out from between them. He stopped and stared; his mouth open.

253

Marla froze. She felt him. She actually felt him. Tialla snapped her fingers, and a branch dropped on the man, smacking him on the head. Issa grabbed Marla's hand and hauled her through the bushes. She stumbled along behind, scrambling to find her footing. The others ran behind her.

They dashed through the forest. Bushes parted for them. Marla charged forward, following Issa. The power grew stronger beneath her feet. They were almost there. What about Dornir and Adris? She didn't dare look back.

She sprinted into the dark among the thickening bushes. There, a cave entrance. Feeling it more than seeing it, Marla plunged into the shadows. Bushes rustled and rattled far behind them. They rushed through without looking back.

Kria touched the cave wall, and the entrance shimmered. "Only those with a high enough level of our magic can come in now." She leaned against the rock.

Marla braced her hands on her knees. "Can they—?" She nodded back at the opening.

"Maybe a few, but not all. Most won't." Kria shrugged. "We don't have much choice."

"The others?" Marla stared into the forest, the full moon beaming down among the trees.

"We give them time. Tialla, let me know if the Light Chargers gather and leave. As long as they stay, we know Dornir and Adris are free." Kria was almost whispering as she walked deeper into the cave.

Beams of light flowed through holes in the rocky ceiling. It was almost a canyon, but not quite, the rock closing over them in part. In the moonlight, she clearly saw the stone path leading around the corner where the tunnel turned ahead.

"They're coming." Tialla stopped. "Adris and Dornir." She leaned against the rock; her arms folded over her chest.

Marla heard the panting first, followed by the footsteps as they jogged over the rock. They emerged from the dark and into a moonbeam, breathing hard. Marla pressed her hand against the solid rock wall. She opened herself to the solid rock. Could she borrow that steadiness?

"There's four of them. Two have horses. We didn't see Marla's captor. We got them scattered, but they gathered to treat a man bleeding from a head wound. None followed that we could tell." Dornir sucked in a deep breath.

Adris squared their shoulders and straightened up. "Let's do this."

Marla walked with them along the stone path, the glowing moss between slabs softening the path under her feet. The path turned and widened. She stopped and gasped. A vast ring of stone, big enough to walk through, stood before the point of power.

"Are you ready?" Kria gestured along the path leading to the standing stones.

Trees formed a ring around the site. Trees down here? Marla nodded. Kria led the way. She followed with Issa. The others came behind, with Tialla guarding their backs. Did the order matter? They didn't cover that in practice, but the group seemed to just fall into place.

Marla walked beside Issa, brushing her fingers over the mossy rock as she passed. Her body pulsed with the power below her. It welled up through her feet and coursed through her veins.

Everyone stopped around the ring, each in their own spot. Kria walked to the middle and stood before the tallest stone pillar. The circle was wide, far larger than any other she'd been to. How did the cavern ceiling stay up, with such a wide span to cover?

Issa pointed to a spot between her and Adris. "Here. We'll guide you. It's just like in practice."

Marla nodded and took her place, feeling for the strongest energy under her feet. This was it. The last point of power. If they managed this, the rains should return. Life will go back to normal, whatever that is.

Arms wrapped around her, yanking her back from the circle. Air rushed from her lungs. Marla gasped, but the air wouldn't pull in. Her arms were pinned. A hand around her wrists held her still. Flashes of light filled the cavern like lightning. Her friends were too far away. She wriggled, lashing out. Her power flared, pulling more from the soil.

Something cold brushed against her neck. No! She writhed and fought. The metal slipped away. He cursed. He crushed her against his side and under his arm as he wrapped his hand around her neck. The metal touched her neck again.

Calling to the soil, Marla softened the ground beneath her. The metal pulled around and up. She gasped for breath as she called to the trees, the wooden sentries circling the point of power. Roots shifted under her, reaching up. Did she have enough time?

The collar snapped closed around her neck. A blinding flash of light dimmed her vision. Not again. Not ever. Marla screamed, pulling a surge of power up through herself. She released it all at once, sending a shockwave up, mixing her creative and destructive magics. The ground rumbled. The collar burst off her, shards flying away from her.

Marla stepped onto the circle, the power giving her strength. She closed her eyes and raised her hands. Tree roots rose from the soil and stretched over the ground. Power burst up to the sky, shooting through the gaps in the rock and heading for the stars.

The standing stones glowed a brilliant green. The trees went still, coursing with energy, waiting for her instructions. Marla collapsed, landing on her knees.

Issa ran over and dropped to her side. She looked Marla over, her power soothing as it flowed through Marla.

The ceiling shook and rumbled.

"Get out. Now." Kria grabbed Marla's arm and hauled her to her feet.

CHAPTER 25

I ssa slung an arm around her and dragged Marla to the tunnel. Dornir grabbed the Light Charger and threw him over his shoulders. Adris steadied the man as Dornir ran.

Kria and Tialla charged for the entrance. They stood, hands outstretched, raised to the ceiling. Marla sensed their power flowing up and along the rock. Issa pulled her past them, deeper into the tunnel. Dornir and Adris rushed behind them. They didn't stop until the cave entrance, staying in the deep shadows just outside.

"They're not too close, but they are here," Issa whispered. "Get him away before you drop him somewhere. They'll find him."

Dornir and Adris snuck into the bushes. Branches shifted for him, easing his way. They disappeared among the trees, the white robe like a beacon in the dark night going dark behind the leaves.

Issa cradled Marla's cheek in her hand. "How are you doing? What happened?" She slid Marla down against the rock wall and kneeled before her.

"Where did he even come from? I didn't think they could come in." A tear rolled down Marla's cheek. "He was just there. I got so scared and angry. My magic flared and went crazy. It was like nature was mad, too. It helped, or something. When both my magics hit the collar, it burst." Marla pressed a hand to her neck.

"He might have got in before the barrier went up. They're not at full strength yet. He also might have some creation magic in him, like you have destruction." Kria kneeled beside her. "Can you stand?"

Marla nodded. "Did we do it?"

Tialla shook her head. "Partly. The energy is there. We didn't complete the ritual, though. A team needs to come and stabilize the cave before we can try again."

"We need to get to the safe house. Come." Kria stood and headed into the forest.

Marla pushed herself up. Her body felt like the ground during a quake. She could do this. Safety wasn't far away. Issa offered her an arm and Marla hung on. She could make it. They passed through the bushes, the leaves strangely silent as they moved through.

Tialla stopped them at the edge of the thickest bushes. "They're just over there. Dornir's past them already, coming back. If we go this way, we might avoid them entirely." She pointed to the thicker bushes nearby.

"Lead the way." Kria nodded.

The old woman weaved her way among the bushes, leading them through the deep shadows. Leaves brushed against Marla as she followed, a warm touch on her chilled skin. Tiny bursts of energy sparked through her with each touch. What happened back in the cave, when the energy burst forth from her?

"They're coming," Tialla whispered. "We'll have to hide."

Kria spun, facing Marla. "If they get close, don't run unless it's your last choice. Hide first. The magic is potent here. It'll help you, not them."

Marla nodded. She pressed her hands to her cheeks.

"They're circling around. Get her out if you can. I'll handle this." Tialla cracked her knuckles.

"Are you sure?" Issa grabbed her wrist.

"My time is short. She's powerful. She can do a lot of good, but only if she gets away. I'll give her that chance." Tialla straightened her cloak.

"No heroics. Slow them down and get out." Kria kneeled and pressed her hand to the ground. "Move now."

Issa dragged Marla through the trees. She scrambled along, using Issa's hand for balance. They left the thickest bushes behind and sprinted across the mossy ground. The others were close, just out of sight.

Something flashed behind her. Trees creaked and branches snapped. Was Tialla alright? Another flash showed a shadow broken by the trees, but recognizable as a woman with her hand up.

"Where's Kria?" Marla burst back into thick bushes behind Issa.

"Helping. Keep going. We're ahead of them now."

They charged around, turning left, circling back towards the road. Marla spun at the sound of hoofbeats. A horse charged after them.

"Hide." Issa pulled Marla down.

She ducked and rolled under a massive log, tucking into a space barely big enough to fit. Issa was somewhere nearby, she could still feel her, but Marla couldn't see through the deep shadows. Branches shifted, dropping leaves in front of her.

The horse charged past, turning to circle around again. Marla peeked out between the leaves. She didn't recognize him, but it was so hard to tell in tiny glimpses. She huddled down and waited. He spun in place once before taking off again, heading towards the road.

Adris crept up and poked their hand into her hiding place, grasping hers. They tugged. Marla wriggled out and crouched beside them. Adris held a finger to their lips. Marla nodded.

Issa emerged from the shadows nearby. They set off towards the road, taking as direct a path as they could. Surely, they wouldn't walk along a road in the moonlight, though? Marla shrugged and followed.

Dornir slipped from the shadows and fell into step beside her. He smiled, though a trickle of blood dripped down his cheek.

They snuck along, listening closely. Something crashed in the bushes to their left. It didn't sound close. Marla sighed and smiled as Tialla joined the group, stepping from bushes to walk beside Kria. Marla glanced between Tialla and the distant sounds of men struggling in the thick forest.

"They're chasing shadows. We'll teach you soon." Tialla winked at her. She slipped away again, lost in the darkness.

Hoofbeats came from ahead of them. Marla glanced at Kria. Was it time to run or hide? Kria raised her hand, and the group scattered.

"Run, Marla. Go." Tialla appeared behind her and shoved her shoulder towards the thicker bushes.

Marla sprawled on the ground. She scrambled to her feet and scurried into the bushes. Please, forest. Help me now. I can't do this on my own. She pelted into the trees, stumbling as she dodged and weaved.

A bright flash of light behind her illuminated the forest. Gold light met it and sparks shot past her. Marla tumbled to the moss and rolled, tucking under a fallen tree. Footsteps pounded behind her, the heavy boots of the Light Chargers, and more hoofbeats from another side. The sounds got closer, and Marla could feel the vibrations through the ground.

Another streak of white light flashed. Tialla hit the ground. She rolled and faced the boots. Marla could barely see, pressed low like she was.

"Where is the girl?" That voice. Kienan. Wait, though. He wasn't commanding. He sounded worried. Was he worried about her?

Marla pressed a hand to her mouth.

"What girl?" Tialla struggled to her feet.

"Do you think we're stupid? Where is she? The others?" Another rough male voice shouted at Tialla this time.

Tialla remained silent. Marla could only see her boots and the hem of her dress now. The shadows grew around her as Tialla's magic flowed.

"You are strong. You will make an excellent resource. Take her," the rough voice commanded.

"I don't think so." Light burst from Tialla, gold and green, turning to blues and reds and every colour imaginable.

"Stop her!"

"How, sir?" Boots rushed forward, the cream boots of a servant. They circled the swirling mass of lights that engulfed Tialla.

Marla stared between the leaves. Tialla shimmered. She dissolved into light, dissipating and floating up towards the sky. What? Where'd she go? Some of the light rained down and soaked into the leaves and soil around her. A tiny ball rolled into Marla's hiding place.

She touched the tiny ball of light. It sank into her fingertip. Warmth flowed through her as the light faded. Marla pulled her hand tight to her chest, her fingertip pressed to her heart. She closed her eyes.

"Find the girl," a man shouted.

"Don't hurt her. She's mine." Kienan's voice shook.

Marla took slow breaths, making them as steady as she could. Something covered her like a blanket, some power she knew, but couldn't explain. She remained still as the feet all scattered. Dare she move? What about Tialla? Where did she go?

The footsteps all faded away, except for one set of boots. Someone crouched where Tialla had been. His hand touched the soil. Kienan. After a long moment, he stood and led his horse away.

Her chest was tight. Marla lay frozen, barely breathing. The hoofbeats had gone. Where were the others? Tears streamed down her cheeks. She pressed a hand over her heart. Tialla was gone. Somehow, she just knew it. That little light was a goodbye, a hug made of energy. She lay quietly in the dark, her hand over her heart.

"Marla, come out," Issa whispered. She was close. Her boots passed in front of Marla's hiding place. "They're gone."

She rolled out and lay on the grass, her gaze up at the sky. "She's gone."

"I know." Issa sat beside her and pulled Marla up for a hug.

"Where'd she go?" Tears kept flowing, dripping onto her clothing.

"She gave herself back to the forest. Her energy and life force returned to nature, as we all will one day." Issa rubbed her back.

"She's gone for good?"

"You'll be with her again when you return to the forest as well. There is no permanent gone for us, though you won't see her again in your lifetime." She hugged Marla tightly.

Kria walked over and kneeled. "She wanted you to have a full life and reach your potential. Why don't we find cover, so you have that chance? They're still looking for us."

Marla let them pull her to her feet. She took Issa's offered hand. "Why do they hate us so much?"

"We have a power they can't control on their own. Destruction is powerful, but it's violent and often explosive. Our power is quiet, and they can't always tell when we're using it. We can help bring new life into being. We can build a new and better world." Kria stopped and listened. "They don't understand us."

Marla and Issa stopped and waited. She couldn't hear anything and didn't have the heart to tap into the power under her yet. After a long moment, Kria nodded. They kept walking.

"Why can't they at least leave us alone?" Marla whispered.

"They need us, like we need them." Issa squeezed her hand lightly.

Marla stumbled. "Wait, we need them?"

Issa nodded. "Some types of forests need fire to regrow. When we die, we return to the soil and plants thrive around us. How full would the world be if everything ever created kept living forever?"

She rubbed her cheek. That never occurred to her before. "They need us because destruction without new life is empty and cold."

Kria smiled. "That's right."

"But the women we rescued. They were cold and empty inside. They were being used, and not as a partner." Marla thought back to those early stories in the book, and the picture of the smiling men and women.

"Yes, when they steal our powers, the balance is altered. If it shifts far enough, the weather can shift. You aren't old enough to remember the last famine. Since then, we've made rescues a priority." Issa squeezed her hand again.

"We no longer work together, but we still have stories about what it was like." Kria frowned deeply. "We still remember. One of our duties is to balance out their power and keep nature strong. We're so busy doing that, we can't always focus on growing the way we used to."

Adris popped up from the bushes and gave Kria a hand signal. Kria nodded. She led them deeper into the shadows, shifting their path to the right.

Marla heard distant movement in the brush, the Light Chargers, most likely. The sounds faded.

They stopped at some overgrown brush. Kria moved it aside, revealing a wooden hatch still covered in moss and soil. She pulled on the ring, swinging it up and open. A dim light glowed inside, just strong enough to show the ladder. Issa went first, swinging herself down with ease. Marla followed.

The rungs were smooth. Soil from Issa's boots clung to the rungs, brushing off on Marla's fingers. She made it to the bottom and stepped back, looking up as Kria followed. Adris was just past her, closing the hatch as they stepped down a few rungs.

Light glowed from down the tunnel, strong and golden. Issa led her on, heading for the light. A lantern hung beside a wooden door. She pushed it open and stepped aside, waving for Marla to go first.

"You made it." Dornir grinned at her. He stood at a counter, pouring steaming tea into mugs. "Sit. Rest."

Marla wandered to the rough-cut table and collapsed into a chair. She pulled the blanket on it around herself and huddled in place. Dornir set a mug in front of her.

"Thanks." She cradled the mug in her hands, the warmth seeping through to her.

He kneeled beside her and rested a hand on her knee. "You should get some rest. A lot has happened, and you need time to settle. We can't go back right away."

She nodded. Words wouldn't come. Tears flowed again, just as she thought she was cried out completely. Tialla was gone. Marla looked at her fingertip. Not gone completely. A tiny warmth still hid inside her somewhere, nestled in near her heart now.

Tialla would be alive if it weren't for her. Was it her fault? She got away, and that's what Tialla wanted. Why did Marla deserve to live when Tialla was gone, though? She clenched her jaw.

It was all those Light Chargers. How could she hope to stop them, though? What chance could she have against people who were bigger, stronger, and better trained? People who would steal power from others to get what they wanted?

This was all too big for her. She couldn't do this. Not alone. But if she didn't help, if she didn't try, who would? What would happen to the next group of kids, the newly awakened and scared, just like she had been? If she didn't try, would things ever change?

Marla touched her fingertip. A tiny glow spread for the briefest moment, gone again when she blinked. No, she needed to help. Even if it was hopeless, even if they failed, she couldn't sit by and do nothing. Tialla protected her because she believed in her. What did she believe in, that she would give her own life for?

Her fingers clenched around the mug. If she could help, even a little, she had to try. If her people worked together, maybe they could succeed. The land was in trouble, though it was already recovering. Maybe she was enough? Maybe together they could do it?

She sipped the hot and sweet drink. Apples and spice mixed on her tongue. She inhaled deeply. At least she could rest first. She could feel the energy of nature all around her, stronger than ever before. Whatever happened at the standing stones, she got the power moving. Her body felt drained, heavy, and her eyelids wanted to drop closed, worse than when wearing a collar. Marla drained her mug.

"Sleep." Kria nodded to a stack of bedrolls in the corner.

Marla stood, taking the blanket with her. She shuffled to the corner and dropped to a bedroll Adris had rolled out for her. Burrowing under the covers, Marla closed her eyes.

***

She turned her face to the sunlight. Her heart still ached from yesterday and her legs hadn't rested. Still, it felt good to be up and moving. The settlement wasn't far. Kria mentioned messenger birds. They could call for help there.

Marla pressed her thumb to her fingertip. Her skin was warmer than it should be. She tilted her head and stared off into the bushes. Marla closed her eyes and felt for it, whatever it was.

"What's up?" Issa whispered. "You feel him, don't you?"

"Him?"

Issa nodded. "A Light Charger. He's coming our way, but not close yet."

"Do we set a trap for him?" Dornir grinned, showing his teeth.

Kria frowned and rubbed her chin. "He's alone and vulnerable, but also not hiding his presence. We can slow him down, but it could be a trap."

"The last point of power is nearly charged. All it needs is an offering. We can afford the risk. Besides, maybe he'll tell us what's happening in the city." Dornir raised his eyebrow.

Adris peered between the trees. Marla could feel him still far off. Was that from whatever Tialla did?

"He's probably still following Marla somehow, or maybe he tagged her with magic we can't detect. We need to get her back to the city," Issa insisted. "We can't lose her again."

"If he's following her, we need to stop him, anyway. You want him to know where the edge of our shield is when she disappears from his awareness?" Dornir rounded on Issa. "We risk exposing everyone if we do nothing."

Issa braced her hands on her hips. "She just got back, and you want to risk her again?"

"I'll do it," Marla whispered, stepping between them. She gripped her shirt as she hugged herself tightly. "Just be sure you're there to help."

Kria rested a hand on her shoulder. "Are you certain? We haven't had a chance to train you to deal with them. You have few defences, and nothing to help you hide once you're spotted."

Her jaw shook. She nodded. "They have to be stopped. If it's him, you protected me once already. We can do this."

"There's a brilliant spot for an ambush just over there." Adris pointed. "Marla can stand in the middle of a clearing, and we can spread around her. He won't get away."

"Show me." Marla wished she felt as confident as she sounded at that moment.

Adris led her over, the others following. Marla looked around the clearing. It was large enough he couldn't sneak up on her. There were plenty of places for her friends to hide. Marla nodded.

Kria gave a signal and everyone else melted into the bushes. After a few seconds, Marla couldn't see any of them. She still felt them, though. Marla closed her eyes and breathed deeply. She opened herself and tapped into the power. Her friends nearly glowed in her senses. She could do this.

CHAPTER 26

Any moment now, he'd show up. He felt like a bundle of static to her, something that didn't fit with the surrounding energy. She gripped the cuffs of her sleeves, her fingers playing with the buttons.

A slender fox darted across the clearing, stopping at her boots. It was almost pure power, strong and steady. Marla smiled as she bent down to pet her. Her fur was soft. Her whiskers brushed against Marla's pant leg.

"That's incredible. Did you call it or use magic to get it close?" He stood at the edge of the clearing, right where she expected him.

"It's a she." Marla straightened up and stared at him.

He raised an eyebrow and watched it dash off into the bush. "Why did you leave? You were doing so well and settling in."

Marla braced her hands on her hips. "Are you joking? You think that was fun for me?"

"Come back and I can keep you safe." He held his hand out to her.

She forced herself to ignore Dornir sneaking up behind him. No, don't give him away. Kienan shifted and started to turn.

"Who will keep me safe from you?" she spat.

"From me? I'm keeping you safe from yourself." He gestured at her. He spun, a ball of electricity in his hand. Dornir slumped to the ground at his feet. "This is the thanks I get?"

"I don't want your help. I don't need your help." Marla raised her hand, calling power up through her.

Kienan pulled a metal collar from under his cloak. "I got you a new one. This one is lighter and should be more comfortable." He took a step towards her.

No. No way. Marla closed her hands into fists. Bushes shook around the clearing as her friends leapt at him, vines and branches speeding towards him.

"No," Marla screamed.

The collar exploded. Fragments flew past her, piercing leaves and embedding in tree trunks. She stared wide-eyed. Her friends all stood frozen, untouched by the shards. Kienan lay on the ground, red blooming over his white robes. Blood seeped from his neck and chest.

The ground rolled. Tree roots stuck up and wrapped around his arms and legs. Anger bled from her, rushing into the soil, leaving her empty.

"Marla, breathe." Issa rushed over and took her hands. "Breathe and focus. Tell the forest you're safe now."

The red spread faster over his robes. Was he dying? Did she cause that? No, she wasn't a killer. She could heal. Maybe not well, but she would try. Marla took a deep breath. "Thank you, forest," she whispered.

Running over, she dropped to her knees beside him. Marla set a hand over his chest. A shard of the collar stuck from the wound. Blood seeped up around it. He met her gaze, his breathing short and gasping.

"I never would have hurt you." He panted, gasping for a deeper breath. "I would have given you anything."

"This is going to hurt." Marla grabbed the shard and yanked.

He screamed. She pressed her hands to his chest and shoved her power through him, pulling more energy from the nearby lines of power. Magic pulsed around her and through her, bringing more healing up as she needed it. The bleeding slowed. She kept going until it stopped.

"Slow breaths now." She circulated her magic through him, feeling for more wounds. "I can't support a way of life where some people don't get to fully live. Out here, we all can be free and grow and learn. We work together as a team. A proper team, where everybody has rights, and we choose leaders for compassion and knowledge, not power."

His breathing eased. He shifted, stretching, though the tree roots still held him. "You'd really pass up a life of riches and comfort for this? What if your magic gets away from you?"

Marla moved her magic around in him, knitting his body back together, healing his muscles and closing the skin wounds. "I can birth an entire forest with enough time. That forest can give me everything I need. What can your riches give you? When the forests die because you're pulling their life away, how will your riches help? My family can help me with my magic."

"But your magic is wild. That's what they taught us. If we didn't rescue you, bring you in and drain the magic away, you'd destroy the forests. Aren't you the cause of the droughts? Don't your people cause the fires and other disasters? That's what wild magic does."

Marla paused her healing and stared at him. "Excuse me? Are you serious?" She stood and paced. Lifting her hands, she saw all the blood on them. Her hands were covered in his actual blood. Didn't her magic just get away from her? No, her friends would have warned her if it were true.

Kienan shifted and groaned. "We were told you were chaos magic, and we were order. Look how we live compared to you. If we brought order to you and your magic, the planet would thrive again." His gaze fixed on her.

She rested her palms against a tree. Energy flowed through her, the beating heart of the planet. Her new family told her the Light Chargers caused the imbalance. They thought she and her people caused it. What was the truth, really?

What would Tialla say if Marla could ask her? She'd seen more life than anyone she knew, other than Ava. Neither woman was available. What was she supposed to think?

Adris touched her shoulder. "What does the forest say? When I can't figure things out, I ask nature. She knows."

Marla looked around and spotted the largest, oldest tree around the clearing, the trunk thick and strong. She rested both palms against the trunk and closed her eyes. Listening closely, she opened herself to the forest.

The wind brushed over her, rustling the leaves and her hair. It was all there, the plants breathing, the animals darting around and searching for food; even the water flowing in rivers and streams around her. Somewhere far off, a lightning storm raged. Each bolt of lightning left a faint tingling in her palms. Somewhere else, a forest lay in ashes, saplings emerging from seeds released by the heat. Water crashed into sand on a distant shore somewhere.

"What if the truth is something else?" Marla whispered.

Adris tilted their head, their eyebrow raised.

"What if both sides helped make the imbalance? What if, when our people pulled away and hid, their people forgot? We weren't there to counter their greed, and their lust for power went wild? Some forests need fire. Lightning rebalances the planet's energy, too, doesn't it? We thought recharging the points of power would bring balance, but what if it doesn't? What if we need to work together to restore the balance?"

Kria smiled. "Tialla was wondering about that. She just didn't know how to achieve something that ambitious. How do you break down the barriers between two separate societies and find common ground again?" She glanced at Kienan. "I'm guessing he'll live?"

Issa kneeled beside Kienan and set her hand over his chest. After a few moments, she nodded. "Marla has become quite the healer in the time she's been training. She needs to learn finesse, but her ability to channel the raw power is remarkable."

"We can't do anything more until the team gets in and stabilizes everything. We should go home." Kria picked up a large fragment of the collar. "Do these work on them as well as us?"

"Those were tuned to go one way, responding to wild magic." Kienan lifted his head to look at Kria. "I don't know how, though. They should only go one way."

Marla took the fragment and handed it to Dornir. "Destroy it, please. I only managed last time because my destruction magic was strong enough to seal away my creation magic."

Kienan's mouth fell open. He stared at her.

"Besides, I know how horrible it is to wear one of those. Nobody deserves that. Not even them." She kneeled beside him. "I think we can use our powers together as proper equals. Just like nature creates and destroys, we can combine our powers to do big things, like in the old days. If I let you up, do you swear not to do anything to harm us or force us back? I want your help to try a few things."

He perked up. Marla knew that expression. He had it when he was puzzling over a design problem sometimes. "What kind of things? Together how?"

She stared off among the trees. "I'm not fully sure. That's one thing I want to try. One of the books I was reading mentioned centuries ago, when all magic was considered one thing. I couldn't finish the book because your people chased me from my childhood home. Kria, can we take him to a library?"

Kria scowled. "We can't risk it. If he knows where things like that are, and who cares for them, they're at risk as well."

Marla rubbed her cheek. "Okay, I understand. We'll just have to try stuff and hope something works."

"Wait, library? You have libraries?" Kienan struggled to sit, but the roots held him down.

Adris kneeled on his other side. "I'm not sure what you're told about us, but we have our own knowledge. We know things about nature you've forgotten or written off as superstition. We're every bit as civilized as you, but it looks different."

Issa shook her head. "The less they know about us, the better."

"Wait, you have actual libraries with proper books? You have group social structure? What all can your magic do if it's not just flowing from you and infecting the land?" He looked around at them all, his eyes wide.

Marla scoffed. "You were on the council. Are you seriously trying to tell me you know nothing at all about the people you've been stealing, using, and discarding?"

Kria smiled. "We hide well. We haven't lost an educated Wood Walker in a hundred annuals. It's possible they really don't know anything about us. If we can get a newly awakened one hidden, and we almost always do, they'll evade detection for the rest of their lives."

"But I've seen it," Kienan insisted. "A girl at the market lost control of her powers. All the vegetables sprouted, ruining the entire supply."

Issa shook her head. "The awakening in his city are most vulnerable to being taken. They often awaken without help, so they're usually identified before we can get to them. They're not as in tune with nature, living in the cold city of stone, so their excess energy isn't absorbed by the land. He could be telling the truth as he knows it."

"We need to get out of here. His friends are still out there somewhere." Kria crossed her arms. "What to do with you?"

274

"How do you feel?" Adris held their hand against his forehead. "Oh, just some pain left. It's distracting him from using his full powers. Do we ease it, and risk him attacking us, or leave it, despite our oaths?"

"What oaths?" Kienan looked up at Marla. "I really thought I was helping you."

Marla held his gaze. "You still can help me. I still want to explore some things with magic, but only if you promise."

He narrowed his eyes at her. "You're not going to set me on fire or anything, are you?"

She glared back. Maybe this was a mistake. Maybe the rift between groups was too big. "No, that's your people. You're afraid we'll treat you like you treated us." She balled her hands into fists. "We don't keep people captive. We don't beat them and drain them and abuse them, destroying them if they resist."

His mouth opened before closing again. He dropped his head back on the soil and stared up at the sky.

"We have to go. Get him up. Dornir." Kria nodded to Kienan. "See to our guest."

"Here." Dornir pushed off from the tree he leaned against. He walked over and took Adris' place beside the Light Charger.

"Help us escort our guest. We'll go to the lake. It is neither sacred, nor secret, and still far from the roads." Kria snapped her fingers. The roots retreated into the soil, freeing Kienan.

Dornir pulled him up and wrapped ropes around Kienan's wrists. The ropes glowed faintly as he tied the last knot. He took Kienan's arm and started walking. Marla stayed with Kria. She didn't look back at the men. She didn't want to. After having to walk with him in those cold stone halls, she was going to choose her own path now.

Kria glanced over her shoulder at him. "Are you willing to work with Marla and help her?"

"Yes, I'm curious as well. Are you telling me you've never lost control of your powers and destroyed anything? What about what just happened?"

Issa frowned. "Her magic reacted to the trauma you caused her. It never would have happened if she stayed with us."

Adris skipped to his other side. "Outbreaks might happen to the absolute newest to their powers, but if we can get to them, they don't have magical outbursts like you mean. We can guide them. Besides, they're not a danger to the forest, where any outbursts might cause flowers to grow. You don't live surrounded by nature, so the magic would flow to the nearest plant or garden."

"Careful, Adris," Kria warned.

"If we don't tell him anything at all, how will he ever overcome his prejudice?"

Marla listened as they walked. He asked Adris question after question. They wouldn't answer anything about the locations of libraries or hidden city, though they admitted the libraries had books going back many hundreds of annuals. No knowledge was ever wasted. He was most curious about their infrastructure, and how her people designed water and sewage systems.

"We're here." Kria stepped through some bushes that parted, revealing a lake spreading out before them.

A few sparse trees grew near the water, but it was mostly grass and shrubs close to the shore. The water stretched away so far that only the strongest swimmer would make it. The sun beamed down on them, warming Marla through.

Kria pulled a marking stick from her pocket, protected inside a leather case. She wrote a quick message on a small piece of paper and rolled it up. Taking a small metal cylinder from another pocket, Kria slid the paper inside and closed it again. She held it by the slender leather ties.

She whistled, the sound piercing the quiet. Kria watched the sky. Marla glanced between her and the deep blue above her, occasionally looking at Kienan as they waited. Within a minute, a sharp cry rang through the air. A hawk circled overhead, dropping towards them slowly.

Kria moved away from the others and stretched her arms out. The hawk swooped down and landed on the ground at her feet. She kneeled and tied the little cylinder to the bird's leg. Taking a small strip of dried meat from her pocket, Kria offered it to the bird.

The meat was gone in moments. The bird stretched its wings out and leapt into the sky, swiftly becoming a speck in the distance. Marla pressed a hand to her heart. It headed for her city. No, he was. It was a he. The city was always there inside her, a gentle pull on her heart.

"You use messenger birds?" Kienan stared at Kria.

Kria shrugged. "So do you."

"Well, yes, but we don't use birds of prey. They're dangerous." He shook his head. "You're not what I expected at all."

"You're everything I was told to expect," Marla muttered.

Kienan turned to her.

She stared at her boots. "Maybe not everything," she admitted.

Issa wrapped an arm around her. "What do you mean?"

Marla looked up and met Issa's gaze. "He wasn't as horrible as the others were. He didn't beat me, and he made sure I always had food, even when I didn't feel like eating. It was bad, don't get me wrong, but it could have been a lot worse. We need to save them. I have an idea."

Kria folded her arms over her chest. "I'm listening."

"We go in and rescue them. Every last one of them. We can start in the city and spread out from there, not stopping until they're all home." Marla curled her hands into fists.

"You have a way around their magic? Our offensive abilities are limited compared to theirs, remember?" Dornir raised his eyebrow. He wrapped an arm around Kienan as the man slid to the ground. "Hey, are you okay?"

Kienan was pale. His eyelids fluttered. Issa kneeled beside him. The splash of red across his robes, drying and darkening now, still made Marla shiver.

Issa rested a hand on his chest. "He'll be fine with time. He's still recovering from nearly bleeding to death. Imagine how you'd feel if you just learned a lot of what you were taught is wrong? Now imagine you're already physically weak while dealing with the emotional fallout."

"Set up camp." Kria looked back at the treeline. "In there. Marla, do you have any idea how we might achieve this glorious rescue?"

Marla nodded. "I learned how to block the collars. Maybe it'll only work for me, but I still got an idea. I used my destruction magic to do it. If we can blend both magic types together, I bet anyone else with help could do it, too. We need to be quiet and sneaky. We can't charge in there and face them all, but we don't need to."

"Sneak in and get them one by one?" Dornir braced his hands on his hips. "How many people are we talking? What kind of guard force will we be up against?"

"Honestly, I saw the twelve with the council people, including me. How many more are there?" Marla took Kienan's hand and poured healing into him, drawing more energy from the sun.

"A handful at most. A dozen more are out in the field. Maybe a few more in the healing wing, ready for processing." Kienan rubbed his temples as he sat. "You lot took most of them recently. Every time we went out on projects, trying to help people, you would steal at least one away."

Marla rolled her eyes. "Maybe we deserve to live, too. Can't you people build things the normal way, with tools and such?"

Kienan opened his mouth, sat motionless for a long moment, and closed his mouth again. He got to his feet, grabbing for Dornir's shoulder as he wobbled. Dornir steadied him.

"Think of all the people we helped. How many more can we still help?"

"So, I have to give up my life just so you can live in luxury? I give up everything, even my ability to speak, just so you can build things faster? How's that fair?" She turned her back and walked to the edge of the pond.

CHAPTER 27

"It's not fair. You're right."

She spun and stared at him, her boots sliding in the mud.

"Do you have any better ideas, though? We've been working on this problem for a few years now, since it started, and we can't fix it. Do you really think you can do better?" Kienan stared out across the water.

"Well, if we never try new things, we won't know, will we? Will you help me? Keep an open mind and work with me?"

Kienan finally met her gaze. He nodded.

She stomped back over to the others, glancing around as she puzzled it through. "If we build a small fire, that might help. It's a natural part of a forest's life cycle, and we both can work with fire." She looked back closer to the lake. "Maybe on that small muddy bank?"

Adris and Dornir cast about for dry grasses and small branches. Using magic, they shaped the wood, breaking it down as they needed. Soon they had a small fire burning. Kienan watched the complete process, paying close attention when Adris showed Marla how to dry the moss and grass fully for tinder.

"You really think we can do this?" He stared at the fire.

Marla snorted. "You showed me the book of our people working together for centuries. Or do you doubt your ability to be my equal?"

He didn't respond right away, staring into the fire in silence. He shook his head. "Fair point. If it works, though, why would we keep using the bands when we could work together? We do, so the bands must be better in some way."

She crossed her arms over her chest. "Maybe those monumental egos got in the way? With everyone scrambling for power and control, there's not a lot of room for partnership."

He opened his mouth, a reply ready, when Adris snorted and laughed. Kienan rolled his eyes instead. "Fine, how do you propose we do this? How long have you even been studying magic, anyway?"

"There's that ego," Dornir muttered. He added another small branch piece to the fire.

Kria grinned like a wolf, all teeth. "That girl you're criticizing has enough magic skill to keep you from bleeding out to a fatal wound. How long does it take your healers to learn that?"

"Decades, if at all. Fine, what do you suggest?" He held his hands out, palms up.

"We'll have to try some things. I've never done this either. We need to try something that will take both of us, right? That way, we'll know it wasn't just one of us. What, though?" Marla tapped her chin.

"I read a lot of books about the time before our current societies formed." Issa stepped beside Marla and faced her. "Everyone lived in smaller settlements, towns like yours, typically. The books talked about the blended magic, and how they'd shape rock to build the old temples. Maybe try something with rock?"

"That's an idea." Adris started looking around. "We rarely manipulate rocks; we work around them. Not since the city was built, anyway." They shrugged and looked at Kienan.

"We break them and shape them with tools, but not just magic anymore. Not the massive blocks used for construction. I've seen some of the ruins. You really think we can do something like that?" Kienan sounded far too doubtful for Marla's liking.

"Well, the books didn't say what magic was used specifically. The authors might have assumed we still know. They did say it was how both cities were first developed, though." Issa shrugged.

Kienan shook his head. "I still can't believe you have a city somewhere we haven't seen yet."

"You'll never find it. Focus," Kria insisted. "Are you willing to try or not?"

"Got one." Adris bent down by the lake shore and grabbed a large rock. They rolled it closer to Marla. "This should be big enough, and it's the right variety of stone. Maybe try to reshape it?"

Marla took a slow breath. "Alright, I'm not sure how, either, but I feel like we can do this. We'll need to experiment."

Kria rested a hand on her shoulder. "See if it works like blending with us, but don't forget to use both magic types."

She nodded. Marla held her hand out. "Rest your palm over mine."

He moved to her side. His hand completely covered hers. "I'm a rock specialist. I can pulverize that in moments."

"We don't want to destroy it. We want to reshape it. Now breathe, relax, and I'll see if I can guide this." Marla closed her eyes, feeling for the rock instead.

She could hear his breathing, slow and steady beside her. His hand was warm on her skin. His energy sparked inside, not flowing like water the way their magic did. Marla pulled her light magic up and touched his energy with it.

"This is incredible," he said softly. "It's not like the bands. It's stronger. Deeper. It's like you can tap into a vast pool of magic we can't touch."

"That's because we can. Focus, please," Marla pleaded. "I'm new at this."

He fell silent. His magic welled up to meet hers. Energy surged under her feet, with the point of power so close. The land around her tingled, the life glowing in her senses, but there was more. She could feel the rock just as easily now.

"You see this every time you do magic?" He was almost whispering.

Marla rolled her eyes. "You're not focusing. I'm the new one here, so help me out a bit? And yes, I feel this every time I use my abilities, depending on what I'm doing."

She stretched their gathered powers over the rock, coating it with magic. Marla paused. What now? She understood erosion, but it wasn't a normal part of their magic. She knew the feel of rock being pressed together by the planet.

"Umm—"

"Allow me to try?"

Marla nodded. "Sure."

He shaped the magic like a piece of abrasive paper rubbed at the stone. Rock dust and chips fell away, landing in the grass. "This is trickier when we're reshaping and not destroying it."

"What about heat and pressure?" Marla suggested. She called to the deep and invited more power up.

"Let him help channel that," Issa warned. "It's too much for you alone at this point. He can handle more magic pressure, since he has more practice."

"I'll concentrate the magic if you want to shape it." His fingers lightly curled around hers. "Shockwaves, heat, and pressure are part of the tools we use. Though you have access to more raw power than we do."

"Pull more than she can tolerate, and I'll return you to the forest early," Issa warned.

"With her willingly open like this, I can keep her safe."

Marla took a few slow breaths. Opening the channel to the soil for him, she focused on the rock itself. Her nose itched as he drew more magic up and shaped it. Heat formed where their hands touched. Marla sent it out into the rock.

She pressed on it with her mind, like when she worked with clay with her hands. The rock moved under her imaginary fingers. The solid form gave way, shifting and forming as she directed it. The familiar feel calmed her as she guided the rock.

Without looking, Marla made the most familiar movements she knew. Pressing in and drawing up, she formed the stone to her mind's shape. The more she fell into the pattern, the easier it got. When she opened her eyes, a stone bowl sat on the ground before her.

Marla pulled their magic back. He guided the excess magic down and away, leaving enough they were both topped up inside. Her hands were chilly after all that heat. He held his hands around hers, warming them again. Wait, why weren't his hands cold?

"Are you alright?" Issa wrapped her arms around Marla.

Marla smiled as she looked at her stone bowl. The shape was pretty even for not having a wheel to throw it on. "Yeah. I think I got this now. Shaping is a creative process, so it's one I should lead, but I need the heat and raw power to do it. I want to try one more thing. I want to try and make it rubble the same way we decompose a log."

"That's easy for me. Can you do that?" He raised an eyebrow.

"I'm still really new, so I'm slow. It's more a combination of the creative and mostly destructive magic, so you might be better leading this one."

He turned to face the stone bowl. "I'll try it."

Focusing on the dried grass near their fire, Marla touched it with her magic and crumbled it to dirt. "Feel that? It's harder when it's a massive tree, but that's the idea, anyway. We don't want to blast it apart, we want a controlled collapse."

"Yes, I can do that. This time I'll guide it, and you bring the power." He held her hand, her palm against his.

"With living things, we ask nature for help. Insects and tiny beasts will break it down more for us. I'm not sure about rock." Marla worried her lip between her teeth.

He smiled at her. "I got this. We cut through rock regularly, and I did it before with her help. I'll add a layer of magic, inspired by your methods, since we're standing so close. I don't want it exploding on us." His fingers briefly tightened on hers before he relaxed again.

She drew power up and directed it through him. He stretched the magic out. Marla followed with her attention, curious. Her grip on the power slipped.

"Sorry." She focused harder on her own task.

"If this works, I'll show you after. Let's see if it works first."

Pulling more power, Marla ignored the itch on her palm where their hands met. She soothed the sensation with a touch of water essence from the groundwater, and her skin calmed. His ability to channel power was impressive, and she kept a steady supply coming for him.

"That's great. Whatever you did, it increased my control."

She pulled more water essence with the power and kept it flowing. The rock cracked and snapped, crumbling before her. It splintered into a fine dust and landed in a pile on the ground. She let go of the magic and it flowed back to where it belonged.

Kienan touched the dust pile with his boot. "That's amazing. You're not limited to magic within you. You can pull power directly from the planet. I had way more control than when I borrowed her power." He looked up at her. His brow furrowed and his lips pressed tight together.

"That's partly true," Kria agreed. "We need the strength and focus to channel it properly. If we're not fit both physically and mentally, it'll burn us up or wash our inner self away, depending on the magic."

He stared across the water. His fingers twitched. "Is that why the people we take lose their energy?"

Kria braced her hands on her hips. She nodded. "We need proper rest and meditation, as well as plenty of sunshine and being outdoors. Living as you do, they lose the strength to passively replenish what you steal, and they'll feel raw and scraped inside."

"But not you." He turned to Marla. "I felt something was affecting the power I could borrow—"

"Steal," Marla corrected.

"Fine, steal from you. I could use it, but something was holding it back. Now I know how much was really there, locked away."

Issa wrapped an arm around Marla. "Now, a snack and a nap. No arguing."

Marla rested her head on Issa's shoulder. "I could really use a full feast."

"One feast, in convenient travel form." Issa pulled something wrapped in wax paper from her pocket. She handed it to Marla.

Taking the offered feast, Marla tore the wrapper off. She held the compressed bar of nuts, nut butter, dried fruits, and oats in her hands. A drizzle of honey shone on the top. She held it to her nose and inhaled the sweet odour. Marla bit a hunk off and chewed, smiling as she savoured each bite. The nut butter was creamy and smooth, the oats holding it together.

A bird swooped down and landed beside Kria. It stared at the woman and cried out once. She bent down, unfastened the message tube, and gave it some dried meat. With a flap of its wings, it took off. Marla admired the sleek spotted feathers as he flew away.

Kria unfastened the tube and unrolled the message. She scanned the page twice before rolling it up again. "They're moving into the city. By the time we arrive, they'll be ready. We're going in, but once we get our people to the door, they'll escort them away."

Kienan shook his head. "With power like what she can access, you could overwhelm us in moments. I'm surprised you're not sending a large group in."

"We don't stop a forest fire. We regrow from the ashes afterwards. We call to life and cause that first burst of green. We don't cause the great winds or fight the tide. We heal those injured as they pass and restore their strength. While we can easily guide the spring floods, we don't make the water any more than you do. We work with what's there, and your city is a desert." Kria stared him down. "Destruction is not our way."

Marla shrugged. "Even with all the destruction magic in me, my powers are strongest when I'm healing and calling to new life." She took another massive bite and chewed, swallowing it. "Your people are the ones who cause cities to crumble or pound the land with fire and lightning."

Kria glared at Kienan. "This is a rescue mission. If we can find a way to change things without making society collapse, we will. Getting our people out is our main concern, though. Not taking over."

"Understood." He bowed his head.

"Now, about that nap—" Issa guided Marla towards the trees, where Adris and Dornir had a camp already set up.

287

"While she sleeps, you will tell me everything about the building. Where are our people likely to be? How many guards will we be facing? If we want to do this without hurting people, I need to know." Kria grabbed his sleeve and dragged him closer to the lake.

"Do you need a touch of a sleep spell?" Issa offered.

Marla shook her head. "I could drop right here."

"One comfortable resting space, ready and waiting." Adris pointed at a few blankets spread out over the soft soil.

"We'll watch over you. Issa needs to go threaten him a little more." Dornir grinned.

Marla smiled as she dropped onto the blankets. She rolled herself up and closed her eyes. Adris sat beside her. Marla drifted off to the sound of the birds and the breeze, like a lullaby from nature just for her.

CHAPTER 28

She stretched, pointing her toes and reaching as far as she could. The soft blankets kept her warm and comfortable. Marla sat and rubbed her eyes. Adris smiled at her and nodded their head towards the lake.

Kria and Kienan sat near the water's edge, their heads close together, huddled around the small fire. Issa paced nearby, watching them closely.

"They've been at it since you fell asleep. They're figuring out how to both save everyone and change things. Now that he's worked with you, he can see so many possibilities, whatever those would be. I think we have an ally," Adris whispered.

"It would be nice to walk around and not worry about running or hiding any moment." Marla eased to her feet and stretched again.

Issa waved her over. "There are a few more things we need to teach you before we go. Fortunately, we have a Light Charger for you to practice on." She glanced at Kienan.

Marla perked up and skipped over. "What do I need to do?"

"Adris will show you, since this is one of their specialties." Issa grinned.

Adris followed, stopping beside Marla. "The best and easiest way to deal with them is simply to put them to sleep. You've seen Dornir and I do this before. If they don't know you're there, they go out fast. You know how many things hibernate over winter?"

Marla nodded.

"Basically, we put a person in hibernation for a short while. They'll wake without harm. This only works if they don't have a shield up, but if you get them by surprise, they have no defenses against it. I'll show you. Light Charger, lay down." Adris pointed at the thick grass.

"What?" He stared at her, open-mouthed.

"Well, if you fall over, you could get hurt. Lay down. She needs practice." Adris raised their hand.

Kria nudged him. "Surely you've helped young mages learn before."

"No, actually. We take the newly awakened to a school outside the city, where some mid-ranked Light Chargers are assigned to teach them. By the time they become an apprentice, they're already nearly fully trained. Mentors just teach them how to apply their magic in a specialty to help society, but they already know the spells." He shrugged. "I'm too useful to be a teacher, and I have mages under me acting as mentors."

"Down, boy, or I'll put you down. You wanted to help her, and she needs help right now." Adris braced their hands on their hips and stared up at the taller Light Charger.

Marla pressed her hands to her mouth, stifling the laugh.

Kienan stepped over to where Adris pointed and sat. "Try to get this right, okay?" He held Marla's gaze as he lay down.

"I'll try." Marla shrugged. "How do I do this?" She kneeled beside him.

Adris took her hand. "Feel what I do. I call to the life inside my target and focus on going dormant. Think about how trees lose their leaves, and their energy slows down. You slow his pulse and breathing and calm his mind. It's like healing when you need to ease pain, but you're easing consciousness instead."

They set a hand on his shoulder and pushed him down. Energy flowed into him in, much slower than usual, but it gave her time to really see it. His face relaxed and smoothed as his eyes dropped closed. His breathing slowed. Even his legs rolled slightly out.

"Feel that?"

Marla nodded.

"I wake him the same way, but in reverse. I call to the energy inside him, like we call to seeds in spring."

Adris' energy flowed into him again, like a burst of power. His muscles twitched. He blinked and opened his eyes. His breathing quickened.

Kienan sat. "Oh, my head." He pressed his palms to his temples.

"You can soothe that for him, though it'll happen each time." Adris shrugged. "It won't last long."

"Do you need—" Marla reached for him.

He waved her away. "It's already passing. Just get this over with." Kienan eased back down, his hands behind his head. He took a shaky breath. "Just don't put me in a coma or anything."

"Are magical accidents common among your newly awakened?" Kria raised her eyebrow.

"Yes. There's a reason our school is outside the city. It's also made of enormous stone blocks, to reduce the damage. They can't burn it down, at least."

Adris grinned. "Well, whenever you're ready, Marla. Go for it. Just do as I did. Take your time for this first attempt. We'll practice for speed once you know what to do."

Marla closed her eyes and took a slow breath. Life slows down in winter. She knew that feeling well. Opening her eyes, she focused on Kienan. He held her gaze. She let the power flow. Did he have to stare at her like that? Marla focused on his chest instead, where the red stain lingered. His brow smoothed and his eyes closed. His breathing slowed.

"That's the way." Adris squeezed her hand. They rested a hand over his heart. "Now, usually we let people wake on their own, typically within a day. You're new, but strong. I'm guessing he'd be out for half a day if you left him."

"That's usually enough time for us to do a full rescue." Issa rubbed her hands together. "We just might manage this."

"Wake him up. We need practice." Adris nudged his shoulder.

"Spring, now," Marla mumbled as she closed her eyes.

"That's the idea." Kria sat beside her on the grass.

Closing her eyes again, Marla imagined the warmth of the spring sun as tiny shoots emerged from the soil. She could almost smell the dampness and see the vibrant green of the tender new plants. Any gardener loved spring.

"Oh, ow." He sat bolt upright, his hands pressed to his forehead.

"Here." Marla set her hand on his back. She let her power flow, easing the ache.

"Thanks." Kienan dropped his hands to his lap and met Marla's gaze. "What did you do to me? His—her—their magic didn't feel like that."

Adris smiled. "She's powerful, but she's a channeler, not a waker. Actually, there's something to that. If you can't get them asleep in time, incapacitate them with a headache. Just flood them with energy. It's harder on the body if they're not already dormant, so use it as a last resort. You could cause bleeding in the brain."

"What?" Kienan stared at Adris.

"It's usually minor and easy to treat." They waved their hand idly. "Beats being taken as a slave and drained until we die."

He glared at them. "I'm trying to help you change that, alright?"

"Relax." Marla pulled her magic back, soothing the last of the discomfort as she went.

"Okay, now he's going to help you with one last thing. You'll try again, and he'll start pulling a shield up. As long as the shield isn't fully up, you should still subdue him. By the time they wake, we're usually long gone." Adris kneeled beside him. "Start forming a shield, but don't close it all the way. She should get you out before you do, anyway."

"How long does it take to put a shield up for you?" Marla rubbed her chin.

Kienan shrugged. "I can do it almost instantly. Most guards and ordinary mages take a breath or more, depending on their inner power. For us, inner power matters more than experience."

"Try it." Adris nudged her lightly. "It'll feel different when they're actively resisting, but you're strong." They stood and stepped back.

Marla pressed her fingertips together as Kienan lay back down. She touched his arm and felt for his power. The instant she felt his energy gather, Marla unleashed a burst within him. His entire body went limp, his head rolling to the side.

Adris cradled his head in their hands. "I think it's safe to say you'll be fine. Maybe go slower when you wake him. Ease him awake. There's no rush."

"Was it too much?" Marla rested her hand over his heart, ignoring the dried blood on his robes.

"Your focus was excellent. You did unleash an unusual amount of power on him. It won't kill him, but be ready to soothe more than a headache." The corners of their mouth quivered. "We'll need to work on how you control your strength this close to lines of power." Adris grinned.

Marla thought of spring, of the lazy melting of snow, and the leaves slowly budding. She sent her powers into him gradually, soothing the rawness her energy blasted in his core. He groaned, his fingers twitching as his eyelids opened. He looked up at her.

"What?" Marla hesitated, her power faltering.

He shook his head. "Nothing. I'm just not used to being touched. Especially not by one of you."

She pulled her hand away. "You want me to stop?"

He pressed a hand to his stomach. "Please finish. Is nausea normal?"

Marla placed her hand over his heart, feeling the soft cloth under her palm. She sought places in him where energy wasn't flowing right and smoothed them out. "Do you have ways to stop people without killing them or actually harming them?" Her hand twitched.

"Yes, though not everyone can. Guards can. I can stun with a controlled lightning burst. I can also temporarily blind them with a burst of light. That might not stop someone, and they might keep fighting, swinging wildly instead."

"She's ready. Well, ready enough. When we team up, Issa, you stay with him and Marla. If he does anything to harm her or try to take her again, stop him however you need. Send him to the planet if you must." Kria stared at him.

Issa stepped beside Marla. "I'll protect her."

"The nearest town will have carts. We can get a ride to the city. Everyone can rest on the way." Kria tilted her head towards the treeline.

Marla stood and stepped back.

"I know what I just felt when we shared magic. We can't draw that kind of power, not even with the neckbands. If I can show them the benefits of working as free partners, maybe that'll change things. I don't care about power for power's sake, but if I had help like that to build irrigation ditches, imagine how much easier the farmers can work." He got to his feet and brushed off his robes.

"Why do you care about farmers?" Marla walked beside him as they followed Kria to the trees.

"I was born in a farming town, but we didn't live in the fertile belt. Some years we barely had enough. One year, our crop failed completely. I know how hard they worked to keep us fed." He shook his head. "Even as a boy, I wanted to help. I began designing irrigation projects to trap and hold the rain. When I made it to the council, I had the power to help farmers all over the country."

"You're a farm boy?" Marla raised an eyebrow.

He smiled and shrugged. "It never leaves you."

"No wonder you worked so hard," she muttered to herself.

"It'll make the biggest difference to the northern communities, where there's naturally less precipitation. If we do this right, we won't harm the many rivers, and the life those support, like the fishery. I avoid using dams. Instead, I designed a system of holding ponds and channels that collect the water. It takes space from cropland, but the remaining land is more productive."

"You care about rivers?" Marla glanced up at him.

"My father was in the fishery. I helped him. I learned all about how the fish grew and lived. I even learned how to keep the land around the rivers healthy to protect them." He smiled as he stared off ahead, his gaze distant.

Adris poked his shoulder. "Maybe you're more Wood Walker than you know. After all, she's got some Light Charger in her, too."

For the rest of the walk, Marla and Kienan shared stories of their childhood. They laughed at how names changed, but the same kinds of people were there. They had different interests, but both loved the land and grew up in small towns led by wise elders. No wonder he differed from the city Light Chargers.

Kria led them to the edge of a town. A couple of carts waited, horses hitched and ready. Issa stayed beside Marla as they climbed in a wagon with Kienan.

"We can keep practicing minor magics along the way." Issa settled onto the same wooden bench as Marla, facing Kienan.

Marla gripped the wagon's side as it started rolling. "Sure. What kinds?"

"You and I will practice shields more. You'll probably need more than a few before we're done today. Their city is harder to draw magic in, so the more practiced you are, the better."

She tilted her head and looked up at Issa. "Is this like the protective spells?"

"It's similar, but there are some important differences. Now you'll call a barrier of energy directly in front of you. Since we'll be in a city of stone, you'll probably need to draw on the power of the sun the most. Fortunately, that's easy for you."

"You have shields of light, too?" Kienan sat straighter, paying close attention.

"We do." Issa met his gaze. "The sun can be one of our most powerful resources, though not everyone is equally skilled in accessing it. It can be tiring to work with, so most of us like easier sources, but we adapt to what we have. Would you show Marla one of your shields?"

"For us to cast a sun shield, I gather the energy and shape it like a disc or globe in my mind. That depends on what I'm protecting. A quick hand gesture like so," he rotated his hand around his wrist, "and the shield is ready."

Marla felt for the shield. It shimmered in front of her like a wall of energy. She poked the shield lightly with her finger. There was something solid in front of him, something her eyes couldn't detect but her abilities could.

"How do ours work?" Marla turned to Issa.

"Similar, but again, it depends on your intention. As always, intention matters most. If you want protection, focus on safety. If you want to pass unseen, think of a shadow. If you want to go unheard, imagine a bubble of silence around you. We don't need a gesture. Just ask the forest for what you want and think of the outcome."

Marla leaned back against the wagon. "Imagine safety. Right."

With her hands together over her heart, Marla closed her eyes. Her thoughts wandered to her childhood bedroom, and the snug feeling of being wrapped up in a blanket near the fireplace. She imagined the safety of a cocoon of pure energy. The surrounding energy shifted and flowed, following her focus. Another energy touched hers, flowed over and around her barrier, but couldn't slide through. She hardened her focus and pushed back. When she opened her eyes, Kienan was smiling.

"That was incredible. Does all magic come so easily to you?"

Issa wrapped an arm around Marla and hugged her tightly. "Yes, she's got a real affinity for working with the deepest powers. Other things are trickier for her. Surely you lot are the same? You can't all do the same things, and some are gifted with more than others."

He shrugged. "Our schools teach a set curriculum, so we all learn the same things. Magic is only taught one way. Only the exceptionally powerful learn anything else from private tutors. If someone is too powerful, they risk being sent to distant parts of the country, so they aren't a threat to those on the council."

Marla raised her eyebrow. "Are you serious? How'd you avoid that, then?"

Kienan laughed. "I always cared more about my projects than power. Someone ahead of me a couple years found himself in the forests far to the northwest, away from research materials, where he still lingers in obscurity."

"What a waste." Issa shook her head. "All our students are gifted in different ways. It's the mentor's job to learn how, so the student can flourish, and everyone can benefit. No wonder culture stagnated under your control."

His cheeks reddened. "If I was in control, there's a lot I would change. More now that I've met you. I'm not, though." He crossed his arms over his chest. "I'm one of many on the council, and not influential outside of my specialty." Kienan closed his eyes.

"Try a few more until you can call a shield in an instant. Don't get tired and tell me when you need a snack. There's even time for a nap." Issa nudged Marla lightly.

Marla straightened up again. She tried different ways, sometimes with eyes closed, and at different speeds. She tried moving her hands to focus and remaining still.

"It's easiest when I blend the methods." She slumped against the wagon side.

"You're doing great. Here." Issa handed her a wrapped bundle.

Marla tore the bundle open and devoured the stuffed bun. She folded the empty wrapper and tucked it in her pocket.

"Sleep if you want. There's time." Issa lay her hand on Marla's shoulder.

She curled up on the bench, her cloak wrapped around her, and her head on Issa's leg. Marla yawned as she closed her eyes.

CHAPTER 29

"We're here. Marla, wake up." A hand rubbed her back.

"Here? Wha—?" Marla rubbed her eyes and sat. She covered her ears and looked out at the crowded streets. Her heart still pounded from the dream. She pressed herself up on shaky arms.

"Nightmares?" Kienan's brow furrowed.

"She's had them since you took her. Here." Issa's voice sounded muffled. She touched Marla's cheek, and her magic flowed in, soothing Marla's ears and calming her heart. "I know this city is noisier than anything you've encountered before."

Marla dropped her hands to her lap. "Our city is big, too. Why doesn't it sound like this?"

Issa smiled. "Don't underestimate how much noise the plants can absorb. This place is like a barren wasteland in comparison. We have plants growing everywhere, even over our walls."

"How big is your city?" Kienan leaned forward, his elbows on his knees.

Issa narrowed her eyes. "Big enough. Maybe, one day in the far future when things changed, maybe we'll let you see it. Maybe not. It's our sanctuary."

Marla looked around. She never actually got to see this city last time. The cart rolled down a crowded street. They followed the cart ahead that was carrying their friends, staying close behind it. Somehow, the crowd always seemed to leave a space for them as they weaved their way among the buildings.

"The horses don't seem to care." Marla watched the big grey mare walk, her head relaxed and her ears floppy, twitching occasionally at a noise. She smiled to herself. The horse was handling this better than she was.

"They come often enough to be used to it, even if they prefer our city. She'll get to go home soon enough. We're stopping part way in." Issa leaned back against the side of the wagon.

Marla noticed someone had given Kienan a cloak to cover his bloodstained robes, though it was incredibly short on him. Despite that, people still whispered as they passed. How did he manage being stared at all the time? The wagons rolled to a stop down a side street, pulling Marla from her thoughts.

Kria leapt down, landing with a spring in her step. "Alright, everyone, we walk from here. Our backup is in place. We probably won't see them, but they're ready." She glanced at Issa, who nodded. "Follow me."

Marla stayed beside Issa. Adris walked on her other side. Dornir gestured at Kienan, who fell into step beside him. They eased into the crowds and joined the steady stream of people heading deeper in.

Someone jostled her shoulder, pulling her away. Marla grabbed for Adris' cloak. They pulled her back in place and glared at whoever it was, their arm wrapped around Marla. Dornir moved closer behind her as well.

Kria turned off on some side roads and threaded through alleys, leaving much of the crowd behind them. Marla looked up and shivered. The building stood over them, up on the hill, towering over everything. Adris took her hand and squeezed it.

"The quietest gate is over there." Kienan pointed ahead and to the left, at a narrow passage between two buildings.

Kria held his gaze. "If this is a trap, we will kill you."

He held his hands up, palms out. "No trap. When I took her in, I swore to protect her." Kienan nodded at Marla. "If we can work such amazing magic as equals, I want that for everyone. Your people, too."

Kria nodded. They followed him between the buildings and through more narrow paths. They reached a metal gate in the high stone wall. It hummed with magic. When he touched it, the gate swung open. He held it while everyone passed through.

Marla pressed a hand to her chest and gripped Issa's cloak. The whole place throbbed with magic. Was she feeling it more since sharing magic with him? Did tapping into the lines of power at the sacred site change her? A few Light Chargers were in a nearby garden somewhere beyond some hedges, but most were inside. How could she feel them through the stone so well now?

Issa took her hand. Soothing magic calmed her senses. Her focus sharpened again, and the people were more like shadows than glowing beacons now. Marla smiled and nodded.

Kienan led them down a path at a brisk walk. The driveway sloped down towards a door. They were somewhere around the back of the building.

"Do you recognize this place?" he asked her.

She narrowed her eyes at the thick wooden doors. When wide open, a few people could walk through together. "No. I only vaguely remember noises, and maybe some shadows, before I woke in the prison."

"It's a medical care facility, not a prison." He set his hand on her shoulder.

"Maybe not to you," she muttered. Marla shrugged his hand away.

301

His brow furrowed. "There are only a few medical staff in here, depending on how many hunts were scheduled. I can go first and distract them, or you can do that sneaking thing you all do so well."

"Do you know exactly where the young might be?" Issa gripped his sleeve.

He nodded. "There are six intake rooms and two treatment rooms for your people. If any of your people are here, they'll be in those rooms. It's unlikely those rooms are full."

"Lead on." Kria pointed to the door.

Kienan stepped closer and set his hand above the lock. Something metal clicked, and the door swung open a crack. He pushed it open and walked in, tall and confident, with Kria right behind him. Marla froze.

Dornir hugged her to his side. "We'll protect you. It's your turn to help your people. We're with you."

She nodded. Marla took a step through the door. She let out a breath. Nothing happened. Nobody rushed her. Her magic stayed active. She was fine. Why didn't she feel fine? She hustled to catch up to the others, Dornir right beside her.

At the first corner, Kria stopped. She held her hand up. Kienan walked around the corner, out of sight. Marla pressed herself to the wall. The cool stone was firm under her fingertips. She was okay. She could do this.

"Sir, we weren't expecting to see you."

Marla gripped the stone. Did it have to be the man in blue?

"I came to see about a replacement." Kienan sounded so confident.

Why couldn't she be that confident? She huddled against the wall between Issa and Dornir.

"We have three here now, but all have been placed. Don't you need to wait another week, in case you find yours?"

"I do. I thought I'd check anyway, in case you can put on hold for me."

"Well, these ones are claimed, but I can set aside the next one that matches your requirements. I don't know when that will be, though. Hunting season is almost over."

"I'd appreciate it. I don't think I'll be getting mine back."

His? Hardly. Marla scowled at the stone wall. No, he was just playing his part. She pulled herself from her thoughts as their voices approached. He wasn't giving them away, was he?

Kienan walked past their hiding place, deep in a discussion about nutrition with the man in blue. Dornir glanced around the corner. He dashed out and touched the man in blue. The man slumped down in his arms; his eyes closed.

"Bring him this way." Kienan pointed at a door down the hall.

Dornir slung the man over his shoulders and followed Kienan. They stopped at a door with a metal grill near the top.

Kienan swung the door open and looked inside. "This'll do."

Dornir lay the man on the thin mat in the corner. Kienan took a thin bracelet from the man's wrist and slid it over his own arm.

"The girls should be this way." Kienan led them from the room, pulling the door closed behind him. He waved his wrist over the frame and the lock clicked.

They walked back, passing that hallway they came in from. He turned another corner and stopped at a door. Kienan glanced through the grill and nodded. The lock clicked open when he waved his wrist over the frame.

"Perhaps one of you should do this?" He stepped aside. Kienan headed for the next door and unlocked that one, too.

"Issa, get this one. Adris, the next. Marla and Dornir, see to the last girl. I'll signal our escorts." Kria pulled a gemstone from her pocket.

Issa pushed the door open and walked inside. Marla followed Dornir to the last door, where Kienan waited. Adris stopped at the middle door and pushed it open. Dornir opened the door for Marla, but stayed with Kienan just outside.

Marla stared at Kienan as she stepped through.

He took the bracelet off and handed it to her. "I'm not here to trick you. I won't lock you in."

"No?" She raised her eyebrow.

Kienan shrugged. "I'd be lying if I said I didn't consider it, but no. I can't now." He tilted his head towards the girl huddled in the corner.

Marla focused on the girl. Dornir had her back. She knew how lost and confused the girl might feel, how vulnerable and scared. Marla took a step closer and kneeled.

"Hey, we're here to help. Come with us. We'll take you somewhere safe." Marla held her hand out to the girl.

The girl peeked out from under the blanket, bright light brown eyes staring at her. She looked Marla over; her gaze stopping at Marla's neck for a long moment. She was Marla's age. Where in the country did they pull her from?

"You're not one of them? Where are we going?"

Marla shifted closer. "We have a safe place. An entire city of people just like us. Come. My friends will get you there." Her skin crawled at how close together the walls were, but she pressed the sensation down. Confidence. She could do this.

The girl's gaze rested on Dornir. "What about him?"

Marla smiled. "He's one of us. He's not a Light Charger. Without his help, I never would have made it here to rescue you."

She nodded, her black hair swinging. Her hand was thick and didn't have callouses. Was she from the city? Marla held her hand and helped her up. They walked through the door together. The girl noticed Kienan as they passed and she leapt into Marla, pressing herself close.

"Easy," Marla soothed. "Let's get you out of here."

Marla led her over to where Issa stood with another girl, this one a little older than her.

"Let's go, darling. We'll get you out of here." Issa's magic was a light tingle in Marla's awareness as she rubbed the girl's shoulder.

Calming magic. She'd need to remember that. Issa herded the girls towards the entrance when Adris and a young man joined them. Kria waited at the end of the hall by the door. The young man glanced back at Dornir, who smiled at him.

Two older women stood just inside the main door beside Kria. They had a bag in their hands. They pulled clothing out, different tops and pants like the city folk wore. It was fancier and better decorated than the chore clothes she had in her town. Her people had more vibrant colours, though.

"Quickly, now. The guards will pass on patrol at any moment, and we want to be ready once they're gone." One older woman pulled a dress over the younger girl. "We weren't planning on a young man, but we'll make do."

The other woman pulled trousers and a tunic from her bag. "You're a healthy young lad. I hope you're not too tall." She handed him the clothing. "We'll take them and go. Another escort team will be ready for any others you find." She nodded to Kria. "Save them."

Kria clasped the woman's hand and bowed her head. "Be safe out there. May the forest hide you."

"And you. Go."

Marla looked over at Kienan. He stood against the wall, arms folded over his chest, his brow furrowed. He watched them stuff the extra clothing back into bags. What was he thinking? Was he regretting helping, or still debating if he should help?

"Not having second thoughts, are you?" Dornir moved beside him.

Kienan shook his head. "This isn't what I expected. You're more organized than we realized."

Adris snorted. "What, you thought we were savages, acting on instinct or something?" They shook their head. "Let's get moving."

"If you give me a moment, I can get spare robes here. This isn't what I'd usually wear, and it might draw attention." Kienan gripped the cloak in his fingers and looked down at himself.

"Make it fast," Kria commanded.

He strode to a room nearby, Dornir and Adris staying with him. Marla shifted from foot to foot. Should she stay and wait? Did she trust him out of her sight? No, but she trusted them, and that was enough. She let out a sigh as he came back out, wearing new white outer robes instead of the cloak.

The women had the young ones through the doors and were gone, not even the bags of clothing remaining to give them away. Kienan now looked like he belonged again, though the robes were just a little short. Were they actually ready? Could they really do this?

At a gesture from Kria, Kienan led them down the halls. Marla followed close behind, staying beside Dornir. He drew so many maps for them, she couldn't even recall them all. This building was immense. From here they had to go up, though, right? She remembered so many stairs.

Only people with rooms on the top floor had her people in captivity. Would they all be there, though? What if they were in a council meeting, or workrooms, or something? Could they possibly get lucky?

Kienan stopped at a door. He turned to the group. "From here on in, we'll find guards evenly spaced along hallways, close enough to hear commotions. Be fast and silent. I can walk ahead and act normally. You can follow and do that sneak thing. The first guards will be on the left."

Dornir and Adris stayed close behind Kienan. Issa tucked Marla back with Kria as they trailed behind. Marla gripped her cloak. Her hands shook. She once walked down this hall, through that door, and up all those stairs. This time she walked by her own choice, her neck wonderfully bare of any adornment. The memory lingered. Swallowing was harder than it should be.

Issa took Marla's hand and squeezed her fingers gently. Marla almost smiled as she wrapped her fingers around Issa's. No, she'd be okay.

Kienan opened the door and strode through. His robes flowed as he walked, blocking some of her view ahead as they moved with his motion. Adris and Dornir stayed back, sneaking along behind between the columns at the side of the hallway. Issa and Kria kept Marla even further back.

He glanced left as he walked, nodding slightly. Dornir and Adris snuck closer to that spot. Dornir nodded, and they leapt forward around the column. Marla winced at the clattering of armour on stone as the guards dropped.

Kienan spun and marched back. He glanced over his shoulder down the hall. "We can hide them in here." He pointed at a spot just down the hall.

"Fewer guards?" Marla touched his shoulder.

He froze for a moment before looking up at her. "Yes. I'm not sure why. If they've noticed any guards outside missing, they'd go there first to investigate. If so, they'll be back looking for intruders soon, and in force. They'll increase all patrols. It's only a matter of time before they find us."

Dornir slung a guard over his shoulder and carried him down the hall behind Kienan. Marla helped Adris drag the other guard. His toe caught on the door frame as they hauled him inside, and Issa kicked it free.

Marla crouched beside the guard they dumped by some barrels. She touched the armour. "Can we use this somehow?"

Kienan snapped his fingers as he closed the door. A ball of light flared to life, illuminating the storage room. "He could. You lot are all too small." He rubbed his chin as he stared at Dornir for a long moment. "If it were just he, Marla, and I, he can dress as a guard and walk with us. I can claim I got her back, and he was escorting us to my quarters. That would leave you three alone, though."

"Would you three keep their attention?" Adris glanced between Dornir and the armour.

Kienan nodded. "Very much so. An unbanded resource gets every guard's attention, as they're most likely to resist or run."

"We could keep sneaking along behind and stunning them?" Adris raised an eyebrow.

"If you're all that good, yes." Kienan met their gaze. "If something happens and too many guards appear, the three of us look like we fit in, though. You three would be vulnerable."

"Dornir, get dressed. It's a risk we'll take." Kria stared at Kienan, that cold assessing gaze on him. "What are you thinking?"

He shook his head. "If you all can do this to us," he gestured at the guards on the ground, "I can see why you can rescue the girls so easily. You've never actually harmed us, though. Couldn't you have stopped us at any time?"

"Our goal isn't to rule as you do and subjugate you. We just want to walk free as equals." Kria braced her hands on her hips. "We want peace and the ability to walk in the sunlight without looking over our shoulders all the time. We want you to stop destroying the land and causing the drought."

"We never caused the drought." He stood straighter, his cheeks turning red.

Marla stepped between them, her hands stretched out. "How about we free everyone first, and argue about the misuse of magic later? Those women are more important than this right now. Trust me. I've been one of them."

"I'm ready." Dornir adjusted the helmet.

Kienan held his hand out to Marla. "Just like before, walk beside me. He will be right behind us. We're heading to the hall where our room is."

Marla glared at his hand. "Your room, my prison." She took his hand. "Let's get this over with."

He shook his head slightly as he opened the door. Kienan guided her from the room, Dornir behind them. The hallway was deserted, so he left the door open. Marla sensed the others behind her, a warmth and comfort she needed right now.

His pace was slower now that she walked beside him. She focused on breathing slow and steady, and feeling for what magic she could sense around her. Her palms were clammy, and her heart kept trying to race as they approached the next guards down the hallway.

"You're safe," Kienan whispered. "They won't let anything happen to you. Neither will I." His fingers tightened over hers for a moment.

"Oh, no," Dornir whispered.

After a long moment, she realized why. The guards were at the end of the hall, standing at the bottom of a wide staircase. There was no cover between the last columns and the guards. They would see her friends before they got close.

"We got this, Marla. I'll take the one on the left." Dornir kept his voice low. "I've warned the others."

She nodded. All she had to do was touch the guard and be fast. She could do this. Suppressing the urge to tremble all over, Marla took a measured breath.

The guards watched them approach. Kienan walked forward with confidence, keeping Marla moving. She clung to his hand and gripped her cloak. Don't fidget, she reminded herself. He shifted their path slightly right, closer to the guard.

They passed between the guards. Marla reached out and touched his arm, gripping his wrist where the glove didn't quite meet the sleeve. Her magic burst forth, pulling some from Kienan, too. The guard toppled.

Dornir crouched beside the other guard, also asleep on the floor. "I knew you were a natural." He grinned at her.

Her legs shook. Marla slid to the floor. Kienan caught her and eased her down, sitting her on a step.

Issa charged over and kneeled in front of her. "You're doing great. Breathe. Nice and deep. It's okay to be scared. You did it."

Marla smiled. Her jaw trembled. She gripped Issa's hand. Magic flowed into her and steadied her. The trembling eased. How can she flip between determined, angry, and scared so quickly?

"The first one is always the hardest, and scariest." Adris rested a hand on Marla's shoulder. "Now, where do we stash these two?"

"Back there or just up ahead." Kienan pointed. "There aren't usually guards here. This is a back stairway in a private corridor."

"Does this change things?" Issa grabbed a guard's wrist and pulled, helping Adris drag him.

Kienan shook his head. "No, we just have to be ready to encounter them anywhere. We still need to check the most likely rooms if you're still determined to continue."

"We are." Marla gripped the railing and stood. "We can't leave them here. They need to come home."

Kria nodded. "We press on." She looked up the stairs. "Are there more guards above?"

CHAPTER 30

Kienan nodded. "Not close, or they'd be investigating already. We should go first. If anyone is nearby, I'll make an excuse and come back down. If you don't hear anything, it's safe to follow."

Marla steadied herself with the railing as she climbed the stairs. Kienan held her other hand again. How was he not tense and on edge? Of course, this was his home. He wasn't in danger if they were discovered.

With the other guards stashed somewhere, she could feel her friends behind them again. Marla forced her legs to carry her on. She didn't realize this place had a distinct smell, but it did. More like a lack of smells she was used to. The familiar odour of growing things was missing, leaving behind the smell of people. The Light Chargers stayed clean, but the guards? Image was less important to them.

"It's not far," Kienan whispered, stopping at the top to wait. "There should be one more set of guards. I have an idea, though."

Kria raised her eyebrow. "Oh?"

They huddled together as he explained, their voices hushed.

"I can do that." Marla nodded.

"Whenever you're ready." Kria gestured at the hallway.

She gripped Kienan's fingers as they headed down the hall, leaving Dornir with the others. The guards were right where she expected them, around the next corner. They stood on either side, watching everyone come and go down that hall.

Marla stared up at the guards with wide eyes. Wait for the signal, she reminded herself. They focused on her as she approached. Not too close now, she pleaded. Kienan lightly squeezed her fingers. Wrenching her hand from his, Marla sprinted back down the hallway.

"After her," Kienan ordered. He spun and followed at a brisk walk.

The guards pursued her down the hall. She squeaked and pushed herself harder. They were getting close quickly. Too quickly. She scrambled around the corner and darted down the hall, past the columns. Fingertips brushed against her back, just missing getting a solid grip.

He hit the floor behind her, his helmet smacking her heel. Too close. She collapsed and huddled on the floor. Her friends leapt on the guards, stripped them of weapons, and dragged them off.

"Did that hurt?" Issa kneeled beside her.

Marla nodded. She stuck her foot out. Issa lay her hand over Marla's ankle. The energy flowed, and the pain eased. Marla sighed and smiled. She eased to her feet, bracing against the pillar for balance.

Kienan strode over. "Are you alright? You did great."

She nodded. "That was close."

"We're almost there. You did it." He smiled and reached a hand towards her shoulder, but stopped short.

"Let's get this over with and get out of here," she whispered, pushing herself away from the pillar.

"Here." Kienan offered her his arm.

Marla wrapped her hand around his arm. Her body still trembled from being chased, and her stomach turned. Leaning against him, Marla walked back around the corner. Dornir and the others followed close behind.

"This way. There shouldn't be any guards in these halls at all, though we'll need to watch for my people." He led them partway down the hall and around a corner. "There. That door." Kienan pointed about halfway down the hall.

Adris snuck up to the door and put their ear to it. They waved everyone over. Issa set her hand over the lock. The wood crumbled, and the lock fell into her palm.

Kria stood beside the doorframe; three fingers held up. She lowered one finger. Marla tensed. Another finger lowered. Slow breath now, Marla reminded herself. The last finger curled up. Dornir pushed the door open and rushed in, staying low. The others followed, spreading out. Kienan followed with Marla, a shield already partly formed and waiting at his command.

"He's not here." Dornir came back from the bedroom.

Kienan shoved the door closed behind them. He went to the desk and shuffled through the papers on top. Marla waited by the door, leaning against the wall.

"No. He's not. The others aren't, either. They're all in an emergency council meeting." Kienan held up a slate piece with chalk writing on it.

Marla glanced between Kria and Kienan. "What now? Is there any way we can take on the whole council in one place like that? Do we wait?"

Kienan shook his head. "Waiting risks you all being found. Going after them is also tricky. The instant they feel their lives are in danger, they might put powerful shields up. That can drain the resources to the point of death. If you want to save them, you need a new plan."

"They're people, not resources, and you mean murder." Marla braced her hands on her hips. "Why can't you even call them people? Is it easier to steal their lives and subject them to humiliating and degrading treatment?" She pulled her hand back and leapt for him.

Adris grabbed her from midair and pulled her close, their arms tight around her. "Breathe, Marla. He's helping us change that. We can't do it alone. We can't cause a revolution big enough on our own. We need their help."

Kienan stopped just out of her reach. "When you were with me, you didn't speak to me. Not once. You interacted with me more than most of the women do. They usually sit on their cushions quietly or sleep. It's incredibly easy to forget you have needs when you don't express them."

She yanked her arm free and swung at him, her fist missing his jaw by a hair. "I couldn't talk. Something in those cursed collars kept words from coming out. All I could do was shout at you inside my head and seethe at the things I saw. Don't you dare try to make this our fault when you stole our voices from us."

He dropped to his knees and caught her fist in his hand. "I didn't know. The bands don't do that to the highborn city girls. They can still talk to us in private. They were always so proud to serve. I just thought you were refusing to talk to me."

"Now you know, so what are you going to do about it?" Kria crossed her arms over her chest. "Your city girls might be deluded into thinking this is their highest purpose, but we will change things, with or without you."

Marla glared at him. She blinked back the tears gathering in her eyes. She took a breath and relaxed her fist.

He let go of her hand. "We need a new plan. Have you considered how you're going to make these changes once we've rescued your people?"

Kria smiled. "The council needs a new leader. Maybe a whole new council. Help us make this smooth and bloodless."

"I'll do what I can." Kienan stood.

Adris relaxed their grip on Marla but didn't let go. "Calm now?"

Marla almost laughed. "Yeah, I'm okay." Everything felt so absurd. She refused to turn and see behind the desk, where a cushion would wait for some unlucky woman. "The council chambers aren't far, but they're down a floor."

"We still need a plan. We can't just charge in and hope for the best." Kria grabbed some paper and a stylus from the desk.

The door swung open. Marla froze. Kria and Dornir were at the desk with Kienan. Issa and Adris were across the room, exploring the bookshelves, their backs to the door. Was she the only one who noticed?

"Kienan?" A man stood in the door. His white robes didn't have the gold border around the neck and sleeves. He looked around at everyone. "What's going on?"

Kienan turned and smiled. He waved him over. "Something big. Shut the door."

The man closed the door. He kept his gaze on Marla and her people. "You brought strangers? Why isn't she wearing her band?"

Dornir took a step towards the man.

"Wait, everyone. Let's do this calmly. What happened while I was out?" Kienan held his hands up, palms out.

"They called an emergency meeting. Why aren't you there? You were called, too." The man shifted away from Dornir a half-step.

"I didn't get the message. I was at a survey site for an irrigation project. We were deep in the forest." Kienan gestured at Marla.

"Well, it's too late now. They locked down the chambers when word spread of someone sneaking around and disabling guards. Chancellor Ginnor asked me to come get something for him. What are you doing here? Who are they?"

Marla reached for Kienan's hand. Would he lend her power?

"They're the townsfolk who helped me find her." He glanced at her as her fingers intertwined with his. When she tugged lightly on his power, he nodded. "I was taking them back to my chamber to arrange their reward, but I wanted to talk to the Chancellor first. When I didn't see him, I came to leave a note."

She pulled a burst of power from him and focused. The shockwave of sleep hit the man. He hit the door and slid to the floor, leaving a thin trail of blood behind. The wound on his head oozed more blood.

Dornir sprinted over. Marla was close behind him. Kienan rushed with her and kneeled beside the man.

"Why? Traitor." His voice shook as much as the hand that gripped Kienan's sleeve.

Kienan took his hand. "I got to experience magic like you wouldn't imagine. Magic like in the old days, big enough to build cities."

"Those days are gone." The man tried to focus on Kienan.

"Here." Marla set her hand on his forehead and sent her magic into him.

The bleeding stopped. He stared right at her now. "I should call the guard." He reached for his pocket. "Who are they, really? Why turn your back on your own people?" The man shifted to get up.

Dornir clamped a hand on his shoulder and held him down.

Kienan reached into the man's pocket and pulled out a stone. "I haven't. They're still my people."

"With her in your care, you could easily be the next chancellor. Isn't that what everyone wants?" The man turned his attention to Kienan.

Kienan held Marla's gaze for a long moment. Marla narrowed her eyes. He wouldn't, would he? Not when he knew how it felt for her. He knows the cost of their system, and what was possible. No, if he tries, she'll never forgive him. Never.

"Think of all the projects you could approve. You're all about helping others. You could make it so everyone has access to resources. No more hoarding them among the most powerful." The man gripped his sleeve. "We can all go out and work on the projects that way."

Marla shook her head slightly.

Kienan frowned. He handed Marla the smooth stone. "What if I told you I could more than double the partnerships out there, and we could complete projects all over the country? We might even bring the rain back."

The man narrowed his eyes as he stared at Kienan. "Did they trick you? Are you thinking straight? Oh, wait. You know where one of their colonies is, don't you?"

"All you need to do is have a little nap. Everything will be fixed when you wake." Kienan nodded to Dornir.

Dornir touched the man's temple. His eyes closed, and he flopped back against Dornir's legs.

"We need to get out of here. The Chancellor will send someone else to retrieve whatever it was, and if they find him, we'll be in serious trouble. They'll call in more guards from the city." Kienan glanced around, his gaze landing on the bathroom door. "Lay him in the bathtub. That'll buy us time."

Adris helped Dornir lift the man and carry him to the bathroom. They eased him through the door and Marla winced at the thump as he landed in the tub.

"Were you actually considering it?" Marla touched his sleeve.

Kienan sighed. "Yes, honestly. I have to consider what's best for the country. However, you've shown me what we can accomplish by working together. I think that's better than a system that exploits people. How are you being used and drained any different from farmers being worked to death in the fields? The law protects the farmers, but nobody is protecting your people. I have to ask, though, will your people willingly work with us?"

Kria stopped pacing and leaned against the desk. "Some won't. You've caused too much harm for them to get over. More will, though. We put the land first. If your projects are good for nature, you'll have an abundance of volunteers. We want a say in the projects we work on, and control over our own energy, though."

"That's fair." He nodded.

"We want laws to protect us and guarantee we won't be coerced." Kria stared him down.

"We have to control the council first."

Marla tugged on his sleeve. "We have to rescue the others first."

Kienan smiled. "Once they're free, controlling the council will be easy. If you help me, that is."

Marla nodded. "Don't forget I do this by choice."

He held his hand out. "Partners."

She clasped hands with him. "Partners."

"He's safe and breathing fine. We should get moving." Dornir strode from the bathroom towards the door, Adris on his heels.

"They called an emergency meeting. Everyone will be in the council chambers. They'll have your people with them. It's probably surrounded by guards. I'm not sure how we'll get in there." Kienan rubbed his chin as he stared at the door.

Marla closed her eyes and listened to the silence in the room, the ticking clock the only noise. "Wait, I have a crazy idea." She smiled. "Maybe."

"Oh, let's hear it." Adris rubbed their hands together. "I love the crazy ideas."

"Is there a room beside the council chambers that might be empty? One we can stand above?"

Kienan stared at her; his brow wrinkled. "Above?"

"Yeah. Together we can move rock, right? We go through the ceiling and drop to the lower floor, right beside the council chamber and past the guards. Who needs a door when you can reshape rock?"

Issa rested her hand on Marla's shoulder. "Are you two strong enough to do that together?"

Kienan grinned. "Easily, especially since we've already tried, and know how to work together. I just need to think—" He walked to the desk and took some paper. Within moments, he drew a couple levels of the floor plan on it. "Here, probably."

Marla shook her head. "You're not sure? I don't want to try digging through a lower wall." She peered over his arm and examined the map.

"I am sure. As long as one of these rooms is empty, we can choose either one." He tapped two of the rooms drawn on his map.

Dornir shrugged. "We'll empty one if we have to. What are the rooms used for?"

"This one is a workroom, but should be empty right now. The other is a storage room. I'm not sure what's in it." He stared at the paper for a long moment. "The workroom is our better choice. Why don't the three of us check it out? If it's empty, can you find your way back and tell them?" He raised an eyebrow at Dornir. "No, I can come back while you protect her."

Kria nodded to Dornir. "Keep her safe." She gripped Dornir's wrist.

"You stay safe as well." Dornir clasped her shoulder in his gloved hand.

Kienan headed for the door. "We should get moving." He gripped the doorknob.

Marla followed and stopped beside him. Dornir joined them. She looked up at him, his face partially covered by the helmet.

"I got your back." He smiled at her.

"I know." Her lips twitched as she smiled back.

"This way." Kienan opened the door and stepped out, letting them pass.

Marla fidgeted as he closed the door. What if someone else came and found her friends? They could take care of themselves, but not if they were outnumbered.

Kienan rested a hand on her shoulder. "Are you alright?"

She straightened up and nodded. "Yeah. Let's get this done."

He tilted his head as he looked down at her. "If you're sure."

"It's a bit late to change my mind," she muttered.

He started walking, going slowly for her. "You could always stay in my care. I can get your friends safely out of the city." Kienan kept his voice quiet.

Marla curled her lip and wrinkled her nose. "Absolutely not."

"I could even get you a band like the highborn wear. Those allow you to speak and interact more." He glanced at her.

She balled her hands into fists and glared at him. "You promised you'd help me free my people."

He held his hands out, palms up. "Just offering. I will keep my promise. Just remember, there are many ways to do what you want. We don't have to choose the most dangerous one."

Marla stared straight ahead, her gaze hard and fixed on the end of the hallway. "Yes, we do."

Kienan shrugged. "As you wish." He quickened his stride.

They passed through the archway leading to the main stairs. Two guards stood on either side, waiting, as always.

"Kienan?"

He turned and faced the guard. Marla stopped with him. The guard nodded towards Marla.

"I just got her back but forgot her band in my room. We're heading down to get it put on in a moment. I need to visit my workshop quick." Kienan turned and kept walking.

The guard nodded. Did he look familiar? No, but they all looked more or less alike in the armour.

Dornir nudged her. "Keep up."

She spun and looked at her feet as she darted after Kienan.

"Wait, I don't know you," the guard called.

CHAPTER 31

K ienan stopped and turned again. "He's from one of my project sites. He helped me get her back, so I had him come and help me."

The guard nodded. They shifted back into the waiting position, standing still and watching.

Marla hustled along, nearly jogging to keep up. It took everything she had not to run ahead. They passed the stairs and headed down a hall. A wide window let light in at the end, brightening up the doors on either side of the hall. So close, and the area looked empty.

Kienan opened the door and walked in. Marla followed, stopping short at the sight of people inside. Three men in cream robes held dusters and spray bottles. They wiped glass equipment on a massive workbench. Each looked over at Marla and her group.

"Gentlemen, I need the room for a bell or so." Kienan walked over to a small desk at the side and went through the papers on it.

"Yes, Sir. The council, though?" The man bowed deeply.

"This is for them. I'm heading down the instant I'm done." He ignored them as he sat and pulled out more paper and a stylus.

"Of course, Sir." The man bowed again.

They scuttled from the room and closed the door behind them.

Kienan stood. "You two wait here. Marla, you should sit." He gestured at the chair. "You should stand beside her like this, your hand on her shoulder. If someone comes in, they'll think you're waiting for me, and won't raise the alarm."

Dornir nodded. "The others?"

Kienan smiled. "I've seen the way you work now. We won't have any trouble getting past the guards. I'll be right back with them."

Marla gripped his sleeve. "Keep them safe, please? I couldn't stand it if anything happened to them. They're my family." She pressed her lips together.

He took her hand and held it between his. "I promise. Now, can you feel below and look for the best place to go through?"

She nodded.

"Good. If you can, that's one less thing to worry about when we come back. I'll get them here safely." Kienan squeezed her hand lightly before letting go.

Marla sat and folded her legs under her. The chair was large and there was plenty of space. She closed her eyes and took a few slow breaths. Dornir lay his hand on her shoulder. His power flowed, ready if she needed it.

Feel around me. Sink into the stone. What's beneath? Marla let her senses roam the area, feeling for the void beyond the stone. It was all fuzzy at first, dark and shapeless and cold. After a few moments, the stone came into focus. There, that would do.

Marla stretched her senses into the room. The stone was above her now as she hovered near the ceiling. Her people were just beyond that wall, their life essences muted by the stone. The room she was in was empty of life, except for a lone potted plant on a windowsill. Maybe she could rescue it when they were done?

324

Dornir's fingers tightened on her shoulder. The door latch clicked, yanking her back into her body. Marla opened her eyes. Was it them, or guards? Did the cleaners come back? She pressed a hand to her chest over her heart.

The door opened, and the others rushed inside. Marla let out the breath and grinned at them.

Issa dashed over and kneeled in front of her. "We're fine. You look pale. Are you alright?"

Marla nodded. "I was worried about you. I found it, though. The best place to drop through." She pointed at the floor. "The chamber wall is right here." She traced the line with her finger. "We want to go down on this side." Marla stepped to the spot she chose over the empty room.

Kienan held his hands out to her as he stepped beside her. "Let's have a closer look."

"I think it's empty." Marla rested her hands over his. "I felt the plant, but no people. My people are over there." She pointed towards the floor where she sensed them earlier.

He lay his thumbs over her fingers, holding gently. Marla closed her eyes and focused on her breath. He matched his breathing to hers. She called on the power from the sunlight streaming through the windows and let it flow between them.

"You chose well. It's empty and clear. Are you ready?" He gave her fingers a light squeeze.

"Ready. It's a high ceiling. How will we get down?" She met his gaze. Why hadn't that occurred to her earlier?

Kienan smiled. "I have a few ideas. Let's get an opening first. One step at a time."

Marla turned her attention back to the stone under her feet. He directed their power into the stone. She kept the power flowing from the sun, an endless supply unless she got tired. He focused the magic into pressure and waited as Marla shaped it.

She pressed and kneaded the floor with the power, softening the stone and mortar. The first stone came loose. Dornir grabbed it and pulled it aside. Marla worked on the gap, easing stone blocks free one at a time. Don't do too much, she reminded herself. We're still standing on this floor.

Adris and Dornir kept moving stones as she widened the hole. Marla didn't stop until it was as wide as her arm was long. A stack of stones sat nearby, neatly piled by the others.

Marla peered into the room below. She wobbled and gripped Kienan's robes. He steadied her and moved her back from the opening, guiding her by the arms.

"You're safe. Don't look. Rock is my specialty, but I'm pretty good with air, too. I think if you loan me power, I can make some stairs for us to walk down. What do you think? Can you help me try?" He kneeled in front of her and offered her his hands.

"What, just hanging in space like that? Have you done anything like that before?"

Kienan shook his head. "No, but when I was a boy, I read a lot of legends from our ancient past. They did amazing things. One man could shape the clouds, with his lover beside him, helping. Another helped his lover reverse a waterfall to save a drowning child. The tales were all of incredible things like that. One man shaped the air."

She lay her trembling hands over his. "You just need power?"

"Yes. I'll shape it this time. Just focus on bringing power."

Marla closed her eyes, sinking easily into that magical feeling. She pulled more power and guided it through him. As much as she wanted to feel what he was doing with it, Marla kept her focus. She could sense the stairs taking shape as the power spiralled down into the room.

"Will it hold us?" Marla whispered, her eyes still closed. Her fingers tightened on his.

"I will test it. You can wait here." Kienan closed the magic in a loop, maintaining the spell. He stood, letting go of her hands.

Marla called a thread of magic from the sun and fed it into the loop, keeping the spell strong. She opened her eyes and watched as he walked to the hole in the floor. He stuck his foot out and stretched it down. Dornir stood beside him, his hand on Kienan's elbow.

Kienan stopped partway down. The stairs held him in place. He took another step, slowly winding his way down the stairs. Marla stared with wide eyes as he walked down the stairs. Stairs made of air. How was this even possible? She shook her head. If anyone told her a month ago that she'd be doing things like this, with one of them no less, she'd have laughed herself silly.

"It holds. If you're uncertain, close your eyes and hold the railing once you're down far enough." Kienan smiled, only his head and shoulders visible now.

Adris laughed. "You made a railing?"

"Well, yes. If she falls from the stairs, that's a problem, right? I promised to keep her safe." Kienan shook his head as he descended the stairs, disappearing from her sight.

Issa slung an arm around Marla and pulled her up. "Let's go. The sooner you're down, the sooner it's over, right?"

Marla nodded. She gripped Issa's arm. The instant she looked down, the world turned under her. She clamped her eyes shut.

"Easy, now. One step at a time." Dornir took her arm. "Feel how solid it is as you step down. Keep those eyes closed. Follow me."

Her legs trembled as she stretched her foot down through the hole. Marla squeaked as she lowered herself to the first step.

"That's it. I've got you. Keep going. I'm already on it, right?" Dornir steadied her as her foot touched something. "That's it. Now another step."

Marla gripped his hands. She forced her body to take a slow breath. A few more steps and she felt the railing beside her. It really felt solid under her hand, like any metal railing. Marla took one step after the other, winding her way down the stairs.

"Almost done." Kienan sounded from beside her.

Marla opened her eyes. She was a couple of steps up now. When she looked down at her feet, she saw the shimmer of magic shaped into stairs.

"Think you can make it from here?" Dornir smiled at her as he let go of her hands and stepped onto the stone floor.

Marla laughed, her entire body relaxing. "Yeah, I think I'll make it some-how."

Dornir backed up, giving her space. Kienan offered her his arm. Marla clung to it as he guided her to a chair nearby.

"Sit for a moment," Kria advised, as she joined them in the room. "We'll figure out where to go through the wall."

Marla curled up in the chair and hugged herself tightly. She just helped make stairs from nothing and walked down them without dying. What else was possible? Maybe she'd find out once the nausea passed.

Kienan joined Kria at the wall.

Kria had her palms flat against the stone. "Our people are over there, away from the door."

"The council meets in a circle near the windows. Everyone has their own chair. There is no large table, though some chairs have a small table beside them. There's nothing to give them cover, but also nowhere for your people to hide." Kienan leaned against the wall.

"What are they likely to do if we burst in?" Adris touched the wall, examining the stonework.

"I'm not sure, honestly. If it were just you lot, they'd attempt to overwhelm you with magic and capture you. With me here, they might still try, and attempt to arrest me as well. Or they could be curious and want an explanation." Kienan shrugged. "I guess we find out when Marla's ready."

"I'm as ready as I'm going to get." Marla got up and joined them at the wall.

She pressed her palms to the wall. The stone bricks were packed tight together. They weren't a consistent size. If she took the wrong ones out, would the whole place fall on her? Which were the wrong ones?

"I'm not a designer," she muttered.

"I am." Kienan moved beside her and rested a hand over hers. "We want to make the door here and include these blocks." He pointed along the line. "Keep the lower edges vertical and we'll arch the top, so it supports itself. I'll help."

Kienan moved behind her, his hands on her shoulders. Marla shivered. She sought nature's power, the ability to erode and wear down. Water could wear away rocks. Wind and sand could scrub things away. Mountains could become hills in enough time.

"So much power. You were holding that back?" he whispered. His power joined hers.

"Nature gives me what I need. I don't take more than that."

Marla directed their combined power into the stone. Her wild nature joined with his ability to shape the elements more easily. She spun the

329

power like a thread, and he placed it over the wall. With one push, the stone dissolved into a fine dust.

The dust hovered in the air, obscuring their view. Marla waved the dust from her nose and mouth as she coughed. What waited on the other side?

A barrier snapped up in front of her, pulling on their thread of power. Marla let the power flow. Sparks burst on it, spraying back into the council chamber. Kienan's hand stretched out before her, pushing the barrier further from her, taking the dust with it. She kept the power flowing as they stepped through the wall.

A breeze blew through the room, pulling the dust away. Kienan kept Marla close, his arm around her shoulders now. She stared at the council, all on their feet with raised hands.

The old man with the long gold chain stepped closer. "Kienan. We were wondering what happened to you. You got her back. Good. People have infiltrated the building. We need your shields." He gestured at Kienan's empty chair.

Kria and the others stepped through the arch behind Marla. She helped Kienan extend his barrier around them, too.

"I can't do that, sir. We're ending the practice of capturing people and draining their magic. Step back, away from the resources, and stand in that corner." Kienan nodded at the far corner by the windows.

"Be reasonable, Kienan. Look at all we accomplished with their help. Imagine what you can do now that you have her back. You're now the world's strongest stone shaper in generations. Think of the monuments you can build. With you as my successor, you'll become the most powerful mage alive one day." The old man took another step towards them, his gaze flitting over the archway behind them.

Kienan's shield wavered.

Marla's cheeks burned. Not again. How could he consider it now? No. She pulled her magic back just enough to tug on his.

"No. In the corner. If we can shape stone together, imagine how powerful our fireballs and lightning are. With her, I bet we could hit every one of you without harming them." Kienan nodded to the people still motionless on the cushions.

One man patted his woman's shoulder before he stood and went to the corner. Another followed. A couple stood and moved to the Chancellor instead, fireballs flicking to life over their palms.

"We need to get those bands off," Kienan whispered. "That'll sap most of their power."

"If we keep the shield up, they can do it," Marla whispered back.

"We can't shield and attack at the same time." His arm tightened around her slightly.

Marla looked over her shoulder at him, her head tilted up. "I'm not planning on attacking. That's not how we do things."

The old man raised his hand. A fireball sped towards them. Marla raised her hands as she called on more power. The massive windows let sunlight deep into the room. The shield glowed as the fireball deflected up and away.

The fireball hit a bookshelf. Old paper caught in moments, dry and brittle as it was. The fire spread along the shelves. Smoke streamed up and across the ceiling. The men split and ran, some shoving past them towards the archway as others ran for the large double doors. A few men tried to smother the flames with their powers, but the fire kept spreading.

Marla dashed to the nearest cushion and dropped to her knees beside the woman. She grabbed her hand. "Come on. We need to go."

The woman staggered to her feet and stumbled after Marla.

Kienan kept a breeze blowing, clearing the smoke for her and the others. "The balcony. We can get out there."

Marla pulled the woman with her, dashing for the balcony. He already had the doors open. She charged through, dragging the woman around the corner. Dornir already had another woman out and was helping her sit. Issa rushed past with another woman. Marla got up and ran back in. How many more?

Adris stumbled past with two more people, both coughing from the smoke. Marla ran to the next cushion, but it was empty. She charged around the chair to the next, where another woman waited. Marla slipped an arm around her and pulled her up.

"One more," Kienan called. He dashed past her, into the thicker smoke.

His breeze still blew, but the smoke spread too quickly. She got the woman to the door, where Kria took her. Marla ran back in. Where was Kienan and the last one? The flames roared over the maps and tapestries, consuming old books and scrolls along the way.

There, two faint heartbeats in the middle of the room. Marla called a breeze around her nose and mouth and ran for them. Her eyes watered. Everything was blurry. She followed those faint beating hearts. Her foot caught on something, and she plunged to the floor.

The rug softened her landing, but Marla still winced as the breath was knocked from her. Kienan lay on the ground. She tripped over his legs. He still had a pulse. It wasn't too late.

Taking his hand, Marla pulled energy through both of them. She called the strongest breeze she could, surrounding them all with it. The air cleared, holding the smoke back a few feet. He coughed as she added a touch of healing. Marla kept the power flowing, even as she swayed, cursing the lack of sunlight now.

He shifted to his knees and looked around. The woman was on his other side, her glassy eyes staring at them.

"Get her. I'll protect us." Marla wobbled as she stood. She focused on the breeze, pushing sparks away with it.

Kienan grabbed the woman and staggered to his feet. He charged for the door on unsteady legs. Marla pushed on his back, towards the sun beyond the smoke. She kept the bubble up as the smoke got lighter. She guided him back to the sun and the fresh air beyond.

CHAPTER 32

D ornir took the woman as they emerged on the balcony. Kienan leaned against the railing and gasped for air. Adris pulled him further from the smoke. Issa grabbed Marla and guided her around the corner as well. Marla fell to her knees and leaned against the building, her head back against the sun-warmed stone.

Issa kneeled beside her. "That's all of them. Here." She gripped Marla's hand as she sent healing through her.

Her lungs cleared. Marla coughed one last time. She took in a lungful of fresh air. Her fingers pressed against the stone as she sighed.

"We got them. Now what? The council got away." Tears rolled down her soot-stained cheeks.

"Now we claim the title of chancellor. The position goes to the most powerful mage, and that's not him anymore." Kienan doubled over, coughing.

Adris touched his back and Kienan breathed easier. He smiled at them as he straightened up.

"She's free, so he can't call on her power." Kienan nodded to the woman Issa was tending. Her damaged collar sat on the stone beside her.

"She'll need extensive care, but it's nothing she can't recover from." Issa brushed tears from the woman's cheeks.

"You know a way?" Kria folded her arms over her chest.

Kienan nodded. "The Right of Challenge. It's a time-honoured custom. The people will accept it. I challenge for the position, if Marla will support me. Together, we are way more powerful than he is, even if he still had her. I will have to issue the challenge, and Marla will need to lend me her power. I can't ever be weaker until we get some rules changed with a new council."

Marla rubbed her temples. Loaning him power wasn't so bad, and it would bring the changes she wants. How long would she be trapped here again, though? She may not wear a collar this time, but she'd be just as stuck, wouldn't she?

"If you agree to make the changes we want, and free everyone. We want to take them home." Marla looked up and met his gaze, her jaw clenched.

He smiled as he sighed. Kienan looked at the column of smoke still flowing from the open balcony doors. "That was our only way off this balcony, though."

Marla shook her head. "There's always another way. Only one exit? What if something happens like that?" She pointed at the fire with her thumb.

He shrugged. "Nobody ever thought stone would burn."

"What about through a window?" Dornir touched the glass. The window led into the room on the other side of the council chambers.

Kienan shook his head. "They spell the glass to prevent breaking."

Adris darted over and set their hands on the glass. "Well, good thing I'm not going to break it, isn't it?" They grinned.

"Do it," Kria ordered.

Marla sensed Adris' power flowing, coating the window. What were they doing? The glass slipped from the top first. With a light push, Adris toppled the glass into the room. It clattered against the floor but remained intact.

Adris smirked. "Ha. I aged the putty. It wasn't spelled against that, just water damage."

"They'll need help to get inside." Kria nodded to the women resting on the balcony.

Dornir leapt through the window. He moved the glass aside. "This will be easier with the glass intact. I'm ready."

Kienan helped Issa get a woman up and to the window. Dornir helped lift her through, easing her down inside. Marla waited as they got everyone inside. She stared out at the city, the bland stone walls and bursts of colourful fabric everywhere. Weren't there any plants anywhere out there? Not a single tree outside these walls?

"Marla, your turn." Kienan held his hand out to her.

She pushed herself away from the railing and walked to the opening. Her body was stiff, and her stomach growled. At least she made it by herself. Dornir reached through the window and helped her through. She clung to him as her feet touched the stone floor inside.

Issa unwrapped a meal bar and handed it to her. "Eat. It'll help until you can get a proper rest and meal."

Marla took the bar and stuffed it in her mouth, chewing a hunk off. With each swallow, she felt a burst of energy. She finished it, licking her fingers clean, as Kria and Kienan joined everyone else inside. Were there more? Her stomach still growled.

The door swung open, and guards rushed inside, their swords and spears pointed at her group.

"Arrest them. They stole my resource." The old man strode in behind the guards, his finger pointing wildly. His face was red as he shouted.

Kienan raised his hand, two fingers pointed at the sky. "I call a challenge for leadership. As a council member, it is my right. Such a challenge is to happen immediately."

"What?" The old man nearly choked on the word. "How dare you?"

"It is his right." Another man Marla recognized from the council stepped through the door. "We will witness."

"It is within my right to take another resource before we do this." The old man turned to the others, his hands out.

"They're all gone," another council member pointed out.

The old man turned to Marla. "I choose her."

Marla crossed her arms and scowled. "No."

The vein on the man's forehead bulged. "What do you mean, no? As reigning Chancellor, I can reallocate resources as I see fit, if anything happens to mine."

Kienan rested his hand on her shoulder. "She's not wearing a band. She's not my coerced resource at this time. You are not entitled to time to hunt and band a new person." He stressed the last word.

Marla reached up and lay her hand over his.

"Neither are you." The old man turned on him.

"I'm not banding her. She's free to help or not. Do you accept the challenge, or forfeit?"

He stomped his foot. "You'll ruin everything." He gripped the chain around his neck. "Start the challenge."

The other man from the council stepped forward. "As called, the challenge has been accepted. We will meet in the proving ground in one hour."

Issa wrapped her arm around Marla. "That gives you time to eat and rest. You want to be ready and give this your best."

"You can safely rest in our room," Kienan offered.

Marla gripped Issa's sleeve.

He held his hands out, palms up. "Use my bed. Your friends can stay and watch over you while I get everyone some food. I'll stay in my reading corner, otherwise."

Issa brushed a lock of hair back from Marla's face. "It's a good idea. You look ready to drop."

"Fine." Marla rested her head on Issa's shoulder.

Kienan nodded to the man who was arranging the challenge. "We'll be in my room. I'll be there on time."

The man nodded back. He turned and began barking orders, sending people scattering.

"Let's go rest. I wouldn't mind a chance to meditate, too." Kienan gestured at the doorway. "Lennor, escort Marla and her companion to my room." He waved at another man in white, one without the gold borders on his robes. "I'll help you get the women out first."

Kria smiled. "Excellent. I will assist you if any magic is called for."

Issa slung an arm around Marla's ribs and guided her behind Lennor. They followed him to the main stairs, and through hallways Marla would rather not see again. The guards on either side of the arch straightened as they approached.

Lennor kept walking, tall and confident. "I'm escorting them for Kienan."

The guard on the left nodded. Marla gripped Issa's shirt as they passed. No, she was safe. He made a promise and was keeping it. Now all she had to do was help him win a challenge that could change everything.

When they arrived, she slumped on the bed. Marla curled up in the soft blankets, wrapping them around herself.

Issa took a book from the smaller bookshelf and settled on the end of the bed. "Sleep. The others will be here soon. I'm watching over you."

Marla closed her eyes.

***

She wrapped her arms around her full belly. Her stomach clenched. Despite passing on the rich foods and choosing the vegetables and bread, eating might have been a mistake. Not eating would be worse, though. Marla took a few slow breaths. Whatever happened, her life was about to change. Again. If she failed, she and her friends might lose everything.

"You'll be fine. You know how to do this. It's actually natural for us to work together. This time, he'll lead, and you just support him, right?" Adris hugged her tightly. "You're a channeler. You were born for this."

Marla nodded. "This time it's my choice. I choose to help. Nobody is forcing me," she whispered. She looked out over the building, crumbling in the middle and falling apart at the edges. "What are we doing here?" Marla glanced back over her shoulder at the city behind them.

"There are three parts to the challenge. The first two are magical and prove I have the power to protect and help people. We hold those here, in the old castle's ruins. I'll need your help with both. The last challenge is when I prove I can manage people and lead."

Marla glanced up at him before letting her gaze wander over the partial walls around them. "Can you?"

He chuckled. "I've been overseeing projects since I was a boy. I manage people every day."

She nodded. "And the challenges you need help with?"

"First, we show we can defend against invaders, taking them out as needed. Don't worry, they're wooden target dummies. After that, we show we can rebuild. We can do this. He must do it all as well and do it alone." Kienan raised his hand as if to touch her cheek before letting it drop again.

"Challengers, assemble." The man walked into the middle of the massive crumbling building.

"Ready?" Kienan raised his eyebrow.

She offered him her hand. "No, but I'm still going to help."

Kienan took her offered hand. They walked together to the man overseeing the challenge. Marla took a slow breath and focused on calming her pounding heart.

"She's not banded. He doesn't have a resource, and he's not allowed outside assistance." The chancellor pointed at Marla.

"Actually, I'm not allowed assistance from another Light Mage. I may use power from her, and she does not have to be banded for me to do so. Check the rules." Kienan stood taller. "It's in the third section, second paragraph." He squeezed Marla's hand lightly.

The man nodded. "I am familiar with the rules. It's allowed. We'll begin. Chancellor, you will be first. We will clear the area and watch from the balcony. Once there, I'll signal the beginning."

They followed the man to a nearby staircase that spiralled up to a balcony that had seen better days. The pillars were all still there, but the railing was falling away in places. She hesitated at the bottom of the stairs.

"It's safe. It's been reinforced by magic," he whispered.

Marla looked up, where Adris waved at her from above already. The others gathered with the watching Light Chargers. Her stomach lurched as she started up the stairs with him. Kienan led her to her people at the top and they stopped to watch the chancellor stand below.

"You don't need to hold his hand for this part," Adris whispered, their mouth right next to Marla's ear.

She glanced up at him before turning back to them. "He's as scared as I am. I have all of you, but he's alone here." That, and she'd never admit it out loud, but he felt like the rock he so easily moved, solid and steady. Being high like this, she needed all the steadiness she could get.

Adris grinned and stared pointedly at her hand in his. "No, he's not. Besides, we're standing with him, too."

A bell rang out, echoing through the stone ruins. Fireballs flew across the space below. The chancellor dodged, running for a pile of wood and stone. He shot fire as each dummy popped up. A fireball hit the first one square, setting the straw hair alight.

The dummy burned as he aimed at the next one. As he hit them, the fire coming from near them stopped. Marla glimpsed the Light Chargers hiding behind the rubble piles, throwing the fire for the challenge. As their dummies were hit, they crept back from the challenge area. Soon, the last one stepped back as well.

"Done. Chancellor, come up. Challenger, prepare."

Kienan led her back down to the rubble-filled room. She clung to his hand. They were about to throw real magic at her, magic like they used when they caught her. Her skin itched over her back. Marla opened herself to the magic below her, drawing it up from the ground. This was her chance to save others from being hurt like that.

His fingers tightened over hers. Marla gathered more magic, tapping into it like a spring. She sensed the men around them, felt their life energy from behind the rubble. They were all gathering power, though it was a fraction of what she could tap into.

He formed a shield around them, ready to snap it into place. Marla ignored the men and focused on her connection with the planet. All she had to do was bring him power that flowed so easily through her. Could she trust him to keep her safe? If she burned, he burned.

The bell rang. Marla unleashed a burst of power into him as the shield flared to life. Flames burst over them, hitting them from every direction at once. She wiped the sweat from her forehead and focused on the power, ignoring the heat that filled her lungs. The flames stopped, though their shield stayed strong.

Kienan snapped his fingers. Lightning shot out, striking all the dummies at once. Marla sighed as the little dots of life energy fled, their power drawing back. They did it.

Or did they?

Something pulled at her, that feeling of being watched by a predator. Marla reinforced the shield, even as Kienan relaxed. Magic was building off to their side. She spun with her hand up, strengthening her shield. He pulled her close and raised his hand, adding his focus to their barrier.

Lightning struck. It glanced off the shield and hit the rubble nearby. Marla kept the shield in place, even as she pulled more power up for him. Her body vibrated with the power. He tapped into the energy and sent it out, a lightning bolt that struck behind a rubble pile. Someone yelped and ran, their robes leaving a smoke trail behind them.

Marla glanced up at him.

Kienan shrugged. "A simple stunning spell, and not even a strong one, at that. I marked him. The guards will get him. Thanks for that."

Marla nodded. She wasn't sure she could speak. Had someone just tried to kill both of them, or only her? She sent the excess power back into the soil, though some still clung to her nerves.

"The challenger showed more finesse and control, as well as more raw power. The challenger wins this round. Now, challenger, you have fifteen minutes to clear this room, restoring the building as much as you can. Begin now."

The gong sounded. Kienan tugged lightly on her power, taking the excess from her nervous system. Marla brought more power up, pulling only enough for what they needed this time. They smoothed broken stones and rolled them back to the walls, setting them in place. Smaller stones and dirt packed into the gaps, holding the larger stones in place. They fused the joins with a little heat and pressure.

Power still surged through her. Marla sent it out as a breeze, gathering the loose dirt and wooden planks and stacking them in a corner. She let some power split off as he reshaped and restored some stone benches by the wall.

"Can you shape wood?"

Marla sank energy into the boards. It was warm and pliable. "Yes."

"Let's make something. Anything you like." His hand squeezed hers briefly.

Marla broke the wood down and reshaped it, blending the fibres together. She kept some energy channeling into him as she formed a statue near the back of the room. Marla worked the soft wood, though the design came from beyond her somehow, from the power she channeled instead. Two trees with intertwining branches formed. A last rush of power burst through, and leaves unfolded from the branches. Marla's body calmed as the extra energy left her.

"Time."

Marla opened her eyes. The room was nearly clear of debris. The walls were intact again, though the clouds were still visible through the partial roof. The rain was coming. She sensed the moisture in the air, though she wasn't sure where it came from.

Kienan smiled as he guided her back up the stairs. They stopped by her friends. Marla leaned against the railing beside him. After all that power rushing through her, she felt both empty and raw right now. She could run across the country or drop to sleep right here. Was this going to happen every time she channeled that much power?

Issa stood beside her. "That was amazing," she whispered. "You've learned so much, and so fast."

"As much as I hate to admit it, he's easy to work with," she whispered back.

His fingers twitched around hers. She didn't dare look over at him.

"You make an excellent partner. You're incredibly perceptive and brimming with enthusiasm." He squeezed her hand lightly.

The bell rang out. The chancellor walked to one of the remaining rubble piles. He kneeled beside a stone block. Marla waited. Was anything happening? He stared at the block. Surely, at any moment, he'll use his power and do something?

"He's nearly exhausted. He's tapped out, unlike you. Without her to draw from, there's nothing he can do." Kienan tilted his head as he watched the chancellor.

"What about you?" She finally looked up at Kienan and met his gaze.

He smiled and shrugged. "You taught me how to use the energy you can draw instead of exhausting myself. I can even pull a tiny thread up myself now, though nothing like what you can access. If I can do it, I bet they can, too. We can recharge ourselves with it without draining one of you. It just means for anything big, we have to work together, right?"

Marla raised an eyebrow. "No more slavery and magical theft?"

"No more."

CHAPTER 33

The sand in the hourglass ran down. The chancellor shook his head. The stone block before him hadn't changed at all, not even dust shaved from it.

"Time. We reconvene in the secondary council chambers for the last challenge in a quarter bell." The man walked down the stairs and examined the stone.

Kienan turned to Marla. "This last challenge might be incredibly boring for you, but I'd ask you and your people to watch over me and guard against any more magical attacks. You seem to feel power as it's building."

Kria wrapped an arm around Marla's shoulders. "We'll help. We're so close to seeing lasting changes without bloodshed and chaos."

Kienan bowed his head. "I'll make certain you come in."

Everyone walked back down to the carriages and gathered in them for the ride back. Marla sat between Issa and Dornir. Kienan sat nearby, across from the man overseeing the challenges, as well as a few others who supported him. Her insides twisted. Here she was, sharing a wagon with people who used and mistreated her. Would that pain ever go away?

The road was smooth. Nobody spoke on the trip back. Soon enough, they pulled up the long driveway in front of the council building. How good would it feel to leave this behind and run among the trees once more?

Marla and her friends walked with Kienan through the doors and to the room. She recognized it as one of the meeting rooms she was in before. Marla wrapped her arms around herself as she and Issa followed Kienan inside. The others waited in the entry hall, tucked in a quiet corner away from the Light Chargers who also waited. Only the council members entered the room.

The chancellor stopped her just inside the door. "You don't need your resource here for this."

Kienan stared down at him. "When have we ever left them unattended, or allowed them to be separated from us?" He braced a hand on his hip. "I swore to protect and care for her. She stays with me."

The chancellor scowled and stormed across the room. A few of the men walked to a wide table on one side of the room. They took papers from a folder and spread them across the table. Marla and Issa stayed beside Kienan near the door.

"Hopefully, this will bore you. If you feel anything is wrong, maybe you sense gathering magic or a possible attack, come stand beside me. Touch my arm or shoulder. Hopefully nothing will happen," he instructed, his voice hushed.

Marla nodded. She closed her eyes and felt around. Issa took her hand and their magic blended, extending how far and well she could feel. The room was quiet and free of magic. There were slender gaps in the wall, barely more than slits, but each had a space behind large enough for a person. Secret chambers? None had anybody in them, but that could change.

"We'll keep an eye on those," Issa whispered.

Kienan waited beside her; his arms crossed over his chest.

Marla lay her hand over his wrist. "You can do this. We'll watch over you and keep you safe."

He smiled, the corner of his mouth twisting slightly. "Thanks. I'm supposed to be the one protecting you."

She shrugged. "Partners? If only for now."

"The challenge will begin. Chancellor, you go first." The man stood behind the table.

Marla and Issa stayed close to the wall. She kept her senses open. He was right, standing here while someone did paperwork was incredibly boring. Nobody moved. Nothing happened. The council members sat in chairs silently, waiting.

"Challenger, your turn." The man gathered the papers from the chancellor.

A council member lay new pages out for Kienan, adding fresh writing tools. Kienan walked over and sat. He surveyed the pages before him and nodded.

"Begin."

Marla pinched herself. She blinked back the tear and focused. There, she was awake now. He was counting on her, and so was every newly awakened Wood Walker who wouldn't have to run in fear. She scanned the edges of the room.

Marla gripped Issa's hand. Someone entered one of the hidden spaces. Issa squeezed her hand back. Their power blended and Issa began shaping it, a combination of erosion and decomposition magic. Was the light she had inside enough to strengthen it? Marla had to try.

Focusing on one brick at the hiding place, Marla sank into her powers. She conjured images of mountains eroding away, taking seconds to do what nature did in ages. With all her intention on that one block, Issa guided her using a new magic. What was it? It was from her people, but she hadn't seen it yet.

347

The stone crumbled, and the block fell from the wall.

"Interference." A council member pointed at the exposed hiding place.

"Guards," the overseer called.

Men in armour rushed in as the council members pulled a barrier around the intruder. Kienan kept writing, ignoring the commotion behind him. He glanced up and smiled at her before turning back to his task.

A quick check proved the rest of the hiding places were still empty. Marla strolled over to the windows and looked out at the darkening sky. The clouds were thick and dark grey. She could feel the moisture in them, like her bones were wet or something. Reaching as high as she could, Marla touched the glass window as her senses stretched to the sky.

A raindrop spattered against the glass and rolled down to her fingers. A few more landed near her, making tiny thumping sounds. Water cascaded from the sky, little droplets landing on the parched soil and stone outside.

The grass and trees perked up, with extra energy flowing into them with each bit of water they absorbed. Marla glanced back at Issa. The woman smiled at her and nodded. Even a light rain could make a difference.

Kienan set his stylus down. He looked out at the rain and smiled. He stood as the councilman took the papers from the desk.

The door opened. Two guards escorted a young man, barely more than a boy, inside. He wore plain white robes. A student? Was someone here his mentor?

Ignoring the men talking behind her, Marla opened the patio door. She stepped out into the blessed rain, raising her hand to the sky. The rain dampened her clothing as she walked to the edge of the patio. Marla leaned on the high stone railing and looked out over the perfectly manicured garden.

Puddles formed on the stone. She turned her face to the sky and closed her eyes. The cool water was a blessed relief after the warm day. Marla walked through a narrow gap in the railing and followed the path into the garden. She stopped under an archway where the water didn't reach. Leaning against the archway, Marla listened to the rainfall.

Issa walked up, a familiar presence in her senses. The woman hugged her close. "You did it."

"We did it. I couldn't have done anything without everyone helping. I wouldn't know how." Marla stretched her hand out into the rain. The cold water spattered on her palm. "It's hard to imagine people choosing to live here, so far from the forests and plains."

Issa laughed. "Some of these city people have never been anywhere else but here. They don't know what the wilds feel like, so they fear them." She looked back over her shoulder. "Someone wants to talk to you."

Marla turned. Kienan stood beside Kria, just inside the patio doors. He wore the gold chain of the chancellor.

"I don't really have anything else to say, I guess."

"We're leaving as soon as another team gets here. Maybe he wants to say goodbye? Sometimes it can heal us just to listen, too."

Marla stared at her boots for a long moment. "Stay with me?"

Issa linked arms with her. "That's what family does."

They stepped back into the rain. When was the last time the city even had a good rain? She wiped her face with her sleeve. Her clothing dripped on the floor as she and Issa stepped back inside the warm and dry room.

The water flowed from her clothing and landed on the floor. She knew that magic. Marla looked up at Kienan. "Thank you."

He bowed. "You are most welcome. Were you staying? I always had hoped we could be partners. We are so strong when we work together."

Marla shook her head. "I have so much to learn still. I'm not ready. Besides, I'm not the only one who can share power. I belong out there, in the forests and the wild places."

His brow twitched. "Will you visit, at least?"

"Maybe, when I'm done with my training. There are also so many books to read, and the library is nowhere near here."

Kienan took her hand. "I want to change things for people like you. For everyone. I will miss your perspective and idealism. You made me see the world in a new way."

Issa draped a protective arm around Marla. "She's only a hawk away. Letters are a thing, right?"

He smiled. "Right. You don't mind if I write? I do still want your perspective on some things."

Marla grinned. "I'm happy to give ideas and suggestions. One thing I've learned, though, is my people have never steered me wrong. I trust them, and the elders are wise. You can trust them, too. If you listen, that is. Treat them like people. They might know things you don't."

He hung his head. "I truly didn't know. Now that I do, we can make things better. We'll start with what we teach our young."

"What will you do with the older ones? The ones who won't change?" Marla stared at the former chancellor, huddled in a corner with a scowl on his face. "Even some of the young ones might resist, if it means not being so special anymore."

"We start by changing the laws. We destroy the bands. I'll choose the new council carefully and will include your people as well."

Kria nodded to a woman, who walked over and joined them. "This is Milla. I know her well. She's wise and powerful and will work as your partner while we sort things out. She follows the centre path, neither blindly adhering to tradition, nor discarding it entirely. Her light is almost as strong as Marla's, and she is also a channeler."

Kienan bowed to her. "I will listen. We need to build the council sooner than later. It gives the stability society needs and prevents power from being abused when balanced right."

Marla glanced around the room at the growing number of people, including older Wood Walkers.

"They've been gathering since I sent word out that we were coming, and what we wanted to achieve," Kria explained. "They'll step in until our own council representatives are chosen officially." She rested a hand on Marla's shoulder. "Oh, and our people stabilized the site. We can get in and finish what we started."

Marla touched her fingertip to where Tialla's ball of light once glowed. How could she want to smile and cry at the same time? Did Tialla know somehow, or was she beyond where she could feel them? Her fingertip warmed, and the warmth spread down her arm. Tialla knew.

"Would you like to eat and rest before you go?" Kienan offered.

Kria narrowed her eyes as she examined Marla. "Yes, I think we should. We'll leave first thing in the morning. The magic is strongest the day of the full moon, but there's plenty of power before and after, too."

"You can stay in the guest's quarters. I'll arrange rooms for everyone." Kienan waved, and a guard walked over. "Take them to the diamond suite and let them rest in peace. See that no one disturbs them. I'll have food sent."

"Yes, sir." The young guard saluted, raising his palm to his opposite shoulder.

Kienan kneeled in front of her and took her hand between his. He pressed something small and metal into her palm. "I should have given this back sooner. I'm sorry."

Marra opened her hand enough to see her pendant, the little gemstone eye staring up at her. "Thank you. I thought it was gone forever."

"I'll come check on you soon. There's much to be done." Kienan bowed to her before walking over to the man who oversaw the challenges.

"Come. You need a chance to unwind and settle. A lot has happened, and we still have the final ceremony to do." Issa guided Marla along behind the guard.

***

Marla walked along the stone path, a small potted plant in her hands. Moss filled the spaces between the stone slabs. Power flowed beneath her feet. The stone pillars almost hummed with power. She passed under the archway, the runes glowing where they were carved in the stone.

She followed the path to the ring of standing stones. Marla stopped between two stones. Adris stood between the next two stones on one side, and Issa was on her other side. The stones still glowed from last time, and the power flowed between her feet. Kria met her gaze and smiled.

Closing her eyes, Marla felt around. Nobody was here who shouldn't be. She sighed and rolled her shoulders. One less thing to worry about, at least. The energy flowing beneath her made her feet tingle. She opened herself, letting the power well up through her. Her friends hummed in her senses, also charged with power. After setting her little plant at her feet, she stretched her hands out towards the stones at her sides, giving the power a path to circulate.

"Today we finish what we started. What Marla started. For the first time in years, we fully charge all points of power. We also say goodbye to a longtime friend and family member. Tialla, may you flow with the planet's energy in peace." Kria raised her hands and touched the central standing stone.

The flowing energy lifted the crushing weight in her chest. Marla blinked back tears as she glanced at Adris, who stood in Tialla's usual spot. Her fingertip warmed, and the heat rushed through her with the energy, easing her aching heart.

Kria began chanting. Power rushed along the circle under her feet. The runes on the stones glowed brighter, pulsing with the energy from below. Marla smiled at the bits of moss that floated down from the ceiling, making the air sparkle. Glancing up, the ceiling was back in place fully. Blue sky brightened the natural gap, letting sunlight in.

The chanting stopped, though the words echoed off the rock walls. Kria placed the offerings at the foot of the middle stone, some fruit and woven baskets and little carved figurines of animals.

A beam of light shot into the sky. Marla squeezed her eyes shut and turned her face away. The light faded, and she opened her eyes. The offerings were gone, though a trace of the light lingered.

"It is done." Kria bowed her head. She seemed to have a glow about her.

Marla looked at the others. Everyone had some glow left over. She raised her hand and examined it. Even she felt the energy still and had that aura of light. She stepped back from the circle and the glow faded. The energy left her, flowing back down into the soil. Somehow, Marla felt empty inside, like only an echo of the power remained.

Kria walked over and took Marla's hands. "You did well. It'll take time to learn how to tap into that much power away from the site, though you've come close before. Give it time. I'll help you develop all your channeling abilities fully."

"Is that why he and I worked together so effortlessly?" Marla brushed her fingers over the small standing stone. It was warm to her touch, like something alive.

"He has more dark inside, like you have more light. Who knows? Maybe after a while, when your training is complete, you two will want to consider working together."

Marla snorted. "I belong out here. If we're so helpful and can do so much, he can come and find me instead. Why should I get uprooted just because they want to live in comfort?" She picked up her little potted plant. A single flower sprouted from among the delicate leaves.

Kria laughed. "That strength will serve you well." She slung an arm around Marla and steered her down the path. The moss was soft under their boots.

"Does this mean we no longer have to run and hide?" Marla took a deep breath. The smell of damp soil and growing things warmed her through.

Issa pushed off from the tunnel wall and stepped into the sunlight with them. "It does. It'll take a while before you'll walk down the street, and your heart won't race if you see one of them. The transition council is there to help both sides adapt to our new partnership."

Marla smiled as she cradled the pot in her hands. The sunlight welcomed her. "Even knowing the next group of awakening is safe, that they're not running for their lives, that's enough. I'm ready to go home."

DEAR READER,

If you enjoyed my book, please consider leaving a review. It helps other people find my books, so they can enjoy them, too.

You can find more information on all my books at www.aliings.com. Sign up for the newsletter for bonus content and scenes, tips and facts, book information, and more.

ABOUT AUTHOR

Ali spends her days with her horses and ponies, dreaming of adventures and magic. She enjoys martial arts, especially swords and edged weapons, though she practices for self-improvement. She also practices meditation, both sitting and moving varieties.

ALSO BY

Forest Guardians

The Last Dragon

Runaway Magic

Facing the Fire

Healer's Strength

Scout's Honour

Shadow Hunter

Apprentice Scout

Chasing Shadows

Tales From Athia

A Healer's Promise

Legends of the Mountain

Phoenix Rising

Other Books

Rogue Magic

A Flash Of Light